WHERE WAS SHE?

Prudence closed her eyes, cleared her mind of fear, and waited. For a moment, there was nothing but darkness. Then a warm light bathed her mind's eye and she felt herself rising above the house, above the fields and forests surrounding the big old house on the hill.

When she was younger, before falling asleep at night, she would seek her family, even when they were all at home. To see everyone's flame burning steadily all around her was like a lullaby. Despite the cost, Prudence would always fall asleep content.

Ignoring Eloise's deep red light, she cast about, extending her awareness farther. There. On the road leading out of the Village of Bartaux. Two fiery lights linked like two bonfires feeding each other—Mother and Father. To the east she found Gemma's cool blue light near Sundance. The twins, Patience and Felicity, she found as orange and green lights at the neighbors' pond, probably skating, since they both had minimal chores this week.

But no Constance.

Cold sweat soaked Prudence's underarms as she searched for her sister. She whispered Constance's name under her breath, willing her sister's steady white flame to appear.

Finally she opened her eyes and looked at Eloise.

"She's gone," she said. Then she slumped exhausted on the scarred tabletop.

BOOKS BY THE AUTHOR

Mendenhall Mysteries series:

The Shoeless Kid
The Tuxedoed Man
The Weeping Woman

Kirwan's Son
Obeah
On Her Trail

BACKLI'S FORD

by

Marcelle Dubé

FALCON
RIDGE
PUBLISHING

BACKLI'S FORD

❧ ONE ❦

FEBRUARY 1911, LOWER CANADA

C-c-COLD...

She shivered and tried to sit up, but her body refused to move, as if a great weight pressed down on her. She lay on her side, her left arm trapped beneath her body, her cheek pressed against something cold and wet. She strained to part her eyelids but could see nothing past the stabbing daylight.

She was lying in snow.

With a grunt, she managed to bring her free hand up to her face and felt a rough scratchiness on her cheek. Wool. She was wearing a woolen mitten.

She reached out a cupped hand and brought snow up to her eyes and scrubbed. The snow burned but she kept rubbing until whatever glued her eyelids shut finally gave way and she opened her eyes to dazzling brightness.

She blinked away the reflexive tears to see snow heaped in front of her nose and beyond that, a tree trunk.

By her constant shivering, she could tell she had been lying in the snow for a long time. Her A'lle genes had protected her so far but she had to get up now or she would die.

She pushed herself into a half-sitting position. The arm that had been trapped beneath her protested with pins and needles as it swung free and she stared down at it numbly, wondering why it hurt so much.

She reached inside her coat—a sheepskin coat, wet and weighted with warmth—and fished under a sweater until she felt flesh. And hissed when she encountered the hard knob of her shoulder out of its socket.

The realization called up a searing throb of agony that lanced through her shoulder and chest, and down her arm. She gasped, fighting the darkness that threatened to rob her of consciousness again.

Get up. Getupgetupgetupgetup.

Clutching her left arm close to her body, she struggled to her knees, then, slowly, to her feet. The world swam for a moment and she took deep breaths, willing herself to remain upright. When the darkness receded, she took stock of herself.

Her body ached with bruises. Those she could ignore. Besides the gut-wrenching pain in her shoulder, she felt as if every other joint in her body had been pulled free and inexpertly reset. Her feet, even inside the sheepskin-lined riding boots, were blocks of ice. But worst of all was the blinding pain in her head, made worse by the glare of fading daylight off the snow.

Using her teeth, she tugged her mitten off and tucked it between two buttons before exploring her bare head. Through the thick, shoulder-length hair she felt a lump on the back of her head that was big as her fist. She gingerly poked it but the bone beneath seemed intact and there was no broken skin.

The lump above her temple was a different story. Though smaller, it sported a deep gash that had crusted over. The hair around the gash was matted with dried blood. She barely touched it, for fear it would start bleeding again.

At last she looked down. The snow was packed tight where her body heat had melted it. In spots, the snow was tinged pink with diluted blood. Her stomach heaved and she quickly looked away.

Tall trees loomed in front of her, still dark and sleepy from winter. Black spruce, willow, aspen, a few pines. Together they formed a forbidding wall that cast long blue shadows in the fading light. It should still be morning... shouldn't it?

She glanced at her body's imprint again, bothered. Where were her boot prints? She studied the disturbed snow all around her body's outline. The snow showed no boot prints. No hoof prints. No carriage sled tracks.

Slowly, she turned to look behind her. A cliff reared at her back, at least sixty feet tall. Its face sloped slightly outward as it reached for the ground and it was covered with snow and brush. A path of broken bushes and disturbed snow gave mute testimony as to how she had arrived at the bottom without leaving boot prints.

She stared up at the cliff, trying to understand. Where was her horse? She'd had a horse, hadn't she?

She couldn't remember falling, but that was a blessing. If not for the bushes and thick snow that had broken her fall, she likely would have died. Her A'lle constitution couldn't protect her from a broken neck.

But even as she thought it, she found herself studying the cliff's edge anxiously, expectantly. Without consciously deciding to, she began moving toward the trees, toward shelter. Someone had been up there, had pushed her off.

Whoever it was would be coming to make sure she was dead.

ও TWO ৎ

Médéric Desautel, Chief Investigator for the Magistrate of the Baudry Region, dipped his nib in the ink well and brought pen back to page to complete his sentence. Normally he dictated all his reports to his secretary, Louis, but this report was different. This one was for the magistrate's eyes only, and the last thing Desautel needed was for Louis Hallepin to learn that he wanted the A'lle girl reassigned to a different region.

A knock at the door interrupted him. He blotted the ink, then turned the page over.

"Come in!" he called.

Louis stuck his head in. "Maître," he said, using the old honorific from Médéric's lawyer days, "there is a boy here for you." His mouth did that pinching thing it did when there was something he wasn't saying but wanted to.

Desautel took in the look, his eyebrows rising in surprise. He'd had very little to do with children since his two boys had grown into men.

"Very well," he said. "Show him in." He sat back in his wooden chair as Louis opened wide the door to his office, allowing the stifling heat from the woodstove in the common room to invade Desautel's cool office.

Louis stepped inside the office, his face a study in barely controlled dismay. A moment later, Desautel understood why.

The boy who entered behind Louis was preceded by a strong smell of manure. He was about fourteen, with the angular awkwardness that heralded a growth spurt. By the size of his booted feet, he had a long way to go before reaching his full size.

The boy's fair hair bristled with bits of straw, and the cap he clutched in his long-fingered hands was worn in spots and dusty with chaff. He stopped in a beam of late afternoon sunlight streaming through the office's only window. Motes of dust danced around his head like a halo.

A stable boy, presumably from the constabulary stables.

Unlike his secretary, Desautel didn't mind the smell of the stables. It reminded him of his childhood on the farm.

Louis opened his mouth to speak, but the boy beat him to it.

"Sir, a horse came back to the stables, riderless."

Desautel's estimation of the boy rose. He liked a man who came straight to the point.

"Which horse?"

"The roan gelding." The boy's clear grey eyes looked serious. "One of your men rode out on it this morning."

A small lump of ice formed in the pit of Desautel's stomach. Renaud.

Desautel had sent Renaud and Dallaire to Backli's Ford, with the A'lle girl, just before the midday meal. They were to investigate the apparent beating of an A'lle boy and bring him back to St. Vincent, unless they could locate his people. No one in Backli's Ford knew him and he apparently spoke only A'lle.

He glanced at Louis, whose thin mouth was pursed in disapproval. Louis had warned Desautel that it was a mistake to send the A'lle girl with Renaud and Dallaire, but his dislike of the A'lle made him unreasonable. Of course Desautel had to send the girl.

She was the only one at the constabulary who could speak A'lle.

Desautel forced a smile for the stable boy's benefit.

"Renaud is usually a much better rider," he said. "We must be sure to tease him when he returns."

But the boy didn't smile in return. "There's something else, sir."

Desautel took a deep breath. "Yes?"

"There was blood on the saddle."

The ball of ice in his stomach shattered into shards.

"Have you touched the saddle?"

The boy shook his head. "I thought you would want to see it first."

Desautel nodded. "Good man. Get back to the stables and make sure no one touches the horse."

The boy flipped his cap back onto his head, sending a small cloud of dust into the air. Louis took a cautious step back.

"Yes, sir," said the boy as he turned to go. At the door he paused to look back. "Mind you make it quick," he cautioned. "He needs a good rub-down."

Desautel smiled, as much for the admonition as for the outrage stamped on Louis's face.

"I will be quick," he promised. Then, as the boy was about to leave, "What's your name, young man?"

"John Lambert, sir."

"Thank you, John Lambert," said Desautel.

The boy nodded and left, trailing straw chaff and the odor of manure into the common room.

"Cheeky bugger," muttered Louis.

Desautel ignored him and picked up the phone. It rang twice before someone picked up at the other end. "St. Vincent exchange," said a familiar voice.

"Is that you, Edna?" asked Desautel.

"Hello, Médéric," said the operator, Edna Filchner. "Haven't heard your voice in a while."

"That's because you keep going to Montreal," Desautel pointed out. "How's that grandson of yours?"

"He is the most beautiful boy in the world," she said. The pride in her voice made him smile, in spite of everything. "When will those boys of yours make you a grandfather?"

Desautel shrugged even though she couldn't see him. "Heaven knows, Edna. You'll have to bring me a photograph the next time you're downtown."

"I'll do that, Médéric," said the operator, recognizing his hint. "Now, how can I connect you?"

"I need to talk to Backli's Ford."

"Hold, please," said Edna automatically.

Louis waited patiently while Desautel listened to the various clicks and pops of the telephone system.

"Ringing you through," Edna finally said and Desautel listened to five rings before the phone at the other end was picked up.

"General Store," said a gruff male voice.

"This is Médéric Desautel. Is this Jacques Patenaude?"

"It is," said the shopkeeper. "Hello again, Chief Desautel. How can I help you?"

Desautel hated dealing with civilians on police matters, but villages like Backli's Ford had no police presence. Most did not even have a mayor.

The shopkeeper had called the St. Vincent constabulary minutes before Médéric arrived that morning. According to the duty sergeant, an A'lle boy had been found beaten and unconscious in Backli's Ford. Médéric had immediately phoned Monsieur Patenaude, who had the only public telephone in Backli's Ford, to speak to him personally. He was unwilling to send constables out on the road in the middle of February without verifying the need first.

"Monsieur Patenaude," said Médéric, "I need to speak to my men. Could you find them and have them call me?"

Louis leaned forward, as if to hear the shopkeeper's answer.

"I haven't seen them yet, Chief," said Mr. Patenaude. "When did they leave St. Vincent?"

Desautel glanced out the window. "About four hours ago," he said grimly.

There was a long silence at the other end. The shopkeeper knew as well as Desautel that it was only a two-hour ride to Backli's Ford. The roads were well-packed and saw a lot of traffic.

"I'll get some of the boys together and go up the road," said Mr. Patenaude. "Probably a problem with a horse."

Desautel nodded to himself. "One of their horses came back," he said, "so they're down a horse. And there's an A'lle girl with them."

"Huh," said Monsieur Patenaude. Desautel knew what he was thinking. To see an A'lle once in this area was surprising. Two in one day was extraordinary.

The shopkeeper's astonishment had been clear in their earlier phone conversation. He had been surprised that an A'lle boy was in his village in the first place, let alone one who had been beaten. Not much happened in a town the size of Backli's Ford without everyone learning of it immediately, and no one had seen this boy before.

And now, Desautel's people were missing.

"What about the boy?" he asked.

"Still unconscious, by all accounts," said the shopkeeper. "The doctor is tending him."

"Thank you, Monsieur Patenaude. Please call me the moment you learn anything."

The shopkeeper promised he would and hung up.

Desautel turned to Louis.

"Are they going to help?" asked Louis. His natural expression was one of disapproval but at the moment, it looked more like the expression of a man who was about to be sick. For Louis, that meant he was worried.

Well, so was he.

"Send Saint-Amand and Johnson out." Saint-Amand was their best tracker. "See if they can find out what happened." He glanced out the window again. "But I want them back before full darkness. If they haven't found them by then, we'll send out a search party in the morning."

Louis nodded, but instead of leaving, he closed the door and watched as Desautel walked over to the coat stand behind the door.

"I warned you that girl would be nothing but trouble," Louis said.

Desautel shrugged into his heavy black wool coat and changed into his wool-lined boots.

"Yes, you did, Louis," he said. "And I would appreciate it if you kept your opinions to yourself when it comes to Miss A'lle." Just because he agreed with his secretary in this particular instance did not mean he could allow Louis to poison the work atmosphere in the constabulary. Any more than it already was. "Now, please, do as I asked."

Louis flushed and nodded stiffly. "Yes, Maître." He opened the door and left.

Desautel hated having Constance A'lle as one of his investigators, but she had been foisted on him by the magistrate and he'd had no choice in the matter. It was hard for the rest of the men, however, who saw only that she had been posted to her home town, where they were all miles from their own homes. To them, it seemed like preferential treatment. To him, too.

Still. The magistrate decreed and Desautel obeyed.

With any luck, he would discover that she was responsible for the delay in reaching Backli's Ford and he would dismiss her for incompetence.

❧ THREE ❧

THE kitchen door burst open, startling Prudence, and Eloise strode in, her heavy leather boots thumping on the wood floor. She slammed the door behind her.

Potato in one hand and paring knife in the other, Prudence stared up at her sister. It was Prudence's week at kitchen duty. She had a pork roast in the oven and was about to add the potatoes, onions, and carrots. In winter, the kitchen was the warmest room in the ancient, sprawling fieldstone house. Even though it was often too warm for Prudence's comfort, she enjoyed the work. Until recently, she had also enjoyed the company of Josella, whom the family had taken in last year when she got pregnant and her parents turned her out. But Josella was gone now, moved away to live with her sister in St. Amable.

"Someone's coming," said Eloise.

Her winter coat was unbuttoned and her mittens were stuffed in her large pockets. She had been out back, splitting wood for the cookstove. Her cheeks glowed ruddy with exertion, and cold air still swirled refreshingly around her.

Prudence set the paring knife and potato down and rested both hands on the tabletop, her fingers splayed over scars made by past generations of A'lle. Five past generations, to be exact.

"About Constance?" she asked when her sister just stood there like a big wooden statue.

"Don't know," replied Eloise. "It's a man, riding."

Prudence nodded and rose from the table. Whoever it was would be coming to the front door. She led the way out of the kitchen and down the long narrow hallway past the dining room and the front room. Eloise clumped along behind her and shrugged when Prudence glared pointedly at the boots leaving a trail of melting snow on the polished wood.

At twenty-two, Eloise was only a year younger than Prudence, but honestly, sometimes she acted ten years younger.

Swallowing a rebuke, Prudence opened the front door and stepped out onto the porch. Eloise came to stand next to her and they both watched the horse trudge up the narrow track that led to their house from the road. In the fading afternoon light, and with his hat obscuring his face, neither one could make out the man's features.

Father said they would buy a car in the spring, but Prudence didn't see why they should go to that expense. It would be much more practical to run electricity up to the house, instead. After all, they couldn't use a car in winter and St. Vincent had had electricity for three years now. It wouldn't cost that much to run it up to the house. And once the electric wires were strung to the house, it would be easy enough to a get telephone line installed. And perhaps buy an electric range.

Not that it mattered. They would never have enough money for any of it.

The man finally brought his horse to a stop at a respectful distance and sat looking up at them. It was only when he swept off his cap that Prudence recognized Chief Investigator Desautel. Next to her, Eloise stiffened, obviously recognizing him, too.

"Mesdemoiselles," said the chief investigator politely. "Are your parents at home?"

Prudence glanced at Eloise but her sister remained grimly silent.

"No, Monsieur Desautel," said Prudence. Then, because she couldn't help herself, "Is it Constance?"

The chief investigator hesitated, and suddenly, Prudence realized that she was standing in what was to him freezing cold in nothing but her thin wool skirt and poplin blouse. No wonder the man was staring at her.

"Would you like to come in out of the cold?" She gestured behind her to the open door. The chief investigator's gaze flicked to the open doorway, then back to her. Humans could never get used to the A'lle ability to withstand the cold.

It was summer with its terrible heat that the A'lle had trouble with, not winter.

He finally smiled. "Thank you." He swung a leg off the horse and got down stiffly, reminding Prudence that he was not a young man. He led the horse to the post at the foot of the stairs and looped the reins around it before climbing the stairs.

Prudence turned and went back inside, waiting for first Eloise, then Monsieur Desautel to go in before closing the door. The inside of the house was not much warmer than the outside, save for the kitchen and its cookstove.

Monsieur Desautel stood on the rag rug, holding his hat in his gloved hands. After a moment's hesitation, he spoke.

"Something may have happened to your sister."

Prudence glanced at Eloise again but her sister merely looked at the chief investigator, waiting for him to continue.

"Tell us," said Prudence, clasping her hands in front of her waist to keep them from shaking.

"I sent her and two of my men to Backli's Ford this morning," said the chief investigator. "A horse belonging to one of the men returned to the stables a little while ago. We have no idea what happened to him, or to your sister and my other man. No one in Backli's Ford has seen them."

Prudence took a deep breath to calm a surge of fear. It was probably nothing. A small accident, likely.

The chief investigator didn't like Constance. The whole family knew it. He didn't like any of them, though Prudence had no idea why. He had only accepted Constance at the magistrate's insistence. He probably hoped Constance was to blame for whatever might have happened to his man. That way he would have reason to dismiss her.

And the family would lose their best chance of acceptance into the community, not to mention an important source of income.

"Well?" demanded Eloise suddenly. "What are you doing about it?"

Prudence winced at her tone and the chief investigator frowned but answered politely enough. "I've sent men to find them, and Backli's Ford has sent out a search party, as well. But..." He took a deep breath. "I am told your parents can find lost people," he said stiffly.

Eloise shook her head impatiently. "They are both in Bartaux. They're trying to find a lost child."

The chief investigator's face closed down and worry slammed into Prudence with a force that almost staggered her. In spite of his dislike and distrust of the A'lle, he had come to them for help. He thought something had happened to his investigators. To Constance.

"What aren't you telling us?" she asked.

He stared at her for a long moment before finally speaking. "There was blood on the saddle." He shrugged. "It may be nothing, but I need to make sure." He tried to hide his concern, but it was there in the tightness around his mouth. "I had hoped they could tell me where your sister is..."

And by extension, where his two men were. Prudence allowed none of her bitterness to show but a quick glance at Eloise's scowl told her that her sister had understood what the chief investigator had left unsaid.

If Mother and Father were here, they could easily find Constance. But Eloise and Prudence were the only ones home. Gemma was still in Sundance. Patience, Felicity... Everyone was out.

Eloise looked at Prudence. It was up to them.

Which meant it was up to Prudence.

Because, despite her gruffness, Eloise's talent was for finding true love, which while embarrassing to her and lovely to the rest of the family, was of no use to them right now.

None of them ever discussed their talents with the humans. Only her parents had let it be known that they could find those who were lost. Prudence didn't know why her parents had chosen to reveal their talent to the humans. When she was first old enough to understand, she had been old enough to realize what a terrible risk they had taken.

A'lle had died for trusting humans too much.

But Constance was missing, and right here, right now, only Prudence could help.

Prudence had always felt her own talent was the most useless one in the family. At twenty-three, her talent should have been fully developed by now. But of all the talents in her family, hers was the one least needed, the one least likely to bring in barter or money. Instead of finding lost objects or people, or water, or that rarest of all Finder talents, truth, all she could do was find her family.

And despite its uselessness, her talent came at the greatest cost. Every time she used it, she was left weak and trembling, unable to move until she rested and ate.

She hated the weakness.

Eloise looked at the chief investigator, her mouth grim. "Come," she said. Then she took Prudence's hand and led her back to the kitchen at the back of the house. She sat Prudence down at the old pine harvest table and pulled out a chair next to her. She glanced around at the chief investigator and nodded him over to the chair across the table. Without a word, he pulled it out and sat down, watching them carefully.

Eloise sat down and pushed the potatoes and cutting board aside before taking Prudence's hands in her big, warm ones.

Prudence swallowed hard and stole a glance at Monsieur Desautel. He did not like the A'lle. He wanted Constance out of his constabulary. That much they knew. But in spite of this, Constance trusted him. Or at least, she trusted him to be honorable.

Was that enough to protect them? She looked at Eloise, who nodded in encouragement.

Did it matter? If Constance needed help, Prudence had to do whatever she could to provide it.

She closed her eyes, cleared her mind of fear, and waited. For a moment, there was nothing but darkness. Then a warm light bathed her mind's eye and she felt herself rising above the house, above the fields and forests surrounding the big old house on the hill.

When she was younger, before falling asleep at night, Prudence would seek her family, even when they were all at home. To see everyone's flame burning steadily all around her was like a lullaby. She could even see Josella's flame, though she was family by love, not by birth. Despite the cost, Prudence would always fall asleep content.

Only once did her seeking betray her. One night, a year ago, she found everyone's flame but Maïta's bright pink one. Maïta was Josella's baby girl and the darling of the household.

Worried, Prudence had crept to the baby's crib, only to find her little body cold in death. Josella's own light had dimmed after that, and soon she moved away to St. Amable. Since then, Prudence only sought when absolutely necessary.

Ignoring Eloise's deep red light, she cast about, extending her awareness farther. There. On the road leading out of the Village of Bartaux. Two fiery lights linked like two bonfires feeding each other—Mother and Father. To the east she found Gemma's cool blue light near Sundance. The twins, Patience and Felicity, she found as orange and green lights at the neighbors' pond, probably skating, since they both had minimal chores this week.

But no Constance.

Cold sweat soaked Prudence's underarms as she searched for her sister. She whispered Constance's name under her breath, willing her sister's steady white flame to appear.

Finally she opened her eyes and looked at Eloise.

"She's gone," she said. Then she slumped exhausted on the scarred tabletop.

❧ FOUR ❧

Thomas pulled up sharply on the lines as a figure stumbled out of the shadowed woods just ahead.

"Whoa there," he said as the horses startled. He kept a firm hand on the lines and the pair settled down, finally slowing the sled to a stop.

The figure—a girl, he suddenly realized—looked up sharply, as if she hadn't been aware of his presence, though it would be hard to miss his sled full of supplies, not to mention the horses, even in the fading light of late afternoon.

"Ho there, Mademoiselle," he called out. "Didn't mean to..."

His voice trailed off as she turned toward him and he got his first good look at her. *Saint Joseph...*

The girl turned away and seemed to be trying to go back into the woods.

"Wait! Mademoiselle!" He quickly looped the lines around the handrail and clambered off the sled. He hurried toward her as fast as his short legs would take him, sinking up to his knees in the wet snow filling the ditch.

"Mademoiselle! Stop, you're hurt." She ignored him and kept heading for the woods but then her movements slowed and she swayed. He caught up to her just as she began to fall and wrapped his arms around her to support her.

She screamed as if his arms were brands. Startled, he let her go and she fell to the ground where she remained, eyes scrunched shut, panting in pain.

Thomas fell to his knees next to her but didn't dare touch her again.

"Mademoiselle?"

There was a gash on her forehead, and a big lump just above her temple was an ugly blue. Blood smeared her eyes and cheeks and her dark hair was snarled and matted with yet more blood. There was dried blood all down one side of her face and she cradled her left arm as if it were broken.

"Mademoiselle, you need help," he said gently when he could no longer wait. "We're within a few miles of my inn. We can get a doctor."

The girl opened her eyes to look at him and it took all of Thomas' fortitude not to flinch. Her eyes were a shade of blue he had never seen before, a rich blue like blueberries with cream. Only there was too much blue, as if the irises were larger than usual. Or maybe it was because the pupil was contracted to a pinprick.

For all of her youth, there was something fierce and unflinching about her gaze. Untrusting. Her cheeks were gaunt with pain and beneath the blood, her skin was too pale for the dark cloud of her hair.

A shiver ran up his scalp, thanks no doubt to the wind that had sprung up as the sun sank. Marie would have *his* skin if he didn't get the child to help soon.

"I'm going to help you up now," he said firmly. "You need warmth and tending. I'll be as gentle as I can, but it may still hurt," he warned.

He eased his arm beneath her shoulders. Before he could lift her, however, she grasped his collar and pulled him closer with surprising strength.

"What—?" Then she released his collar and clamped an icy hand on his face. A jolt ran through him and he gasped and tried to pull away but her hand moved with him. A wave of dizziness swept over him.

Then she released him and dropped her hand back to support her injured arm.

Thomas rocked back, lost his balance, and found himself sitting in the snow. What was that? Eying her warily, he removed his mitten and touched his face. It felt normal, with no trace of whatever it was she had done.

"Forgive me," she said, her voice a croak. "I had to know."

Thomas shook his head, trying to clear it.

"Know what?" That he was real?

"If you planned to harm me."

The suspicion was gone from her eyes. With a sigh, Thomas decided to work it out later. Right now, the seat of his pants was getting wet. He could imagine how uncomfortable the girl must be.

Working together, they got her upright, though he knew it hurt her. The walk back to the sled was slow but they managed it. It was when she was standing by the sled, looking at what must seem like the impossibly high seat that Thomas finally asked about her arm.

"Is it broken, Mademoiselle?" he asked.

"The shoulder is out of true," she said through tight lips. "I do not think anything is broken."

Thomas sighed unhappily. He could wait until they returned to the inn and call for the doctor, but the girl would be in agony the entire trip. Even with runners instead of wheels on the sled, even with the potholes smoothed over with snow and ice, the county road was bumpy and rough.

"I think we need to reset the shoulder before we leave," he said gently. He explained his reasoning and she listened, her eyes narrow. Still, he saw no suspicion it them. Whatever she had done to him back there, it had convinced her he meant her no harm.

She heard him out and nodded. "You've done this before?"

He had, when Jerrod was still at home. The boy had fallen off the roof of the inn and howled with pain, which was nothing like the pain he experienced when Thomas grasped the arm, pulled and twisted it back into place.

And that was when the injury was fresh and there was barely any swelling. There was no telling how long ago the girl's injury had occurred. Whatever the case, waiting would only make it worse.

"I have," he finally said. "It won't be pleasant."

She nodded again.

"All right," he said. "Come round to the back of the sled." He put his arm around her waist, careful to stay on her good side, and led her around to the back.

She was a tall one, easily a head taller than he was, but young enough that her frame was just starting to fill out. He judged her to be maybe sixteen summers.

At the back of the sled, he quickly untied the stays and pulled off the tarp protecting the food and hay he had bought in St. Vincent. He lowered the gate and shoved his supplies around to make room for her.

He should do this as quickly as possible. The less time she had to think about what was coming, the better.

She leaned against the gate and he helped her slide the sheepskin coat off the injured shoulder. The coat went to mid-thigh and was split up the back. The kind of coat you wore if you were riding. Beneath it, she wore a heavy pullover in the light grey of the local sheep, and heavy wool pants tucked inside mid-calf leather boots. Hardly the fancy dress and button-up leather boots a city woman might wear, but definitely appropriate if she were going to be on a horse for a while.

"Now, why don't you tell me what happened?" He ran his fingers lightly over the knob of the injured shoulder. She gasped but didn't flinch away. The shoulder was swollen and rigid.

This was going to hurt a lot.

"I fell down a cliff," said the girl. "Knocked myself out. I expect that's when I hurt the shoulder."

"Grab on to the side of the sled," said Thomas, pulling her sleeve up. He hesitated. She wore a thin muslin shirt beneath the sweater. Bare skin would be better, but he was reluctant to touch her skin. At least the shirt would give him better purchase than the sweater.

She began to shiver.

"How did you fall off a cliff?" he asked as he grasped her arm midway between the wrist and elbow. His other hand slid gently up her arm, ready to grasp firmly. He wasn't truly paying attention to her answers, only trying to divert her attention from what he was doing.

"I don't know," she said after a moment.

He blinked, momentarily distracted from his task. She looked at him, her eyes troubled.

"Well, let's start with first things," he said finally, shaking off his sudden discomfiture. "What's your name?"

She frowned and opened her mouth. Now, he thought, just as she said, "I don't know."

He pulled with all his strength and twisted.

She half-shouted, half-screamed in pain, then cut it off abruptly. He gently released the arm, praying he had done it right.

The girl slumped unconscious against him, her face gray.

Yes. That had been Jerrod's reaction, too.

❧ FIVE ❧

"THIS will be better than bumping around on the seat with me," Thomas muttered to himself, rearranging his supplies even more to make the unconscious girl a little nest. He placed a blanket over the flour and sugar bags and then hauled her onto the makeshift bed, trying desperately not to jar her any more than he had to. Finally he placed all his remaining blankets—new ones from the mill in St. Vincent to replace the worn ones at the inn—over her and jumped off the sled.

He quickly secured the gate and threw the tarp over the hay and the rest of his supplies, covering her up, too. It would cut the wind, if nothing else.

When the tarp was tied down, he clambered up to the driver's seat and freed the leads. "Ho, horses," he said softly and they obediently started off again. By the look of the sky, he would not make it home before dinner. Marie always worried if he was late.

The sled's runners shushed reassuringly on the snow covering the road. In another few weeks, the road would be a mess as spring melt began, but for now, the weather was good for travelling.

Had the girl truly fallen off a cliff? The nearest one was at least half a mile away. That meant she had managed not only to survive the fall, but also to make her way half a mile through the woods to the road.

Those strange eyes of hers marked her as clearly as if she wore a sign. She had to be from that family near St. Vincent. Wouldn't Marie be surprised when he brought home an A'lle girl?

His cheeks were growing cold again after the warmth of his exertions. The sled's runners caught in a frozen rut and jerked the sled into place, rattling his teeth and shaking his bones. He hoped the girl was still unconscious.

He caught a whiff of wood smoke on the wind and breathed deeply. Ah. Almost home. The town was ahead, just down a shallow valley.

Then, the horses' ears twitched and they blew gusts of hot breath into the cold air. Over the creaking and rattling of the sled, he heard it, too. The thudding of hooves moving fast. He glanced up the road but nothing moved in that landscape of white and gray and dark green. Then he looked over his shoulder and saw two figures on horseback round the bend, riding hard, hauling a riderless horse behind them.

They caught sight of him at the same time and slowed to a stop. They were too far away to distinguish if they were male or female, but something about the way they sat their horses told Thomas they were men. Unconsciously, his hand reached under the seat to feel for the shotgun he kept stowed there.

The two men, if that's what they were, leaned toward each other, obviously talking. Then they straightened and urged all three mounts forward again.

Thomas spoke soothingly to the horses but didn't slow down. They were indeed men, unshaven and rough-looking. Their whiskers were covered in white. Frost covered their horses' noses, too, as if the beasts had been ridden hard for a while.

The men caught up to him and passed him, only to stop in the middle of the road, forcing him to pull up.

"Afternoon," said the bigger one on the left. He held the reins of his horse and those of the riderless horse with a relaxed hand and he smiled easily, but Thomas saw the coldness in his eye and wasn't fooled. He glanced at the smaller one, a sharp-featured man with narrow eyes and a narrow mouth.

They looked like highwaymen.

Thomas' heart beat faster at the thought that these two might be ruffians. He didn't see any weapons on them, but with a sled full of goods, not to mention the sled itself and the horses, he didn't want to take a chance. There hadn't been highwaymen in this area in a decade, not since the new chief investigator set up a police force for the region.

But that hadn't stopped all crime. Look at that poor young fellow who'd been beaten and left in the village square. It was only luck that someone had found him and brought him to the doctor.

The big man rested his big hands on the pommel of his saddle and smiled. "We're looking for our niece," he said, nodding to the third horse behind him. "She wandered away from camp this morning." He leaned forward conspiratorially. "She's a little tetched, if you know what I mean, but she's one of ours."

Americans. The border was less than ten miles south of Backli's Ford, across the river. These men were probably up from Albany or Freemont and on their way to Montreal to do a little drinking. Thomas had heard from a guest that New America government agents were now in Cornwall and many other border towns to watch for Americans returning home with alcohol. He even knew a few merchants in Cornwall who did brisk business supplying these rum runners. After all, there was no Prohibition in *this* country.

He didn't approve, but then, he wasn't in the business of providing alcohol.

He glanced at the smaller man and was rewarded with a flash of teeth that looked nothing like a smile. They had come up behind him. Had they seen where he had pulled up and chased the girl?

Something about the small man was familiar, but Thomas couldn't place him. He'd been an innkeeper for over two decades.

Perhaps the man had stayed at his inn once. Thomas relaxed into the hard wooden seat. He had learned that his jovial, inoffensive-looking face could defuse most fraught situations. He shrugged at the big man.

"If you don't mind my saying so," he said with a grin, "that's not something you hear every day."

The big man smiled in response, but the little one just stared at Thomas as if he were steak and dinner was served. Thomas cleared his throat. He must be mistaken. He would have remembered a face like that. "No, I haven't seen any children wandering about," he said. "Where is your camp?"

"Just a few miles away," said the smaller one before the big man could reply. "What's in your wagon?"

So they *had* seen his tracks.

Thomas allowed his smile to falter. "Supplies. Why?" He glanced from one hard face to another. "You're not highwaymen, are you?"

The big man laughed out loud. "No. At least not for a while now." He winked at the other man, who stared back at him stonily. "We'd like to see those supplies, if you—"

Before the man could finish speaking, Thomas pulled the shotgun out of its hiding place and pumped the shells into place. He pointed the shotgun in their direction. Both men's arms automatically rose, their hands spread to show they were empty.

"I don't think so," Thomas said grimly. "Get off your horses." The big man looked astonished at this turn of events, while the little one looked furious, but both of them obeyed.

"In the ditch." Thomas waved to one side of the road. "Leave the horses," he added, when both men tried to lead the horses to the side of the road. With a look that promised retribution, they left the horses in the middle of the road and climbed into the ditch. Then Thomas fired the shotgun over the men's heads. They threw themselves into the deep snow while their horses bolted down the road with frightened whinnies, with his team right behind them.

❧ SIX ❧

SHE woke up in a warm bed and opened her eyes to lamplight. Her head immediately throbbed with pain, but something cool and soothing rested against her forehead. Someone had strapped her arm snugly to her ribs and placed a pillow beneath her shoulder.

Heart racing, she glanced around without moving her head. She was in a bedroom. A small table rested against one wall. A gray sweater hung from a hook on the wall, next to stained and torn pants. Hers. She frowned and pulled the blankets away with her good hand. Someone had undressed her and put her in a soft muslin nightgown. Blood pounded in her temples as she wondered who that someone was.

A window in the wall opposite her bed stood curtained against the night. A small mirror hung on the wall by the door, reflecting the lamplight. Next to the bed was a stand with a white washbasin with crocuses painted around the edge, a matching pitcher, and the lamp. A straight-backed chair sat next to the bed.

The lump on the back of her head felt tender and sore and the other lump above her temple kept it company. Her shoulder still hurt, but not nearly as much as before. And her thighs hurt. She reached down only to discover bandages—another invasion of her privacy. She put the thought aside for now.

Her entire body ached, but she would live.

The cloth on her forehead slipped with her movements and she removed it, placing it in the washbasin.

The door opened and a girl peered in. She looked about fourteen years old and had thick, black braids that fell halfway down her back. Her eyes widened in alarm and she ducked back out, but kept the door open.

An aroma of stew and baking bread wafted into the room, instantly making her mouth water.

"Madame!" called the girl. "She's awake!"

A moment later, an older woman, even shorter than the man who had rescued her, bustled in, wiping her hands on a plain white cloth pinned to her dress at the waistband. She looked harmless enough.

"Good!" she said with approval. A gray bun sat primly at the nape of her neck. "You look much better."

"Where am I?"

"This is the Bartolomée Inn," replied the woman. "In Backli's Ford. Our home. I am Marie Pelletier. My husband Thomas found you."

"How long have I been here?"

"A few hours," replied the woman, examining her face closely. "You fainted when Thomas fixed your shoulder."

A wave of nausea threatened to overwhelm her and she closed her eyes for a moment.

"Did you...?" She opened her eyes and indicated the nightgown she was wearing, the bed, the washcloth.

"Yes," said the woman without hesitation. "Your boots and socks are downstairs, as is your coat, drying by the kitchen woodstove."

The woman had touched her, seen her naked...

"You have been tending me," she said after a while. "I am grateful," she added stiffly.

"A little ice to reduce the swelling of your shoulder, your head." The woman shrugged, as if it was of little importance. "Do you remember your name?" she asked gently.

Her name? She looked at the woman in alarm. A flurry of images raced through her mind: waking up at the foot of the cliff, stumbling through the woods, trying to run from the little innkeeper. Then the blankness when he asked her name.

Before panic could set in, a name floated through her consciousness and with it, her memory returned in a rush.

"Constance," she said with relief. "My name is Constance."

The woman's face relaxed. "It was the knock on the head that shook it out of you," she said. "We hoped you'd remember after a bit of a rest."

Constance took a deep breath, ignoring the twinge in her shoulder. Her name was Constance A'lle, from St. Vincent. Her parents were John and Lily, and she had five sisters: Gemma, Eloise, Prudence and the twins, Patience and Felicity. She was an accredited investigator assigned to the Baudry Region and to Chief Investigator Médéric Desautel, who did not want her as part of his constabulary.

Constance sighed softly. St. Vincent was her first posting. She knew the magistrate was watching keenly from Quebec City to see how she would work out, since she was the first A'lle to ever become an investigator. But in the six months she had been in St. Vincent, this was the first assignment Chief Desautel had given her. And even then, she was to translate, not investigate.

In sudden apprehension, she glanced at the woman standing over her. "What of the two men who were with me?"

The older woman blinked.

"We have not found them yet," said Marie Pelletier gently. "Your chief has been on the phone with poor Mr. Patenaude all day, trying to direct the search party from St. Vincent."

Alarm shot through her. "Is he coming?"

"Not yet. At least I do not think so," said Madame Pelletier.

"We told him that we had found you. He wanted you to come to the telephone but I refused to let them wake you up. Tomorrow will be soon enough."

Tomorrow. Constance glanced at the window. There was no daylight beyond the curtains. "How long...?"

"Thomas found you late this afternoon. It's seven o'clock."

She had left St. Vincent just before the midday meal. She, Dallaire, and Renaud had eaten their meat sandwiches as they rode. She remembered sunshine glittering on the snow, her breath pluming in the still air as she followed the two men who rode abreast. Remembered how they ignored her.

Then, nothing.

What had happened to knock the memories out of her head? She woke up at the bottom of a cliff. Had she fallen? Been pushed? If she had fallen, surely Renaud and Dallaire would have come looking for her. They might not like her—no one at the constabulary liked her—but it didn't matter. All constables looked after each other, unless they couldn't.

She was thinking nonsense. She had been confused when she woke up at the foot of the cliff, and frightened. If she had waited, Renaud or Dallaire would have found her. Maybe they had found her tracks and had followed her, only to lose her when Mr. Pelletier took her in his sled.

She had to find them. She pushed the wool blankets off and made to swing her legs out of bed. The room spun wildly and she clutched the bedsheets to keep from falling out of bed.

"Non." Madame Pelletier shook her head firmly and stood against the side of the bed to prevent Constance from getting out. "You must remain in bed."

Constance shook her head, then regretted it. "Madame, I must find my colleagues." As soon as the room stopped spinning.

"Mademoiselle A'lle," said Madame Pelletier firmly. "You are in no condition to go traipsing around the woods at night." She placed a chapped hand against Constance's good shoulder and gently pushed her back against the pillow. "Besides," she added, "there's something else."

The woman's tone immediately made Constance wary. "What do you mean?"

"Thomas said two men on horseback accosted him on the road. They were looking for their niece, but Thomas did not believe them."

Constance's heart sank. "What did Thomas do to them?"

Madame Pelletier smiled. "He separated them from their horses. They will have a merry time rounding them up."

"They must have been my colleagues," said Constance. "I must speak with Thomas."

"Mademoiselle," said Madame Pelletier, "They said they were looking for their niece, not their colleague. These men were ruffians."

"Ruffians?" Constance considered Dallaire and Renaud. They might be rough-looking at times, but they were always clean-shaven and polite. She looked up at the little woman.

"Can you describe them?"

"Thomas said one was big with pale hair and the other much smaller, with a sharp nose, dark hair and narrow eyes."

Before she even finished speaking, Constance knew. "They are not my colleagues. Dallaire is in his forties and Renaud in his thirties, about the same size. Dallaire has grey hair and Renaud's hair is red."

The two women stared at each other. The concern in Madame Pelletier's eyes echoed Constance's.

"They could be hurt," said Constance. She couldn't waste time on strangers looking for a niece. She tried nudging the woman away but Madame Pelletier refused to move.

"There is nothing to be done until morning," she said gently. "The men have already been out looking. Two of them are camping out near where Thomas found you. They will build a fire. If your friends are out there, they will see it." She patted Constance gently on the arm. "The searchers will be out again in the morning," she promised. "They will find your friends."

She didn't meet Constance's gaze and Constance knew why. February nights could kill an unprotected man. An unprotected human man.

"As for you," continued the woman, "you are lucky to be alive Thomas tells me you fell off a cliff? How did that happen?"

Constance did not want to talk. She wanted to look for Dallaire and Renaud. On the A'lle homeworld, she would have used a machine to locate them, a machine to reach them, a machine to heal them, were they hurt. On the *A'lle*, the ship that took them from their home and brought them through inhospitable space to this place, there were sensors that could pick up the least particle of carbon in a vast space.

Here, on this backward world, she would have to rely on her eyes to find them.

Tomorrow could be too late for the men. But Marie Pelletier was right. Nobody could do anything tonight but prepare for the morning. Constance was in no shape to travel an unfamiliar road at night, even with her A'lle eyesight. She didn't even know where the cliff was.

There was no help for it. She would have to speak to the chief. They had to coordinate the search effort.

"Where is the telephone, Madame?"

Marie Pelletier crossed her arms and looked down at her. "You are certainly a stubborn one," she said. "The telephone is in the general store, but Mr. Patenaude closes at dinnertime. He'll be open again tomorrow morning."

There. She would have to wait until morning to report in. For the first time since she woke up, she allowed herself to relax. She did not want to talk to the chief investigator before she absolutely had to.

Renaud and Dallaire were grown men, used to traveling these roads in winter. They would seek shelter. She would find them tomorrow.

But they were kith, and surely she owed them more than leaving them to the cold and dark. Even if they hated her.

"Now then," said the innkeeper, "how did you come to fall off a cliff?"

Try as she might, Constance could bring up no memory of the fall or the events before the fall. She only knew that a sense of urgency, if not fear, had prompted her to get up and move, to get away from the cliff before... before what?

She frowned. "I don't remember."

Madame Pelletier smiled in sympathy. She settled herself in the wooden chair by the bed and folded her hands in her lap. "The doctor may be able to help. We sent for him as soon as Thomas brought you in." She frowned. "I can't imagine what's taking him so long."

At least she was in Backli's Ford. Renaud and Dallaire would look for her here, if they could. In the meantime, she could interview the A'lle boy.

A shadow blocked out the light from the doorway and both women looked around. A man filled the doorway, his curly gray hair brushing the lintel.

Madame Pelletier jumped up. "Père Noiron!"

The man stepped in and Constance finally saw the white collar of the black cassock under the heavy black wool coat. The effect was formidable. Only the patched woolen socks on the priest's feet marred the effect of a slab of granite come to life.

"Madame," acknowledged the priest abruptly. His accent betrayed him at once as English. He turned a cold gray gaze on Constance. They examined each other in silence for long seconds while Marie Pelletier fidgeted uncomfortably.

Father and Mother had taught their children to be polite to the clergy. The entire family attended mass every Sunday, though they sat at the back of the church and never partook in communion or any of the other sacraments. It was the uneasy balance they had struck with their community. They showed respect by participating in St. Vincent's religious rituals, but did not push the Church further than it was willing to go.

When the A'lle starship had crash-landed on the shores of the St. Lawrence, two hundred years earlier, the Church had not known what to make of these Others. Like humans, the A'lle were created in the likeness of God, and yet they did not believe in God's existence.

At first, the missionaries had attempted to convert them in the same way they had converted the aboriginal people they had found on this new continent. But they could not get through the A'lle genetic predisposition for logic.

No A'lle could "believe." Faith made no sense to them. Either a thing existed irrefutably, or it did not. There was no A'lle concept of "God."

Since that time, Rome had held off taking a formal position regarding the A'lle, but a strong sect within the Church warned that the A'lle were sent by the Devil to confuse and lead astray God-fearing Christians, while another sect stated that the A'lle were sent by God as a test of Christian love.

By the look on Père Noiron's face, Constance suspected he sided with the former.

"Do you know what you harbor under your roof?" asked the priest quietly. While his words were directed at the innkeeper's wife, his cold gaze remained fixed on Constance.

In the golden glow of the lamp, Marie Pelletier's face paled. Nevertheless, she looked at the priest directly, even though she had to crane her neck to do so. His attention remained on Constance.

"Père Noiron," said Madame Pelletier formally, "allow me to introduce Constance A'lle." She took a step closer to the bed. "My husband found her injured outside the village and rescued her. He felt it was his Christian duty to do so." Her faint emphasis on the word "Christian" brought the priest's head up. He turned to look at Marie.

"Indeed. Thomas is a good man. I do not fault his charity, only its object." His big hands were balled at his side. Now one hand rose to sweep the air in Constance's direction. "She does not belong here," he said firmly. "She must leave."

He was no better than the St. Vincent bullies who had bedevilled her as a child. What made him worse, however, was the fact that he was willing to toss her out at night, in the cold. She didn't know if she should condemn him for his bigotry or admire him for speaking his mind.

She cleared her throat, drawing their attention before Marie Pelletier could speak and possibly endanger her immortal soul.

"I am here on behalf of Chief Investigator Médéric Desautel to investigate the beating of an A'lle boy." There. It would be interesting to see if the good father was ready to challenge the authority of the magistrate.

"All that matters right now is that you are injured," said Marie Pelletier. "Isn't that right, mon Père?"

Père Noiron frowned. "Madame, I know you for a God-fearing woman. Do not allow your kindness to blind you to the danger here." He turned to stare down at Constance from what seemed like a terrible height. "She is not a woman, as you think of it. She has no immortal soul. Her presence here endangers yours and that of everyone in town."

Marie Pelletier's hand flew to her mouth in shock.

"Mon père!"

Surprise left Constance momentarily speechless. The man's complete lack of logic left her flailing for where to start rebutting him. Perhaps it was the headache that fuddled her thinking.

"Madame...?" They all turned to face the door. The serving girl hovered in the doorway, obviously reluctant to come in.

"Oui, Camille?" asked Madame Pelletier.

"Le docteur est arrivé."

"Merci, Camille. Fais-le monter." She turned back to the priest. "The doctor has come to examine her. We can continue this discussion over a bowl of stew. I made fresh bread to go with it."

With a firm hand on the priest's arm, she led him away from the bed. At the door, both turned to give Constance a last look. Madame Pelletier's smile was troubled but reassuring, but the look the priest gave her was fierce and uncompromising.

✑ SEVEN ✑

DESAUTEL'S horse resisted turning up the A'lle road and Desautel could not blame her. It was very cold and even beneath the thick woolen scarf, he could feel his cheeks growing stiff. The house itself loomed atop the hill like a stone and wooden beast guarding against attack, its roof line hard and straight against the starry night.

He did not want to be here, either.

He urged the mare onto the road with a click of his tongue, silently promising her an extra long rubdown when he got her back to the constabulary stables.

He could have sent one of his constables—*wanted* to, in fact— but honor forbade it. He had alarmed the two young women need-lessly, earlier. The least he could do now was inform the family in person that their daughter was safe.

The main floor windows were lit with the soft glow of oil lamps. It was becoming an uncommon sight, with most of the countryside converting to gas or electricity. But the A'lle house was outside of town and isolated. It would be expensive to bring the power line up the hill.

He'd been told that the A'lle had moved here from Upper Canada years ago. He wondered what they had left behind that they would willingly settle in a community that was not exactly welcoming to them. That they'd had a hard go of it, he had no doubt. Yet the house was kept up, its shingles snug and aligned, its steps solid, its windows sparkling with cleanliness.

The little he'd seen of the inside spoke of pride of place and hard work.

These should be welcome attributes in any new arrivals.

Desautel did not blame St. Vincent for its reserve. These people did not fit anywhere. They did not belong.

Even as he thought it, he could hear his grandfather's words echoing from the past.

"They are refugees, Médéric," he would say patiently. "They have lost everything. Their entire *world.*"

Hughes Desautel had been a forbearing man, willing to extend a hand in friendship to these strangers, these intruders. But he had never had to work with them. It was much easier to dispense charity than to welcome the objects of your charity into your every-day life.

He had always thought of himself as being like his grandfather, but as he grew older, he saw much of his father's distrust of the A'lle in himself. There had been no reason for it—not in his father, nor in himself—yet there it was. He did not like them. They were strange, with their huge eyes and their odd ways.

They were *other.*

A soft nicker sounded from behind the house. The mare's head lifted in interest. Then the slap of a leather guide against a rump sounded in the still night and amidst the jangling of bells and swooshing of runners, a two-person sled rounded the corner of the house.

The driver caught sight of Desautel and pulled up on the lines.

"Good evening," said Desautel, trying to make out the figure in the dark. Fairly tall—was it the tall sister? What was her name? Eloise.

"Chief Investigator," came a man's voice.

The father, then. With those damnable A'lle eyes that saw in the dark.

"Mr. A'lle," said Desautel. "Where are you going?"

There was a long silence while Desautel tried to make out the other man's features. His ears were growing cold, despite the sheepskin flaps covering them. He shied away from the thought of Renaud and Dallaire out in this cold. Of Saint-Amand and Johnson, who had yet to return.

A faint whiff of woodsmoke reached him and he was obscurely reassured. It seemed these A'lle did want warmth of a cold night.

"I am going to look for my daughter," said John A'lle finally. His tone was cool and reserved, yet Desautel could sense anger beneath it. Or perhaps he was imagining it.

"There is no need." Desautel was glad to finally divest himself of his good news. "Your daughter is safe in Backli's Ford."

Only when the other man's shoulders slumped did Desautel realize the tension that had been holding him up.

"Come inside," said John A'lle. "You can tell us all at the same time."

The last thing Desautel wanted was to go back inside that house. His experience there earlier in the day had shaken him. If he hadn't known that the girl's parents were well-known in these parts for their ability to find lost people, he would have taken the girl, Prudence, as a charlatan. As it was, he believed her when she said she could tell where the various members of her family were, but it disturbed him.

Then it occurred to him. Perhaps she was a charlatan, after all. Constance A'lle was alive, according to Monsieur Patenaude and that irritating woman, Marie Pelletier. Why then, hadn't Prudence A'lle been able to find her?

John A'lle took Desautel's acquiescence for granted and stepped down from the sled. He tied the lines to the porch railing and waited for Desautel to climb down from his horse.

Desautel tried not to grunt as he lifted his leg over the saddle to swing down. He was stiff with cold and tension and wished he was in Backli's Ford, looking for his men.

John A'lle led the way up the wooden stairs and Desautel clumped along behind him, trying to regain the feeling in his toes. Before the man could reach for the door, it opened, spilling light onto the porch.

"John?" came a woman's voice.

"It's all right, Lily," said A'lle. "She's safe."

There followed a flurry of activity as Desautel was ushered into the house and surrounded by women demanding information. He tried counting them but they were all moving and he kept losing track. At one point, he caught John A'lle's eye and was surprised to see laughter in them.

"Now you see what my daily life is like," said the elder A'lle.

"Girls!" said Lily A'lle firmly. "Let the man breathe!" In the sudden silence, she turned to Desautel and smiled. "Now then, Chief Investigator. May I offer you some tea?"

Desautel desperately wanted something hot inside him while his feet thawed. But he even more desperately wanted to say his piece and leave. He looked down into Lily A'lle's strange eyes and opened his mouth to say no.

"Of course he will have some tea," said Prudence firmly. She was at the back of the group, standing next to the tall one. With a gentle nudge, she made her way through the female barrier and faced him.

"Chief Desautel, come to the kitchen. It's warm and I have pie."

In the end, his stomach betrayed him. He had yet to have his dinner, and if there was one sweet he could not resist, it was pie.

"Thank you, Mademoiselle," he said solemnly. "That is a handsome offer."

The tall one—Eloise, definitely—rolled her eyes and headed down the hallway toward the kitchen.

Five minutes later, they were all seated at the table and Desautel had a mug of hot, sweet tea in his hands. While Prudence cut up the pie and set pieces in front of everybody, he told them what he knew.

The joy in their faces slowly faded as his story unraveled. Despite the excellence of Mademoiselle Prudence's apple pie, he found he could eat only a few bites. At last, he pushed the plate away. It scraped loudly against the scarred table.

He waited and watched while they absorbed his words. Two of the girls were twins and seemed to be the youngest ones. They sat close to each other, their heads slightly bent toward each other, whispering. Lily A'lle's hand had crept into her husband's as the tale unfolded and now she frowned at the table. The middle child sat between Eloise and Prudence, and kept her hands clasped together tightly in her lap. Her hair, like that of the twins, was bound in two tight braids that fell on either side of their faces. Eloise and Prudence exchanged a glance and there was no disguising the relief in their faces.

They had had to live with the fear longer than the others.

At last John A'lle leaned toward Desautel.

"You say she fell?" His eyes were the same strange blue as the others, but paler.

"It would appear so," said Desautel cautiously. He did not want to alarm them needlessly, but they had to be prepared for serious injuries.

"We will go for her," said Lily A'lle. She released her husband's hand but not his gaze. "We will bring her back."

John A'lle nodded at her.

"There is no need," said Desautel firmly. "She is being well looked after at the inn. Backli's Ford has a doctor. She will profit from a good night's sleep. My men and I are going at first light. We will bring her back."

"What of her companions?" asked Eloise, drawing every eye. She had not spoken a word since he arrived, and the first words out of her mouth filled his chest with dread. *What of her companions?*

He took a deep breath. Every eye was on him and in the sudden silence, the fire in the cookstove popped and hissed as flame found moisture.

"They have yet to be found," he said finally. He stood up. His feet were as thawed as they would get. It was time to go back to the constabulary.

"Mademoiselle," he bowed slightly to Prudence, "thank you for the tea and pie. They were most welcome."

John A'lle was on his feet, too. He led Desautel back down the dark hallway to the front entrance. His wife and Prudence followed behind.

"Thank you for coming to tell us," said John A'lle. He stuck his hand out and Desautel hesitated a bare second before taking it, but it was long enough for the warmth in John A'lle's eyes to dim somewhat.

Desautel shook the man's hand firmly and released it. "I will keep you informed," he promised.

"I will accompany you in the morning," A'lle said.

Desautel would have sighed but that would have been rude. Of course the man wanted to come. This was his daughter, after all.

"Sir, there is no need. We will leave before first light and bring her back to you."

John A'lle exchanged a look with his wife before turning back to Desautel.

"In that case, we will wait for her here. Thank you."

Desautel slid his feet into his hard leather boots and shrugged into his sheepskin coat, accepting his hat and thick gloves from Madame A'lle. He had his hand on the door handle when he remembered. He turned to look at Prudence A'lle.

"Why is it you could not find her?" he asked softly. She knew exactly what he meant. He could see it in the troubled look in his eye.

She took a deep breath and clasped her hands in front of her waist.

"She must have been unconscious," she said softly. "Else I would have sensed her."

Desautel nodded, filing the information away for future thought. A decidedly strange family. With a final goodnight, he stepped into the cold night. The door closed firmly behind him and he took a moment to breathe deeply of the woodsmoke-laden air. Fat gray clouds had moved in from the north, heavy with snow. A few flakes had begun to fall. It was going to be a cold ride back to town.

The mare whinnied softly as he came down the steps and it was only as he was untying her reins that he noticed Eloise A'lle standing by the other horse. She was waiting for him to leave so she could turn the sled around and return it to the back of the house, where presumably there were stables.

The faint glow from the windows, reflected back by the snow, was enough for him see her watching him. Without a word, he climbed into the saddle and urged the mare back down to the road.

* * *

The snow fell harder and faster as he made his way back to town, and by the time he reached the stables, he was thoroughly chilled. The stable boy raised his head from the straw pallet where he slept, but Desautel waved him back to sleep.

He took his time wiping down the mare, making sure she was dry and warm. As he worked, his mind kept coming back to his unholy fascination with the A'lle.

They hadn't seemed particularly concerned that Constance was injured. Beyond asking what had happened, they brushed past the state of her injuries as though it meant nothing.

He should not have gone there this afternoon, and didn't understand why he had. It was foolish to involve the family when he knew so little. Had he waited, he could have sent one of his constables with the information that Constance A'lle had been injured but would be all right. There would have been no need to involve himself in their affairs.

It was the girl. She should not be working in her home town. Too many conflicts and ties. And the fact that she looked sixteen—

though she and the magistrate assured him she was actually twenty-one—did not help him or any of his constables to take her seriously as an investigator. Intellectually, Desautel knew the A'lle matured slower physically, but he could not help thinking of her as a child.

God *bless* the magistrate.

* * *

Doctor Saunders was much younger than Constance had expected.

She watched him rummage through the black leather bag he had set on the chair by her bed. His hands were fine, his fingers long.

The door had been left open a crack and Constance was sure the girl, Camille, was loitering in the hall. Madame Pelletier understood the doctor needed privacy for his examination, but apparently she was also mindful of the proprieties.

He was tall, though not as tall as the priest, and his black hair gleamed in the light of the lamp. How did Backli's Ford warrant a doctor? And such a young one, at that?

He found what he was looking for and held out a small instrument with a lens at one end. When he finally turned to look at her, she saw that his eyes were blue.

"I am told your name is Constance A'lle. Is that right?"

"Yes, that's right."

"How old are you, Miss A'lle?" He brought the lamp closer to the bed and leaned in toward her, angling the instrument so that he could peer through it at her eyes. His breath smelled of China tea.

"Twenty-one," she answered.

He straightened and looked down at her. She knew exactly what he was thinking, having dealt with it all her life. To humans, she only looked sixteen. Nevertheless, she *was* twenty-one, a grown woman by law.

Then the doctor smiled at her. The smile crinkled his eyes and caused dimples to appear on either side of his mouth.

"When I was at university, my roommate was A'lle. He was much older than I, but looked my age. Most unfair." He replaced the instrument in his bag. "Do you have a headache?"

"Yes." She wanted to ask him more about his A'lle roommate but at that moment, a knock sounded at the door and Madame Pelletier came bustling back in. She had removed the cloth at her waist and a few more hairs had escaped the bun at the back of her head.

"How is she, Docteur?"

"I am still examining her, Madame," replied the doctor. "Perhaps you would assist me by holding the lamp up."

Madame Pelletier hurried to the bed and grabbed the electric lamp by its ceramic base. The movement set shadows dancing on the walls. Doctor Saunders straightened, waiting until Madame Pelletier steadied the light before resuming his examination of Constance's head.

Where was the priest? Off to harrass another parishioner? Organizing a lynch mob?

The doctor took her chin in one firm hand and turned her face toward the light so that he could see the injury above her temple. Next to him, Madame Pelletier leaned in closer.

"Seigneur..."

"What is it?" asked the doctor, peering from the woman to Constance.

"It looks much better than when Thomas brought her in," murmured Marie Pelletier.

"Yes," said Doctor Saunders. "The A'lle heal quickly." He examined the gash carefully. "You cleaned it?"

"With warm water and soap," replied Madame Pelletier.

"Very good," he murmured. "It looks clean."

Nevertheless, he removed a brown bottle from his bag and a small cotton pad, upon which he then poured a clear liquid. There was no smell and Constance didn't turn away when he applied the pad to her gash. They used peroxide at home, too.

"With anyone else, I would stitch this," he said under his breath.

"No need," said Constance. And there wasn't. Left alone, the gash would be gone within three days, with no scar.

"Indeed." He straightened to look down at her. "What other injuries?"

Before Constance could speak up, Madame Pelletier said, "She has a terrible lump on the back of her head. And Thomas had to reset her shoulder—the left one. He suspected she might have some broken ribs, though I think he's wrong. That's it, save for her legs."

Constance looked up at Madame Pelletier. "What happened to my legs?"

"The gashes, ma fille. Probably from broken branches when you fell."

"What happened?" asked the doctor. He pulled the blankets off Constance to expose her legs. It was done so quickly and impersonally that Constance didn't have time to reflexively clutch the blankets to her. Madame Pelletier frowned, but the doctor was already bending over Constance's legs.

"Raise your gown, please."

Constance hesitated and he waited. Finally she hitched the muslin gown up to the top of the bandages.

She was at the mercy of these people. For the first time, she realized how vulnerable she was without Renaud and Dallaire. She did not like to admit it, but she had been fortunate to fall in among kind strangers. What if Madame Pelletier's two strangers had found her first? She shivered and the doctor, misunderstanding, said, "I will go as quickly as I can. Madame, would you hand me the scissors from my bag."

Madame Pelletier rummaged inside the bag and finally emerged with a small pair of scissors, which she handed him. In two snips, he cut the binding off her bandage and pulled the cloth away. Madame Pelletier peered around him to see.

"Multiple lacerations," murmured Dr. Saunders. "Also healing well."

Constance didn't bother looking. She knew what they would find. Madame Pelletiers's lips pursed while the doctor removed the bandages from the other leg.

"Less damage here," he said. "Madame, the disinfectant, please."

Madame Pelletier handed him the brown bottle and a fresh cotton swab. As he daubed the lacerations, Madame Pelletier looked at Constance.

"The gashes were deep," she said. "One so deep I was surprised it had stopped bleeding on its own." She took a deep breath. "All of them are scabbed over. And the deep one is almost closed."

Constance nodded. "We heal faster than..."— she almost said "humans" but reconsidered—"...you. There is something here that helps us heal even faster. We think it is a mineral in the soil." She stopped talking when Madame Pelletier moved back.

There it was. That look. The look that said, OTHER.

Once again, she had reminded Madame Pelletier that she was from another world, as if the woman couldn't tell just by looking at her. No A'lle ever went unnoticed. If their above average height did not give them away, their eyes did.

Every A'lle on Earth had the same shade of eyes, a cross between blueberry and cranberry. Compared to humans, A'lle eyes had too much color, as the iris was larger than in human eyes. It did not help that A'lle pupils were always contracted to a pinprick. There was too much light on this world for them.

Grandmother Esther had once told her that only their clan had that colour of eyes. The other ships had contained different clans, but none of them had crashed on Earth.

"I wish all my patients would heal as quickly," said the doctor with great satisfaction. He straightened. Reaching across Madame Pelletier for his bag, he said, "Pardon me."

Marie Pelletier took that as her cue to step even further back.

The doctor finished bandaging Constance and began putting his bottle and cloths away.

"Thank you, Docteur," said Constance. "Now I wish to see your other A'lle patient."

He paused with his back to her, then finished putting everything away. "That's right. I was told you were with the St. Vincent constabulary." He finally turned to look at her. She could not always tell what certain expressions meant on human faces. His perplexed her until he explained.

"I'm very sorry, but the boy died. That's why it took me so long to get here."

Constance's mind went blank. She glanced at Madame Pelletier to find her looking unmistakeably surprised.

"How did he die?" asked Constance finally.

The doctor took a deep breath. "He died of his injuries," he said in a low voice. He looked away, fiddled with the clasp of his satchel. He finally looked at her again. "I could not stabilize his internal injuries."

The anger that always simmered just below the surface threatened to boil over, but she controlled herself. It would not be fair to take it out on this man. He obviously cared deeply that he had not been able to help the boy.

"It must have been a severe beating," she said. So severe that the A'lle ability to heal could not cope with the amount of damage.

"Yes." He frowned. "Broken ribs, nose. I suspect a fractured cheekbone. Cracked fingers, extensive bruising..."

He stopped. Madame Pelletier looked as if her dinner wanted to escape.

"Who beat him?" asked Constance calmly. Until Renaud and Dallaire arrived, she was the only law in Backli's Ford. Whether Chief Desautel liked it or not, she was now in charge of her first investigation.

The doctor shrugged. "I don't know, Mademoiselle. A few boys found him on the square and went to fetch their parents. They brought him to me, unconscious." He picked up his satchel and stood looking down at her. "He never regained consciousness."

Constance nodded. Already the headache was beginning to recede. "I will need to examine the body."

She heard the innkeeper gasp softly but ignored her. This was a constabulary matter now. A person was murdered, perhaps accidentally, but murdered nonetheless, and in the absence of her superiors, it was her duty to investigate.

"Certainly," said the doctor. "I am keeping his body in the stone shed in my backyard. Backli's Ford does not have a mortuary," he added.

"Where is your surgery?"

"Just the other side of the church," said Doctor Saunders. "I will come by in the morning to see how you are feeling. I can accompany you back to my surgery then if you are feeling up to it."

"I am feeling up to it now," she said and made to swing her legs out of bed.

At once, Madame Pelletier objected. "Docteur, she is not well enough!"

The doctor placed a hand on Constance's good shoulder and gently pushed her back down. "I must agree with the good lady," he said sternly. "You may be A'lle, but you suffered serious injuries. You need to rest, at least tonight. The boy is not going anywhere."

∂ EIGHT ∾

CONSTANCE glanced out the window before leaving her room. The window gave onto the inn's stables. She could hear the whinny of horses and the soft thudding of hooves stamping the straw. It was dark, but enough light spilled from the downstairs windows to reveal a heavy snow falling.

Once in the hallway, she counted five doors on one side, four on the other, two on either side of the staircase. Electricity had come to Backli's Ford but the conversion was apparently haphazard. While her bedroom was equipped with an overhead electric light fixture and a small electric beside lamp, two oil lamps bracketed her bedroom door, which faced the staircase. Aside from that, there were no other lights on upstairs. Apparently, she was the only guest. Not surprising, really. Backli's Ford only sprang to life once the ice left the river.

She stood at the top of the stairs, her good hand clasping the banister, her bare feet on the cold pine floor. Already the waves of dizziness receded as her body healed itself. Madame Pelletier's beef stew—all three bowls of it—had gone a long way to fuel her recovery. The girl, Camille, had stared in fascination as Constance polished off bowl after bowl, but Constance hadn't cared. Her cells had been starved after expending so much energy to repair her injuries.

Now she wanted to find her boots and socks. Her clothes, having dried on the wall pegs, were stiff and scratchy, but she felt enormously better with them on. Madame Pelletier had said her coat and boots had been set to dry by the woodstove in the kitchen.

The inn seemed very quiet. A faint smell of wood smoke permeated the air.

From the top of the stairs, she could see the empty entry hall. The main dining room would be off the hall, which meant the kitchen would be at the back of the house. A pair of closed doors separated the hall from what must be the sitting room.

Once Camille had left her room, Constance had gotten out of bed and dressed. Her shoulder was tender and stiff and she tried not to jostle it. Of all her injuries, it would take the longest to heal. Other than that, and the occasional dizziness, she felt well enough to be out and investigating.

Once she found her boots.

She made it down the stairs without a problem. As she reached the last step, she heard a murmur of voices from beyond the double doors. Without thinking, she headed for the doors and leaned against the crack, the better to hear. Men, many men, speaking low and serious, with an undercurrent of concern in their voices.

The search party? She leaned her forehead against the door. After a moment, she straightened. She could do nothing for Renaud and Dallaire tonight. She hoped they had found shelter against the falling snow. And the cold.

As she turned away from the doors, she glanced at the front door with its expensive bevelled glass inset. A dozen pairs of boots rested on either side of the door, slowly melting snow onto thick braided rag rugs.

She headed the other way, toward the back of the house. A lone electric lamp on a narrow shelf kept the darkness at bay. Despite the long narrow rug running the length of the hallway, it was cooler in the hallway than upstairs. Heat emanated from the far end, and Constance didn't need the strip of light at the bottom of the door to know that beyond was the kitchen.

Behind her, in the common room, the men's voices rose in pitch. They were getting ready to leave.

She reached the kitchen door in three long strides and pushed it open. The heat in the room stopped her in the entrance and she blinked furiously against the sudden blaze of light, her eyes watering at the stab of pain. The aroma of beef stew tickled her nose and her stomach rumbled hopefully. When her eyes finally adjusted, she found herself staring down into the stern face of Madame Pelletier.

"Why are you out of bed?" The woman stood with her fists on her hips, a large wooden spoon, forgotten in her hand, dripping stew juice onto the scarred pine floor. Beyond her, a large black gas cookstove had various cast iron pots simmering and steaming on its top.

Constance took a deep breath, noting the aroma of cooking apples and cinnamon, as well as the stew. The heat in the room was almost overwhelming. On the large table, a mound of bread dough rose under a clean cotton cloth.

"Madame," said Constance, "I am looking for my boots."

A flicker of the innkeeper's eyes told Constance where to look. She turned toward the far end of the room where a large wood cookstove—obviously relegated to back-up duty now that they had a gas cooker—kept a kettle of water simmering and moisture in the air. Next to the woodstove was an alcove in which her boots, socks, and coat were arrayed on various pegs and hooks.

Madame Pelletier watched her with consternation as she took her dry socks off the drying hooks.

"Mademoiselle A'lle," said the innkeeper. "Please—you must return to bed."

Constance leaned against the wall to pull on her socks. They were warm. "Madame," she said. "Please call me Constance."

"Constance," Madame Pelletier tried again. "Please…"

Constance pulled on her boots. Mostly dry. She straightened and took her coat from the peg. "The men in the common room." She nodded at the connecting door. Clearly the searchers hadn't found Renaud or Dallaire.

Madame Pelletier finally set the spoon down on the table next to a large pottery bowl. "They are discussing tomorrow's search." Her gaze slid away from Constance's. She had no faith the men would be found in time.

Constance did, in spite of the falling temperature and falling snow. Dallaire and Renaud were experienced men. They would find a safe place to spend the night. She carefully pulled the coat over her tender shoulder and then slid her right arm into the other sleeve.

The door connecting to the common room swung open and Camille backed into the kitchen carrying a tray filled with cups and glasses. Constance caught a glimpse of figures milling around at the far end of the common room before the door swung shut again. Camille turned around and stopped when she saw Constance. She looked at Madame Pelletier.

"Thank you, Camille," said Madame Pelletier. "You can go home now."

The girl nodded and set the tray on the counter before hurrying out.

Constance looked at Madame Pelletier. The innkeeper had a wary expression on her face. Constance sighed.

"Madame, you and your husband have been more than kind, but if I cannot look for my colleagues, at the very least I can do my duty." She nodded to the door at the far end of the kitchen. "That door leads to the stables?"

Madame Pelletier resisted a moment longer, then nodded.

"And the doctor's surgery?"

"East of the house, beyond the graveyard. His house is set back from the street but he always keeps a light burning on the porch."

"Merci, Madame." Without another word, Constance stepped

into the night and closed the door behind her. She wondered if she would be allowed back in.

She took a deep breath of cold night air and expelled it on a gust. Her ribs ached but walking wouldn't harm them.

A horse nickered in the darkness of the stable as she stepped away from thc inn.

Please be safe, she sent out to the night. *Just stay safe and we'll find you in the morning.*

She walked around the corner of the inn, past a chicken coop with sleepy hens. About twenty feet away, a tall iron fence separated the inn's property from the church yard. A few marble headstones gleamed in the faint light from the back of the inn. Beyond the cemetery, the back of the church loomed in the darkness, its stabbing steeple gentled by the falling snow.

A dog trotted out of the darkness and she greeted it with pleasure, pausing to rub its jowls with her bare hands and let it get a good sniff of her. A mutt, no taller than her knees, but bright-eyed with intelligence. Male. His coat could be gray or dun—hard to tell in the dark.

They'd had a dog when she was little, before the twins were born. Then one day the dog was gone and Father never discussed what had happened to it. Years later, she learned from Prudence, who was two years older and remembered, that some boys from St. Vincent had stoned the dog to death and left its corpse by their front door.

Constance gave the dog a last pat before straightening up again.

"Stay, little one," she said softly. "I'll come visit again."

The dog woofed softly and sat on the frozen ground, as if prepared to wait for as long as it took.

The snow now fell with greater insistence although it wasn't cold. Constance studied the sky as she walked the rutted path alongside the inn. Snow meant clouds. In February those clouds usually kept the temperature from dropping too far.

At the corner, she stopped. The men were leaving the inn, calling out their goodbyes to Thomas Pelletier, who stood at the top of the porch, storm lantern in hand. Constance counted ten men, all on foot.

She waited, expecting the dog to trot to the front of the house to check on the activity, but he stayed put. Perhaps he did not belong to the inn, or to one of the visitors, after all.

The men reached the main street and dispersed to their various homes. Thomas waited until the last man had disappeared before going back inside, still unaware of her presence. As soon as he closed the front door, she strode down the path to the street and turned left, toward the doctor's surgery.

The breeze sent snowflakes down her collar to melt. Brick and wood houses loomed like ghosts in the snow, set back from the road behind picket fences. Most had lighted windows on the main floors. Dogs barked in the distance. Behind her, the dog barked in response. At one house, across the street, a young boy tromped up the side porch stairs with an armload of wood. As if sensing her attention, he paused at the top to look around at her. After a moment, he nodded in acknowledgment and Constance nodded back.

Unlike the inn, with light blazing from almost every main floor window, the church stood dark. Did Père Noiron live on site? Was there a rectory? Was he in there now, plotting how to save his parishioners from her?

A moment later, she stood in front of the doctor's home and surgery. As Madame Pelletier had predicted, a lantern hung from a hook by the front door, illuminating a wide porch that ran the width of the house and disappeared around both corners. Fieldstone posts at the corners supported a balcony at the second level. The good doctor was doing well for himself, in spite of Backli's Ford's small population.

As far as she could tell, Backli's Ford had only one reason for existing: the presence of the only safe ford of the Bartolomée River for miles. That, and its proximity to the American border. The river acted like a natural border and the town ran a small ferry for travelers going between Montreal and Albany. Travellers could save half a day by using it. From Backli's Ford, it was only thirty-three miles to Montreal.

As perfect a set-up for smuggling to and from the American States as Constance could imagine. It was becoming such a problem that the chief was considering setting up a satellite constabulary in the village. No doubt he would exile her here if he thought he could get away with it.

Otherwise, Backli's Ford was nothing but a collection of surrounding farms and maybe a few orchards. The village itself couldn't have more than two hundred people.

By comparison, St. Vincent was the biggest town in the region, with almost ten thousand people, and there were not enough doctors to fill the needs of the townspeople.

How had Backli's Ford managed to attract a doctor?

Fragrant smoke poured out of the chimney and warm light filled the main floor windows. A front walk, recently shoveled but now coated with an undisturbed, thin layer of snow, led straight to the front door. The doctor obviously used a different door to go in and out. She made her way to the front door, where a neatly painted shingle placed beneath the lantern read:

DR. EPHRAIM SAUNDERS
DOCTOR OF MEDICINE

Constance reached for the plain brass knocker and knocked three times. A moment later, the door opened, spilling light onto the porch. Docteur Saunders stood before her, his boots on and a scarf wrapped around his neck, as if he had been about to go out.

"Miss A'lle!" he said. "You shouldn't be up!" He gestured her inside.

"Were you going out?" she asked, stepping inside.

The doctor closed the door behind her.

"I just got in, actually," he said. He studied her face, frowning. "You should really be in bed."

Constance tamped down a spike of irritation. Why did they insist on judging her by their frail standards?

The front hall was warm and redolent with a faint smell of the chicken the doctor had no doubt eaten at dinner. To her right, an open door revealed a horsehair settee and a few hard-back chairs.

"I've come to see the body." She waited patiently, trying to make her face as expressionless as Chief Desautel's.

The doctor stopped trying to guide her into his sitting room and stood looking down at her. He was quite tall, considering she towered over most men. The serious expression his face wore naturally took on a deeper cast, as if something pained him.

For a moment, Constance thought he was going to refuse, but after hesitating, he contented himself with a nod.

"I'll get my coat," he said.

The body was in his shed, she remembered him saying. Not a respectful way to treat a person, she thought as he disappeared into the back of the house, but the practicalities surrounding death were rarely dignified.

Moments later, he emerged from the back of the house dressed in a heavy coat and gloves and carrying a lantern that he'd already lit.

"Through here," he indicated.

She followed him down a hallway carpeted with a flowered runner. Prudence would have been upset that she hadn't removed her boots.

As she passed the open door, she saw that what she had thought was a parlor was more of a waiting room. On the other side of the hallway was another door. That one probably led to his clinic. Hopefully it was better furnished.

Then she found herself in a kitchen much smaller than the one at the inn. She glanced around and gained an impression of starkness before the doctor opened the back door to lead the way outside. She followed him down two wooden steps onto a path worn deep between two banks of snow. Her boots squeaked on the hard-packed snow. A trick of acoustics allowed her to hear the river running beneath the ice, a deep, *shushing* sound that was oddly comforting, despite the fact that the river was on the other side of the main street.

The doctor's lamp illuminated a small stone building with a padlock on the rough wooden door. The building would barely be tall enough for her to stand in. The doctor handed her the lantern, then removed a mitten to fish through his pocket for the key. In the lamplight his hair was the color of brass.

He unlocked the padlock, took the lantern from her and went inside. A faint smell like copper mixed with manure wafted out and she wrinkled her nose. The doctor's stooped back obscured her view until he shifted. In the light of the lantern, she saw that the shed was lined with wooden shelves set against the back wall, and a narrow table that was pushed up against the long wall beneath a small, square window. On the table lay a still figure draped in an old, stained, bed sheet.

Constance swallowed hard. This was part of her job. As an investigator, she would have to see dead bodies. Touch them. She swallowed again. She had witnessed an autopsy when she trained. It had disturbed her, despite her fascination at the differences between human and A'lle anatomy.

"Please remove the cover," she whispered.

The doctor hung the lantern on a hook in the low ceiling and shadows swung wildly in the small room, illuminating his face, the bed sheet, the mostly empty shelves. In the reflection from the window, she saw her own face staring back at her before the swing of the lantern obscured it. Then the doctor pulled the sheet down to the corpse's waist and stood back, watching her.

Constance forced her feet closer, her gaze downward. The corpse might be that of a young man, but it was hard to tell because of the bruising and swelling about his face. His shirt had been ripped open. He was thin in the way of young men—human and A'lle—before they reached full maturity. Dark, shaggy hair that would have fallen over his ears. Thin chest. Thin arms but wiry.

His lip had been split. His cheekbones were scraped raw and swollen. His eyes were swollen shut. Blood had pooled and dried in his ears. Through his torn, parted lips, she caught sight of broken teeth. The flesh of his face, where not discolored by scrapes and bruising, looked pale and translucent.

Death made him indistinguishable from humans. She removed the mitten from her right hand and without giving herself a chance to hesitate, touched his eyelid. The flesh was cold and resistant, and when she finally pried the eyelid open, she found the eye clouded and flat looking. Even in death, however, the iris looked large. She didn't need to see the color to confirm he was A'lle. Had been A'lle.

She released the eyelid, but it stayed open.

Ignoring the taste of bile at the back of her throat, she forced herself to examine his chest and belly. White bandages were wrapped tautly around his rib cage but his belly was swollen and discolored.

His hands... his hands were big and blue, the knuckles scraped. At least two fingers were broken. He had fought hard for his life. The palms were callused. He had been used to hard work, this one.

"Help me remove his clothing," she said tightly.

"Pardon?"

She turned to the doctor. "I must examine his body."

"Miss A'lle..." The doctor gestured at the corpse. "I can assure you—"

"Your assurances mean nothing." At the look on his face, she sighed. "Forgive me, Docteur. This is upsetting. What I meant was that I am the representative of the chief investigator for the Baudry Region and this is now an official investigation. I must be able to report back what *I* saw, if at all possible. I must be able to testify in court to what I saw."

The doctor looked at her silently, then finally nodded. Together they removed the sheet, then proceeded to disrobe the corpse. Rigor mortis had fully set in and by the time they finished, both Constance and the doctor were sweating.

The boy's knees were scraped, as if he had fallen on a hard surface, or had to crawl through something rough. The feet were also blue, but the toenails were pale. She ran her hand over his shins. The right shin bone was obviously broken.

There was a jagged, white scar on his left shoulder, clearly from an old wound. A'lle rarely scarred—it must have been a serious injury.

"Help me turn him over, please."

The doctor stared at her a moment. Finally he took the hips and Constance took the shoulders. Together they turned the corpse onto his side. Blood had pooled to the underside of the body, turning it a livid purple. The skin where Constance pressed the shoulder turned white.

In the gloom of the little shed, it was too hard to distinguish anything but the purplish color of the skin. She would have to return in the morning.

Without a word, they redressed the corpse and then draped the sheet over it. The doctor took down the lantern and gestured for her to leave ahead of him. He locked the shed door before leading the way back into his kitchen, where he extinguished the light and set the lantern on the floor by the door before turning the overhead light on.

"I prescribe a pot of hot tea for both of us," he said, hanging the padlock key on a hook by the door.

Hot tea seemed most appealing. She nodded.

"Sit," ordered Docteur Saunders, waving at the kitchen table with its mismatched chairs. "How do you feel?" He glanced at her, examining her critically in the quick look.

"I'm fine," said Constance, but taking her boots off took a long time as she fought off waves of fatigue and nursed her bad shoulder. Finally she walked across the pine floor in her stocking feet and sat down in the chair closest to the woodstove.

Dr. Saunders busied himself filling the kettle from the pump and setting it on the cookstove. He opened the door to the stove and from a huge basket next to the stove picked out three split logs that he proceeded to stuff inside the fire box. He waited until the fire caught, then closed the door. No gas stove for him, but then he probably didn't do much cooking for himself.

Constance welcomed the heat. She felt unaccountably cold, chilled to her core. Where the doctor had removed his coat and hung it on the back of a chair, she huddled inside hers.

While he busied himself with cups and cutlery, Constance considered the facts. She did not know the A'lle boy, which meant he wasn't from around these parts.

Most of the A'lle's escape pods had landed in the southeastern corner of Lower Canada. In the two centuries since then, A'lle had spread throughout Upper and Lower Canada. Some had gone to the New American States. But wherever they had settled, A'lle knew each other, or at least *of* each other, within their region.

It was hard *not* to know the other A'lle within reach. At first, A'lle had kept track of each other out of necessity. In some areas, A'lle had been persecuted and chased out. In New America, some had been drowned or hanged as witches.

Father thought those days were gone, but in this one thing, Constance thought him foolish. No A'lle should ever trust that the bad days were gone. All she had to do was look into Madame Pelletier's troubled eyes, or face the priest's fear-fueled fanaticism.

It was all too easy for humans to keep track of the A'lle. Too easy to blame them when things went wrong. A'lle had to know where other A'lle were. In case they needed to be warned.

Whoever he was, this young man—a boy, to human eyes— didn't come from anywhere near St. Vincent. Perhaps he came from Montreal, or Upper Canada, or even New America. She suddenly realized she should have checked his pockets for anything to help identify him. She should have examined his boots—the wear pattern could have told her if he had walked far. Had he had a coat?

This was all basic—how could she forget her training like that?

"I am sorry, Docteur," she said. "I must see the body again."

The doctor looked over his shoulder at her and frowned. "No." He studied her eyes and mouth, the droop of her shoulders, and shook his head. "No more tonight. You will be stronger tomorrow." He turned back to what he was doing at the counter and Constance opened her mouth to argue, only to close it again.

She didn't know if she could even get up, let alone walk to the shed again. And the thought of manipulating that body again...

The doctor was right. Tomorrow would be better. In daylight.

The boy had been found this morning, probably early, since a village square was usually well-travelled. So, say around eight o'clock. Whoever found him would have run home, or to the doctor, depending on the age of the discoverer. Then help would have been summoned to bring the boy to the doctor, who would then have examined him.

By mid-morning at the latest, the doctor would have known what was happening. The call to the constabulary had come close to the midday meal. Why had it taken almost two hours for the call to be made?

The doctor set a plate down in front of her, startling her.

"Eat," he said.

On the plate was a slab of bread, slathered with butter and spread with molasses. Obediently, she picked it up and took a bite. The sweetness of the molasses spread through her and she closed her eyes in bliss. She was starving.

She ate in silence for a few minutes, then the doctor brought the tea pot and two cups to the table. He dragged a clay container from the middle of the table toward her and nodded to it as he poured tea into her cup. "That's honey. Add some to your tea."

For the next little while, they were occupied with fixing their tea. Finally, bread eaten and the first sip of hot tea warming her, she sat back.

"Thank you, Docteur. I feel better."

He nodded. "You look better. For a while, I feared you would faint. And it's Ephraim."

She blinked. Oh. His given name. She nodded in acknowledgement.

"Tell me again how he came to you." She nodded toward the back door and the shed in the backyard.

The doctor sat back, his big hands cradling the china cup. His face looked grave.

"A couple of boys found him on the square," he said. "This morning. They told their parents, who brought the boy to me." He nodded toward the front of the house and his surgery. Then he looked down at the tabletop. "I'm afraid there wasn't much I could do for him." He looked up at her, his eyes full of regret. "He was badly beaten."

Badly beaten and left to die on the square, with no more regard than her dog had been given. Her dog's death had been a message, one that said, *We don't want you here.* What message did the boy's death send?

She clamped down on her emotions, refusing even to identify them. "Tell me about his injuries."

His mouth tightened and he took a moment to respond. "The injuries to his face were caused by fists, I believe, although I suspect a kick to the mouth broke his teeth." His voice grew dispassionate, as though the only way he could get through the litany was by distancing himself from what he was saying. "Broken ribs. One punctured a lung. I suspect his spleen was ruptured." He took a deep breath. "Broken leg, broken fingers." He set the cup down on the saucer very gently, then looked up at her. "I may have missed some."

What could he possibly have done to warrant such a beating?

"Do you know him?"

The doctor shook his head. "No. I've only been here a little while, but I am certain I know everyone in Backli's Ford and he is not—*was* not—from this village or the surrounding area." He sighed deeply, regretfully. "Poor boy."

Not such a boy, really. At least twenty, though he looked younger by human standards.

"Perhaps it's a blessing that he never woke up," continued the doctor.

The blessing would have been to not be murdered. Constance kept the thought to herself and drank her tea. Finally she stood up. He immediately stood up, too.

"You said a few boys found him. Do you know who they are?"

He shook his head. "I never saw the boys. Two of the fathers carried the boy over."

"Who were the fathers?"

"Joseph Amirault was one. He lives at the far end of town, on the north side of the square. And Sam Henderson. He's the ferry operator."

"Thank you, Docteur." She put out her hand and he took it. They shook formally. "I appreciate your help, and your kindness." She nodded to the teapot and the crumbs on her plate.

His hand was big and warm, as was his smile. "My pleasure, Miss A'lle." He released her hand and fetched her boots, carrying them and his own to the front door. "I will accompany you back to the inn."

"No need," said Constance firmly. "I am quite recovered, thanks to your ministrations." She smiled to make it clear it wasn't a rebuff. Well, not meant as a rebuff, in any case. She eased her feet into her boots. It wasn't far to the inn—she would leave them unlaced.

"I would feel much better if I saw you home," insisted the doctor, his boots in hand.

"And I would feel foolish if you did." She smiled again to take the sting out.

The doctor hesitated, then finally admitted defeat by depositing his boots on the carpet by the front door. "Very well. You are a stubborn one." He went to one knee and laced up her boots quickly and efficiently. Constance thought of objecting, but didn't have the heart to rebuff his kindness again.

When he stood, she smiled her thanks and his eyes crinkled up in an answering smile. He reached across her to open the door and she suddenly remembered what she had meant to ask him.

"Why did it take so long to call the constabulary?"

He looked at her, his hand on the doorknob. He was very close. Then his puzzled expression cleared.

"About the boy?" He shrugged and straightened.

In the yellow light of the hallway, she saw him flush.

"I was busy trying to save him," he continued. "By the time it occurred to me to send for the constabulary, I was told St. Vincent already knew. I don't know who called, or when."

Constance turned away to hide her involuntary smile. Likely it was because she was a magistrate's investigator—or perhaps it was because she was herself—but she had managed to fluster the good doctor.

❧ NINE ❧

THE flurries had turned into a full-fledged snowstorm by the time Constance came down the doctor's front porch, and she blinked against the sting of flakes in her eyes. Across the square, a few lights burned in house windows. Hopefully the Pelletiers wouldn't have locked the inn door against her.

Head down against the snow, she turned right at the gate and headed for the inn. The wind had picked up and drove the snow almost horizontally into her eyes so that she could barely see. A few flakes found their way inside through a gap at her collar and she shivered as they melted.

Her thoughts lingered on Renaud and Dallaire, who had no real shelter against the storm, and no A'lle genes to help them withstand the cold.

She hid her hands inside her pockets. Was it only hours ago that she had trudged, broken and bleeding, through the snow, trying to escape some unknown threat? Her day had been full of concern for herself, for kith and kin. First she lost Dallaire and Renaud, and now here she was, trying to figure out what had happened to another A'lle.

Who was he? And why was he in Backli's Ford? Had he been

attacked here in the village, or somewhere else and then dropped at the square?

She would need to interview the boys who had found the victim, and get them to show her exactly where he had been found.

As if to taunt her, a snowflake landed on her nose and melted. Tomorrow would be soon enough to interview the boys. Even if they brought her directly to the spot, any evidence would be hidden under all this new snow.

Stupid. She was being incredibly unprofessional. No wonder the chief had yet to assign her a case—which reminded her that she would have to telephone him in the morning.

The wind soughed through the fir trees in the cemetery. Something creaked noisily and she peered up, her heartbeat quickening, but it was only the cast-iron gate that led to the cemetery. The wind had pushed the gate open and now it swung on hinges that needed oiling.

She turned up the path that led to the gates and reached for the swinging gate to fasten it securely. Before her hand could close on the cold metal, something wet clamped over her mouth and pulled her off balance.

Startled, she flailed to regain her balance, jolting pain through her shoulder. She pulled at the gloved hand over her mouth, but a hard arm clamped hers to her sides, jarring her ribs. She gasped in pain, and fear flashed through her. Then her feet were swept from under her. There were two attackers and now the second one had her legs. They dragged her into the cemetery even as she struggled against them.

Thoughts and images flew through her mind too quickly to grasp and hold on to: the cliff, Madame Pelletier telling her about men looking for her, Renaud and Dallaire missing, the dead boy.

Finally—*finally*—her training kicked in. *Your legs are your most powerful weapon,* her instructor had said.

She twisted in the men's grip and managed to free one leg. Her grunts of effort muffled by the hand over her mouth, she lashed out with all her strength and had the satisfaction of landing a solid kick somewhere on the second man's back. He stumbled and his hold on her other leg loosened as he jerked forward.

Constance kicked him again and suddenly her legs were free. The jar of her feet landing on the ground loosened her first attacker's hold on her mouth and she bit down as hard as she could on the gloved hand. The man cursed and jerked his hand back. She took a breath and shouted with all her might.

Then a fist struck her on the injured side of her head, and only the fact that the fist was muffled by a glove saved her cheekbone. As it was, she reeled in the man's hold.

"Stop it or I'll kill you right here." The voice came from above her. She hadn't had a look at either attacker yet, but this one was taller than she was.

"Let's do it anyway," said the second attacker and there was no mistaking the fury in his voice. She heard a soft snicking sound over the sound of the wind and suddenly lost the strength in her legs. She'd heard that sound before. That was the sound of a switchblade opening up.

Nearby a door slammed against a wall and light spilled over the snow-shrouded gravestones.

"Who's there?" came the unmistakeable voice of the priest. He filled the doorway, lamp held high. "Who's out there?"

The man holding Constance tried clamping a hand over her mouth again but she twisted in his arm and her heel ground his instep. He cursed and the arm around her dropped away. She was free! But before she could run, a heavily-booted foot lashed out and caught her in the hip, sending her crashing against a headstone. Her shoulder and head hit hard and she slid to the frozen ground, fighting the darkness that threatened to overtake her, waiting for the knife to slip between her ribs and end her life.

It never came.

For a while, all she heard was the wind in the trees and the roaring of her blood through her veins. Snowflakes landed on her cheeks and melted. Her hands were cold—she should have worn her mittens. Then a pair of hands gently pulled her up to a sitting position and she groaned at the pain in her ribs and shoulder. Someone was talking to her but she couldn't make out the words. Then a hand forced her chin up. She blinked up at the priest. She couldn't make out his words, but the angry expression on his face was unmistakeable.

"Père Noiron," she said, unable to resist. "It would seem you are destined to save me, after all."

ঙ TEN ড়

CONSTANCE stood in the dark by the bedroom window, staring out at the snowstorm. She hugged her arm to herself, trying to hold the weight off her shoulder. Her ribs hurt when she breathed and she couldn't put her weight on her left leg, her hip hurt so much. Her head pounded with every beat of her heart. A concussion, no doubt, from hitting the gravestone.

She could see nothing but swirling flakes. The tracks in the cemetery would be covered over soon, if they weren't already. She wanted to throw her coat on and hurry back to the graveyard to follow the tracks were they led her. But her new injuries, on top of the earlier ones, would take a while to heal. She needed food and rest before she could attempt to track the men.

And by the time she was fit to do so, it would be too late. The trail would be gone.

A trembling began deep in her stomach and spread outward until she hugged herself to keep from shaking apart. She clenched her jaw to keep from screaming.

They had tried to *kill* her! If the priest hadn't appeared when he did, she would be lying in a pool of her own blood, as dead as the young man in the doctor's shed.

Who were those men? Were they responsible for her falling off the cliff? Had they *pushed* her? Had they attacked Renaud and Dallaire? What did they *want*?

The questions pushed her rage down as she tried to understand what was happening in Backli's Ford. She had too few facts.

One. Someone beat a young A'lle man and left him in the square. Perhaps the guilty party had meant to kill him, perhaps not.

Two. Something happened to her and her party on the way to Backli's Ford.

Three. Two strangers confronted the innkeeper, looking for her.

Four. Two men accosted her in the cemetery, presumably the same two. They seemed willing to kill her when she fought back, so it was safe to assume that they had already planned to kill her in a more secluded place.

She leaned her good shoulder against the wall. The facts meant nothing right now. She needed context. She needed to talk to whoever had found the boy. Maybe he had said something to them. And she needed to search his clothing.

And she needed to find Renaud and Dallaire before Chief Desautel came looking for them.

Whatever else she found out, it seemed clear that Backli's Ford was at the center of something unsavory.

A knock at the door startled her and she winced at the flare of pain in her shoulder. The pain made her voice sharper than she intended when she said, "Yes?"

The door opened to reveal the innkeeper, Thomas Pelletier.

"Mademoiselle A'lle?" he said hesitantly and she realized that while she could see him clearly, he could not see her.

"One moment," she said and went to the bedside table where she turned on the lamp.

The innkeeper stood blinking in the sudden light. He looked uncertainly at her.

"My wife tells me you would not let her look at your injuries. We need to know if we should call the doctor."

He did not say it, but Constance heard the unspoken "again" at the end of his sentence.

Constance controlled a sudden spike of irritation. She had not asked him to help her!

And yet he *had* helped her, and her thanks had been to bring trouble into his home. She could offer to leave, but they both knew she had nowhere else to go. This man had done nothing wrong. In fact, in her brief, forbidden reading of him, she had seen nothing but concern and compassion.

The memory eased her somewhat. Not all humans distrusted A'lle.

Not all humans wanted them dead.

Which brought her to Fact Number Five: Thomas Pelletier was the only person in Backli's Ford that she knew she could trust.

"I do not need the doctor, Monsieur Pelletier," she said gently. "I need food and time to heal."

He searched her face as if looking for deception, then nodded. "Then you shall have them. But first I must know who those men are."

She wanted to straighten and come closer but fatigue robbed her of strength. It was all she could do to keep the pain from showing on her face.

"I'm sorry, but I don't know. I don't know who they are or why they attacked me."

He nodded again, as if he had expected her answer. Without a word, he came up to her and, wrapping an arm around her back, gently pulled her toward the bed. As if sensing the damage to her ribs, he kept his touch feather light.

She wanted to protest, wanted to tell him she was fine, but knew he wouldn't believe her. She allowed him to guide her to the bed and lower her down.

"Lie back," he ordered kindly. She stifled a gasp as her ribs adjusted to her position and didn't argue when he pulled her legs up onto the bed.

She let go of her injured arm to lay a cold hand on his. "I need food," she said. "Or the healing will take much longer."

He nodded, then gently took her hand off his arm. He pulled the blankets over her and left.

Constance was asleep before he could close the door.

* * *

Marie Pelletier stood in the middle of her impeccably clean kitchen, arms folded, staring at nothing. She no longer knew what was the right thing to do. She believed in charity, in looking after those who could not look after themselves, but Père Noiron's reaction to the A'lle girl had put her off balance. It was one thing to look into those strange but lovely eyes—she had been to Montreal; she had seen A'lle before—but to be confronted by the girl's alien abilities...

Was the girl truly a danger to their household? Marie knew what Thomas would say. He would say they should take care of their own business and let the Church take care of its own. Thomas did not believe in giving the Church too much sway.

But sometimes, Thomas' generous heart blinded him to the truth.

* * *

Constance awoke sometime in the night, ravenous. The inn was quiet and dark. She would have to make her way to the kitchen to find something to eat. By the time she had struggled to a sitting position, however, she realized that someone had placed food on the table by the door. The smell had awakened her.

She cautiously made her way to the table and removed the plate covering a large bowl of leftover stew. The stew was cold, but she didn't care. She ate it all, then polished the bowl with the bread she found on the plate. When that was done, she ate the cheese— mild, with some kind of seeds. She drank directly from a pitcher of water and then crawled back into bed.

* * *

By first light, the clouds had cleared out nicely, leaving behind clear skies and eight inches of fresh snow on the ground. A perfect day for staying inside in front of a warm fire, especially after spending the night on the settee, startling awake at every little oound. Thomas hadn't wanted to be tucked away in his bed upstairs should the girl's attackers attempt to enter the inn.

He sighed and turned away from the window.

Six of his neighbors had already gathered in the kitchen and were helping themselves to tea.

Marie, bless her, had been up for hours preparing food for the searchers.

Zach stuck his head in the parlor. "Any sign of Gaston and Jonathan?"

Thomas shook his head. "Not yet. They'll be along. Is everyone ready?"

Zach Castonguay had a shock of black hair that always looked as if a wind storm had riffled through it, even when it was freshly combed. But he stood straight, looked you in the eye, and did an honest day's work. Thomas would have been proud to call him son-in-law, if he'd had a daughter.

Zach, along with the other men gathering in the inn's kitchen, was single. None of the married men had wanted to leave their families unprotected while the girl's assailants were roaming about Backli's Ford. Neither had Thomas. The single men would go look for the missing constables.

"We're ready," said Zach. He hesitated a moment. "Thomas, we all understand why you need to stay behind."

Thomas stared back gravely. None of them were comfortable with the kind of violence Backli's Ford had seen these past few days.

"We will gather the families at the inn," he finally replied. "Half of us will stay behind while the other half will try to pick up the trail of the men in the graveyard." He shrugged. "We probably won't find much of a trail, with all the snow."

Zach came fully inside the parlor, letting the door swing shut behind him. "And you called St. Vincent?"

Thomas nodded. "Yes. The chief investigator himself is coming. I told him about last night's attack and he'll bring reinforcements." He glanced out the window again. "It will likely take them until mid-morning to reach us, with all the snow. Hopefully, you will have found the missing men by then."

Zach said nothing. They both knew the chances of the two men surviving were slim.

"I'll see you off," said Thomas and headed for the kitchen, where the murmur of voices seemed to throb with excitement. He felt no excitement. He had been on a few of these search parties in the past ten years. They rarely ended well.

"Monsieur Pelletier."

He and Zach stopped at the kitchen door and turned at the sound of the A'lle girl's voice. She stood at the foot of of the stairs, dressed in the clothes in which he had found her, holding on to the post.

"Mademoiselle," he said gently. "You should not be out of bed."

Indeed she shouldn't. She was pale, except for the livid reddish purple bruise that extended from temple to jaw. A big fist had done that and Thomas knew the owner of that fist. Or at least, he would recognize him if he saw him again. That she had slept in her clothes was evident and her hair looked like someone had set it on fire and extinguished it with a towel.

Zach Castonguay stared at her as if she had just descended from the heavens. Thomas almost rolled his eyes but remembered his manners.

"Mademoiselle A'lle, allow me to introduce Zacharie Castonguay. Monsieur Castonguay owns the stable in town."

The girl nodded politely at Zach but he stepped forward and stuck out his hand.

"Enchanté, Mademoiselle." He had to look up at her.

The kitchen door pushed open and Marie looked in. "Thomas, they are leavin—" Her voice trailed off when she saw the A'lle girl, standing big as life in the hallway.

The men looked at each other, then at Marie. Thomas found himself holding his breath.

The girl broke the tension with a raised hand.

"I do not plan to ride with them, Madame," she said stiffly.

Marie nodded brusquely and Thomas would have sworn she bit her tongue on a sharp reply.

"Good. Now, Zacharie, you should be on your way."

Although he wasn't leaving with them, Thomas hurriedly made his escape from the parlor with Zacharie.

Madame Pelletier eyed Constance unfavorably.

"If you did not plan to join them, why are you out of bed?"

Constance wanted desperately to lean on the post, but she dared not show any weakness. It had taken everything she had to make her way downstairs without falling.

"Madame," she said in a low voice. "I am very hungry."

All suspicion fled from the woman's face, to be replaced by surprise. "Mais, voyons donc!" She crossed the room and tucked her arm in Constance's. "I have never met anyone who could eat as much as you do, and you so thin!" She led Constance into the kitchen, which should have been too warm for comfort but wasn't. Another measure of her body's struggle to regenerate itself. While muscles, ligaments, and bones healed, her energy reserves were growing dangerously depleted.

"Sit," said Madame Pelletier. She left Constance to sit and went to the counter, where a loaf of bread awaited cutting. She spread molasses on a slice and brought it to Constance at the table. "Start with this," she said.

In the next half hour, Marie Pelletier proceeded to ply Constance with oatmeal, honey, and cream, followed by three eggs, scrambled, rashers of back bacon drizzled with maple syrup, a ladle-full of baked beans, also drizzled with maple syrup, and slice after slice of freshly-baked bread slathered with butter. She brought a pitcher of milk from the cold room and filled glass after glass to wash the feast down.

At last, Constance put up her hands in surrender.

"Enough, Madame. This will suffice."

Madame Pelletier nodded—in relief, thought Constance—and helped her up the stairs and back to bed. Once again, Constance was asleep before the door closed behind the woman.

❧ ELEVEN ❦

DESAUTEL turned at the sound of his office door opening.

Louis stood framed in the opening, still clad in his overcoat and tall boots. The preposterous black beret he affected lately was clenched in one hand. "Why didn't you send someone to fetch me?" he demanded. Behind him, the duty room was almost deserted. The overhead electric lights did very little to chase the pre-sunrise gloom.

Desautel shrugged. "What could you do that I could not?" he asked. "I saw no point in disturbing your sleep." He raised a hand to forestall the argument he saw forming on his assistant's face. "Now that you are here, however, can you arrange for food? It will be a hard ride."

Louis' eyebrows rose. He recognized a dismissal when he heard one. He left, closing the door smartly and leaving behind a puddle of melting snow.

Desautel sighed. He was tired and irritable, never a good combination when dealing with Louis. He reached for the cup of tea on his desk, but it had grown cold.

Someone had attacked Constance A'lle last night. That one fact cast an even more sinister light on the events of the previous day, especially when he considered the death of the A'lle boy. Now it was much easier to believe that someone had lain in wait for his people, and that Constance A'lle had been lucky to escape whatever fate had befallen Renaud and Dallaire.

He decided it would serve no purpose to inform the A'lle about this most recent event. The girl was safe. He would bring her back to them.

There'd been no word from Saint-Amand and Johnson, the two men he'd sent out yesterday to find his three missing constables. Two constables and one investigator, he corrected himself. He had wanted Saint-Amand and Johnson back before nightfall. Likely, they had found shelter for the night when the weather turned.

He closed his eyes briefly. He hoped he was not now searching for four constables.

It was time to bring the scrutiny of the law to bear on Backli's Ford.

* * *

As the sun worked to crest the trees, Desautel squinted against the glare of the snow. Finally, he pulled up on the lines and the sled came to a shushing halt. Behind him, the six riders following in his tracks stopped, too. He sat on the padded bench, taking in the rise of land to his left, the finger of snow-covered pines jutting out of the forest, and the expanse of gleaming snow between the road and the trees. The gray of the sky was turning blue and the wispy clouds pink and gold. The horses blew irritation into the cold morning.

Bérubé nudged his horse forward until he was abreast of Desautel. He nodded at the road in front of the sled, his breath fogging in the crisp morning air.

"Problem?"

Desautel said nothing, only studied the road and the hint of a ditch on either side. They were almost halfway to Backli's Ford and he had seen no sign of his men.

Despite his sheepskin gloves, his hands were cold and stiff. He finally admitted to himself that he had half expected to see a set of hoof prints or even the track of a sled. He would not have been surprised to learn that John A'lle or even his tall daughter, Eloise, had headed for Backli's Ford as soon as he left their place last night.

But he'd seen nothing. So what had made him stop?

The sun finally rose above the trees, flooding each wrinkle in the blanket of snow with blue shadow. Behind him, horses stamped impatiently and his men murmured among themselves. He wanted to snap at them to stop complaining.

Bérubé sniffed deeply of the cold air. "Smoke," he said.

Desautel took a deep breath, too. Yes. Very faint, but definitely smoke. That must have been what caught his attention. He and Bérubé glanced around to find the source. They were still too far from Backli's Ford for the scent to come from there. Desautel spotted the thin column of smoke rising in the air above the treetops just as Bérubé did.

"Maître," said one of his men and Desautel turned to see Alphonse pointing toward the trees. Desautel turned back to peer at the black trees. A movement, then a figure emerged from the finger of trees and waved at them.

Bérubé blew out a sigh of relief. "Johnson."

And so it was. The knot in Desautel's chest began to loosen as he watched Johnson plodding through the knee-high snow toward them. A couple of the riders dismounted and handed their reins to others before descending into the ditch to go meet him.

Desautel tied the lines to the brake and clambered down stiffly from the sled. He couldn't tell if it was age stiffening him or the cold. He joined the others at the side of the road to await Johnson.

The two men reached Johnson and paused. They were still too far away for Desautel to overhear what they were saying, but the two men finished talking with Johnson and then headed for the trees while Johnson resumed his trudge toward the road.

The knot in Desautel's chest began to tighten again.

By the time Johnson arrived, he was met with a grim silence.

He was an older man who always seemed to be growing a beard even when he was freshly shaven. He came to a stop in front of Desautel.

"Maître," he said in acknowledgement. His gray eyes were bloodshot and the lines bracketing his mouth were deeper than usual. He had stuffed his hat and mitts in his capacious pockets and the sun's rays now gleamed on the scalp showing through the man's thinning gray hair.

"Saint-Amand?" said Desautel.

Johnson hooked a thumb toward the trees. "Back there." He took a deep breath, as though girding himself. "We found 'em."

Desautel nodded grimly. "Report."

"They were shot in the back, sir." Johnson's voice carried anger. "There wasn't much light left by the time we got here," he continued, "but it looks like the three of them were forced off the road, probably at gunpoint. There," he pointed a little further up the road. "Can't see it now because of all the fresh snow." He dropped his hand to his side. "We followed the tracks beyond the cover of trees. Horses moving fast. Saint-Amand says Dallaire was shot first, then Renaud." He pulled out his gloves, as if the cold had finally registered now that he had stopped moving. "Looks like Investigator A'lle made a run for it, but there's a cliff just beyond." He pointed again. "Just past the trees. It's hidden by a scrub of bushes. The horse stopped at the edge and sent her flying."

The cold seeped through the soles of Desautel's feet and he suddenly felt every day of his forty-six years.

"Maître," continued Johnson, "it's a miracle she survived. The cliff is over sixty feet high."

Bérubé whistled. "And she managed to walk to Backli's Ford? That's miles from here."

Desautel shook his head, still trying to wrap his mind around the facts as they were becoming clear. "She made it to the road. The innkeeper found her and took her in."

"I guess that makes her pretty lucky," drawled a voice behind him.

Desautel turned a cold look on the speaker. "Charlevoix, stay behind with the sled and the horses. The rest of you, grab two horses and come with me."

Without waiting, he stepped down into the ditch and up again.

* * *

Desautel followed Johnson's tracks into the trees. Johnson walked behind him, followed by Bérubé. The others trailed them. The only sound to be heard was the tromping of their feet in the deep snow and heavy breathing. The way grew easier, if no warmer, when they entered the forest. The sun had yet to reach here, either with warmth or light, and Desautel was grateful when the trees ended in another clearing. The sound of a horse nickering told him he was close.

He emerged from the woods to find Saint-Amand waiting for him. They had built a small fire and dragged a couple of logs next to it. Desautel nodded to the tracker. A hundred feet beyond them, his two men searched the ground, although Desautel could have told them to save themselves the effort. Last night's snow had covered the ground with at least six inches of snow. Any tracks would have been covered.

To his right, three horses stood saddled and tied to trees. Two of them would belong to Saint-Amand and Johnson. The third would be Dallaire's or the the A'lle girl's.

"Report," he said.

Saint-Amand nodded at the ground beyond the campfire and only then did Desautel notice the two side by side mounds in the snow. He wanted to close his eyes against the sight, deny the truth, but he did not have that luxury. Without a word, he circled the fire and trudged to the bodies. There was only a faint path leading to them, covered in undisturbed snow.

The rest of his men emerged from the trees, and Bérubé ordered them to stand back.

Crouching, Desautel brushed the snow off the nearest mound. The body was covered by a gray wool blanket, standard issue any time a constable travelled on horseback. Saint-Amand and Johnson had spent a cold night huddled around a fire in order to pay this respect to their colleagues.

And in order to preserve as much evidence as possible from the snow.

Desautel found the edge of the blanket and pulled it away from the body. Snow cascaded off, mounding on the other side. It was Renaud. His thin face was pale and covered in blond stubble, in stark contrast to his red hair. His eyes were closed, as was his mouth, but there remained on his face a faintly grim expression.

A shadow moved next to him and Desautel looked up to see Saint-Amand's own grim-looking face.

"It happened near the cliff," he said, nodding toward the two men still examining the ground. Beyond them were willow and wild rose bushes with rosehips swaying in the breeze. From his vantage point, it was impossible to tell that the ground gave way beyond the bushes.

"We think they were galloping toward the cliff when they were shot. That would explain the blood on Renaud's saddle."

Desautel nodded. "How long ago?"

Saint-Amand shrugged. Like Johnson, his eyes were sunken from lack of sleep and his face deeply lined. When he was not speaking, his mouth pressed closed in a tight line.

"We found them at dusk, just as the snow was beginning to fall. We searched the grounds but there were too many hoofprints. No footprints at all. We managed to catch Dallaire's mare, but the investigator's horse is long gone."

Desautel glanced at the cliff but Johnson shook his head. "No sign that any horse went over the cliff. Only the investigator."

Desautel nodded. Without a word, he began to unbutton Renaud's heavy sheepskin coat, then pulled up the man's gray wool sweater and finally, his wool shirt. Renaud's muscled, hairless chest gleamed palely in the morning light. No wounds, no blemishes.

"Help me turn him over," he said.

Saint-Amand tramped over to the other side of Renaud's body and crouched next to him. Grabbing Renaud's far arm, Johnson pulled as Desautel pushed. Together they got the body resting on its side.

The snow beneath the body was stained pink. Desautel pulled up Renaud's clothes and stared grimly at the small, deadly hole in his back. Either the shooter had been lucky or he was a marksman because the shot had entered Renaud's back just below his shoulder blade to the left of the spine. One clean shot, straight to the heart.

The bullet hadn't gone through the body. It must have been fired from a rifle at a distance, or perhaps closer, from a hand gun. He would have to wait for the autopsy to know more.

Desautel pictured Renaud's horse, as he had seen it at the stables the day before. Blood on the saddle and on the horse's rump. Rifle still in its scabbard. Renaud never saw the attack coming.

Dallaire had. Whoever had shot him was not as gifted a marksman, or had been more hurried. The first bullet had caught Dallaire in the side, below the rib cage. Likely it had missed all vital organs, giving Dallaire the chance to turn around and shoot back.

Desautel had already seen that Dallaire's rifle was missing from its scabbard. Had it fallen into the deep snow when the killing bullets slammed into his back?

Desautel looked up from the two holes in Dallaire's back and tried to picture what had happened. The three of them had been on the road, heading for Backli's Ford. Had they been followed? No—they would have noticed someone following them. A trap, then. A trap right here. The finger of forest jutting out from the main part of the forest, the wide open space before it... A rifleman lying in wait in the woods would have ample opportunity to see the three riders coming.

How had Renaud been shot in the back? Something had caused him to turn around, turn his back to the shooter in the woods. An accomplice?

He worked at the problem while Saint-Amand silently replaced the gray wool blanket over Renaud.

An accomplice could have emerged from the forest on the other side of the road once they had passed. He glanced back toward the road, where Charlevoix, hidden by the finger of trees, waited with the horses.

Yes, it would make a perfect spot for an ambush. A second gunman, waiting for them to pass. He had picked off Renaud first, then perhaps he had shot Dallaire in the side when he turned toward Renaud. Dallaire would have realized the trap and then what?

And what of the A'lle girl? There was much to fault in the girl, but she did not lack courage. Had she tried to help her colleagues?

Desautel shook his head in frustration. He settled Dallaire's body back into its depression and Saint-Amand replaced the blanket. They both stood up stiffly.

"How were they found?" Desautel finally asked.

Saint-Amand nodded in the general direction of the trees. "The killers dragged the bodies to the trees," he said. "Bad job of hiding them. Anxious to find the investigator, I expect." He cleared his throat and spat off to the side. "Found traces of blood on the road where they shot Renaud. They had to chase the other two but they got Dallaire near the cliff. I think he and the gir—the investigator were looking for cover." He nodded at the scrub brush hiding the cliff. "My guess is the investigator's horse saw the cliff's edge and reared. She didn't stand a chance."

He turned back to the gray-shrouded bodies. "Then the shooters had to hide the bodies, and hide the evidence of the murder. And then they had to find a way to reach the bottom of the cliff. Would have taken hours, I expect."

That was the longest Desautel had ever heard Saint-Amand speak.

"Did you find where the shooters hid?"

Saint-Amand shrugged. "Yes, but they didn't leave anything behind." He pointed across the road. "One waited there, the other there." He hooked a thumb over his shoulder to indicate the finger of trees.

Desautel nodded his agreement, then frowned down at the shrouded bodies. There was nothing left to do here.

"Très bien," he said loudly, attracting everyone's attention. "Saint-Amand and Johnson will take the bodies back to the morgue." He looked at Saint-Amand. "Get Docteur Rivard to do the autopsies. He has a better eye." Turning back to the rest of the men, he said, "Charlevoix will accompany them back in the sled and take Dallaire's horse back. The rest of us go on to Backli's Ford."

He supervised the wrapping of Dallaire and Renaud's bodies, making sure the blankets were tightly wrapped around their frozen bodies. He didn't want to lose any evidence in the transport.

It took close to an hour to carry the bodies back but finally they were settled on the floor of the sled. Then it took another fifteen minutes to turn the sled around on the narrow road. Finally, Charlevoix slapped the lines on the horses rumps and the sled, with its weary escorts, took off for St. Vincent.

Without another word, Desautel mounted Charlevoix's horse and led the rest of his men toward Backli's Ford.

❧ TWELVE ❧

Marie scooped a bit of the broth onto a spoon and tasted it. Bland.

"Camille, bring me the salt cellar and my basket of spices, please."

The girl left the unshaped bread dough on the floured board and wiped her hands on her apron. "Oui, madame." Her mother was among the women and children in the common room. Some had brought their darning. Others were helping the young ones with their lessons. Madame Sansouci was teaching a few of the younger girls how to knit. All were trying to occupy themselves as best they could.

Marie had had to insist that she did not need help in the kitchen. As big as it was, it would soon be overwhelmed by the number of women wanting to help.

The half dozen men who had stayed behind were outside, patrolling the town and guarding the inn.

Camille brought over the basket with it dried herbs in muslin bags and Marie plucked out the one containing oregano and drew open the drawstring. She pulled the dry leaves out and crumbled a healthy portion into the soup.

She had soup, a bit of last night's stew and bread, and Camille's loaf would be ready to pop into the oven, in time for lunch. Surely the men would be back by then.

She looked up as the hallway door opened, ready with a smile to rebuff yet another offer of help, but it was the A'lle girl, Constance, too tall, too gaunt, too strange. Camille stopped kneading to stare and Marie poked her in the ribs to get her back to work.

"Sit," she told Constance. "I'll heat up some stew."

* * *

Thomas felt guilty at leaving Marie alone to cope with the dozens of women and children, but she could have as much help as she wanted. His time was better used in trying to find the ruffians.

He and a dozen or so of his neighbors had set out from the graveyard on their snowshoes. As he had suspected, the men's tracks had disappeared under a thick blanket of snow. Even the shadowy dimples of their passage had all but been smoothed out by the wind. They were left to split up, two by two, and go off in different directions.

Thomas broke out of the cover of the trees and stood high above the riverbank, his legs apart because of the snowshoes, his cheeks and nose the only parts of him still cold after the exertion.

"Anything?" Barnaby puffed as he came abreast. Barnaby was of an age with Thomas, but he seemed older. He had been the ferry master when Thomas first came to Backli's Ford. Now he did carpentry work. Barnaby adjusted the rifle across his back so that it didn't bump against his head.

Thomas shook his head. "No sign." He reflexively shrugged his own rifle into a better position across his back.

Here, the Bartolomée River was a smooth blanket of white, broken only by snow ridges created by the wind. The two men could have crossed over elsewhere along the river, but he'd seen no tracks along the river bank.

"Maybe the others had better luck," said Barnaby.

Thomas looked at him, but the carpenter was staring at the

river, frowning under his beaver hat. He didn't like the idea of two murderous ruffians wandering around Backli's Ford any more than Thomas did.

If anyone had found tracks, they would have returned to the inn and waited for the others to return.

It was time to turn around and go back. He and Barnaby hadn't found anything, but surely someone else had. Unless the ruffians were hiding in someone's house, they would find them. No one was missing, no one had reported anything amiss.

"What was that?" said Barnaby suddenly.

Thomas looked at the man questioningly, but Barnaby held up a hand for silence, then pulled up his ear flaps to hear better. Then Thomas heard it, too. Men's voices, coming from the road.

* * *

Constance sat back and sighed. She felt much better. Madame Pelletier was a very good cook.

"Would you like more, Mademoiselle?" asked Camille. The child had huge brown eyes and dark hair that she apparently always kept in tight braids. Constance self-consciously touched her own hair. She couldn't remember the last time she had combed it. It must look like a rat's nest.

"Thank you," she said, "but no. However, I would like to borrow a comb. Do you think Madame Pelletier has one?"

The girl looked uncertain and Constance began to regret asking her, but then Camille's face brightened. "Un moment," she said and scooted out the hallway door.

The innkeeper's wife had brought the kettle of soup into the common room and was serving lunch there. The gabble of female voices had risen sharply for a few minutes but now seemed to have abated. Constance was happy to be alone in the kitchen with Camille. The girl was quiet but efficient and the room was warm. Warmer than her bedroom upstairs.

She closed her eyes, content for the moment. She could have eaten another bowl of stew but the girl's eyes had grown larger with each helping, so she decided against a fourth. It was enough, for the moment, to be dry and warm and in no great pain.

She would comb her hair, then put on her boots and her coat, and go back to the doctor's improvised morgue to examine the boy's clothing. Her chin touched her chest and she startled awake. There would be time for sleep later. But her body knew its own imperative. Eat and sleep, and thus heal.

She stood up and walked to the window next to the back door. The snow had stopped and there were footprints in the yard leading to the stables and the chicken coop. If she leaned just so, she could see the path alongside the house, the one she had taken last night. The thought brought back last night's terrifying attack and her certainty that they would kill her if she allowed it. A shudder coursed through her and she turned back to the kitchen, looking for a weapon.

There. By the old woodstove. A series of cast iron tools for tending the cook fire. She walked over to the tall box in which they were stored and pulled each tool out until she found the poker. She hefted it, wondering if her tender ribs would allow her to wield it over her head, if she needed to.

"Mademoiselle?"

Constance looked around. The girl was back, a fancy mother-of-pearl comb in her hand. Her gaze fell on the poker in Constance's hand and her face filled with uncertainty.

Constance smiled reassuringly and set the poker down to lean against the wall by the door.

"Thank you, Camille," she said gravely, putting her hand out. The girl placed the comb in Constance's hand and returned to her cleaning duties, stealing glances at Constance as she pulled the heavy comb through her snarls.

"Will the doctor be coming to see you today?" asked Camille hesitantly, not looking up from the table she was scrubbing.

Constance fought with a knot deep in her thick hair. "I don't think so," she replied. "There is nothing more he can do for me."

"Oh." The disappointment in the girl's voice was clear and Constance turned to look at her. The girl was perhaps thirteen or fourteen. Too young for the doctor. Did she harbor feelings for him?

Human emotions were often difficult to identify. Especially the ones that were quickly masked. Grandmother Esther had taught them to ask questions as a means of identifying which emotion was predominant.

"How long has the doctor been in Backli's Ford?" she asked.

Camille looked up from the exceedingly clean table. "Almost six months. He came from Montreal, you know." The words came out on a rush of breath as though pent up too long.

Constance blinked. "Why?"

Camille looked confused. "Why what?"

"Why did he come to Backli's Ford?" Presumably a doctor would be better compensated in a big city like Montreal. "Does he have family here?"

"No. I think his family is all in Upper Canada, near York." She leaned forward and lowered her voice. "I think he left Montreal because of a love affair gone bad."

Constance tried to keep her skepticism from showing. A love affair?

A swell of noise arose from the common room. Then the door to the common room opened and Madame Pelletier came in, wiping her hands on the towel tucked in her waistband.

"The men are back." She went to the gas stove and turned the heat up under the stew. "Camille, slice more bread and take the molasses out of the pantry. They will be hungry." Her long skirt swished around her legs as she bustled around the room. Constance watched her and Camille move around each other between the work table, the stove, and the ice box, and for a moment, she envied them their obvious ease with each other.

Then she put the comb down and went out into the hallway and to the front door. Hearing someone in the hallway, the women in the common room burst out of the double doors only to halt when they caught sight of her. Constance nodded politely to the group, then pulled on her boots and went out the front door.

The day was brighter than she had expected, and warmer. She squinted against the midday glare, momentarily blind. Down the road came the sound of many horses snorting and neighing, their hoofbeats muffled by the deep snow. She blinked away the tears to see a dozen riders walking slowly toward the inn.

Behind her, the door opened and Madame Pelletier stepped out onto the porch. She placed Constance's sheepskin jacket over her shoulders then came to stand beside her, herself wrapped in a heavy grey wool coat. They stood at the top of the steps, watching the silent group of men approach. Constance picked out Thomas' friend, Zach, first. Then she saw the erect figure of the chief investigator riding next to him and her legs almost gave way.

Not yet. She hadn't found Renaud or Dallaire. She hadn't had time to examine the body properly or search the boy's belongings. She hadn't identified him yet or interviewed the boys who found him on the square.

The chief investigator would think her incompetent. And he would be right.

Madame Pelletier blew out a soft sigh and Constance looked at her.

"It's not good," murmured Madame Pelletier, her gaze going from face to face. Then, as if realizing who she was addressing, she looked up at Constance. "I could be wrong. We'll wait to hear what they have to say."

But even an A'lle could read the pity on the woman's face. She had read something in the men's expressions. In their silence.

Of course. The silence was the clue. Had they found Renaud and Dallaire, they would have called out, sent for the doctor, made demands. The way they sat their horses... Most of them sat up straight, but it seemed to take an effort, as if they would rather have slumped in the saddle.

Constance swallowed against a dry throat, suddenly aware of

the woodsmoke in the air, of the faint smell of exertion and beef stew clinging to Madame Pelletier. She felt more than heard the press of women and children at the large common room window.

It was as if the world held its breath for a long, fearful moment.

Then the horses turned into the inn's yard and Chief Investigator Médéric Desautel halted in front of the porch. Behind him, men and horses did the same, all of them staring at her, it seemed.

Chief Desautel's words fell on her as if he wielded a bludgeon. "They're dead. Both of them."

* * *

Desautel accepted the bowl of stew from the child and smiled his gratitude. Bérubé was still at the stables, along with two other constables, ensuring the horses were rubbed down and fed. He would have to remember to tell Louis to reimburse the innkeepers for the feed. And the food for him and his men. And the room for Constance A'lle.

As though conjured by the thought, she pushed open the door from the common room and entered, bearing a tray full of dirty bowls and crusts of bread. Her hands shook but she made it to the counter by the deep sink and set the tray down carefully.

Her appearance had shocked him. The coat over her shoulders had been bloodstained, as had the heavy wool pants that all his constables wore in winter. Hers had been torn, and expertly repaired along the front, but bloodstains were hard to wash out.

Now that he saw her without her coat, he knew that it was more than exhaustion that had hollowed out her face. She looked gaunt. Her eyes were shadowed, as thought she hadn't slept in a week. Her sweater hung on her like a scarecrow's rags.

What in God's name had happened to her? In two *days*? She looked as if she had lost twenty pounds.

"Mademoiselle Camille," he said gently and smiled when the girl turned those doe eyes on him. "Would you give us a moment, please?"

The girl looked confused then blushed when she realized what he was asking. With a half curtsy, she fled the kitchen for the common room where a half dozen women still awaited the return of their husbands.

Apparently, the men with families had gone out to try and find where the men who had attacked Constance A'lle were hiding. On foot. At least they had gone in pairs, and armed. What did they think to do if they did stumble across the ruffians? He almost shook his head in despair. And yet, he could not fault them for their actions. He would want to find the men threatening his family.

The A'lle girl leaned against the counter, her back to him, scraping leftovers into a slop pail. She dropped a knife, which clattered noisily on a plate. She was trembling. Out of fear? Of him? Or out of weakness?

"Sit down before you fall down," he ordered.

She gave him a look that was a cross between resigned and angry, but he was never sure with her. She made her way to the work table, pulled out a chair, which scraped noisily on the scarred pine floor, and sat down across from him. She sat straight but kept her hands hidden in her lap.

"Tell me," he said.

She stared at him unblinkingly for a long moment, then took a deep breath. And for the next five minutes, she gave him as concise and complete a verbal report as he had ever heard. When she finished, she sat looking at him, waiting. Outside, voices could be heard in the back yard.

"You have no memory of the first attack?" he asked.

She shook her head. "The last memory I have, before waking up in the snow, is of riding behind Renaud and Dallaire. They were talking to each other. After that, nothing."

He nodded. He had suffered several knocks on the head. Sometimes the memories had come back, but not all. In the common room, voices rose in greeting but he ignored them.

"And last night? Would you recognize the men who attacked

you? Are you certain they are the same men who attacked you on the road?"

She stared down at the tabletop for a moment, considering. Then she looked up at him. "I can't say if they are the same men who attacked us on the road." Her voice was very low. "But they match the description the innkeeper gave of the men who were asking about me. One was very big, the other shorter, slighter. I didn't get a good look at their faces. But I would recognise their voices."

Desautel stood up and went over to the coffee pot staying warm on the stove. He poured himself another cup and came back to the table.

There was no help for it. Until the men were found, he could not leave this village unprotected. He had been arguing with the magistrate for two years that Backli's Ford needed a police presence on site. The location of the village, so close to New America, made it a tempting spot to smuggle alcohol. He did not understand why New America insisted on prohibiting the use of alcohol. It did not curb the amount of alcohol that found its way to their towns and "tea rooms." And it created huge headaches for police services on either side of the border.

No doubt the two ruffians belonged to that unhappy class of entrepreneurs, the bootleggers. With the river frozen, it would be easy enough for them to cross, obtain liquor, and return to the New American side with no one the wiser. If he were to travel far enough up or down river, he would no doubt find evidence of their crossing.

But why would they call attention to themselves by murdering two officers of the law? And trying to murder a third? What had Dallaire, Renaud, and the girl seen that made them such a danger?

Desautel sipped his coffee while he thought. It was bitter stuff and had been on the burner over-long, but he didn't mind. It reminded him of his younger days and travelling on horseback through the wilderness, eating the fish he caught and drinking coffee made over the camp fire.

Bootlegging was a profitable business. So profitable that criminals had organized it into a business model, with suppliers and distributors on the payroll. Freelancers were discouraged, sometimes permanently. Had these two ruffians mistaken Dallaire and Renaud for crime lords? But strange as she was, there was no mistaking the A'lle girl for anything but a girl.

He shook his head in frustration. It made no sense.

Constance A'lle waited patiently for him. Her hands had emerged from under the table and now rested quietly on the tabletop. Outside, more voices could be heard. Clearly, more of the men had returned from trying to find the ruffians' tracks. Bérubé would interview them as they arrived, but Desautel did not hold out much hope. Wherever the men were, they were well hidden.

A heavy knock on the hallway door and Bérubé stuck his head in, looking around until he spotted the two of them sitting at the table.

"That's the last of them, Maître," he said. "Did you want to see the innkeeper?"

Desautel shook his head. "In a moment." Bérubé nodded and ducked back out.

He glanced at Constance A'lle. She hadn't seemed particularly worried over the men still out there, but now her shoulders seemed to relax.

As if she felt his gaze on her, she turned back to look at him. "I need to examine the boy again," she said, leaning forward. "And his clothing." She looked down and took a deep breath. "I should have done so last night," she said firmly.

A twinge of sympathy almost made him smile. She sat before him, gaunt, exhausted, bruised, and injured, and she castigated herself for not examining the boy well enough. She was very young, despite her claim to the contrary.

"The clothing will still be there," he said gruffly. "As will the boy. I want to speak to the men who have returned, first."

She nodded. "Yes, sir." She hesitated a moment, then said, "I've been trying to see the connection between the boy's death and the attacks, but I can't."

Desautel tried not to show his surprise. The girl assumed there was a connection. It hadn't occurred to him to see the attack on the road as linked to the boy's death, but perhaps it was. Perhaps there was something about the boy that the two men did not want discovered. Perhaps the boy had seen something.

Wait. What if the only reason the boy had been beaten was because he was A'lle?

But still, why attack officers of the law? Surely they must have realized that such an attack would bring more investigators to Backli's Ford?

He hadn't given this enough thought. If the boy was linked...

"Do you know him?" he asked.

She shook her head. "No, sir. He is not from here."

By that she meant that the boy was not known by her or her family. He could well believe that they would know every other A'lle in the area.

"Very well," he said, getting up. "We must try to establish his identity, learn why he was killed, who those men are. But first," he added sternly, "we must get you back home to recover."

Dismay filled her face. "Sir, I would prefer to stay here and help with the investigation."

He looked down at her and shook his head. "I promised your father I would bring you back."

She stood up, too, and he found himself eye to eye with her. Damn, but these A'lle girls were tall!

"Chief Investigator," she said formally, "I can assure you that I am capable of performing my duties." The words came out stiffly and he suddenly realized that he had embarrassed her, called into questions her abilities. Treated her like a child.

Something he would never have done to another constable, even a young one. Female constables were becoming more common in Lower Canada, but he had never worked with one. Not only did he have to get used to having an A'lle investigator among his staff, but he also had to accustom himself to a *female* A'lle investigator.

He sighed. "We will be bringing the boy back with us," he said carefully. "I will need a sketch done to help in his identification. I may need you to liaise with other A'lle communities."

Constance A'lle looked into his eyes, searching for what, he couldn't say. Whatever it was, she did not seem to find it. She nodded and looked away.

* * *

Constance walked to the end of the upstairs hallway and tried the door handle to the last room. It turned easily and she walked in, leaving it open behind her. The room was furnished similarly to hers but as she had hoped, the window opened onto the graveyard next door.

She stood at the window and looked down at the crisscrossing snowshoe patterns in the graveyard. Whatever tracks her attackers had left had been obliterated by well-meaning searchers. She shook her head slightly. After last night's snow fall, there had been little enough chance to follow the trail. Now it was impossible.

Her stomach rumbled and she wanted to growl back at it, having grown tired of its constant demands. Instead, she turned around and went back downstairs. She had to appear fit if she was to convince the chief investigator to let her participate in the investigation.

Downstairs, the double doors leading to the common room were wide open and she could hear Bérubé's familiar drawl as he reported to the chief. He fell silent when she walked in, but the chief drew a little circle in the air with his index finger, indicating that he should go on.

There was no one else in the common room save for Thomas,

the innkeeper. He sat on the settee, his short legs stretched out before him, a cup of something steaming resting on his little potbelly, supported by both hands wrapped around it. He looked sound asleep, but the moment she set foot in the common room, his eyes opened and he sat up, placing the cup on his knee.

He smiled at her while studying her critically. Apparently satisfied with her appearance, he patted the seat next to him in invitation.

Constance glanced over at the chief but he was still listening intently to Bérubé, so she made her way over to the settee and sat down next to the innkeeper.

"You are looking much better," he said in greeting. "Would you like some hot cider?" He lifted his cup and for the first time she noted the strong, rich aroma of mulled cider.

She shook her head but smiled her thanks. He seemed completely at ease in her presence, never staring overlong at her eyes, never seeming nervous. He relaxed her.

"I take it you will be leaving us," he continued, nodding at the two men talking in the corner.

Constance didn't want to think about it. She would be forced to leave before she had even begun a proper investigation.

"And I take it you found no trace of the men?" she replied.

The little innkeeper shrugged. "Too much snow," he said. There was a hard edge to his voice.

Constance could imagine how he felt, knowing there were two probable murderers in the vicinity and being unable to find them. She thought of the boy in the doctor's shed and felt her own anger return. She couldn't sit here and do nothing. The chief was busy.

She leaned over to Thomas and he obligingly leaned closer, presenting his ear.

"Once he is free," she said, "could you tell the chief investigator that I have gone to the doctor's?"

Immediately he turned to look at her, his face filled with unmistakeable concern. Before he could say anything, she smiled her reassurance. "For the boy," she said simply.

The concern turned to sadness and he nodded. "Of course."

With that she rose and headed for the front door, where her coat still hung on the peg and her boots waited on the braided rug. As she donned her boots, she wondered where the rest of the chief's men were. Had they already taken the boy and headed back to St. Vincent? Perhaps they were performing their own search.

She closed her eyes against the knowledge that Chief Investigator Desautel had not kept her informed. Was it deliberate? Either way, it spoke to the little regard he held for her.

She grabbed her coat and went outside, closing the door behind her before she put the coat on.

Either way, she didn't figure as anything but a victim in the chief's plan for investigating this assault. This murder.

A boy had been beaten to death, her colleagues had been murdered, and she had come very close to the same fate. She did not plan to antagonize the chief investigator, but she was not going to sit idly by while others tried to learn what had happened and why.

It was well past midday but the sun felt warm on her face. The street in front of the inn was suspiciously busy with neighbors working at clearing the snow from their walks. She saw faces turn toward the inn and men pause in their shovelling to look at her.

She had lost track of the days but thought it might be Friday. Except for the general store, the day of the week hardly mattered in winter. Many of the inhabitants of Backli's Ford either worked on farms or orchards, or on the ferry—all occupations that would keep them fallow in winter.

Ignoring the curious looks, she went down the steps, her hands deep in her pockets. A joyful bark greeted her from the side of the house and last night's dog bounded through the deep snow to greet her.

She leaned down to rub his face, smiling. He had a soft golden coat with warm brown eyes.

"Hello, boy," she murmured. He practically vibrated with joy and she could tell he wanted to jump up, but he was a well-mannered dog. "What's your name, eh?" she asked him. "Surely you belong to someone."

In answer, the dog licked her hand and wagged his tail. She gave him a final scratch behind the ears and straightened. "I have to go," she said regretfully. But when she started down the walk, he followed her.

The doctor was not home. Constance knocked once more, for good measure, then followed the wraparound porch to the back of the house and knocked at the back door, too. When there was still no answer, she turned to face the yard. In daylight, it seemed much smaller than it had last night. Snow was piled waist deep in wind-sculpted drifts, highest next to the tall white fence that surrounded the doctor's property.

She blinked in amazement at the proliferation of snowshoe tracks on either side of the path leading to the stone shed. Clearly the doctor had joined the search party. Had he tried to scale the fence in his snowshoes only to return and head for the front of the house? He had fallen in a few spots.

Constance smiled. It was brave of him to join the the search when he was clearly ill-suited to do so. Finally she looked at the doctor's makeshift morgue.

The stone shed looked much smaller. She considered its contents for a long while before turning back to the door. She placed her bare hand on the doorknob and took a deep breath before turning it. To her surprise, the door opened. She had expected that it would be locked, given the events of the past few days.

"Docteur?" she called. Silence was her only answer. She stepped inside and found the key to the stone shed hanging from the hook, exactly where the doctor had left it last night. He knew she had planned to return to examine the boy in daylight. She didn't think he would mind if she helped herself to the key. At least, she hoped not.

Closing the door behind her, she took the steps down to the well-trodden path that led to the shed, the dog following behind her. When she reached the shed, she immediately unlocked the padlock without giving herself a chance to think. It fell open with a heavy clunk and she removed it from the staple. It felt cold and unwieldy in her hand. She pulled open the hasp, then hung the lock back on the staple before stuffing the key in her pant pocket.

Then she took a deep breath of the cold, woodsmoke-laden air and pushed the door open. The dog barked once, then sat down, apparently unwilling to go inside.

The smell of death was stronger today, despite the cold. It was a smell of old, congealed blood. Of tainted meat. She breathed through her mouth.

The body was as she had left it, under a stained sheet. It wasn't rational, but for a moment, she wished she had placed a warm blanket over him before leaving last night.

The inside of the shed was also as she had remembered it—dark, cramped, and chill. Still, between the open door and the window over the table, she had enough light to see what she needed to see. She pulled the sheet off and balled it onto the shelf below the table.

In the harsh light of day, the boy looked much paler than she remembered. She stared at his clothed body and wondered what she had been thinking last night. Surely it would have made more sense to leave the body unclothed, rather than go through all the work of redressing him. But the same impulse that had her wanting a warmer blanket for him had guided her decision to redress him.

It was bad enough he had to spend the night alone in a stone shed. She didn't want him to be cold.

The A'lle did not cry. They shed tears to rid their eyes of dust or other foreign objects, but the human ability to weep for grief, or for joy... that they did not have. For the first time in her life, Constance envied humans that ability.

The dog barked sharply, startling her, and she turned to see Chief Investigator Desautel coming down the back steps. She watched him make his way toward the shed on the narrow path. His boots squeaked on the hard-packed snow. The dog backed up until he was in the shed with Constance and began to whine. As soon as the chief stepped to one side of the door, the dog leapt out of the shed and back onto the path.

The chief smiled grimly. "You didn't undress him?" There was a note of censure in his voice and she looked at him in surprise.

"Of course I did. The doctor helped me and we examined him."

He frowned at her. "And then you redressed him."

She nodded, but said nothing further, and he contented himself with examining the boy in silence. "I need more light," he said finally and reaching past her, picked up a lantern she hadn't noticed. She turned around and saw that it had been on one of the shelves behind her.

The chief reached past her again and straightened, holding a box of matches in his hand. He proceeded to light the lantern and hang it from the ceiling hook before continuing with his examination.

Constance blinked away sudden tears as the light stabbed into her eyes. There must have been an extra lantern in the shed. Or else the doctor had returned to the shed after her departure and left the lantern.

"Help me undress him," said the chief.

With a silent sigh, Constance set about undressing the boy for the second time. It was just as awkward as the first time. When they were finished, they examined the body in silence. Constance darted glances at the chief investigator, trying to determine what he was looking for, but his gaze roved carefully over the body with no pause or seeming concern.

"Help me turn him over," he said finally and she grabbed the boy's near shoulder and placed her palm under his back. The chief investigator stared at her but she couldn't decipher his expression. Then he placed his hand under the boy's hip and nodded at her.

Together, they pushed up until the boy was resting on his side.

Constance kept one hand on his shoulder and the chief investigator kept his hand on the boy's leg to keep him steady. The blood had pooled to the bottom, discoloring his body all along his back, except for where their hands pressed against his cold, unyielding flcoh. There the pressure of their flesh on his caused a displacement of the blood, leaving a lighter area.

Constance closed her eyes, all at once sickened by what they were doing. Surely he deserved better than to be disrobed, poked, and prodded. Grandmother Esther had told her that their people had respect for the dead, that it was an honour to wash and prepare the dead for journey to the crematorium, where the loved one's ashes and bones would be added to the soil and thus feed the next generation.

Humans clung to a belief that something existed beyond death, that a person somehow continued once shed of the bonds of flesh. But A'lle did not believe. Could not believe. Either God was, or he wasn't. No A'lle could ever believe in the existence of a God that left no evidence of his existence.

And if God did not exist, then neither did Heaven, or Hell. A'lle believed what they could see, measure, and explain. They all accepted that there was nothing beyond death, therefore each death was mourned as a terrible, permanent loss. The death of one so young, especially at the hands of another, was an abomination.

"This work is not pleasant," said Desautel quietly, "but it is necessary."

She opened her eyes but he was still examining the boy's body, inch by interminable inch. She knew he was right. They had to learn as much as they could, as quickly as they could, before the body gave up the bonds that kept it intact. Perhaps he had done this so many times that it no longer affected him.

She almost objected when he pulled the sheet over the boy's naked body, but there was logic in the decision. They needed to examine the boy's clothing.

The dog barked and they both turned to see the doctor emerge from his house onto the back porch.

"Hello," he called. He was dressed in loose tweed trousers, a heavy woolen sweater, and a pair of plain mukluks laced up the leg with rawhide. Constance stared at him for a moment before turning to the chief investigator.

"That is Dr. Saunders," she told him in a low voice. "He tended the boy's injuries. And mine."

Desautel stepped out of the stone shed and headed toward the back porch. The dog walked ahead of him and went up the stairs, finally sitting on the top step. Desautel and the doctor shook hands. The doctor's hair was tousled, as if he had removed a hat and not had time to comb it.

Constance folded the boy's clothes and placed them next to him before going out. She closed the door and slipped the padlock through the hasp, but didn't lock it. No matter what, she was not leaving the boy's body here, to be buried like a pauper in the place he was murdered.

When she joined the two men, they stopped talking at her arrival. Wordlessly, she handed the doctor the key to the shed. He sighed and looked at the stone shed. "I will examine him more carefully before burying him. I will send you my report."

Alarmed, Constance looked at Desautel, but he was already shaking his head.

"Thank you for your offer, Docteur," he said, "but we are taking him back with us. For the autopsy."

Constance's empty stomach did a slow heave. She swallowed.

The doctor's did not look pleased, but he nodded his understanding. As though sensing her distress, the dog stood up and came over to lean against her leg. She automatically leaned down to scratch the top of his head.

They were all curious about the A'lle, these human doctors, about how the A'lle differed from humans. There had been autopsies of A'lle before and the information gained had been published in journals. Was that not enough? What was this obsession with seeing for themselves?

There were differences, of course. Of course there were. The species had evolved on different worlds. But the similarities were vastly greater than the differences. Both had blood based on hemoglobin. Both needed oxygen to fuel their hearts and brains. Both ingested and excreted in similar fashion.

Why wao that not enough for them?

"I will go back to the inn," she murmured and stepped around the chief investigator. The dog fell into step next to her and she rounded the corner of the house without looking back.

❧ THIRTEEN ❧

CONSTANCE walked slowly toward the inn, mindful of stepping carefully on the hard-packed snow on the sidewalk. A tall berm of snow separated the sidewalk from the road, with narrow inroads at irregular intervals to allow access to the road.

She could feel them watching her, the women behind their curtains, the men clustered outside their homes, talking with each other, more frank in their stares.

She couldn't blame them. Their lives had been tossed into the air and now they all waited to see where the pieces would fall.

In St. Vincent, horses and cars would be travelling the streets, shoppers would be entering and leaving stores, businessmen would be hurrying to appointments, children would be playing in school playgrounds.

In contrast, Backli's Ford gave the appearance of idleness, with no one busy except for Mr. Patenaude at the general store. She knew that was wrong, however. Many of the men would be out on their traplines, looking for marten and fox, and maybe even the elusive lynx. Other men would be in the deep woods, at lumber camps, cutting down trees to feed the growing needs of Montreal and its surrounding townships.

The men left behind were likely farmers, repairing and preparing for the planting time. She hadn't seen a school here, but surely there must be one.

The sun warmed the top of her head and shoulders, while a breeze off the river brushed cold against her cheeks. She took a deep breath, noting the scent of wood smoke. Soon the snow would melt and the ground would thaw, releasing the fecund smell of spring. The crocuses and daffodils would poke through the last of the snow to herald the coming of the warm season. And she and her family would steel themselves against the encroaching, dangerous heat.

She had lost track of the dog. He had been behind her when she left the doctor's place but now he was nowhere to be seen. Probably he had gone back home to eat. Her stomach rumbled in sympathy.

As she came abreast of the church yard gates, her shoulders tensed. Where were they? Had they found an abandoned cabin? Were they holed up in a cave?

In spite of her earlier uncharitable thoughts, she knew that Monsieur Pelletier and the men who had gone out searching knew this area much better than she or any of the chief investigator's people did. And with all the snow on the ground, they should have found traces of her attackers' passage.

Why hadn't they?

"Mademoiselle?"

Startled, she looked around to see Camille coming up behind her.

"Bonjour, Camille," said Constance with a smile. The girl smiled back and stopped when she reached Constance. She was dressed in black lace-up boots and a blue, boiled-wool coat that was tight at the bodice but flared out as it descended to a few inches below her knees. Her gray woolen skirt hung to mid-calf and her starched white petticoat a few inches below that. Hand-knit mittens and a matching hat, also in blue and also felted, completed the outfit.

Despite all the layers, the girl shivered with the cold.

"Where are you off to?" Constance asked.

Camille showed Constance the empty net bag she clutched in one hand. "To the general store," she said. "Madame Pelletier needs a few more supplies."

Constance glanced at the inn. "No doubt she doesn't normally have to feed so many people," she said. From the back of the inn came the sounds of a harness bell and the voices of men calling to each other.

"Not at this time of year," agreed Camille cheerfully. Her dark braids emerged from the hat to fall down the front of her coat.

"Do you not go to school?" asked Constance.

Camille laughed out loud. "I am fourteen, Mademoiselle," she said, as if that explained everything. And perhaps it did, here. Father and Mother insisted that their children spend some part of every day in learning something new. Even Prudence, the eldest, had been studying the effects of various grains on A'lle physiology for ten years, keeping meticulous notes. Father dreamed of a day when all A'lle would be able to share what they had learned of this world with each other.

"Are you going back to the inn?" prompted Camille when Constance remained silent too long. The girl seemed to have gotten over whatever shyness she had been feeling.

"Not right away," said Constance, making a sudden decision. "Can you tell me where the ferry master lives?"

"Monsieur Henderson?" Camille turned and pointed at a small house down the street, on the river side of the square. "But he is probably working to get the ferry ready."

"And where...?"

Camille nodded at the ferry master's house. "Walk past his house until there are no more homes. You will see his workshop on your left. It's right on the river."

"Merci, Camille," said Constance. Now that she was decided, she headed for the nearest low point in the berm and crossed over.

Clearly someone ran a log across the road regularly, but after yesterday's snow, it was now a churned and rutted mess. She picked her way across until she finally reached the square. It was nothing more than a wide space in the road, forcing the road to either side of it. There were half a dozen oak trees and a large fir tree in the center, and by the number of tracks and well-trodden paths crisscrossing it, it was also a favorite short cut.

She hesitated, then stopped to examine the square more carefully. It took a moment but she finally saw the mess of tracks by the largest oak tree near the center of the square. There was also a round imprint in the snow, just the size of a curled up body. She imagined that it was tinged pink with diluted blood, but of course it was impossible to tell beneath the fresh snow.

Someone had beaten the boy nearly to death and left him on the square to be found. Or had he managed to escape and made his way to the square, hoping for help?

A tide of bitterness rose in her, leaving a taste like soapberries in her mouth. How desperate he must have been, to look to humans for help.

She turned away abruptly and walked away as fast as the terrain would allow. At any moment now, the chief investigator would call out and stop her. Or worse, Bérubé, his right-hand man. Bérubé disliked her even more than did the chief's assistant, Louis, though he always treated her fairly.

She passed a man shovelling his walk and nodded politely when he touched his hat. A pair of girls emerged from a house, arm in arm and giggling. They stopped to watch her walk by until an older woman came out and boxed their ears.

The sun glinted off the snow, forcing her to squint against the glare. The houses were growing farther apart, and between them she could see the long, unbroken expanse of the frozen river. It was hard to believe that in a month, the snow and ice would be gone and the water would be flowing again.

Here and there, she spotted cleared-off areas on the ice, ideal for skating. And there were holes hacked in the ice for drawing water. Clearly, not everyone had a well.

At last, she reached the house Camille had pointed out. Like many of the others, it was made of fieldstones, probably cleared from the fields in preparation for planting. The house was small but well tended, with bright red shutters and a matching red door. The front walk had not been cleared, but a path led to the back of the house.

There she found a henhouse and a small barn, just big enough to house two horses and a sled. Its doors were closed, but she could smell the warm, comforting smell of horses. She turned toward the house just as the back door opened, revealing a heavy woman near Madame Pelletier's age. The scowl on her face was nothing like Marie Pelletier, however.

"Yes?" said the woman. She crossed her arms over her bosom, an awkward looking movement that reminded Constance of overdressed children in winter.

"Madame, my name is Const—"

"I know who you are," said the woman abruptly. "What is it you want?"

Was the hostility for the office she represented or for the fact that she was A'lle? A black labrador poked his nose out the door and quickly retreated.

"Madame," began Constance again, "I am investigating the murder of the young man who was found—"

"Murder!" The woman's arms uncrossed and she stepped down onto the top step of the narrow porch. She seemed unaware of the cold. "I was told he got a whuppin', that's all."

Constance's chin rose and her tone sharpened. She did not like being interrupted. "It was more than a *whuppin'*" she said. "He was beaten to death."

In spite of the cold wind putting roses on her cheeks, the woman's face paled. She suddenly seemed to lose all animosity. A calico cat rounded the corner of the house, hugging the wall where the snow edged away.

"I would like to speak to Monsieur Henderson," continued Constance. The hens clucked in annoyance behind her, whether at the sound of their voices or the appearance of the cat, she didn't know.

"He's workin' on the ferry," said the woman, her voice subdued.

Now that she wasn't scowling, Constance could see the prettiness of her, though her features seemed to drag down her round face, as though she was constantly being disappointed. "And your son?" she asked.

At that, the woman's head jerked up. "Joshua? Why do you want to talk to him?"

"It's part of the investigation," said Constance calmly. The woman had finally started shivering, but she still didn't invite Constance in. Fine. Constance could endure the cold much longer than this aggravating woman could. "Your son found the victim. We need a statement from him."

The woman rubbed her arms. "It wasn't just him," she said. "He was with a bunch of the lads, on his way to school."

Constance took a step closer and the woman's chin tucked in. "Where is your son now?" she asked.

"At school," said the woman quickly.

Constance nodded sharply. "In that case, I'll return later."

Without another word, she turned and headed back toward the street. She put the woman out of her mind, refusing to allow her antagonism to have any effect on her. She had grown up seeing that half-fearful, half-angry look on people's faces, especially strangers' faces. At least now she could tell herself that perhaps it was because she was an investigator that people did not like her.

* * *

She followed the sound of hammering past the last house on the river side and down a wide, tamped path to a large, box-shaped building with double doors large enough to accommodate two sleds side by side. There was a series of short, wide windows along the width of the building, just below the roof line.

Beyond the workshop, down a small embankment, a wooden pier jutted into the Bartolomée River, like a hair clip on a white ribbon of snow and ice.

When Constance finally rounded the workshop, she found a smaller door with a window next to it. Peering in, she saw a big man, presumably Monsieur Henderson, pounding fiercely and with great concentration on a board. She tried the doorknob, and finding it unlocked, pushed it open. The man had his back to her and seemed oblivious to her arrival.

The smell of fresh sawdust filled the air, as did the dust motes swirling in the sunbeams. There was a matching series of windows on the other side of the building so that the workshop was flooded with light. At the far end, a barrel woodstove fought vainly to keep the cold at bay. Split logs were stacked neatly against the wall, ready to be fed to the stove.

The ferry itself was up on a low scaffolding that would allow a crouching man access to its underside. It was a flat-bottomed construction, with hand rails and a gate at one end, and a low structure at the other end, presumably housing an engine.

How they had managed to hoist the thing up on the scaffolding was a mystery to her.

She finally returned her attention to Henderson, watching the sure swing of the hammer as it aimed for and struck a protruding nail. He seemed to be removing nails from a plank, rather than inserting them, and was lost to his work. Despite the fact that she could see her breath in the building, he wore a plaid wool shirt with the sleeves rolled up to reveal an undershirt. His pants were held up by black suspenders that had gone gray with age. He wore a flat, billed cap made of tweed that was covered in sawdust. Clearly he had been crawling under the ferry.

"Monsieur Henderson?" she finally called.

The man jumped and whirled, his hammer out to his side as though it were a live thing that might bite him if held too close.

"Forgive me," she said, herself startled at his reaction. "I did not mean to…"

He laughed, a great booming laugh that brought a smile to her lips. "Mademoiselle, you scared me out of a year's growth!" He set the hammer down on the board and walked toward her.

He was a few inches shorter than she was, with the broad shoulders of someone who worked hard every day of his life. His broad, craggy face was creased in lines that suggested a humorous outlook on life. He was clean shaven and what she could see of his thinning brown hair was flecked with gray.

"My name is Constance A'lle," she said. Before she could say anything more, he nodded and stuck out a big hand for her to shake.

"I heard what happened to you," he said gravely. "I hope they find the bast— men who attacked you."

She hesitated a moment, then placed her hand in his. He shook it firmly but gently before releasing it. It was hard to believe this man was married to the antagonistic woman she had just left.

"Thank you," she said. They stood staring at each other for a few moments. His eyes were blue and serious, though laugh lines radiated from their corners.

Finally she remembered why she had come. "I am told you brought the boy to the doctor."

He nodded and waited.

"Did your son find him?" she asked.

The man's chest rose and fell in a great, silent sigh and sadness filled his eyes. "Yes. He and two other boys were on their way to school when they found him on the square."

She nodded, suddenly realizing she did not have a notebook on her. Was there no end to the mistakes she would make?

"When did you become involved?" she asked.

As though realizing this might take some time, Samuel Henderson opened one arm to welcome her in. "Let's sit by the fire," he said.

Which was a gentle way of reminding her she had not closed the door behind her. With an apologetic smile, she closed it and followed him past the ferry to the back of workshop. She hadn't noticed before, but there was a stack of rough-hewn sawhorses against the far wall, next to a pile of two by six planks neatly stored on wooden brackets nailed to the wall. He pulled a sawhorse off and set it close to the woodstove. He nodded her over to it and Constance accepted the kindness as it was meant, even though proximity to the woodstove was uncomfortably hot for her. She removed her mittens and opened her coat.

Henderson pulled a second sawhorse off the stack and brought it near to hers. "I can't offer you anything to drink," he apologised.

She waved him off and waited for him to settle himself. He sat down and stretched his legs toward the heat of the woodstove.

"Now," he said, crossing his burly arms over his chest. "Josh came running to the workshop a few minutes after he left for school. I'd just gotten here. I was starting the fire." His eyes lost their focus as he looked inward, remembering. "He talked so fast I couldn't make heads nor tails out of what he was saying. And then I did." He sighed softly. "I ran as fast as I could to the square. A couple of other men were there ahead of me."

Constance nodded encouragingly but didn't say anything. She cursed herself once more for not thinking to bring a notepad with her.

"The boy was still alive," said Henderson and his fists clenched. "His eyes were open, but he weren't talking. I'm not sure he was aware of what was going on." He shook his head. "He was beat up pretty bad."

He lapsed into silence, his gaze on the sawdust-covered floor.

Constance waited. After a moment, she prompted him. "And then?"

Henderson shook himself and uncrossed his arms. He placed his hands on either side of the sawhorse and leaned back. "And then we picked up the boy and carried him to the doctor's." He shrugged. "We sent the kids off to school."

Constance nodded again. Inside the woodstove, a log shifted

noisily and sent a belch of smoke through a crack in the belly of the stove. The chimney rose a good ten feet, to bend and exit through the wall, near the roof. Metal flashing had been fashioned roughly to line the hole and block cold air from coming in. Drying lumber, sawdust, wooden construction, and a woodstove. It was only a matter of time before Henderson's workshop went up in flames.

"Who were the other men?"

"Matthias Esterbrook and Jonas Miller." Before she could ask, he continued. "Matt is probably gone back to his lumber camp but Jonas lives directly across from the general store. The house with the green door."

"I will need to speak to your son," she said. "And to the other children he was with."

Henderson's lips pressed together, but he nodded. He glanced up at the windows. "Josh'll be home in an hour or so," he said. "I'll get him and the other boys together. Come by my house."

Constance thought it through before speaking. "Could they come to the inn?" she asked. "The chief investigator may want to speak with them." She stood up to signal the end of the interview and her head spun a little. She leaned back to let the sawhorse support her. Henderson stood up, too, and brushed sawdust off the seat of his pants.

"All right, Mademoiselle. I'll see to it."

He walked her to the door and opened it for her.

She smiled her thanks and closed the door behind her. She stood in the cool air and breathed deeply as the hammering resumed inside. It had been stifling in the workshop.

"Maître Desautel wants to see you."

Constance whirled to find Bérubé leaning against the corner of the workshop. Her hands had risen automatically to ward off a blow and now she lowered them. They were shaking.

Bérubé's gaze followed her hands down, then lifted to her eyes. He stared at her stonily for a moment, then turned and walked back up the path, leaving her to follow.

How long had he been there? Why hadn't he come in?

Her heart still beating fast, she took long strides to catch up to the man. The sun was still high and warm and she left her coat unbuttoned, although she felt a little chilled. Her hands were still shaking and finally she realized she needed to eat. Right now.

Constance caught up to Bérubé at the square and they walked side by side back to the inn, in silence.

The main street was still mostly deserted, although Monsieur Patenaude was outside, sweeping the snow away from his front porch. He wore a shapeless brown cardigan and a hat with ear flaps.

When they turned in to the front walk, Bérubé pointed wordlessly at the front door, indicating that she should go that way. Constance paused for a moment, half expecting the dog to show up. When he didn't, she walked up the steps and pushed open the door with Bérubé right behind her.

The number of boots littering the front hall had gone down considerably. The doors to the common room were closed, as was the kitchen door, though she could hear movements behind the door. With a silent sigh, she sank onto the bench and slowly pulled her boots off. Bérubé stomped the snow off his boots and swiped them on the carpet, then stepped onto Madame Pelletier's clean, waxed floor.

Constance did not give much for his chances if the innkeeper caught him. Oblivious to his danger, he knocked at the double doors and entered, leaving Constance alone for a blessed moment.

Her shoulder still ached, but she was regaining mobility. The headache was all but gone and when last she checked, the gashes along her thighs were nothing but thin red lines. Her body was healing itself but at the cost of her alertness and strength. She needed food and sleep. Since the latter was not likely, she would settle for the former.

But first, the chief investigator.

With a slight grunt, she pushed herself up and dropped her

boots under the bench. She hesitated to remove her coat, but in the end she hung it up on one of the available coat hooks. Finally, she padded silently to the double doors to the common room and pulled them open.

Bérubé and Desautel had been standing by the front window, leaning in to each other and talking in low voices. Now both stopped talking and turned to look at her.

Damn, damn, and triple damn.

The chief investigator nodded to Bérubé, who nodded in silent confirmation before pulling his hat out from under his arm and moving toward the door. He glanced at her as he passed her, but she couldn't read his expression.

And then she was alone with the chief investigator. Desautel stood with his back to the big window, his hands clasped behind his back. She could barely make out his expression against the glare from the window. He did not look happy.

"Mademoiselle A'lle, where have you been?"

She did not need to be human to sense a trap. But she answered him truthfully. "Interviewing the ferry man, sir. He was one of the men who carried the boy to the doctor."

Chief Investigator Desautel nodded. "And did you think to tell anyone that you planned to do that?"

She blinked at him, unsure of how to respond. She hadn't wanted to be forbidden to do it, which he would have had he known what she planned. No matter how this assignment had started, it was now her case and she didn't want to be told she couldn't investigate.

He clearly expected an answer but she suddenly found herself distracted by the smell coming from the kitchen. Baked beans. Her mouth watered and her stomach growled.

"I... knew everyone was busy, sir," she said, forcing herself to concentrate on him. His stern expression grew even grimmer. "I knew we would have to speak to these men before we left."

"Indeed," he said, cutting off the word with a near snap of his teeth. "And so you thought to walk to the end of town and disappear into a building with no one knowing where you had gone. You. Who had twice been attacked by men still at large."

The blood drained from Constance's face and she swayed. With a muffled curse, Desautel took two long strides and grabbed her elbows.

Much as she hated appearing weak, Constance was grateful for the support as the room began a slow dance.

The kitchen door suddenly opened and Madame Pelletier stood in the opening.

"What are you doing to the girl?" she demanded.

"Send for the doctor," said Desautel almost angrily. "She feels faint."

Madame Pelletier stepped into the common room, her eyes narrow as she examined Constance's face. The aroma of baked beans filled the world and flooded Constance with longing.

"Bring her into the kitchen," she ordered and turned to lead the way.

"She would be better to lie down," argued Desautel.

"She needs food," said Madame Pelletier shortly. "Again."

Desautel looked uncertainly at Constance, who barely managed a nod. Looking unconvinced, he placed an arm around her back and led her into the redolent warmth of the kitchen. He pulled out a chair at the work table and guided her into it. Almost instantly, a bowl of baked beans, brown and rich with the smell of pork and maple syrup, appeared before her.

"It's hot," warned Madame Pelletier and it was all Constance could do to blow the worst of the heat away from the first spoonful before she put it in her mouth.

Bliss.

She applied herself to the bowl with the single-minded devotion that only the starving could attain. At one point, a thick slice of bread, slathered with butter, appeared in front of her and she polished it off, as well.

A glass of water, followed by more bread, leftover ham, scrambled eggs, and more beans.

Two more slices of bread.

At last, Constance closed her eyes and breathed a sigh of relief. "Thank you, Madame," she said in heartfelt gratitude. "You may have saved my life."

"She left."

Constance opened her eyes to find the chief investigator staring at her. She glanced around the kitchen to find that he was right. They were alone.

"I have never seen anyone eat like that," he said, as though he could not help himself.

Constance blinked once, twice.

"My body repairs itself," she explained. "I need the food as fuel."

He stared at her a moment longer with something akin to wonder. "Is that why you look so thin?"

She nodded. "Our injuries heal fast, but only if we eat copiously. Otherwise, we grow dangerously thin." So thin that the body ceased all but essential functions, until the vital organs shut down one by one and the brain died from lack of oxygen.

But he did not need to hear that.

"Why didn't the boy heal?"

Constance leaned back against the hard chair and rested her hands on the edge of the table.

"His injuries were too severe," she said softly. "There were too many of them. His body could not cope."

Whatever anger the chief investigator had held against her seemed to have dissipated. He sat back in his chair, resting his forearms on the table, and drummed his fingers absently.

"Tell me what you learned from the ferry master," he said finally.

Constance pushed the bowl away. "His son, Joshua, was walking to school with two friends at approximately eight o'clock yesterday morning. They found the boy injured on the square."

She swept up the bread crumbs into the palm of her hand and dropped them into the bowl. "All three ran for their fathers. Those would be Sam Henderson, the ferry master, Matthias Esterbrook, and Jonas Miller. Monsieur Esterbrook returned to camp this morning but Monsieur Miller is still in town." She sipped at her water and continued. "The men carried the injured boy to the doctor's surgery. Mr. Henderson said the boy's eyes were open but he did not speak." Her hands began to shake as anger rose within her. The boy did not speak because he had been beaten senseless, because his cracked ribs made it difficult for him to breathe, because he now knew better than to trust the humans.

"Anything else?" asked the chief investigator. His mouth closed on the words, forming a hard line.

"No," she replied.

Desautel nodded. His drumming fingers stilled on the tabletop as he thought. Constance glanced out the window. The day was wearing on. They would have to leave soon in order to make it back to St.Vincent before nightfall.

"Sir," she said, interrupting his thoughts. "I would like to interview Mr. Miller. And Mr. Henderson promised to send his son and his friends to the inn as soon as they return from school. Someone should speak to them if I am not back."

"You are to stay here," he said. He raised a hand as though to forestall her objection, although she hadn't said a word. "I'm leaving Bérubé and St-Jean behind to continue the investigation. I want to bring the boy's body back to St. Vincent and you back to your family so you can recuperate."

"Sir, I am recovering well. I can help—"

He stood up abruptly, silencing her. "No. You were attacked twice. The first time might have been because you were with Renaud and Dallaire, or because you were from the magistrate's office, but last night... last night's attack was directed at *you*, personally. I will remove you from this place until we learn the reason behind these attacks."

She took a deep breath to calm herself before standing up, too.

"If I am the object of their attention, then I should stay, to flush them out."

He studied her face for a moment, then smiled, an action so startling that she forgot to be angry.

"Those two are probably long gone," he pointed out. "The manhunt revealed no traces of them."

Constance laid her palms on the table and leaned forward. "Do you not consider that strange, Chief Investigator?" She lowered her voice. "No trace at all. With all this fresh snow?"

Desautel shrugged, but he looked troubled. "They could have made their escape last night, under cover of the snow."

"True, but what if they are still in the village?" she asked softly. "What if they have found refuge with someone here?"

She saw at once from his face that he had already considered the possibility.

"That's why you are leaving Bérubé and St-Jean behind," she said accusingly. "You think the men *are* hiding here." Her hands rose of their own volition and spread wide, beseechingly. "Let me stay, too. Three stand a much better chance against those ruffians."

He shook his head decisively. "Non, non et non. You are returning with me and the others. Tomorrow I will send reinforcements to help Bérubé and St-Jean. If those two are still here, they will find them. You are not fit to stay behind."

And there it was. She straightened slowly and looked him in the eye. His face slowly turned a dark shade of red.

"A poor choice of words," he said stiffly. "Nevertheless, it is true. You have been injured and need to recover. Your memory still hasn't returned. And consider this, Mademoiselle. Do you not think it strangely unlikely that two A'lle were attacked in this small village? It beggars belief that it would be a coincidence."

And despite her anger and her resentment, she had to admit that he was right.

It beggared belief.

* * *

Desautel obtained the use of the sled from the the innkeeper with the promise that it would be returned the following day. Monsieur Pelletier did not seem to mind, especially as his inn now had two additional guests, Bérubé and St-Jean, and the promise of at least two more coming tomorrow, better prepared for an indefinite stay.

Madame Pelletier took Desautel aside and managed to extract a promise out of him to send one of his constables to her regular supplier in St. Vincent with a list of her requirements before returning to Backli's Ford. After all, she pointed out, she needed to feed his men, and Mr. Patenaude would not be able to supply her needs for much longer.

As Madame Pelletier busied herself preparing her list, Constance returned to the doctor's house, accompanied by Joliette and Mackenzie. Two more taciturn men she had never met, and she did not even attempt to talk to them as they walked the sort distance to the doctor's.

The sun was still high and warm and the breeze was just enough to keep her from growing too warm. She saw more children on the street now that school was out. The chief investigator was interviewing the boys at the inn while Bérubé had gone across the street to find Monsieur Miller. He would bring the sled around to the doctor's surgery when he was done.

This, then, was the last useful thing she could do here—make sure the boy was treated respectfully on this last journey.

As she passed the church, she thought again of Père Noiron and the irony of him being the one to save her from the two ruffians. She peered at the building, but the priest did not magically appear.

She turned up the doctor's walk, followed by the two constables, and went up the stairs. She used the knocker to announce her presence, and a moment later, the door opened to reveal Ephraim Saunders. He glanced at the two men standing behind her then turned his smiling attention on her. He was coatless, and his shirtsleeves were rolled up to his elbows. To her surprise, he wore a pair of wire-rimmed spectacles that he removed and tucked into his vest pocket.

"Mademoiselle A'lle," he smiled. "You are looking much better."

"Thank you, Docteur," she said formally. "We are here for the body."

The smile faded from his eyes. "Ah."

"We will go around," she said, obscurely sad to see the light leave his face.

He nodded. "I will meet you there."

She turned away as he closed the door and glanced at her companions. At nearly forty, Joliette was the older of the two, with unruly brown hair that ate combs. He was tall and thin with a prominent Adam's apple. Everything he wore always had too-short sleeves and pant legs. He reminded her of a scarecrow. Yet someone had found him attractive enough to bear him five children.

Mackenzie was shorter and wider, with the red hair of his Scottish ancestors and the burly arms and powerful shoulders of the Vikings who had invaded his homeland. As far as she knew, he was not married, which was not surprising. She couldn't remember ever seeing him smile. Mackenzie carried an old woolen blanket rolled up under one arm. Monsieur Pelletier had handed it over it wordlessly as they were leaving the inn.

The two men stared back at her stoically and she wondered what they were feeling. Then she decided it was best she didn't know.

Without a word, she turned and led the way down the wraparound porch to the back. The doctor was already at the stone shed, standing in front of the open door. Taking a deep breath, Constance walked down the steps to the path and joined him.

It wasn't often she had to look up at anyone and she struggled against an urge to step back, but the constables were crowding her and she had to choose between entering the shed or stepping off the hard-packed path.

She did not wish to re-enter that place of death and stepped off the path. At once she sank up to her calf and would have lost her balance if not for the doctor's steadying hand on her elbow. She smiled her thanks as the men brushed past them, and noticed again how blue his eyes were. They were almost A'lle in their intensity.

"Are ye keepin' this sheet?" asked Mackenzie from the depths of the shed and she turned back to the task at hand.

Ten minutes later, the A'lle boy was placed in the blanket and wrapped loosely. Mackenzie and Joliette carried him carefully down the path to the back porch and around the house. Constance and the doctor followed behind and it struck her that they formed the only mourning party the boy was likely to get in this place. At the back door, she shook hands with the doctor.

"Thank you for your help," she said gravely.

He nodded and looked away. "I'm sorry I couldn't save him."

Constance looked away, too, to the doctor's yard and its crisscrossed pattern of snowshoe tracks. Some of the tracks overlaid boot tracks, as if he had struggled with the snowshoes, removed them, and tried again. She might have smiled, had it not been such a sad occasion. The doctor was not an outdoorsman.

The stomp of boots on the porch announced Mackenzie's arrival before he emerged from around the corner of the house.

"The sled is out front," he said.

She nodded and with a final smile at the doctor, left.

৯ FOURTEEN ৩

"What the hell...?" murmured Joliette.

Desautel saw them, too. Seven dark figures standing still at the foot of the drive. A lit lantern rested on a tree stump by the road.

"My family," said Constance A'lle, sitting next to him on Monsieur Pelletier's sled. He thought he detected patience in her voice, but it might have been resignation.

Mackenzie and Joliette slowed their horses and allowed him to pull up to the foot of the long, narrow road leading to the A'lle house.

He called "Whoa" to the horses and John A'lle stepped forward to meet them.

"Monsieur A'lle," said Desautel in greeting. There was a half moon tonight, but it remained stubbornly hidden behind more snow clouds. At least it wasn't snowing. He peered into the night to pick out Prudence A'lle but the rest of the family remained clustered and obscured to him. How had they known he was coming? Or had they been out there for hours, waiting?

"Chief Investigator," replied John A'lle formally. "You return our child to us."

An odd way of putting it. Desautel nodded. "Injured, but recovering. She is to remain at home until she is fully recovered." A small sound from the A'lle girl told him what she thought of his edict, but he ignored it.

Madame A'lle stepped forward, nearly as tall as her husband, and placed a bare hand on Desautel's arm. He could feel the heat through his coat but before he could do more than register the oddness of it, she removed her hand.

"Thank you, Monsieur Desautel. We feared her lost."

She said it strangely and he tried to make out the expression on her face but the moon failed him. A breeze had picked up during the last mile but it lacked bite. There would be more snow tonight but there was also a smell in the air, more a promise, really, that spoke of warmth and green growing things.

"Not lost for long, Madame," he said seriously. "I will leave it to Mademoiselle A'lle to relate her adventures. I must return to St. Vincent." There was no mistaking the faint sigh of relief next to him. This much at least he could do for the girl. Let her choose what she wanted her family to know.

Prudence A'lle's clear voice floated out to him. "Surely you and your men can stay for a cup of tea? And there is fresh prune cake."

His traitorous stomach betrayed him with a loud rumble but he shook his head regretfully. "Thank you, Mademoiselle, but we must get on." He peered into the cluster of figures and made out her shorter figure at the front.

"Who is this?"

It was the quiet one. Eloise. She had moved to the the sled without making a sound on the hard-packed snow. Now her tall figure leaned over the side.

"He is A'lle," said Constance A'lle and before he could move, she jumped down from the bench onto the road and joined her sister. Mackenzie's horse, less than five feet away, snorted unhappily and at once Eloise moved to his side and placed a calming hand on the beast's nose. She murmured in its ear while Mackenzie fidgeted in his saddle. It occurred to Desautel that the man could use someone murmuring calming words in his ear, too.

John A'lle joined his daughter at the back of the sled and Desautel finally gave up. He wrapped the lines around the handrail and clambered down from the sled. Not as gracefully as Constance A'lle had. The snow squeaked under his boots.

"Maître?" asked Joliette uncertainly, and Desautel waved at him to stay where he was. By the time he rounded the sled, Constance A'lle had removed the pins and lowered the gate. Her father climbed in and pulled the blanket away from the boy's face.

After a long, silent moment, Desautel could bear no more.

"Do you know him?" he asked.

John A'lle covered the face once more and climbed off the sled. He nodded at his daughter to replace the gate. While she did, he turned to Desautel.

"I had never met him," he said softly. "But I believe he was coming to meet us."

"Father?" That was Prudence. She approached, leaving behind her three siblings.

Lily A'lle was the one who replied. "His father wrote to us," she explained, and there was real grief in her voice. "He hoped that his son would find a mate among you."

Desautel felt rather than saw Mackenzie's start of surprise and managed to cover his own better. He had heard that the A'lle arranged marriages, but hadn't believed it. Arranged marriages were a relic of another era. The whole idea was distasteful. And surely against the law.

Then something else occurred to him. He turned to Constance A'lle. "Why didn't you tell me?"

Before she could do more than straighten her back, John A'lle spoke up. "She didn't know," he said, and his voice carried the weight of sadness. "Only Lily and I knew."

Desautel cleared his throat, wondering why he was always so ready to blame the girl. "What is his name?"

"Frederick," replied the man. "He lives... lived with his father outside Montreal. If it is him." He left unspoken the fact that the boy's face had been severely altered by the beating.

"You were expecting him?"

"Yes," said Lily A'lle. "His father wrote to tell us Frederick would be on the afternoon train on Wednesday. John was delayed getting to the station and when he arrived, Frederick wasn't there. We thought he hadn't been on the train. We expected a note today explaining that he had been delayed."

So, the boy—not a boy, not if he was looking for a mate—must have been on the train. But how had he gotten to Backli's Ford? And why hadn't he waited at the station?

He sighed, more tired than he could ever remember feeling, and suddenly Prudence A'lle was by his side and patting his arm. The simple gesture made him feel absurdly comforted and he smiled down at her.

"I will need the name and address of his father," he said finally.

"Of course," said Madame A'lle, reclaiming his attention. "Do you want to wait for me to fetch it?"

Desautel's gaze fell on the sled's sad cargo. "Non. Constable Mackenzie will accompany you back to the house."

Lily A'lle nodded. "Constance."

Constance A'lle looked to Desautel, who nodded.

"Thank you, sir," she said formally. "I will see you tomorrow."

"Only if you are recovered," he warned.

Constance did not reply. Instead, she tucked one hand into the crook of her mother's elbow. Prudence took hold of Constance's free hand and the three women turned up the long drive.

Only as they passed by the lantern did he realize what had been bothering him. Not one of the A'lle was wearing a coat. Lily A'lle had thrown on a shawl but the rest were in shirt sleeves and bare hands.

"Mademoiselle A'lle," he said.

All three stopped and turned, letting go of each other. He was suddenly struck by their wariness, as though they were ready for anything. What were their lives like, that this should be their instinctive reaction?

"Sir?"

"You've forgotten your jacket." He picked it up from the floor when it had fallen when she jumped out.

Constance A'lle made a move toward him but Eloise gave Mackenzie's horse a final pat on the neck and in two strides was next to him. She took the jacket from him without a word and headed for her sister. She nodded as she passed the younger sisters and one of them grabbed the lantern and the family turned away and walked up the road. All except for John A'lle, who remained standing next to Desautel at the back of the sled.

A strange family, thought Desautel.

Mackenzie dismounted and, without a word, led his mare up the road, following the women.

John A'lle's silence began to weigh on Desautel and he finally turned to look at the man. Either his eyes had grown accustomed to the night or the moon emitted more light, because now he could clearly see the man's face and the troubled expression it wore.

"Maître?" said Joliette.

"Go on ahead," said Desautel. "Fetch Dr. Rivard. Tell him I'm bringing him a body that I want him to look at tonight."

"Yes, sir," said Joliette with relief. He turned his horse around and prodded the animal into a walk.

The doctor would not be happy to be roused from his warm bed for what promised to be a long night, but so be it. The magistrate paid the doctor a handsome sum to be available to perform autopsies as needed. And tonight, he was needed.

"He is not the only one," said John A'lle in a low voice when Joliette was out of earshot.

Desautel looked up at the man. The blue of his eyes could be discerned even at night.

"I beg your pardon?"

A'lle nodded at the body in the sled. "Other A'lle have been murdered."

Desautel stared at the man in astonishment. "I would have known if such a thing were happening," he said firmly. "No such cases have crossed my desk, or that of any other constabulary in the region."

But John A'lle was shaking his head. "Not here. Not until now, in any case." He took a deep breath and looked up at the night sky. "Montreal. Small towns near Montreal."

Desautel swallowed hard. He had thought those days were long gone.

In the early years after their arrival, depending on where their escape vessels had landed, A'lle had been stoned to death, or hanged for crimes they did not commit, often at the instigation of local priests. Even today, if the Church had its way, the A'lle would be rounded up and forced to live on reservations. In the New American States, A'lle had been burned at the stake. What few A'lle survived that pogrom had come to live in Upper and Lower Canada, which were both more accepting of the strangers.

Relatively speaking.

"How do you know this?" he asked slowly. If he, who had law enforcement contacts throughout both provinces, hadn't heard of a resurgence of violence against the A'lle, how could this man, who lived isolated with his family?

John A'lle lowered his gaze until he was looking directly at Desautel.

"It is in our best interest to remain in contact with one another," he said simply.

Yes. Desautel imagined it would be.

"Do you have details?" he asked. "Names of these murdered ones?"

"Not just murdered," said John A'lle. "Some have disappeared."

How had he not heard of this? "How many?" he asked gruffly.

"Five are still missing," said the man. He placed a hand on the side of the sled, almost protectively. "Three have been found dead."

Eight? Eight A'lle had gone missing or been killed, and this was the first he'd heard of it?

"All men?"

A'lle shook his head. "No. And all ages."

"How long?" asked Desautel, then cleared his throat. "How long has this been going on?"

"Almost a year. Until today, I had thought this was localised in the Montreal area." He left unspoken the thought that must be clamoring through his mind, just as it was clamoring through Desautel's. How safe was his family?

"I will look into this," he promised. I won't let anything happen to your family, he wanted to say, but that was one promise he couldn't make. "Can you get me their names and where they were from?"

"Not all of them. I will write down those I know for certain, and whatever I know of the remaining. Do you need them tonight?"

Desautel hesitated. He could ask John A'lle to give the information to Mackenzie, but he knew his constable would be eager to leave. In any case, he wouldn't be calling anyone tonight.

"Tomorrow will be soon enough."

* * *

The ride back to St. Vincent was a lonely one. John A'lle's allegations were troubling. Was someone attacking the A'lle again? He had read extensively on the history of the A'lle, ever since he learned the magistrate was assigning the A'lle girl to him. Depending on where their ships landed, the A'lle were either welcomed in and sheltered by people like his own ancestors, or chased and murdered.

He was uncomfortably aware of his conflicting feelings for the A'lle, and his grandfather's words echoed in his memory. "How would you like to be torn away from everything you know, and have to depend on the charity of strangers?"

Those first decades had been hard ones for the A'lle, but they had adjusted, especially in the big cities. In Montreal, the A'lle ran businesses, owned farms, even ran in local elections. He had been to York and Quebec City and seen how accepted the A'lle were.

The A'lle had made a home for themselves on this planet. Had found a way to make themselves useful. They no longer depended on the charity of the settlers who found them wandering the woods after their escape ships crashed.

Why would the winds of hatred be blowing again? There was no cause, no trigger.

But an A'lle boy had been beaten to death just a few hours south of St. Vincent. And Constance A'lle had been attacked, too. If John A'lle was right, whoever was attacking the A'lle was coming closer to St. Vincent.

» FIFTEEN «

In the room she shared with Gemma, Constance stepped out of her bloodstained pants and slowly peeled off the ragged bandages on her thighs. The gouges were almost completely healed over.

"Those pants will never be the same," said Prudence from the doorway.

Constance sighed. No, they would not. And the family could ill afford to replace them. Worse was the state of her sheepskin coat, on which she had bled as well. The coat she might have to live with for a few years, before she could save enough to replace it.

She glanced at her sister. Prudence leaned against the door jamb, her arms crossed, exuding the smell of anger. Or perhaps it was concern. She was too tired to distinguish between the two.

The bed beckoned and Constance longed to crawl under the worn quilt and sleep. It felt like an eternity since she'd slept in her own bed but she had only spent one night in Backli's Ford. Except for last night and the six months she had spent in Quebec City training to become an investigator, she had never slept away from her family.

She tried to pull off her sweater and winced in pain as her abused shoulder protested.

"Let me help," said Prudence, coming into the room. She took the right sleeve and pulled carefully. Constance eased her arm out, then Prudence pulled the sweater over her head and off completely.

Constance closed her eyes as a wave of fatigue buffeted her. She needed sleep. And food.

"Mother is drawing a bath," said Prudence as she unbuttoned Constance's shirt. "Is there any piece of clothing upon which you didn't bleed?" she asked plaintively.

Constance looked down at her older sister and grinned. "Madame Pelletier removed the worst of the bloodstains."

Prudence blinked. Without a word, she pulled off one sleeve, then the other, leaving Constance in her undershirt and underwear. She shivered slightly and Prudence frowned.

"Father is heating up the tourtière and there are baked beans. But first, a bath." She pulled the robe off the hook from the back of the door and helped Constance into it, then she led her to the bath room at the end of the hall. While they had no electricity, Father had set up a small windmill behind the house. It powered a small heater that provided the house with hot water, as long as they were frugal with it.

Constance walked into the washroom to find Mother pouring the precious Epsom salts liberally in the steaming water.

Mother straightened and looked around. "Ah. Good. In you go."

"The wallpaper will come off," warned Constance, concerned over the amount of steam in the small room. Already mother had beads of sweat on her forehead. But for Constance, the heat was blissfully welcome.

Behind her, Prudence laughed. "Just get in."

Mother helped her with the sash, as if she were still a child, and then had to help her remove the undershirt. Finally, she was naked and cold, but before she could climb into the bathtub, Mother pulled her close and held her.

Mother was tiny compared to Constance, but she was very

strong. Constance didn't try to free herself. Besides, Mother was warm.

Mother took a deep breath, fanning warm air over Constance's neck. Then she turned her face so that her mouth was against Constance's cheek, and licked her.

Constance almost pulled back. Mother hadn't tasted her since she almost died in the measles outbreak of 1901. But she'd been a child then, not a grown woman.

At last, Mother released her and she and Prudence helped Constance over the high lip of the tub. She sank into the hot water, groaning half in pain, half in relief. The water closed over her shoulders as she slid down the slippery enamel.

She looked up to find Mother and Prudence staring down at her. Mother studied her from the healing gashes on her thighs to the fading bruises on her temple.

"I'll be fine," said Constance. "Some food. Some rest. That's all."

Mother said nothing and Constance knew she hadn't fooled her. The damage had been serious enough to affect the chemical balance in her blood, which Mother had tasted on her skin.

Mother and Prudence had great sweat stains beneath their arms and down their chests. Their faces ran with sweat and their hair already looked curlier, thanks to the humidity in the room.

"Go," she said. "I am strong enough to survive a bath on my own."

The two women remained silent for a moment longer. Then Mother nodded and left. Prudence gathered up the underwear and straightened. She looked at Constance for a moment before speaking.

"I'll come back to help you out," she said calmly. "After the kin *st'ah*." Without another word, she left.

Constance stared unseeingly at the closed door. A kin *st'ah*. In which the clan met to decide for one who could not decide for herself.

She suddenly felt cold again and leaned forward in the bath until her breasts rested against her raised legs. But that left her back and shoulders exposed and she shivered. Prudence had sought to warn her that her fate was being decided as she sat unknowing in the tub.

To call a *st'ah* meant that the clan—in this case, her family— felt that the individual—in this case, *her*—was incapable of making a reasoned decision. It normally applied in cases where the individual was too sick to make a rational decision, was about to die, or was unconscious.

The question was, a decision about *what*?

Everyone who could meet joined in the *st'ah*, so that all could be informed before a decision was made. She had never heard of anyone being excluded from the *st'ah*. Unless they were the subject of it.

What decision was her family contemplating?

Constance swallowed a hard lump of anger. No. Surely her family wouldn't ask her to abandon her work. Not after everything she had suffered to become an investigator.

Not *now*, when an A'lle boy lay dead, demanding justice.

She slowly maneuvered herself around until she was on her knees, then grasped the rounded edge of the tub and pulled herself up. Her arms strained but supported her weight. Water ran off her body, raising goosebumps and causing her to shiver. She stared at the floor, considering whether she could trust herself to simply step over the lip of the tub. Finally, she leaned over and, hanging on to the tub, lifted one leg over the rim. Only once she had her foot solidly planted on the towel on the floor did she lift the other leg out. After that, she quickly wiped the water off her body and eased into the heavy cotton robe Prudence had left behind. Then she opened the door, letting all the steam out, and shuffled barefoot to the top of the stairs. She took a deep breath. It seemed lately that she was forever going up or down stairs.

Grimly, she worked her way down the stairs, making sure

to hold onto the railing as she descended. The aroma of tourtière wafted up to meet her and she began to salivate.

Unlike the inn in Backli's Ford, there were no doors on their front room, and long before she reached the foot of the stairs, she could make out the low voices of her family.

"She sustained damage," Mother was saying softly. "It is pure chance that she survived the attack."

Constance paused on the steps. They knew about the attack? How could they? The chief investigator couldn't have told Father or he would have said something when he came in. And then she realized her mother was referring to the original ambush, the one that took Renaud and Dallaire's lives. The one she still couldn't remember.

"And now we have Frederick," said Father. Frederick. The boy who came seeking a bride and found only death.

"What does one have to do with the other?" asked Eloise.

Constance walked into the ensuing silence and every face turned to look at her. Mother sat in the wide, overstuffed chair next to the dead fireplace while Father stood in front of the closed curtains. Gemma and the twins sat on the horsehair settee and Prudence and Eloise had moved two of the remaining oak chairs to be able to see everyone, which meant they had their backs to Constance when she walked in.

Prudence twisted to see behind her and jumped up to lead Constance to her chair. "You should have called for me," she scolded.

"I'm fine," said Constance, refusing to shiver. The only light spilled from the kitchen, the door to which stood open. She had a sudden image of Chief Investigator Desautel squinting in what to him would be gloom. "Why didn't you wait for me?" she asked her father.

But it was Mother who answered. "You are the reason we are holding this kin st'ah," she said calmly. "We need to decide whether or not you should return to the constabulary."

And so they didn't want her there to bend the discussion one way or the other.

Constance considered her words before speaking. "Why?" she asked calmly. "Why is this even in question?"

It was Father who answered. "Because you almost died, child!" His big hands tightened into fists. Gone was the placid face he had presented to the chief investigator. The father who stood before her now had fear written plainly on his face.

Constance glanced at her mother. Lily A'lle controlled her expression better than her husband, but the concern was there in the tightening of her jaw, the frown lines etched between her brows. A quick glance at her sisters revealed the same concern.

Except for Eloise. Eloise looked back at her calmly, her expression reflecting nothing.

Constance took a deep breath. She had to speak clearly and persuasively or all her work would be for nothing. And Frederick A'lle's killers would go unpunished. The constables at the St. Vincent constabulary would not go out of their way to find an A'lle's killers. Too many of them had the same attitude as the chief investigator's secretary and Père Noiron, in Backli's Ford.

"Yes," she said at last, looking back to her father. To her relief, her voice was calm. "I could have died." Father frowned and opened his mouth but she kept going, not giving him the chance to interrupt. "That is the risk every investigator, every constable, takes when investigating a crime or upholding the law. You both knew this when you asked me to take the training in Quebec City."

Father looked away, his gaze seeking his wife's. As though by unspoken agreement, Lily A'lle took up the argument.

"A risk, yes," she said calmly. "But many constables have long careers of enforcing the law without ever encountering violence. This work is too dangerous and we are too few. We cannot risk losing you."

Cannot risk losing my womb, you mean, thought Constance. Every A'lle woman was expected to breed, if she could. Bitterness welled up in her. It hadn't been her choice to train as an investigator. Long months away from her family, exposed to the hidden and not-so-hidden bias among her peers, her instructors… only the magistrate had kept her from giving up at least half a dozen times. But he had been unable to ease the anger that had built up over those long months.

After all that, all the taunts, the rebuffs, the loneliness, she had returned home only to find the same bigotry waiting for her in the St. Vincent constabulary.

And now her family wanted her to quit? Make all that time and sacrifice be for nothing? She might not love working for the humans, but she she knew—*knew*—she could be a good investigator.

Prudence had remained standing when she gave Constance her chair. Now she shifted closer to Constance, as if to lend silent support. The twins glanced at each other but remained silent. Gemma looked at Mother with a puzzled expression.

"You are not making sense, Mother. This is what Constance trained for. Now, at the first test, you want her to quit? The purpose of putting her through all this was to gain an entry into the humans' day to day world. You no longer want this?"

Constance could have hugged her sister. Gemma had managed to sum up clearly the unfairness of the situation.

All faces now turned to Mother and Father. While the A'lle had adopted many human mannerisms over the two centuries they had been on Earth, they had never learned to fidget. Mother and Father stood very still, and yet Constance always imagined an invisible bond linking them, stronger than the thickest rope she had ever seen.

She doubted she would ever find a match as strong as Mother and Father's. She would be lucky to find any kind of match.

"Of course we do," said Mother finally. "We must show them that we can be valuable to them, and not only as finders, or engineers. But…" Her voice trailed off and she looked to Father.

Eloise, who had sat quietly throughout the discussion, staring down at the leg she had crossed over the other, now uncrossed her legs and sat up. She placed both hands on her knees and looked at her father.

"Tell us the real reason."

Mother's hands clasped each other in front of her waist, a sure sign of surprise.

"What do you mean?" asked Constance, turning in her seat so she could see both her sister and her father clearly. "What reason?"

Eloise turned her attention to her mother. "Mother?"

Mother blinked once, twice. Then she looked at her husband. "It's time, John."

Father nodded and his fists finally relaxed. He moved closer to Mother's chair and rested his hands on the doily covering the high back. Mother reached up to touch his hand briefly before clasping her hands in her lap again. In the kitchen, a log dislodged loudly in the cookstove, releasing a puff of smoke, but still no one moved.

"A'lle are being killed," he said bluntly. "For about a year now, we've been getting reports of A'lle disappearing from the Montreal area. Then a few bodies were found."

Constance's heart lurched and then began to pound so loudly in her chest that she had trouble hearing Father's next few words. She became aware of Prudence's warm hand on her shoulder and the comforting pressure of her sister's hip against her arm.

"How many?" she finally managed to ask.

"Eight," said Mother. "Four men, three women, one girl."

Her chest felt tight and her vision grew spotty. She became aware that she was trembling at the same time as Prudence's hand tightened on her shoulder.

"We can continue this in the kitchen," said Prudence. "She needs to eat."

Without waiting, she pulled Constance out of the chair and with an arm around her back, led her into the kitchen.

It wasn't just her, Constance realized suddenly. Prudence was trembling, too.

The warmth of the kitchen enveloped Constance in delicious

heat and she almost groaned in bliss. Her bare feet absorbed the heat of the wood floor like a rock absorbed the heat of the sun. Prudence settled her in the chair at the head of the table, even though that was where Father normally sat. It was the chair closest to the cookstove.

The rest of the family followed silently and arrayed themselves around the table.

The smell in the kitchen was so good it was almost unbearable. Prudence busied herself with the cookstove, pulling the warming box open to retrieve the reheated tourtière and pulling the lid off the cast iron pot that had been pushed to a cooler area. After a moment, she set a plate in front of Constance and placed a knife and fork next to it.

Constance's hand trembled as she reached for the fork. "Tell me about the deaths," she said, and forked meat pie into her mouth. It was the best she had ever eaten.

Father remained standing at the far end of the table. His expression was very still, as though he was working hard at containing his emotions. His fingertips rested on the surface of the table.

"As near as we can tell," he said, "it started a year ago. All from Montreal and surrounding areas. All ages. Men, women, a child."

Constance scooped up some beans and put them in her mouth. Prudence set another plate next to her, with a thick slab of bread slathered in molasses and a chunk of cheddar cheese. A moment later, a glass of cool milk appeared next to it.

"You said some bodies were found," said Constance before downing half the glass of milk.

Father nodded. "Two men. A woman. They had been tortured. Their bodies were found accidentally, and nowhere near where they had disappeared."

Constance continued eating, feeding her body the fuel it so desperately needed, while her sisters reacted. None spoke, but the twins glanced at each other in fear and Gemma looked down at the tabletop, swallowing hard. Prudence remained behind Constance but Constance didn't need to see her to know that her older sister would be standing very still and staring at their father with eyes huge with concern.

Only Eloise remained expressionless, waiting for Father to continue.

Constance swallowed the last bite of bread. "How were they tortured?" she asked calmly. "Were investigations conducted?"

Father answered the last question first. He smiled thinly. "Perhaps 'investigation' is too strong a term," he said softly. "The murderer was never found."

Constance paused in her dedicated attention to the food her sister kept placing before her. This dish was a hearty soup thick with chicken and root vegetables, savory with the dried oregano and thyme Prudence had stockpiled for the winter.

"You think one person is responsible?"

Father shrugged. It was a habit he had lately begun to affect. Constance had caught him practising the movement in front of the mirror in the upstairs hallway. It looked odd on him, not at all the way it looked when humans did it. A'lle shoulders were not built for it.

"The damage was consistent from one person to another. Flesh and muscle tissue cut away. Organs removed." He took a deep breath and his hands balled into fists again. "Five haven't been found."

"And now you think this trouble has moved closer to home," said Eloise.

Mother looked up at that, her eyes troubled. "Don't you?"

Her question dropped into the room like a stone in a pool, sending out cold ripples of silence.

Constance pondered her father's story. Frederick A'lle had been beaten to death, a form of torture, certainly, but nothing like what Father described.

"Have you told the chief investigator?" she asked finally.

"Just now. He promised to investigate." His tone was flat. Clearly, he remained unconvinced.

Constance sat back. If Chief Investigator Desautel had said he would investigate, then he would. She didn't like the man, but she respected him. Still, he had no jurisdiction in Montreal, and the constables there were probably as prejudiced against A'lle as the constables here.

He would need the collaboration of the A'lle population to investigate what was going on, and that wouldn't happen. It would take an A'lle to investigate this crime. These crimes.

The chief investigator would need her.

❧ SIXTEEN ❧

"Absolutely not," said Desautel firmly.

Constance A'lle stood before him, still wearing her blood-stained sheepskin coat, her boots dripping melting snow on his pine floor. She looked as bad as he felt—like she'd been run over by the milkman's cart and left to dry out overnight. Her cheek bones were still much too prominent and there were great dark smudges beneath her eyes.

It was so early that the sun had yet to crest the tree tops and he still had the overhead light on. It gave her face an unhealthy yellow cast. How could her father have allowed her to leave home when she so clearly needed more time? Surely she hadn't *walked* from her house?

Despite his disapproval, a small part of him admired her for her fortitude. He didn't know many grown men who could have survived the physical injuries she had sustained and still want to go to Montreal to pursue an investigation.

He hadn't gone home. After bringing the remains to the medical examiner, he had gone to the office to await the results of the autopsy. He'd managed an hour nap on the settee by the window while the half dozen constables on the night crew went about their business, but the nap made him feel worse so he rose, shaved, and changed into the clean set of clothes he always kept in his office—a habit left over from his days as a lawyer.

And now Constance A'lle stood before him, looking down at him with those strange, troubling eyes. She had brought him the list of the missing or murdered A'lle from Montreal. The sheet of paper lay on his desk, slightly crumpled from its trip in her pocket.

"I have no jurisdiction in Montreal," he continued when she remained silent.

Her face grew very still, as if she did not dare show what she felt. When she replied, her tone was cool.

"Three A'lle dead. Five still missing. All in one year. At best, there have been cursory investigations. Certainly no one has been charged."

She had left the door open behind her and he could see a few constables craning their necks to see inside. Soon the day shift would arrive and the common room would become loud and chaotic. And it was getting hot in here. Someone had overstuffed the damned woodstove again.

Desautel was surprised that she hadn't removed her coat yet. If his office was overly warm for him, it must be stifling for her. He stood up suddenly and walked over to the door, his heels heavy on the wood floor. He closed the door on the curious faces beyond. Where was Louis? His secretary would have shoed them away— and then hovered nearby, out of his line of sight but within earshot.

Constance A'lle turned her head to follow his movements but otherwise did not move.

He regained his seat and leaned back, studying her. Her lips were pressed tightly together. She had more to say but dared not. He had sensed a great anger in her before, but she wasn't the first investigator he had known who carried anger like a shield. Still, what must it be like for her and her family, knowing that someone was targeting them? Perhaps not them specifically, but their species certainly. Not only targeting them but torturing them and then throwing them away like animal carcasses.

"I spoke to Docteur Rivard earlier this morning," he said finally. "He found that the boy died of his injuries. From the beating." The doctor had listed all the injuries impassively, as if he were reading a grocery list his wife had given him. Broken ribs and arms, broken nose and cheekbones, massive internal bleeding, ruptured spleen-like organ, brain hemorhage... it was amazing the boy had lived as long as he had. "He was clearly murdered, but there is nothing to link him to the Montreal killings."

"Except, of course, for the fact that he was A'lle."

Heat flooded his face in a tide of embarrassment. What did she want from him? Did she want him to manufacture a connection?

He took a deep breath and tried not to expel it too loudly. "I despatched four more constables to help find the men who killed Renaud and Dallaire and attacked you. While we don't know for certain, they probably killed the boy."

That damnable stillness of hers was unnerving. Her arms hung loosely by her sides. She held her mitts in one hand and hat in the other. He knew—*knew*—that she was angry, but nothing in her demeanor spoke of it. And she kept staring at him.

It was an effective technique, he realized suddenly. It made him want to keep talking, if only to fill the silence.

Clever girl.

"Thank you for bringing me the list," he said. "Now if you'll excuse me?" He glanced at the door but she didn't seem to understand the hint.

"Sir, allow me to go to Montreal," she said, as if he hadn't said a word in the past five minutes. "I can speak to the A'lle there. I may—no, I am certain that I will learn more than the investigators there did."

Abruptly, Desautel had had enough. "Investigator A'lle, I will call the chief investigator's office in Montreal and obtain more information. But there is no compelling reason to believe that the two cases are connected. Now, since you insisted on coming in, you might as well get to work."

The hand holding the mitts half rose, then dropped to her side, but still her face showed no expression. Then she spoke.

"Yes, of course, Chief Investigator. There is no doubt important filing awaiting my attention." She turned on her heel and left his office, closing the door behind her without even a hint of a slam.

Another investigator might have slammed the door, but none would have dared be sarcastic. He shook his head, half ruefully. The woman was driving him to distraction. Even his most impulsive constable was not as much trouble as she was.

She was young and she was inexperienced. Had she truly expected him to let her take over the Backli's Ford investigation? And yet, her pointed remark made him uncomfortable. Had he been so bent on keeping an eye on her that he had never really given her a chance to obtain the experience she needed?

Perhaps it was time to give her more rein. She had acquitted herself well in Backli's Ford, managing to inspect the dead boy's body and begin the investigation while seriously injured.

She clearly was not back to normal. Whatever normal was for her and hers. Her face was so thin that she actually looked older. The unnatural pace of her healing had obviously taken a toll on her.

Many would consider this ability to heal quickly a gift from the Devil, but Desautel didn't. He was a scientific man, not a man of God, and his curiosity was aroused by the A'lle body's ability to mend itself. How far did it go? Would an amputated finger grow back?

The sun had finally crested the treetops and light now flooded his office. On the other side of the door, he could hear the bustle of men arriving and others leaving as the day shift took over from the night shift. It was still too early to call Montreal. He would wait a few hours.

Restless, he stood up and pushed his chair away from the desk. This whole affair left him unsettled and strangely uneasy. That boy. He could see someone deciding to beat him, but to death?

He walked over to the window and stood staring out. Rue Ste-Anne was beginning to stir, with merchants pulling back their shutters and sweeping the dusting of snow from the sidewalk in front of their shops. On their way to banks and offices, men in heavy wool overcoats and fedoras brushed shoulders with workers in lined, serge jackets and flat caps with ear flaps and carrying metal lunchpails on their way, no doubt, to the new construction site on the corner of St. Jovite. Soon mothers would appear, walking their children to the school three blocks south.

The A'lle girl was upset because he wouldn't allow her to go to Montreal and investigate a case that was in no way related to the Backli's Ford case. Except in the fact that both cases involved A'lle.

But really, was that so extraordinary a coincidence? Strange coincidences occurred often. One took note of them, and carried on. Slowly and methodically—that was the surest way to find a killer. Not by jumping to unwarranted conclusions.

With a sigh, he returned to his desk and sat down. He glanced down at the list on his desk, imagining John A'lle writing the names down with a heavy hand. Eight names—first names only, of course—and dates. With the names were the names of the parents and an address. Next to three of the dates was another set of dates. That would be the date the bodies had been found. His eyes narrowed as he studied the dates, then he plucked his fountain pen out of its holder and unscrewed it. He pulled a fresh sheet of paper out of his top drawer and began jotting down the names and dates, rearranging the information in the order of disappearance. Then he created a separate, shorter list of three names, in the order of the bodies' discovery. The second list matched the first one in order. The first three to disappear were the first three to be found. Each of the three had been found roughly two months after they disappeared. He studied the dates again. If this were a pattern, then the fourth body should have been discovered at around Christmas.

Its absence meant nothing. The body could be covered in snow and hard to see. It was now February. The fifth body was due to be discovered.

A chill coursed through him. Two months from kidnapping to discovery. Did that mean that they were held somewhere and tortured for two months?

What kind of monster would do such a thing?

❧ SEVENTEEN ❦

DESAUTEL clutched the telephone to his ear, wishing he could fly down the line to the speaker at the other end and throttle this latest in a series of fools he had been dealing with. Finally the idiot stopped speaking to take a breath, allowing Desautel a chance to reply.

"Thank you, Constable," he said politely. "I understand that Chief Investigator McReady is busy. I have been trying to reach him for an hour." The constable who was, Desautel presumed, Louis' equivalent in Montreal tried to protest, and in all honesty, he was only the last in a series of barriers Desautel had had to breach before getting even this close to the chief investigator. How did the man function if no one could speak to him?

"However," he continued, ignoring the constable's attempt to interrupt, "I need five minutes of his time. Surely he can spare that for a colleague."

"Of course," said the constable. Desautel had lost his name already. He was the fifth person Desautel had spoken to since Edna Filchner had rung him through to the Montreal constabulary. "The problem is when the chief constable will be available to speak to you."

"Is he in his office?" asked Desautel as calmly as he could.

"Yes, sir," replied the constable. "But I have strict orders not to disturb him."

Desautel felt his shoulders tightening. His hand hurt from clutching the receiver. "Constable," he said reasonably, "I am certain that the chief investigator would be willing to speak to a fellow officer calling long distance. After all, it isn't as if I am trying to call the magistrate of Lower Canada."

There. That was his last card to play. If invoking the magistrate did not give him access to the damned man, he didn't know what would.

There was a long silence at the other end. Finally the constable said, "If you'll hold the line, sir, I'll see what I can do."

Desautel heard the telephone receiver being deposited on a hard surface and the scraping of a chair, and sighed. He stood up and, picking up the telephone, walked over to the window to stare out at the street.

The day had warmed up nicely and the sun had real warmth to it, even an hour before midday. He could see icicles glistening wetly on the eaves of the rooming house across the street as the sun melted snow off the roof. He could hear the dripping of melt water into the gutter above his window. He could almost imagine the smell of thawing earth.

Horse-drawn sleds vied with automobiles on Rue Ste-Anne, not always pleasantly. The mayor had mentioned to him in passing that he was thinking of designating certain streets horse traffic only and leaving the main thoroughfares for the increasingly popular automobiles. Desautel could imagine the protests should that suggestion become public. Personally, he thought the city should invest in traffic lights, like the ones in Montreal. The lights controlled traffic without the use of a constable, all day long. Amazing concept.

There was a click on the line and a gruff voice said, "McReady."

Desautel jumped and almost dropped the receiver.

"Hello?" asked the voice at the other end.

"Chief Investigator McReady," said Desautel. "Thank you for taking my call."

"According to my assistant," said McReady drily, "it was either that or suffer the wrath of the magistrate."

Desautel smiled in spite of himself. "I am certain it wouldn't have come to that."

"How can I help you, Chief Investigator?"

Desautel explained what had happened in Backli's Ford and described the condition of the A'lle boy's body. Frederick A'lle's body.

When he was done, McReady made a noncommittal sound deep in his throat. "Ah, I see. I suppose you will want my office to do the notification of the next of kin."

Desautel found himself staring in mid-space, going back over what he had just told the chief investigator, wondering if he had left a vital piece of information out. He had expected the man to volunteer information about his own A'lle dead. Yet the best he could do was offer to notify the next of kin. If it was an offer.

"Chief Investigator?" prompted McReady. In the background, a cup clinked on a saucer and Desautel imagined the man setting his cup of tea back down after taking a silent sip. The image bothered him.

"Forgive me, Chief Investigator," he said slowly, "but has there not been a series of A'lle disappearances and murders in the Montreal area?" Still standing in the middle of the room with the telephone in one hand and the receiver in the other, he found himself holding his breath, waiting for the man to answer.

McReady took his time before finally saying, "Oh. Yes, of course. I wouldn't call it a "series," really," he said dismissively. "Probably some kind of internal squabble among themselves. That happens in all the immigrant neighborhoods."

It was Desautel's turn to be silent. He pulled the receiver away from his head and breathed deeply for a few moments before bringing it back.

"Excuse me?" he finally asked. "I'm not sure I understood you." Surely he had misunderstood.

"The A'lle here have formed a bit of an enclave," said McReady. "A very insular people, you know. It was only a matter of time before they started turning on each other."

A few seconds ticked by while Desautel tried to assimilate the information. Finally he sat down, rolling a few inches with the force of his descent.

"I have never known A'lle to commit violence," he said. "Have you any evidence?"

"Of course not," said McReady and Desautel heard the shrug in his voice. "These people refuse to talk to us. In any case, I fail to see the connection with your case."

These people?

How could the man fail to see the connection? Frederick A'lle was from Montreal. The fact that he had been killed miles away did not negate that fact.

A slow anger began to form deep in Desautel's heart. "What of other leads?" he asked slowly. "Surely there must be other avenues of investigation?"

McReady sighed impatiently. "We followed the leads and they lead us to the A'lle community," he said sharply. "Where we hit a wall of non-cooperation. If they do not wish to help us, they have only themselves to blame if their people keep dying."

The anger turned to cold dismay. "Surely you are joking, Chief Investigator."

"You are more than welcome to try your own hand, Chief Investigator Desautel," said the Chief Constable coldly, "if you think you can do better."

Well, I could certainly do no worse. "Thank you for the invitation, Chief Investigator," said Desautel crisply. "You may expect me tomorrow. And I will take care of the notification myself."

* * *

The constabulary's common room was a vast space with clusters of scarred oak desks clashing with newer, heavier, metal ones.

Constance used one of the older desks, with drawers that protested every time she opened them. The desk was at the far end of the room, as far from the centrally located woodstove as she could get, and by a window. She often cracked the window open, even in winter, as a consequence of which she found herself isolated in the corner, with the other constables huddling closer to the warmth.

She had spent the better part of the morning in the basement file morgue, looking for any incidents relating to Backli's Ford. She had pulled out several reports, dealing with smuggling, mostly, but they dated back a decade. She found nothing that might give her a clue as to what was happening in the village.

It being Saturday, most of the constables were out patrolling, making sure pickpockets were kept in check and motor vehicles weren't travelling too fast on the slippery streets. In the common room, there were a half a dozen constables and investigators. Some were busy with their typewriters, others were interviewing witnesses, but all of them stopped what they were doing to watch her. Conversations stilled or dropped to whispering. Her chin rose as she looked from face to face. She didn't need to hear the whispers to know that they all blamed her for Dallaire and Renaud's death. It didn't matter that she had almost died—twice—only that she was here and they weren't. She wasn't even sure it had to do with her being A'lle. They might have felt the same about any constable who walked away, leaving two colleagues behind.

The floor was marble, a remnant from when the mayor's office and the meeting hall were on this level, and her boots clicked on the marble as she headed for her desk. In winter, they all wiped their boots carefully before walking into the common room or risked a nasty fall. The ceiling was fourteen feet high, so high that the pendant lights had trouble lighting the space below on night shifts. As a consequence, each desk was equipped with a gooseneck lamp. Constance often wondered if night shift was more peaceful than day shift. As an investigator, she had yet to be required to work at night, principally because she had yet to be assigned a case.

As she reached her desk, constables returned to work and she drew a deep breath.

Louis Hallepin's desk was to one side of the chief investigator's office, facing into the room. Chief Investigator Desautel's door was always closed. When she first arrived, the door had been always open, leading her to suspect that the chief kept the door closed more to keep the stifling heat out than to keep his constables out. Louis liked it hot.

As though suddenly aware of her scrutiny, Louis Hallepin looked up from the papers he had been shuffling on this desk to find her looking at him. His face first went white, then flushed a pale pink.

This human reaction to emotion fascinated her. How terrible must it be to advertise to the whole world that you were uncomfortable, or embarrassed.

Hallepin was a small man, barely five feet six inches, and she judged him to be under twenty-five. And yet he behaved like an old, fussy man, guarding the chief investigator's door like an old maid guarded her virtue. Constance suspected that he had tried and failed to meet the requirements of the constable exam and being the chief's assistant was the closest he could get to becoming a constable.

How galling it must be for him to see her working as an investigator when he could not even become a constable.

"Investigator A'lle," called Chief Investigator Desautel.

Constance and Hallepin both jumped as if on strings. They had been so intent on each other that neither had noticed the chief investigator open his door and step out into the common room. The common room fell silent once again, only to resume its noise level at a meaningful glance from the chief investigator.

"Sir?" said Constance. She dropped the dusty files on her desk and cut across the common room so they would not have to shout at each other.

The chief investigator waited until she stood close enough that he did not have to raise his voice. He looked at his assistant.

"Louis, I will will need two train tickets to Montreal."

Before Constance could do more than mirror Hallepin's raised eyebrows, Desautel turned to her.

"Pack your bags, Miss A'lle. We are going to Montreal."

ન EIGHTEEN ન

THE train station on Rue de la Gare in St. Vincent was shrouded in steam as the big engine warmed up for the trip to Montreal. Constance waited on the outside platform, watching as crates were loaded onto the container car. She could have waited inside the station with the other thirty passengers but she couldn't abide the press of people in the small room. Besides, it was too warm inside.

A man walked up to the workers at the far end of the platform and waved his arms at them, obviously urging them to hurry. He glanced at a pocket watch and shook his head.

Neither he nor the workers wore coats. Last night was the first night that the temperature had remained above freezing. Constance and Gemma had slept with the window open and Constance had awakened refreshed and excited. She hadn't even wanted breakfast but Mother forced her to sit and eat before allowing Eloise to take her to town in the sled. It had still been dark when they left the house but by the time Eloise waved goodbye to Constance, the sun was already making the sky blush with its approach.

The air smelled of coal and woodsmoke and beneath it, the faint, faint smell of earth thawing.

Constance didn't know why she was pleased at the smell.

Thawing earth meant spring and spring meant summer, when she and her family would grow stupid with the killing heat and look for every chance to cool off. Yet, there it was. The promise of spring pleased her.

This was only the third time she had taken a train. The first had been to go to Quebec City to attend the Lower Canada School of Police Arts. The second had been to return home, six months later, when she graduated.

The man who had berated the workers—the conductor, she thought—hurried past her on his way to the front of the train where she could see the engineer working in the small compartment. The conductor glanced at her as he passed, a smile hovering on his lips. He did a double take at the sight of her eyes and his step faltered. Then he nodded politely and kept going.

Would the A'lle ever become so common a sight that they did not merit a second glance? Grandmother Esther had thought not. She had spoken to Constance of the declining birth rate among the A'lle. On their home world, they had had as many children as they had wanted. Here, large families like hers were an anomaly. Father believed it had something to do with the lack of certain nutrients.

"There you are," said the chief investigator, suddenly appearing beside her. Like her, he was wearing his dress uniform, the one reserved for parades, dignitaries, and travel. The winter uniform consisted of a heavy, worsted-wool tailored jacket and pants, navy with gold buttons, a pale blue long-sleeved wool shirt, and a tie patterned in blues and grays. Designed for a man's body, the uniform fit Constance well enough once Prudence had finished altering it. Unfortunately, the color made her eyes stand out all the more.

Unlike the chief investigator, she had folded her heavy overcoat over her arm, unwilling to wear the warm thing. The chief investigator looked different in his uniform. His thinning hair was covered by the billed cap and for the first time, she realized that his eyes, too, were blue. The cut of the uniform, and of the overcoat, hid his small paunch and made him look taller.

As though his arrival had set off an alarm, the doors to the station opened and people began to stream onto the platform.

"We're off," said the chief investigator.

Constance could barely contain a smile as she leaned down to pick up her tattered overnight carpetbag.

* * *

Desautel fell asleep soon after their departure. It was the rhythmic movement of the car, the lulling sound of the steel wheels on the rails, the enveloping warmth of the passenger car after the cold on the platform.

And the fact that he hadn't slept well the night before.

He startled awake at the sound of the train's whistle and opened his eyes to find Constance A'lle watching him. He suddenly felt at a disadvantage. How long had he been sleeping? Had she been watching him the whole time? Had he been *snoring*?

To his surprise, she smiled at him and for a moment she wasn't a strange alien girl that the magistrate had decreed would be a burr under his saddle—she was simply a lovely young woman sitting across from him.

"We are approaching St. Adolphe," she informed him. "Still an hour to go."

He nodded his thanks and rubbed his hand over his chin. He had shaved before leaving but the straight razor he kept at the office needed sharpening and now he could feel the bristles on his chin. He'd only slept thirty minutes, then. He stood up to remove his overcoat and fold it on the seat next to him.

Outside the window he could see farmers' fields covered in a snowy expanse broken only by the posts of fences. In the distance, a farmhouse with a red barn and several outbuildings nestled against a buffer of evergreens. Smoke escaped from the farmhouse's chimney. A few clouds dotted the sky, leaving the sun free to cast its light like diamonds on the snow.

The whistle blew again. They must be getting nearer to the village of St. Adolphe, although Desautel saw no indications of it. He tried to remember the last time he had taken the train. It must be five years now. He usually preferred to travel on horseback.

This train contained no private berths, being on the short run between St. Vincent and Montreal. He had expected the passenger car would be full but he counted at least a dozen empty seats in his cursory glance. Perhaps the one behind was full. He sat down again, making sure to pull up his pant legs so the knees wouldn't bag when he finally got off the train.

The A'lle girl had a drawstring bag on the seat next to her and now she pulled it onto her lap and rummaged through it. It was only when she pulled out something wrapped in wax paper that he realized the bag was full of food.

"From Prudence," she said, handing him the small wrapped package.

He automatically accepted it and then realized it was a piece of pie. He looked up quickly at Constance A'lle.

"Prudence makes the best apple pie I have ever tasted," she said solemnly, biting into a slice of bread wrapped around a chunk of cheese. "You would be a fool not to eat it."

Part of him wanted to bristle at her familiarity but the smell of apples and cinnamon reached him just then and his mouth watered embarrassingly. It might be only mid-morning, but at that moment Médéric Desautel wanted nothing more in life than to sink his teeth into a delectable piece of apple pie made by the delectable Prudence A'lle.

He unwrapped the piece of pie, and using the paper as a plate, brought it close to his mouth. He sank his teeth into it and tart sweetness filled his mouth, sprinkled with the heady taste of cinnamon. He closed his eyes to savor it more fully and then opened them again to be able to see which bite he would take next.

It wasn't until he he had completely devoured the piece of pie that he looked up to find Constance A'lle watching him knowingly. She was only halfway through her bread. She smiled.

At once he was uncomfortable, as if he had inadvertently shared something intimate with her.

"Please thank your sister," he said formally. "She is most kind to think of me."

Constance A'lle nodded and although he couldn't read the look in those strange eyes of hers, he found himself wondering if it was amusement.

He crossed his arms over his chest and concentrated on the scenery. They had finally reached the outskirts of St. Adolphe and the train had slowed down to make sure the way was clear before crossing the main road. Soon the village disappeared behind them. Apparently they were not stopping today.

He had received Docteur Rivard's autopsy report late yesterday and had had time to review it. There was nothing in it that he hadn't learned from the doctor in Backli's Ford. Docteur Rivard could determine, however, that the boy had suffered bruising from two different sets of boots.

Desautel shook his head once, as if that would shake the memory of the boy's mottled skin out of his head. The beating had been personal. No one administered that kind of punishment without a desire for vengeance. Or perhaps not. Fear was also a great motivator.

Louis was under strict instructions to call the inn if and when Bérubé and St-Jean reported in from Backli's Ford. Desautel pursed his lips in frustration. He doubted his men would find anything in the village. The ruffians were long gone. Still, they had gotten a strong description from the little innkeeper and even Constance A'lle had been able to provide information about their heights and relative size.

They would come to the notice of police again. Of that he was certain.

Which brought him to the reason he was sitting in this train, going to Montreal on what was certainly a fool's errand.

Desautel would like to think he had worked out a logical reason for taking his investigation to Montreal and that it wasn't just a desire to tweak the nose of that ass of a chief investigator,

McReady. But truthfully, he had nothing more than a niggle, an irritation in the flow of logic. Why had the boy been in Backli's Ford? According to John A'lle, Frederick had been expected in St. Vincent days earlier, which meant he had made a detour. Why? Whom had the boy been planning to see in Backli's Ford?

And yet, just because the boy had come from Montreal did not mean he was connected to the disappearances and murders in the city. No matter what Constance A'lle thought, and despite his own doubts.

The door at the far end of the car opened and a porter backed into the car, pulling a narrow wooden trolley behind him. He stopped at each set of seats and offered coffee from a silver urn. When he got to their seats, the porter offered Constance A'lle coffee in a lovely china cup on a matching saucer.

"Café, mademoiselle?"

"Non, merci," she said, and smiled. The porter offered her tea and then, finally, water, which she accepted.

When it was his turn, Desautel gladly accepted the coffee and asked for two sugars. He would need help remaining awake.

The porter left, returning the way he had come. Desautel sipped his coffee, content for the moment, and watched Constance A'lle. Her attention was on the snowy fields passing by the big picture window. There was a small smile on her face. He could not recall ever seeing her look so peaceful.

Sensing his attention, she turned to look at him and for the first time since he had known her, there was an openness in her expression. Not quite an invitation—more a willingness to listen. To hear.

It warmed him, that openness, so that when he spoke to her, his tone was gentle.

"You do not like coffee, Mademoiselle A'lle?"

She blinked and he could see his question had surprised her. Two men sitting at the back of the car burst out laughing and she waited until they were done before answering him.

"It is more that coffee does not like me, sir."

His raised eyebrows invited her to go on, and she smiled slightly. "The effects of coffee are exaggerated in us," she said. "Where a human will feel reinvigorated after a cup of coffee, we will feel—and act—as if we had been drinking alcohol."

Just as he was growing accustomed to her, she had to point out the differences between their two species, emphasizing just how alien she was. He swallowed a sigh but as he kept sipping his coffee, a thought wandered through his mind and he voiced it before he could close his mouth on it.

"Then, how do you act after you have drunk alcohol?"

Instead of being shocked, however, she merely looked amused. "Like anyone else," she said promptly. "Like a fool."

Desautel laughed and they both retreated into their own thoughts.

* * *

Constance stole glances at the chief investigator. Despite the coffee, she could see his eyelids growing heavier. Before long, his chin bumped against his chest and he began to snore softly.

She did not know what to make of this new Desautel, this man who smiled as if he meant it and asked questions about her and her people. Was it the fact that they were in an in-between kind of space, neither work nor leisure? Or the fact that she was the only person he knew in the car? There was nothing they could do on the train to advance their investigation, and short of ignoring her—or falling asleep—he might feel duty-bound to engage her in conversation.

Still mulling over the new circumstances, she turned her gaze to the window. Since going through St. Adolphe, they had passed a few more villages and were now going through the outskirts of a town—St. Lambert, she thought she had heard the conductor say. The railroad followed the roadway for long stretches and it amazed her the number of cars and trucks rolling along them. She had yet to see a single sled, or even a horse, for that matter, except in farmers' fields.

Her attention strayed back to the chief investigator in time to see the coffee cup begin to slip from his grasp as his nap deepened into sleep. She lunged for it and caught it before it could spill the dregs onto his folded overcoat.

Easing the cup from his fingers, she righted it and carefully slid the saucer off his lap. She stood up and with cup and saucer in one hand and her empty glass of water in the other, began to make her way down the car toward the far door. They had passed a small kitchen area in the previous car on their way to their seats. She could leave the dishes there.

It was nice to stretch her legs even if the lurching motion of the train constantly threatened to unbalance her. Every person in the car followed her passage, even those deep in conversation. She was accustomed to it. Every A'lle was accustomed to it. Sometimes she wondered if the A'lle disposition for being law-abiding simply reflected the awareness that no A'lle could ever go unnoticed.

It was not a question she had ever thought to ask Grandmother Esther.

She reached the far end and tucked the glass between her arm and her ribs to open the door. The noise level immediately increased and she quickly closed the door behind her. She stood for a moment in the no man's land between the passenger cars. Two waist-high locked gates on either side prevented anyone from falling to a grisly death beneath the speeding wheels—a necessary precaution since the connecting plates upon which she stood shook with every turn of the wheels, threatening to unbalance her. The narrow space gave her a dizzying view of the passing trees and houses, and despite the refreshingly cool air, the acrid smell of burning coal burned her nose.

Pushing the next door open, she entered the second passenger car and found herself face to face with a portly gentleman in a black worsted suit who stood to one side of the aisle next to a closed door—which was the water closet, judging by the unpleasant smells emanating from it.

He nodded bruskely and she moved past him quickly. This car was fuller than her own, and noisier, thanks to two families with seven children under six between them. The children served to distract the passengers from her arrival and barely anyone looked up.

One little girl with pink bows in her blond ringlets shrieked loudly as she darted across the aisle in an attempt to catch the young boy who had taken her doll. The child bumped against Constance just as the train lurched and the cup threatened to slide off its saucer. She frantically moved the saucer about in an effort to stabilize it and finally plunked the empty glass inside the cup.

At the far end was the door that led to the engine and just before it, a curtained alcove that served as pantry and kitchen. She eased the curtain aside, spied the steel tub filled with clanking crockery and deposited her dirty dishes inside with relief.

When she turned around she had attracted the notice of several men. She did not need to be human to recognize the look in their eyes. It always amazed her that human males were always willing to copulate with an A'lle female, even one wearing the magistrate's uniform.

She managed to avoid yet another child who seemed destined to be trod on and gave the nervous mother a reassuring smile when the young matron whisked the child up and scolded it.

With relief, Constance reached the door and pushed it open. A man stood on the platform between the cars, his back to her, watching the scenery. He was smoking a cigar, which explained why he was braving the cold.

Constance edged past him and had her hand on the door handle when a hard shoulder shoved her against the gate, knocking her off balance. The force of the blow folded her over the waist-high railing and for one perilous moment, her toes were off the platform and she could see the railroad ties flashing by. Sparks flew off the wheels where they touched the rail and the stink of coal smoke wrapped itself around her head. She scrabbled against the gate to push herself back upright, praying the gate would hold. Her grunts of effort were lost in the clanging of the wheels on the metal rails.

Then a hand grabbed her by her bun and yanked her up only to slam her against the side of the door. Stunned, she tried to twist around to face her attacker but he caught her left arm and twisted it up behind her back, causing excruciating pain in muscles only recently healed. She bit off a cry and redoubled her efforts.

Then something sharp dug into her side and she grew very still.

"That's right, girl," said a familiar voice in her ear. "Behave and you won't get hurt."

She'd heard that voice once before, in the church yard. This was the man who'd had her by the legs, who'd wanted to kill her.

Her knees buckled and only the weight of him against her back kept her upright. Infuriated at her own weakness, at having allowed herself to be caught yet again, Constance twisted her head to see him. "Let me go!" she demanded and cried out when he twisted her arm up a little further. The blood pounded so loudly in her ears that she almost missed his next words.

"Shut up and listen," he said, digging the knife a little deeper for emphasis. "I'm gonna tell you once. Make sure that boss of yours don't find nothing."

Constance was having trouble concentrating on his words through the pain. She considered stomping on his foot, but he had her off balance. And there was the knife.

"What?" she managed to ask. His breath smelled of tobacco and mint, as if he had been chewing on a leaf, or drinking mint tea. She suddenly realized that she could see his reflection in the small window in the door. He was shorter than she was, and thin-faced, with a receding hairline and small bright eyes. He looked like a ferret.

"You heard me," he said, "Make sure he don't learn a damned thing in Montreal."

Or else what? He would kill her? He'd already tried once. Twice.

Sudden rage gave her strength and she redoubled her efforts to get free.

"Let go!" she shouted.

The knife in her ribs was suddenly at her neck, a very real and immediate danger. She stopped struggling, furious and afraid. Why didn't he just kill her and toss her body over the side?

He leaned in close to her ear. "You remember my big friend, don't you? He's been watching your family, little girl. Do what I say and they stay safe. Don't, and one of your sisters dies. But first he's gonna have himself some fun with her."

Constance's mind went completely blank.

"You hear me?" he asked. The cold metal of the knife point pressed into the flesh of her neck. Any deeper and it would break the skin.

"I hear you," she said thickly, not daring to move. The moment he released her, she'd have him. There was nowhere for him to go. He was trapped on the train.

"And just so's you don't get any ideas," he continued harshly, "we've got a man in the Montreal constabulary. So if you try anything funny, we'll know. 'Course," he added, "you got a bunch of sisters so you can afford to lose one. Or two."

Constance remembered the size of his accomplice all too well, the strength and ruthlessness of him. She didn't know if this man was telling her the truth, but until she could check with her family, she would have to assume the worst.

"An' the minute he sees a copper sniffin' about, he won't wait for my call. Got it, girl?" he asked. "You stop this investigation or one of your sisters dies. You call in your friends at the constabulary, same thing. Maybe he'll pick the twins. He likes 'em young."

For a moment, Constance forgot how to breathe. He knew Patience and Felicity... The fear caught at her throat, strangling her words.

The door behind them suddenly opened and the knife disappeared. His hands on her turned gentle.

"There now, Miss," he said solicitously.

Constance turned around to find the porter looking at them

in surprise. Her released arm swung to her side, throbbing with agony. She bit off a groan.

"Everything all right, Mademoiselle?" he asked. He glanced at Constance's attacker, suspicion in his eyes.

"I startled her when I came through," he said smoothly, stepping away from Constance. The small space between the cars was getting crowded. "She tripped and fetched up against the wall." He studied her critically. He had light green eyes and a sharp nose in a narrow face. "I'm afraid you might have a bit of a shiner," he added regretfully. He turned to the porter. "Got some ice for the lady to put on it?"

Thoughts chased each other in Constance's head like summer lightning. Tell the porter? Tell the chief investigator? Arrest him on the spot?

But what if he were speaking the truth? What if his partner would hurt Felicity or Patience? She could never get back in time to ensure their safety. Or get to a telephone to warn the St. Vincent constabulary in time.

"Mademoiselle?" asked the porter uncertainly. He glanced at the man, who was dressed in worn canvas pants and a heavy work jacket and work boots. He didn't look like any of the other passengers.

He looked like someone who had jumped on the train as a last minute decision.

Constance took a deep breath. "I'm fine," she told the porter. "A little clumsy, that's all."

"Would you like me to bring you some ice?"

She shook her head firmly, aware of the other man's eyes watching her carefully, aware of his hands twitching by his sides.

"No, thank you." She smiled. "I'll return to my seat now."

"All right, Mademoiselle," said the porter. "We're almost in Montreal," he added, nodding to the slice of view between the cars.

Constance glanced at the Ferret man. He was staring back at her, his eyes full of silent menacing promise.

❧ NINETEEN ❦

It was close to eleven o'clock before the train finally pulled in
to Bonaventure Station in downtown Montreal. Desautel walked
up the stairs from the platform area, Constance A'lle a step behind
him, and emerged into the huge marble hall of the station, with its
shops lining both sides and the bronze clock taking pride of place
like a sentinel in the middle.

The hall thronged with people, as did the shops. A newsboy
near the main entrance did brisk business selling the *Montreal
Daily News* and *La Presse Nationale*. Desautel felt remarkably rested, due no doubt to his long nap. Constance A'lle, on the other
hand, looked like she had made the trip from St. Vincent on the
top of the train rather than inside. Her hair was dishevelled and
she had a suspiciously red splotch on her cheekbone. In a man, he
would have suspected that a fist had caused the incipient bruise.
When asked, however, she had told him that she had hit her face
against the door frame when she was returning the cup and glass.

He had remained silent, though he hadn't believed her. Whatever had happened, perhaps it explained the change in her attitude. He had fallen asleep thinking they had reached an *entente*,
and awakened to find the relaxed Constance A'lle gone, replaced

by a young woman whose expression was guarded and whose gaze would not meet his.

He noticed her glancing around the great hall, her gaze resting on first one face, then another. She examined the hall as if she expected ruffians to leap out of shadowy doorways.

He caught a glimpse of himself in one of the shop windows, in between the impatient passengers passing him, and ran his fingers through his hair, trying to look less like his father.

"Chief Investigator Desautel?"

Desautel turned to see a constable in uniform standing a few feet away. The young man had shockingly red hair and brown eyes and looked as if his mother should be calling him in for the night— an impression not dispelled by the fact that his uniform sleeves and pants were too short for his gangly frame.

"Oui," he replied, continuing his inspection of the lad. Pants pressed, uniform jacket neat, boots recently shined. He would do.

"Chief Investigator McReady sends his regards, sir," said the boy. His glance fell on the A'lle girl and he blinked in surprise before returning his attention to Desautel. "He has placed me at your disposal as a driver for the length of your visit."

Desautel concealed a smile. At his disposal, eh? More likely McReady wanted to keep an eye on Desautel's movements. Still, it would be good to have a car. He nodded at the constable, who proceeded to sweep up Desautel's overnight bag and would have taken the A'lle girl's as well, had she but relinquished it. With the faintest of blushes, the boy turned and led the way out through the main doors onto Rue de la Gauchetière. A black Parker with four doors, a hard roof, and actual windows stood at the curb in six inches of slush. The wheels and bottom of the vehicle were caked in the dirty snow but the remainder of the vehicle displayed a gleaming wax finish.

He could not help a twinge of envy as he compared this modern example of the automobile to the ancient Model T that the St. Vincent constabulary used... weather permitting.

While the boy and the the A'lle girl placed the bags in the back, Desautel stood by the Parker and breathed in the smells of the city of his youth. From upwind came the yeasty smell of bread baking. That would be the Model Bakery—or perhaps that was wishful thinking, since that particular bakery was all the way in Westmount. If the wind were blowing the other way, he would be smelling a different kind of yeasty smell, from the Molson brewery, which was much closer. The port and the St. Lawrence were to the south, behind him and hidden by the station. To the north, he could just spy the cupola of the Oratoire St. Joseph on top of Mount Royal.

He sighed silently, but happily. No matter what reason brought him here, he was always glad to return to Montreal. Here he had met and wooed Françoise and here they had raised their two sons, Yves and Olivier, while he built up his law practice. A practice he had abandoned to become an enforcer of the law when his beloved died.

He glanced around at this city that had been home to him. The sun shone warmly, melting the banks of snow that had accumulated over the winter. The snow hid the melted salt that the city sprinkled liberally on the icy streets and ruined the boots of the unwary. Rue de la Gauchetière was filled with passenger cars and trucks and he thought he could hear the clanging of the tramway that ran a street above, on Dorchester.

The city had grown taller since he left, with a number of five- and ten-story buildings replacing the predominantly two-story buildings of his young manhood. He had been surprised to learn that the city now boasted over three hundred thousand inhabitants, almost rivalling Quebec City's five hundred thousand.

"Are you ready, sir?" said the young constable.

Desautel returned his attention to the young man and smiled. "What's your name, constable?"

"Murphy, sir."

"Then yes, Constable Murphy, I am ready." Constance A'lle

was already in the back seat and he slid in beside her, careful to step over the slush at the curb. He closed the door of the Parker just as Murphy closed his, and his ears popped.

Murphy let out the choke, put the car in gear, and they joined the traffic on de la Gauchetière.

"Where to, sir?" asked Murphy. Cars and trucks passed them, going much too fast for Desautel's liking.

"Take me to see Chief Investigator McReady," he said. He wanted to meet this man to get a sense of him. A better sense.

"Yes, sir," said the constable.

A truck passed them in the next lane and sprayed slush all over the driver's side of the car. Undaunted, Murphy glanced up and then swerved into the next lane, forcing Desautel's shoulder against the A'lle girl's. He straightened with a murmured apology only to find himself off balance once again as the constable turned abruptly onto a side street.

Constance A'lle straightened from where she had been pushed against the door and turned her alarmed gaze onto him. He tried to look reassuring but just then, Murphy took a sharp right and forced Desautel up against his own door and Constance A'lle against him. He straightened once more and grabbed the strap hanging above the door.

Chief Investigator McReady had sent this boy to kill them.

He glanced at the A'lle girl to see how she was faring. Like him, she had found the strap above her door and was hanging on. Her face was turned away.

The constable took another sharp turn and Desautel discovered a rumble of laughter threatening to escape him. He cleared his throat.

"Only a few more minutes, sir," Murphy assured him cheerfully.

"Thank you, constable," said Desautel gravely. He wanted to assure the young man that there was no need for haste, but he did not want to embarrass him.

For the first time, Desautel realized that a mirror—it looked like a woman's hand mirror—was clipped to a metal clamp that was in turn soldered to the metal frame of the car, just where the roof met the windshield, to the right of the driver.

What possible use... and then he saw the constable look in the mirror just before changing lanes and finally understood. How ingenious.

The constable turned onto Ste-Catherine, cutting off a lorry, the driver of which objected loudly with his horn. From Ste-Catherine, he turned left onto St-Denis. A moment later, he pulled up in front of a tall, narrow building built of brick and steel. A set of wide concrete steps led up to double doors beneath a brick arch. In the keystone of the arch was inscribed the year 1891 and above the keystone, a carved sign read, MONTREAL CONSTABULARY No. 1.

A set of tall black poles with electric globes provided illumination at night.

The heavy glass-and-wood doors were constantly opening and closing as a stream of civilians and constables came and went.

Murphy jumped out of the Parker and opened Constance Alle's door before she could. She nodded a stiff thanks and climbed out. Desautel emerged from the vehicle without aid and stood on the sidewalk. Unlike St. Vincent, every street in Montreal—except, perhaps, for the port district—was paved, and most of them boasted sidewalks.

"Right this way, sir," said Murply, leading the way up the stairs. The main hall of the constabulary was a study in brass and marble, with a tall oak desk barring the way deeper. A short swinging door to the right of the desk allowed access beyond.

Murphy nodded politely to the desk sergeant who barely grunted a reply—although he did examine the A'lle girl with undiguised interest—and led them through the swinging door and down a short, wide hallway that opened up into a common room much larger but otherwise similar to the St. Vincent constabulary's. A few constables looked up at the new arrivals but otherwise the dozen or so constables were busy at typewriters or taking statements. A row of six holding cells lined the back wall, all full. Two had three men in them, while the rest had two each.

Murphy paid no attention to the activity in the room, heading straight for a staircase that led to a second floor. When they emerged onto the second level, they were in a different world of oak floors and doors with frosted glass and names stenciled in fancy letters. A few office doors were open and Desautel could hear men talking on telephones or to other men. Once he heard a woman's voice murmuring but he couldn't see the woman as he passed by. He wondered idly if she were a visitor, or an investigator. He had heard that Montreal had several female investigators, as well as constables, though he had seen none downstairs. Hard chairs lined the hallway on both sides. Evidently for people waiting for appointments.

Murphy led them to the office at the far end of the hallway, with a door barring any further access. He rapped sharply on the window upon which was stenciled "Chief Investigator Alastair McReady" and opened the door.

They were in an ante-room of sorts. There was a small desk outfitted with a typewriter, a pen and inkwell set, and a blotter. The desk was unoccupied. A small window let in the light, which fell warmly on the polished wood floor. A further door apparently let to an inner sanctum.

Desautel tried not to be judgemental, but it was becoming harder and harder. How could the man keep his finger on the pulse of the common room from up here?

Before Murphy could knock on the inner door, it opened to reveal a big, sandy-haired man with brown eyes and sideburns that swept down and across to meet over his upper lip in a fanciful curve. Desautel had never seen anything so... pretentious. Yes, that was the word. The man's eyebrows met over his nose in a frown that mirrored the mustache.

"Sir!" said Constable Murphy. He stepped back smartly, as if he were still at the barracks. "This is Chief Investigator Desautel and Investigator A'lle. This is Chief Investigator McReady."

"Ah!" The frown left McReady's face and he stepped forward with his hand out toward Desautel. "Chief Desautel, come in. I was expecting you later." He shook Desautel's hand and ushered him inside his office.

"Perhaps you should have told Constable Murphy," said Desautel drily but the other man didn't seem to hear.

"That will be all, Constable," said McReady. "You can wait downstairs." And with that, he closed the door to his inner office.

Desautel frowned. The man hadn't even looked at Constance A'lle.

"Sit, sit," said McReady cheerfully.

His office was big but utilitarian. A large desk covered with paper and another inkwell. A four-drawer filing cabinet, its wood faded on the side facing the window, stood against the wall closest to the desk. Two padded chairs sat in front of the desk. Except for the horsehair sofa, this office was remarkably like his own.

McReady waved to one of the chairs and took his own seat behind the desk. Desautel smiled politely and placed his overcoat, cap, and gloves on the second chair before taking the one offered.

"Good trip?" asked McReady.

Desautel shrugged. "Good enough. Thank you for sending Constable Murphy to pick us up."

McReady's eyebrows rose at the "us." Was it possible that the man simply hadn't noticed Constance A'lle's presence?

"It was the least I could do for a brother constable," he said and Desautel fought hard not to roll his eyes.

"May I presume on your generosity and request his assistance for the duration of my investigation?" he asked.

"Of course." McReady waved as though the request was inconsequential. Then he leaned his elbows on the desk and steepled his fingers under his chin. "Exactly what are you investigating here, Desautel?"

Desautel smiled politely and folded his own hands in his lap, since there were no arms to the chair. The office was too warm. He noticed another door off to the side—a closet or a water closet?

"Forgive me, Chief McReady," he said, "I thought I was clear on the telephone. I am investigating the murder of a young man in Backli's Ford. It would appear he is from Montreal."

McReady nodded. "Yes, you did say. And I can see why you would send your A'lle constable to investigate her own. What I don't understand is why you felt it was important for you to come in person."

So. He had noticed Constance A'lle but chose to ignore her. Like he chose to ignore the A'lle population in his jurisdiction.

Desautel smiled again. "She is actually an investigator," he murmured. "And you misunderstand me. There is no reason to believe that an A'lle is responsible for the boy's murder."

McReady leaned back in his chair and shook his head slightly. "Are you a betting man, Desautel? If so, I'd be willing to wager a week's pay that you will find an A'lle at the bottom of your crime."

Desautel's eyebrows climbed halfway to his receding hairline. "Do you have a crime problem among the A'lle?" he asked, shocked. In all his years as first a lawyer and then an officer of the law, he had never seen an A'lle willingly commit a crime.

There was too much at risk for them.

McReady shrugged. "As I mentioned to you yesterday," he said, "they keep to themselves. They deal with their own problems, in their own way."

Meaning that the A'lle boy's horrible death was just? Retribution for a crime against another A'lle?

Was it possible that McReady was right? After all, there was only one A'lle family in St. Vincent—he really didn't have much experience with them. But he had lived and worked in Montreal until he had chosen to become the magistrate's man and he had never heard of—or seen—any violence among the A'lle. He hadn't thought they were capable of it.

"How big is the A'lle population here?" he asked slowly. He noticed that he was clenching his fingers into fists and forced himself to relax.

McReady looked up at the ceiling, as if the number lived there. "About two thousand," he said finally. "Give or take."

"Out of a population of...?"

"According to the last census figures, over three hundred and thirty thousand people."

Desautel blinked. A drop, then. In a sea of humanity. In a way, it was similar to the situation of Constance A'lle's family in St. Vincent. He tried to imagine John A'lle beating the boy to death and couldn't.

He shook his head. Nonsense. This man spouted nonsense as truth.

"You haven't answered my question," continued McReady. His smile was still friendly, but there was something flat in his eyes. "Why did you choose to come yourself?"

For a mad moment, Desautel considered telling him the truth: that he had chosen to come because he didn't trust McReady to place any kind of importance on the investigation and because he would no more have let Constance A'lle come alone into McReady's jurisdiction than he would have allowed a lamb to wander into a wolf's den unprotected.

Then sanity reasserted itself and he stood up with a smile. "This is my home, Chief McReady," he said. "I raised my family here. I come back every chance I can."

McReady stood up, too, the flat suspicion gone from his eyes.

"Well, in that case, I won't keep you," he said warmly. "Let me know if you need anything else."

"As a matter of fact," said Desautel, gathering his hat and gloves, "I would like to see the files on the A'lle complaints."

The smile remained fixed on McReady's face, but the warmth disappeared from his voice.

"There are no files," he said coolly. "I told you. They look after their own."

Desautel held the man's gaze for a long, silent moment, until McReady's gaze dropped and his face flushed.

* * *

"We are staying at L'Auberge Maillet, on Ste-Famille," said Desautel, from his seat in the back of the Parker.

"No problem, sir," said Murphy. "It's not that far from here."

He pulled out into traffic, earning an irate honk, and began weaving his way up the mountain toward Sherbrooke Street. Next to him, Constance A'lle kept her eyes firmly closed. He longed to do the same, but a sort of morbid fascination kept them open.

After a few more turns, or "shortcuts," as the constable referred to them, they crossed Sherbrooke Street and found themselves on Ste-Famille. Moments later, Murphy pulled up in front of a two-story, greystone building with a wide porch leading to a beautiful red wooden door with an oval window set in it. An overhang over the porch protected visitors from the elements. The window was etched with a design of flowers. A discreet sign hanging from the overhang read: AUBERGE MAILLET.

Armande and Claude Maillet had been his close friends for many years. He and Françoise had watched the three Maillet children grow up side by side with their two boys and had been there to help Armande pick up the pieces when Claude died. Desautel had given Armande the downpayment on the auberge a year later and within five years, Armande had been doing so well that she had paid him back with interest.

Now, whenever he came to Montreal, he stayed at her inn. In a way, it was almost like touching Françoise again.

The door to the inn opened as Desautel was getting out of the car and Armande Maillet flew down the steps to clasp him in a fierce embrace.

"Médéric! It's been too long!"

Desautel hugged her back and released her. He stood smiling down at her, inordinately pleased to see her again. Wrinkles radiated from her lovely green eyes and deepened her dimples, and her once blonde hair was now silver. She had put on a few pounds since he'd last seen her—was it really two years?—but they only succeeded in rounding out her sharper edges. When had they both gotten so old?

"Bonjour, Armande," he said. "It's good to see you, too." He turned to Constance A'lle, who had gotten out of the car but now hovered at a discreet distance with Constable Murphy. "Allow me to introduce Investigator A'lle and Constable Murphy."

Armande's eyes widened slightly at the sight of the A'lle girl's eyes but she nodded and smiled. "Investigator." She turned her smile on Constable Murphy. "Will you be needing a room, too, constable?"

"Non, madame," said Constable Murphy politely. "I live here. I am the chief investigator's driver."

"Ah, bon," she said. "In that case, let's bring their bags inside, shall we?" But before she could reach for Constance's bag in the boot of the car, Constable Murphy, having learned from earlier experience, stepped forward quickly and picked up the two bags. Constance A'lle frowned slightly but he merely grinned at her, drawing from her a reluctant smile.

Well, well, well.

Desautel closed the boot and followed Armande up the stairs and into the lobby of the Auberge Maillet. The hotel had six guest rooms on the second floor and a maid's quarters in the attic. Armande's suite was off the lobby and consisted of a sitting room and bedroom. The rest of the main floor was taken up by a large kitchen, a dining room, and a sitting room at the front of the house, across from the lobby. A man was sitting in an armchair by the fireplace in the sitting room, reading a newspaper. He looked up in curiosity when they came in and nodded when Desautel looked at him.

"You have your usual room, Médéric," said Armande over her shoulder as she climbed to the second floor. "And Mademoiselle A'lle, I have placed you in Room 6. I have lunch waiting on you."

At the landing, Desautel took his bag from the young constable. "I know my way from here," he said. "Take Investigator A'lle's bag to her room, please." He looked at Constance A'lle. "I shall meet you downstairs in fifteen minutes." She nodded and the three of them trooped down the hallway to the last room. Desautel smiled to himself as he opened the door to Room 1. Armande had placed them as far apart as she could, for the sake of propriety.

The room was as he remembered it from his last visit, wallpapered in some kind of small flower design that always made him feel he should be sneezing. The two windows were bordered with white embroidered curtains and brought in a lot of light. They gave onto the street. He liked being able to see who was coming and going. Right now, however, the windows were still covered with light frost. The single bed with a new bedspread and the familiar quilt folded at the foot, the water basin on the bureau, the painted glass lamp on the nightstand... all seemed like old friends to him. But best of all was the small desk tucked between the windows.

He set his bag down on the narrow settee at the foot of the bed and pulled it open. He fished past his change of clothes until he felt the sheet of folded paper that John A'lle had sent him through his daughter. This he brought to the desk and smoothed it open.

At the top of the sheet, in a bold scrawl, was Frederick A'lle's name and the address of his family. Below that, a list of A'lle families in the city, all of whom had lost a family member mysteriously, and their addresses.

How could this have transpired for a year without him hearing of it? Why had it not been in the magistrate's report? Only four months ago he had met with all the other chief investigators of the various regions—including McReady—and no one, *no one*, had breathed a word of the disappearances and murders.

ॐ TWENTY ॐ

I⊤ took them almost two hours to find Frederick A'lle's home, despite the map Constable Murphy pulled out of a side pocket in the driver's door. Desautel was beginning to despair of ever finding it amid the farms and orchards of the north island when the young constable slowed suddenly and turned onto a long laneway hidden from the road by a screen of elm, aspen and pine trees. It was only as they approached the cottage that Desautel realized there was a farmhouse beyond, and beyond that, a red barn that stood out in stark contrast to the white fields.

The laneway was rutted with vehicle tracks, and with the warming temperatures, the snow had grown unstable and punchy. Desautel and the A'lle girl jostled against each other as Constable Murphy struggled to keep the Parker on the road without getting stuck.

Desautel glanced at the girl beside him but her face told him nothing. He tried to think what he might have done or said to effect this coolness in her but he could think of nothing. Was she offended that he had napped on the train? Perhaps she was in pain from hitting the door? Yet her face showed hardly a trace of the redness he had seen on the train.

A man stepped out onto the stoop as they drove up to the cottage and Desautel gave up the puzzle of the girl.

Roland A'lle was a big man, easily over six feet tall, with wide shoulders and strong arms, as revealed by his rolled up shirt sleeves. He wore heavy woolen pants and suspenders, and his feet were shod in heavy work boots. The outfit of a manual laborer. Whatever Roland A'lle did for a living, it kept him fit and strong. A set of wide wooden skis rested on the stoop next to the open door.

Murphy stopped the car and all three got out. It was colder here than in town, but perhaps that was because there weren't so many buildings to reflect the sun's heat.

Desautel kept studying the man whose strange, violet eyes were trained on Constance A'lle; she in turn stared back at him.

Desautel cleared his throat, drawing the man's attention. "Mr. Roland A'lle?" He opened his overcoat to reveal the Magistrate's badge pinned on the inside pocket.

The expression on the man's face shifted from cautious curiosity to dread. His legs shifted as if to brace himself better.

"My son," he said, and there was a finality to his tone that tore at Desautel. He didn't know what he would do if someone showed up at his door to tell him one of his sons was dead.

"Sir." Constance A'lle stepped forward, drawing Roland's attention away from Desautel. "My name is Constance A'lle, from the St-Vincent constabulary."

"I know who you are," said Roland A'lle.

Of course he did. There was only one A'lle investigator in all of Lower Canada. Every A'lle would know of her.

Which meant that he would know that his son had been coming to see her family. Desautel's chest felt heavy with pity for the man.

Without a word, Roland turned away and went inside, leaving them to follow.

While they removed their boots at the door, Desautel studied the cottage. It had one main room that served as the living space. A counter fitted with a sunken basin had red tiles covering its surface, protecting it from water damage. It fit the length of the narrower wall. Judging by the hand pump on the sink and wall-mounted oil lamps, this cottage had none of the modern amenities.

A woodstove against the far wall was cold. It stood on a four-inch stone platform that was wide enough to store two armfuls of split wood in small wooden cribs on either side. Two doors at the back of the room probably led to bedrooms, or maybe one bedroom and a bath room. There was probably an outhouse out back. The doors were made of wide planks with plain black metal bands near the top and the bottom. A narrow loft was reached by a beautifully designed staircase that used oak branches as the spindles and handrails.

Desautel looked at Roland A'lle's big, scarred hands. The man was a craftsman. There must be a workshop out back, as well.

Roland indicated the table next to the icebox and pantry, and they sat down. Like the rest of the cottage, the table showed evidence of good design and care in execution.

Desautel wondered if his boy had inherited his abilities.

"Tell me," said Roland, but he was looking at Constance A'lle. His hair was so black, it looked almost blue, and he kept it long, brushed away from his face and tied back at the nape of his neck in a short ponytail, the way a man did who did not want to be bothered with regular haircuts. It was an old-fashioned look. His face was broad, with high cheekbones and thin lips. Like all A'lle men, he had no facial hair.

Constance A'lle took a deep breath before starting. Where Desautel and Murphy had kept their coats on in the frigid cottage, she had removed hers.

"Describe your son to me," she said and both Desautel and Murphy turned to look at her in shock.

Good lord, what was she thinking?

But Roland A'lle nodded and began matter-of-factly. "Frederick is twenty, a few inches shorter than me. Thin. He has his mother's mouth, my cheekbones."

Desautel looked away from the man, remembering the boy's torn lips and swollen face.

"His hair?" asked Constance. Desautel noted approvingly that Murphy had quietly removed his notebook and was taking notes as they spoke.

"He likes it short," continued Roland, "but has trouble keeping it that way." His hands had curled into fists on the smooth honey-colored tabletop.

Constance nodded. "Any distinguishing marks?" she asked softly.

Roland A'lle swallowed hard and closed his eyes. "A scar on his left shoulder from when he fell against a sharp stone when he was a lad. He was sick at the time, and the wound never healed properly."

Desautel glanced at Constance A'lle and saw the same confirmation in her eyes. The body they had examined in Backli's Ford had had an old scar on the left shoulder. Roland A'lle's son Frederick was dead.

"I am so sorry," whispered Constance finally.

Roland's eyes opened and Desautel almost shrank back against the anguish in them.

"When?" he asked. "How? He was on his way to meet your family!"

The girl's eyes closed as if she couldn't bear to see his pain, but almost immediately she opened them again.

"We received notification on Thursday morning that an A'lle boy had been found in Backli's Ford," she said, and proceeded to tell him in detail the sad tale of his son's murder. She ended with learning who the boy was.

Then she fell silent and allowed the man to absorb her words.

Desautel found himself breathing shallowly. He would not have told a grieving father how brutally his son had been beaten, how his fingers had been broken, ribs shattered, his face battered into a swollen mask of itself. He would not have left that image in the man's mind.

He would not want that image in his own mind, if it were his son.

"Do you believe the two men who killed your constables attacked my son?" he asked finally, turning to Desautel.

Desautel shrugged. "We don't know," he said. "We must find them first."

"Where is my son?" asked Roland A'lle.

"In St-Vincent," said Desautel. "We had to do an autopsy," he added gently.

"Yes, I'm sure you did," said Roland A'lle and the bitterness in his voice stole Desautel's voice. He glanced at Constance A'lle but there was a hard look on her face and she did not meet his gaze. Something was going on here, something more than the terrible loss of a child. Before he could pursue it, however, Constance A'lle spoke to the man.

"Why was he in Backli's Ford if he was coming to St-Vincent?"

Yes, that was the correct question. On that question rested the mystery of the boy's murder.

But the man's answer was a disappointment. "I do not know," he said. "There was no talk of going to Backli's Ford. There are no A'lle there."

As if that would be the only reason to go to a place. But perhaps if you were singled out as different wherever you went, you would seek out the company of others like yourself.

"He took the train to St-Vincent?" asked Desautel.

The man's face was expressionless but there was a resentment in his eyes. "I put him on the train myself."

"When?" asked Desautel. He struggled to remain patient. The man had just learned that his son was dead, horribly dead. Was it any wonder he was resentful of having to answer questions?

"On Wednesday," said Roland A'lle. He turned to look at Constance. "He should have been sitting down to dinner with your family that night."

The anguish in the man's voice caught at Desautel's heart but what filled him with pity at that moment was the man's inability to weep for his child.

The A'lle could cry, but but they could not weep. Desautel had seen Constance A'lle's eyes blink away tears when dust irritated her eyes, or in bright light, but the A'lle could not weep, whether in joy or grief.

How could one survive such grief without the release of tears?

"Sir," said Desautel, "did your son have any enemies?"

Roland A'lle seemed smaller suddenly, diminished from the virile man who had allowed them into his home. The look he gave Desautel would stay with him for the rest of his days.

"He was A'lle, Chief Investigator. Of course he had enemies."

Unaccountably, Desautel felt ashamed. For what, he wasn't sure.

"Do any of these enemies have cause to want him dead?"

Roland A'lle shook his head. "Who knows when someone will take it upon themselves to teach one of us a lesson?" he asked bitterly. "We are in a war of attrition, Chief Investigator, and our casualties are counted one at a time. Even the Bishop of Montreal has preached against us."

Next to Desautel, Murphy made a small sound of protest but otherwise there was no sound in the room. Roland A'lle held Desautel's gaze for long seconds and once again, Desautel experienced shame.

"Do you believe he knew his attackers, sir?"

"I do not know!" Roland A'lle rose abruptly, startling them all. Constance raised an arm as if to prevent Desautel from moving but he had seen many people receive terrible news. And human or A'lle, they all at one point raged against the knowledge that one they loved would never be coming back.

Roland began pacing up and down the wide-planked pine floor, his boots striking heavily.

"From the time he was small, he was bullied by the other children. Most of them outgrew this pasttime, but some grew into worse bullies." He turned a fierce gaze onto Desautel, clearly having fixed his ire on him. "But he was hardly unusual in this," he said.

"What about his employer?" asked Desautel, trying a different tack.

Roland rubbed his face with big, scarred hands. His hair was coming undone from its ponytail, adding to the wildness of his look.

"We worked together," he said sadly. "We built furniture, houses, anything that needed building."

There was such a lost look on his face that Desautel turned away, unwilling to be witness to this man's most vulnerable moment.

"How would he have gotten from St-Vincent to Backli's Ford?" asked Constance A'lle after a moment. The question seemed to penetrate the fog of misery that had isolated Roland from them. He blinked and looked at her.

"What?"

"It's a good two-hour horse ride in winter," said Constance. "There is no train, and no cars use the road in winter. So some time between getting on the train on Wednesday and being found on Thursday, Frederick left the train and made his way to Backli's Ford. How did he get there?"

"I don't know. Perhaps I should be grateful that he was found at all," said Roland, finally stopping his pacing and staring at the floor. "Some never learned what became of their children."

Desautel stood up and walked around the table to stand before Roland A'lle. "Sir, I don't know why your son was attacked, but I have men scouring Backli's Ford, looking for the persons who did this. I promise you I won't rest until I find out who killed him."

Roland A'lle looked down at Desautel, his large eyes narrowed by pain. In them Desautel saw skepticism and distrust. Then Roland A'lle blinked and turned to Constance. They spoke for a few minutes in their own language. When he fell silent, she nodded stiffly and stood up.

Roland A'lle walked over to the door and held it open. "Thank you for telling me about my son," he said formally, looking at Desautel. "Please return him to me."

Murphy looked uncertainly at Desautel but the request seemed clear enough. Roland A'lle wanted them out of his house. With a nod, Desautel stood up and gathered his cap and gloves. The other chair scraped as Murphy scrambled to stand up. There was an awkward silence while all three put their boots back on.

"I will have Frederick's body shipped to you tomorrow," Desautel promised.

"And his dog," said Roland.

Desautel looked up from the boot he was lacing. "I beg your pardon?"

"He took his dog with him," said the other man. "Did you not find him?"

Constance A'lle straightened from pulling on her boots. "What does the dog look like?"

"He's a cross between a golden lab and a bear dog," said Roland. "About yea high." He lowered the palm of his hand until it was about a foot off the floor. Brown eyes." He took a deep breath. "Smart."

Desautel sighed. A dog. Now he had to look for a dog. "There was no dog with him, but we will keep an eye out," he promised. He considered shaking the other man's hand, but nothing in Roland A'lle's face invited the courtesy. "Thank you for your time, sir, and please accept my condolences."

With a stiff nod, Roland A'lle saw them out the door and closed it firmly behind them.

* * *

Halfway to the car, Constance turned around. "I forgot my coat," she said over her shoulder. "I'll be right back."

As she climbed the stairs, she heard the car start up and knew she only had a few minutes. The idea had come to her as she watched Roland A'lle absorb the news of his son's murder. She couldn't stand idly by while the murderers threatened her own family. She had to do something.

She had to beg a grieving man for his help.

The door opened before she could knock and Roland A'lle stood in the doorway, looking at her. There were lines of pain in his face and a groove between his eyebrows. She felt as though they had dealt him a death blow.

"I've left my coat," she said out loud and then, in a softer voice, in the old tongue, "Please, I must speak with you."

He stared at her a moment longer then stepped away without a word. Once she was inside, he closed the door and turned to face her.

"What is it?" he asked. His eyes were dark with pain, a pain so vast she could see his struggle to contain it. And yet he waited patiently for her to speak.

She took a deep breath and tried to calm herself. She had to speak quickly, before Desautel grew curious.

"My family is in danger," she began and told him as quickly and concisely as she could what had transpired on the train.

If nothing else, her tale seemed to bolster his efforts not to succumb to his own pain.

"You have no way of contacting them?" he asked.

"No safe way," she said. "I may be being watched. He said they had a man in the Montreal constabulary."

Roland A'lle looked at the door behind her, as if he could see through it to the car beyond. "Do you think it is the constable? Or perhaps the chief investigator?"

Constance shook her head. "Not the chief investigator. At least, I don't believe so." Chief Investigator Desautel had clearly shown his bias against the A'lle and she could not afford to trust him. And yet, part of her believed him to be honorable. "As for the constable..." She hesitated. "I do not know."

"You could find out," Roland said softly.

Constance nodded, unsurprised that he knew of her particular gift. "But they would know. Besides, the man could have been lying." The Ferret had probably killed Renaud and Dallaire. He had definitely wanted to kill her that night in the church yard. It was not much of a stretch to suspect him of lying.

Nevertheless. She could not take that chance.

"Very well," said Roland and there was compassion on his face. "I will get word to your father."

"How...?" asked Constance. "If they see you, they will know I was talking to you." Had she made a mistake in trusting Roland A'lle?

His eyes closed briefly. "It will not surprise anyone if I go," he said softly. "Tell your chief investigator that I will go to St-Vincent and accompany my son back."

Constance reviewed the train's timetable in her head. "You will have to stay overnight," she said slowly. "There is only one train from St-Vincent and it leaves first thing in the morning."

Roland A'lle nodded. "It will be expected that I spend the night with your family. Ask your chief investigator to get word to your father. I will try to make tonight's train, but if I miss it, I will be on tomorrow's."

It was dangerous. If the big man watching her family grew suspicious... and yet, what Roland A'lle proposed was perfectly normal, by human standards. Any human would expect a father to want to accompany his son back home, even if it was illogical.

All depended on how well the murderers knew the A'lle.

Finally, she nodded. It was risky, yes, but it was a risk she would have to take to protect her family.

❧ TWENTY-ONE ❧

THE port district was the oldest part of Montreal and it showed. Low stone buildings stood cheek by jowl with long, fired-brick warehouses on cobblestoned streets. Soot and gloom covered everything, especially at this time of day, at this time of year. Even with the car's heater on at full strength, Desautel could barely feel his toes. The temperature had dropped with the loss of the sun, and night made lie of day's promise of spring.

By the time they had returned to the inn and pored over their maps to formulate the most efficient plan, it was dinnertime. Armande had roasted a chicken and winter potatoes and had creamed some corn from her canned supplies. Delicious. But it was her fresh bread and molasses that almost closed his throat with emotion. Françoise had always served him molasses at the end of the evening meal, with warm bread slathered with butter.

The farther they drove into the port district, the farther back in history they delved. He remembered coming to the port as a lad with his parents to see the Queen Theresa sail into her berth. Today there were no more sailing ships. They had all been replaced by steam engines, more's the pity.

Desautel winced and bit off a curse as the constable hit yet another pothole created by a missing cobblestone. This was his fault. He had told the young man to hurry.

Every once in a while, he would catch sight of a dark figure slinking furtively around a corner as they drove by, but for the most part, the streets were deserted. They had driven on Water Street briefly and it had pleased Desautel to see a dozen freighters, their hulls rusted and barnacled, moored in their slips.

Next to him, Constance A'lle sat quietly, taking it all in. Her huge eyes looked luminescent in the faint glow of the ancient gaslight street lamps. With her pale skin and dark hair, she looked like an ethereal heroine in some Romantic painting.

The fact that the young constable kept stealing glances at her in his makeshift mirror did nothing to improve his driving.

"Almost there," said Constable Murphy.

Desautel wanted to look at the list again, but the lighting was too uncertain. He wanted to look at his pocket watch again, just to reassure himself that it was not too late, despite the dark, deserted streets.

By the time they finished dinner, there was only one address they could reach by a decent hour, that of Eliane A'lle's family. All the others were further away, in the "Alley," as Constable Murphy shamefacedly called it—a neighborhood near the Jubilee bridge. Those would have to wait until the morning.

The car swerved abruptly, sending the girl into his shoulder before she could restrain herself.

"Here we are," said Constable Murphy cheerfully. "901 Jubal Street."

While the constable jumped out and held the door open for the A'lle girl, Desautel peered out his window uncertainly. There was a building there, certainly, and there was a door with a dim light over it, and he thought he could make out something painted on the building, but squint as he might, he could not make out numbers.

Before the lad could hurry around to his side of the car,

Desautel opened the door and stepped out, careful not to step into slush. The cold immediately reached for his nose and cheeks and tried to crawl down the collar of his overcoat. He closed his door a moment after Constable Murphy closed Constance A'lle's and the sounds reminded Desautel of gunshots. He shook off his unease and looked up at the building. It was a two-story affair that had clearly been a place of business in the past. Perhaps it still was, but if so, it was not a successful one.

The crumbling stone steps had long ago been overlaid by wooden slabs, which were now uneven with ice and clumps of frozen snow. Above the light was painted a faded sign that read Smith and Smith, Importers for Her Majesty. He had no idea what that meant.

Constable Murphy came around the car with Constance A'lle.

"Are you certain this is the place?" asked Desautel.

The constable shrugged. "It says 901 on the building. And this is Jubal Street."

Very well, then. Desautel climbed the steps and tried the doorknob. It was locked. He suspected that no single family lived here. Probably the building had been converted into apartments many years ago. Now that he was closer, he could see that the door was solid, reinforced with metal strapping, and that the knob was solid, as well. The occupants of 901 Jubal Street invested in their security.

"Let me, sir," said Murphy, pushing past Desautel to knock on the door with his fist. The sound was shockingly loud in the narrow street and Desautel had to control an urge to look over his shoulder.

They waited in silence for long seconds. Desautel became aware of the fishy smell of the port district, overlaid by the pungent smell of the tar used to paint the posts before they were sunk into the water to form the framework for the piers.

He glanced up at the dark windows but there was no movement, no sign of life. Constance A'lle moved up to stand next to him on the lower step as the constable pounded once more on the door. Where Desautel had rearranged his muffler to keep the cold at bay, she had unbuttoned her sheepskin coat. Her gloves were stuffed in her pockets.

Suddenly she stiffened. And then he heard it, too, the sound of laborious steps on wooden treads. Inside. Someone was coming down the stairs.

Constable Murphy stepped down to allow Desautel to take the lead.

Yet the windows remained dark. The empty street at his back pressed against him and he squared his shoulders to keep it off. The sound of footsteps stopped, only to be replaced by the sound of a bolt being drawn. At last, the door creaked open, accompanied by sudden light.

All three of them instinctively drew back as light spilled out, revealing the creature within.

"Yes?" quavered the woman. She had thin, wispy, white hair floating around her head and wore a heavy, dark wool dress that went down to her feet in the old-fashioned way. A flowered shawl covered her shoulders and crossed in front, tucking into her waist-band in a way he hadn't seen since his grandmother died, thirty years earlier.

By the sagging skin of her jowls and the hundreds of wrinkles on her papery skin, she had to be at least ninety. But it was her eyes that kept them all mute. She had one watery blue eye that peered at them uncertainly and the other had a lid that drooped lazily over a milky white orb. It was as though the eye could see through him, see every one of his sins, judge every one of his thoughts.

He shook himself mentally and stepped forward, so that she could see him better. If she could see at all.

"Pardonnez-nous, Madame," he said politely. "My name is Mé-déric Desautel. I am the chief investigator for the Baudry Region. I am looking for the family of Eliane A'lle." The girl had been sixteen when she disappeared and had yet to be found.

The old woman blinked and the milky orb disappeared momentarily, only to reappear again. A wave of heat rolled out the door, carrying with it the smell of woodsmoke and stewed tomatoes.

"Gone," she said. "Gone, gone, gone."

Constance A'lle stepped closer, too. "Do you know where they went, Madame?"

The old woman peered closer at the girl's face and sadness filled every one of her wrinkles. "You look like her," she murmured. "Little Eliane."

Desautel closed his mouth on a sharp order to Constance A'lle. He was miffed that she had inserted herself into his questioning, but the old woman was looking at the girl with tenderness. Clearly she'd had a fondness for the missing girl.

"Did she grow up here?" asked Constance A'lle, keeping the woman's attention.

"From the day she was born," said the old woman. "I looked after her when her parents were at work."

Constance A'lle smiled and took the old woman's hands, surprising Desautel. And the old woman, too, for she jumped at the contact. He had never seen the girl make any kind of physical contact with anyone. Not willingly, in any case. But it was a cold night, and the old woman was shivering. Constance A'lle's hands would be warm. The woman would have been warmer inside, but she did not invite them in.

"My name is Constance," she told the old woman.

The woman smiled up at Constance, her eyes almost disappearing in wreaths of wrinkles. "Call me Mère Hubert," she said. "Everyone does."

To Desautel, the woman looked more like a crone than a mother, but that was being unkind. He himself did not look nearly as appealing as he had twenty years ago.

"When did her parents leave?" Constance asked the old woman.

The smile faded into a sigh. "Six months ago," she said. "When they realized that little Eliane would not be back, they packed up and left. I don't know where they went."

"They never wrote?" asked Constance gently.

The woman shook her head. "Non. As I told the other man, even if I could see well enough, I can't read."

Murphy started, reminding Desautel of his presence.

"What other man?" asked Desautel, drawing the woman's attention back to him. She was shivering now, her bird-boned hands still wrapped in Constance A'lle's bigger ones, but still she did not invite them inside. Perhaps she was ashamed of the state of her home. After all, if she couldn't see well...

"The big one, bigger than you, even. He came by a few days ago, asking the same questions."

"Did he say who he was?" asked Desautel. He glanced at Murphy but the constable shrugged. His cheeks were ruddy in the dim light over the door.

"My memory, you understand..." The old woman gently extricated her hands from Constance A'lle's and crossed her arms over her bony chest. "If he said his name, I don't recall it now."

"Was he a police constable?" asked Constance.

"Non." The answer was immediate. "His hair was too long and his clothes too shabby."

For someone who was supposedly half-blind, she had a good eye for detail.

"Merci, madame," he said finally. If they kept her on the stoop much longer, she would die frozen. "If you think of anything that would help us find Eliane's family, please send a message to the Auberge Maillet. That's where we are staying."

The woman nodded, patted Constance A'lle's hand, and closed the door on them. A moment later, the light in the window went out.

They stood on the stoop, listening to her shuffling footsteps climb back up the stairs. Eventually, Desautel grew aware that the other two were staring at him. He pulled out his pocket watch. It was eight-thirty, time to return to the inn.

He needed to think. Who else was asking about the missing A'lle? And *why?*

* * *

Constance stood in front of the open window of her bedroom and stared out at Rue Ste-Famille. The inn had long ago settled down for the night, including Madame Maillet who had retired soon after they returned. There were only two other guests, aside from Constance and the chief investigator—the man she had seen in the parlor when they first arrived, and a woman on her way to Quebec City to visit her mother.

Constable Murphy had dropped them off and left, promising to return early the next morning. The chief investigator had telephoned St-Vincent to arrange for Roland A'lle to pick up his son's body, and he had sent the stable boy to Constance's home to let her family know that Roland would be arriving the following evening.

Surely that should be safe enough? The stable boy couldn't possibly be mistaken for a constable.

She crossed her arms over her chest, fingers digging into her arms. Had the Ferret lied to her? Was his large partner truly in St-Vincent, watching her family, or was he the man the old woman had spoken to yesterday, here in Montreal?

She tried to remember what the big man had looked like but all she had were impressions of size and the feel of his big hands keeping her prisoner. She would never be able to identify him, unless he spoke.

Below her, Rue Ste-Famille had settled down for the night, too. A car had driven by half an hour ago and since then, nothing. The last few lights in the homes across the street went out one by one until only one light burned in an upstairs window of a brownstone. Likely someone's bedroom.

What luxury to be able to stay up so late. There must be no chores awaiting them early in the morning.

She sighed. It all looked so peaceful. Yet somewhere in this throng of humanity, someone was kidnapping, torturing, and murdering A'lle.

And the troubles that were haunting Montreal's A'lle were

coming to St. Vincent. She needed to get back home to protect her family. And she couldn't tell the chief investigator. Not yet, at least. Unfortunately, Desautel held the train tickets. She had seen them in his overcoat pocket. She only had two dollars, for emergencies, and couldn't buy another ticket home.

If she told Desautel that she wanted to go home, he would immediately know that something was wrong. She had seen him work—he would not rest until she told him what was going on.

Which she couldn't. While she did not believe he was behind the A'lle murders, or even tacitly supportive of them, she could not take the chance. Not yet, at least. The Ferret had said he had a man in the Montreal constabulary. Desautel was working with Chief Investigator McReady. The moment Desautel told McReady, her sister's lives would be in jeopardy.

Could Constable Murphy be the one? If he was the Ferret's spy, what had he made of Roland A'lle's sudden decision to accompany his son's body? Would Murphy think it suspicious that Roland had changed his mind after Constance returned to fetch her coat?

The more she thought about the Ferret, the more she doubted her initial assumption that he was in charge. Everything about Frederick A'lle's death spoke of impulsive violence. His body was found in Backli's Ford, not in Montreal, as every other body had been found. From what Father had said, the recovered bodies had shown signs of surgery but very little other sign of violence.

No, the Montreal disappearances were calculated, part of a plan. Frederick's abduction—if it was one—was spontaneous, unplanned.

What had prompted Frederick A'lle to go to Backli's Ford? Somewhere between getting on the train and arriving in St-Vincent, his plans had changed. Something on the train had made him change his mind. Or someone.

Had he seen the Ferret and his big partner? She had presumed that they had come up from the United American States, but what if they had arrived in Backli's Ford from St-Vincent, and had arrived in St-Vincent on the train from Montreal?

But why would Frederick have followed the Ferret and his partner? Had he recognized them from Montreal, and associated them with the disappearances?

But why would Frederick do this alone? Why not wait until Father came to get him at the train station?

She took a deep breath of the cold air and blew it out on a gust. The air smelled faintly of car exhaust and coal.

Enough. She would need to gather more information before she could decide what to do. And she would need her sleep if she was to make a clear-headed decision.

Just as she reached for the curtains to draw them closed, a movement on the street below caught her eye and she glanced down.

Across the street, half-hidden by the corner of a brick-faced, three-story house, someone was smoking. She saw again the red eye brighten as whoever it was drew on the cigarette. Then the cigarette flew in a graceful arc into the snow in the shallow front yard of the house and the half-hidden figure stepped out from his hiding place into the pool of light cast by the street lamp and looked up at her window.

It was the Ferret.

❧ TWENTY-TWO ❦

AMANDA A'lle's home was in a dilapidated but respectable area of the Alley, on a tiny residential street sandwiched between two busy avenues. The walk-up was actually the top floor of a large home. They found her by knocking on the front door of the main floor, only to be told by a human boy that the A'lle lived upstairs.

Constance and Murphy climbed up the spiral metal staircase, Murphy's metal-tipped boots clanging occasionally on a tread. The chief investigator had stayed behind at Madame Maillet's inn to make phone calls. He didn't volunteer whom he was calling and Constance was so grateful not to have his watchful eye on her for a few hours that she asked no questions.

Mature oak and elm trees lined the residential street, which was cobbled under the thick layer of snow and ice. In summer, the trees would provide welcome shade but at this time of year, their stark, bare lines blended with the faded paint and grey stone of most of the buildings.

And yet, the bright blue sky and sunshine added lightness to the shabby grey street.

Constance spotted a small grocery store on the corner, in front of which a young boy hawked that day's *La Presse Nationale*. A dark-paneled Eaton's delivery truck drove by leisurely.

She glanced at her pocket watch. It was nine-thirty.

They found Amanda A'lle with her sleeves rolled up and wearing an apron of the type Prudence often wore, with a fitted bodice and round pockets, in a pretty blue flower pattern that made her eyes look almost navy. Two young girls, no more than nine or ten in A'lle years, peered from behind her skirts. Constance told Amanda in the mother tongue that they were here to talk about her husband Ezra's disappearance. The woman studied Constance's bloodstained sheepskin coat for long seconds before stepping back to let them in.

"I usually take the girls to the playground in the morning," she said as they removed their boots. The girls watched them solemnly. To humans, they would look four or five years old. Constance wondered why they weren't in school, but didn't ask. Amanda herself could be anywhere between thirty-five and fifty-five. By either standard.

The upper level of the house was too cold for humans, but Constance found it quite comfortable and removed her coat. She hung it on the doorknob behind her.

"If you permit, Madame," said Constance, "I'm sure Constable Murphy would be happy to accompany them to the playground."

Murphy glanced at her but she kept her gaze on the other woman. This was a golden opportunity to speak to Amanda A'lle alone. Constance could then control what information she relayed to the chief investigator. The less he and Murphy knew, the better. At least for now.

Amanda A'lle didn't speak but her huge violet eyes studied Murphy as if she wanted to commit his face to memory. She glanced at Constance, who nodded imperceptibly.

Finally, Amanda nodded and turned away to see to her children.

Constance heard Murphy sigh softly behind her.

Fifteen minutes later, the girls were out the door with their red-headed chaperone and Constance finally sat at the table at

Amanda's invitation. The kitchen was small but clean and functional. The ice box sat in the corner by a door that led to a back balcony. Amanda A'lle picked up a kettle from where it had been keeping warm on the electric cooker. If she had running water, she probably had a flush toilet. Amanda and her family had done well for themselves.

Except for losing Ezra, her husband and the father of her children.

Amanda finished at the range and brought a teapot to the table, followed by a small tray with tea cups and a jar of honey.

"Rosehip tea," she explained, setting a cup before Constance. "It will need honey."

Constance nodded her thanks and added a generous dollop of honey to the bitter tea. A little honey drizzled onto her finger and she licked it.

"Madame, I am investigating the disappearance of a number of A'lle in this region." She spoke in the mother tongue again and caught the older woman's wince.

"Speak English," said Amanda A'lle.

Constance looked down at her cup in dismay. She and her sisters had spoken A'lle consistently when they were little, but as soon as they moved to St. Vincent, they had begun to speak more and more English, especially after Grandmother Esther died. She was losing her mother tongue. She wondered if Amanda sent her children to an A'lle school. She had heard that a few towns in Lower Canada now allowed them.

Amanda A'lle blew daintily on her tea and took a sip, her expression unreadable.

Constance studied the other woman with curiosity. She had met other A'lle in her life, but infrequently. Until she left for the academy in Montreal, she had hardly ever been outside St. Vincent. Over the years, A'lle had stopped in to visit when they were passing by, but those visits were few and far between. Most of their contact with other A'lle was in the form of letters between Father and Mother and the A'lle they knew.

Constance had never had an A'lle friend, although Prudence and Eloise remembered another A'lle family from before they moved to St. Vincent.

Now she knew two A'lle, besides her family: Roland and Amanda.

"You are John and Lily's daughter," said Amanda.

Constance blinked. "You know them?"

Amanda nodded. "We were raised in the same village. They are older." She sipped again, not taking her gaze from Constance. "How do they feel about you working with the constabulary?"

Constance hesitated, uncertain as to what the woman was asking. "It was their idea," she said finally. "They felt it would be an advantage."

Amanda stared at her for a long time before finally nodding. "The humans have a saying: Keep your friends close, but your enemies closer."

Shocked, Constance tried to protest that the constabulary was not the "enemy," but Amanda kept talking.

"I find it curious that the constabulary is finally taking an interest in these murders," she said calmly. "Ezra has been missing for six months and you are the first to bother—and that is only because you are A'lle yourself."

Constance shook her head vigorously. "Do not paint all constabularies with the same dirty brush. We only just learned of the disappearances when we began investigating the attack on an A'lle boy in Backli's Ford, four days ago." It was only as she spoke the words that she realized why her parents had chosen not to share information about the missing and murdered A'lle. They hadn't wanted to worry their children.

The realization disturbed her. It was yet another way in which the A'lle were assimilating human customs and habits, even when they went against A'lle traditions. Grandmother Esther had never kept information from the children, no matter how hard.

Amanda had grown very still. "The boy?"

"Roland A'lle's son."

Pain etched lines in the woman's face. Of course she knew the family. Here, every A'lle would know every other.

"What do you wish to know?"

"Tell me what happened when your husband disappeared," said Constance.

Amanda took a deep breath and spread her hands on the clean surface of the maple table, keeping her gaze focused on them. The tile floor was beginning to wear in places but it, too, was scrupulously clean.

"It was September second," she began. Her voice was calm but her hands were white with the pressure she was applying on the table. "A Saturday. I had taken the girls to the Atwater Market." She glanced up at Constance. "Do you know it?"

Constance shook her head.

"It is the best place to obtain fresh produce," said Amanda. "And bread. And cheeses." She smiled slightly.

"The girls loved going there. Usually Ezra came with us but he was feeling poorly so he remained at home."

The smile faded and she dropped her gaze back to her hands, which were now clenched. Constance raised her tea cup finally to take a sip but the cloying scent of honey rose from the steam and she set the cup back down without drinking.

"When we returned, two hours later, he wasn't home. He hadn't left a note. I waited until dinnertime then asked the neighbors. One told me that Ezra had left an hour after we had but didn't know where he'd gone."

Constance waited, but that seemed all there was to her story.

"When did you report him missing?" asked Constance finally.

"The next morning. A group of men had formed a search party that night to look for him and I went to the police the following morning, when they couldn't find him."

"What did the police do?"

It suddenly occurred to Constance that she should be taking notes. She went to the door and fetched a small notebook with a pencil from her coat pocket. Feeling like the novice she was, she returned to her seat, opened the notebook to a fresh page and began recording the date and time of the interview.

"They told me it was not the first time a man walked away from his family," said Amanda. Her hands were now in her lap. Constance stole a glance and saw that they were bunching up the fabric of her apron.

Constance opened her mouth to speak, then hesitated. Finally, she leaned forward and spoke softly.

"You must forgive them for their insensitivity, Madame, but it is true. Most human men who go missing do so deliberately. They do not know this about us."

The two women looked at each other.

Constance knew about marriage among humans. It, too, was supposed to be for life, but men and women often strayed from each other. Among the A'lle, that was not possible.

Until they found their mates, A'lle men and women would take as many lovers as they pleased. Once two A'lle were bonded, however, none could come between them. It was both the greatest source of joy and the greatest tragedy.

There were so few of them left now, that some A'lle never found the right combination of scent and pheromones that told them this one, this one, was the right match. There were legends of A'lle who had mated a second time, after the loss of a first mate, but those were either just stories, or incredibly rare. Once the right mate was found, their bodies adapted to each other, closing off any other possibilities.

On Earth, with so few A'lle from whom to choose, an A'lle was very lucky to find a compatible mate even once.

Amanda would never have another husband.

The older woman smiled tightly. "So the parish priest tells me."

Constance stared at her in surprise. "You have spoken with a priest?"

At that, Amanda A'lle actually laughed. "It would be more accurate, perhaps, to say that the priest spoke to me." Her tone became mocking, almost brittle. "Apparently even a creature with no soul deserves comforting."

The thought of a priest intruding at such a time, imposing the Church's half-formed prejudices on a woman frantic with fear...

"Is there anything else you can add?" Constance asked to break the dreadful silence in which Amanda's laugh still rang like a dirge. "A sign or clue that would indicate where he might have gone?"

Amanda sighed deeply, then shook her head. "No. I do not know what happened to my husband, but I know he is dead. Only death would prevent him from coming home."

Constance nodded. She had accepted that she would be one of the ones left unmated. When she saw the depth of this woman's grief, she wondered if that were not a better thing.

"Thank you for your time, Madame, and for the tea." She stood up.

Amanda stood up, too, and absently brushed the wrinkles out of her apron. "This chief investigator of yours," she said, "why did he not come himself to speak to me?"

Constance knew what she was asking. Did the chief investigator not want to be bothered? Constance shook her head. "We are only three," she said. "And there are many avenues of inquiry to follow."

Amanda hesitated, then spoke slowly. "There is one other thing."

Constance paused as she was shrugging into her coat and looked at the older woman expectantly.

"I have heard from some of the others that a man has been asking questions of them. Questions like yours. I have not seen him," she added, "but he's already approached three of the families of the disappeared."

Constance stared at her for a long moment. "Can you tell me which families?"

"Gabriel. His brother Albert was found a few months ago. Clémence and Thibault, whose daughter Edith was taken nine months ago. She was found soon after. Bertrand, whose wife Mathilde was taken at Christmas time."

Constance had nodded at each name until Amanda got to Bertrand's name. "Bertrand?" she said. "He is not on my list."

Amanda smiled a small, hard smile. "Many will not be on your list," she said. "It became clear early on that the constabulary would not help. So why turn to them?"

But the list had not come from the Montreal constabulary. It had come from her father. But Amanda A'lle did not know that.

Constance almost turned away from the accusation in the older woman's eyes. This, then, was part of the cost of donning the constabulary uniform. She would never be fully accepted by her fellow constables and would be mistrusted by her own people.

"Thank you," she finally said. "If you think of anything else, I am staying at the Auberge Maillet on Ste-Famille."

"There is nothing else. For six months I have gone over and over the facts and searched everywhere I could think. I hope you find what you're looking for, but for me it will make no difference. My Ezra is gone."

* * *

"What did you learn?" asked Murphy as they settled into the Parker. "Where are we going now?"

Constance wanted to go see Chief Investigator McReady and shake the man. Setting aside the fact that he had forsaken his sworn duty to protect the citizens of Montreal, was the man an idiot? Did he think he could simply ignore an entire segment of the population that was being preyed upon and that no one would notice?

Or was he part of of it?

McReady was Desautel's problem. Her problem was that she had to learn everything she could while making sure Murphy and the chief investigator learned very little. The Ferret had told her to make sure the investigation came to nothing, and this she would do until she was certain her family was safe.

And somehow, she had to find a way of returning to St-Vincent without arousing the chief investigator's suspicions.

"Hello?" said Murphy, waving a hand in front of her face.

She smiled perfunctorily. "She told me nothing that we didn't already know."

"Really?" said Murphy, clearly surprised. "You were in there for a long time."

Constance glanced at him. She longed to place her fingers against his skin and read him but this was the strongest taboo Grandmother Esther had drummed into her. Her grandmother had feared the humans' reaction to Constance's talent, and hence, Constance feared it, too.

Murphy's brown eyes shone with intelligence and curiosity, but all A'lle had learned—to their chagrin—that humans could lie with their faces as well as their words. Touching him would reveal his emotions and would give her a solid clue as to whether or not she could believe him.

It would also reveal her mistrust. She couldn't risk it.

"She had much to say about the Montreal constabulary," she said instead, looking him in the eye. "Did you want me to repeat it?"

Murphy flinched a little and started the car. He sat in silence while the heater began to fill the car with unwelcome heat and Constance cracked open the window.

Finally he looked at her. "Where to?" The smile had left his eyes.

She pulled the list out of her pocket. "Gabriel A'lle," she said finally.

She could feel Murphy's gaze on her and looked at him.

"Leaving aside the fact that there's been no investigation done on these disappearances, what do we know?" he said slowly.

Constance sighed. She had gone over and over the information until it was almost meaningless—just facts rolling around in her head. Still, Murphy wasn't as steeped in the case as she and the chief investigator were. Perhaps he would have a fresh insight.

"Eliane A'lle disappeared almost a year ago in broad daylight, on her way back from the clothing factory where she worked. It was a half-mile walk. Granted it was through some rough sections of town, but it was daylight and there were many people around."

Murphy nodded for her to keep going.

"Ezra disappeared on a Saturday last Fall. Again, in daylight. He was home alone while his wife and daughters went to the market. She came home to find him gone. Nobody heard or saw anything untoward."

"They could both still be alive," Murphy pointed out. He didn't sound convinced.

Constance didn't bother rebutting him. "Frederick A'lle was found beaten to death in Backli's Ford, many miles from his destination of St-Vincent." She turned her attention from the street where a young mother was trying to persuade a recalcitrant child to remain on a sled.

"A young woman, a father and a boy. Two missing, one dead. I see no commonalities, except that they are A'lle," said Murphy softly.

"Except that they are A'lle," agreed Constance. "According to the list, and without counting Frederick, eight are missing and three have turned up dead." But Amanda had said that there were more. Constance stared unseeingly at the street. "We will learn more when we speak to the others."

Murphy remained silent for a moment. "I don't understand why they didn't make a fuss," he said finally.

Constance looked at him, not sure what he meant.

"Eliane and Ezra, anyway," said Murphy. "If someone tried to take them in broad daylight, why didn't they make a fuss and get noticed?"

Constance stared at him until he fidgeted uncomfortably.

"You're right," she said. "They would have fought back if someone tried to take them against their will."

"They went willingly," said Murphy, his tone tinged with excitement.

"With someone they knew, or had reason to trust," added Constance.

"And that might work for Frederick, too," Murphy pointed out. "What if he met someone on the train that he knew?"

"We need to interview the porter, the conductor... anyone we can find who was on the train with him." Of course they had to— why hadn't she thought of that before? Then she caught herself. This was exactly what she should not be doing—exploring possibilities, imagining what could have happened. This was what the Ferret had warned her against.

"Should we report to Chief Investigator Desautel?"

Constance hesitated. Her first impulse was to run back to the chief and tell him their theory. But she couldn't. In fact, she shouldn't be sharing information with Murphy. She studied his freckled face, his wide brown eyes. It would be so much simpler if she read him. Then she would know if she could trust him or not.

But even if he was trustworthy, he could still inadvertently cause the death of her family. He reported to Chief Investigator McReady, and him she could not trust.

It was still early. She would have to report to the chief investigator by lunch time, as he wanted to accompany them in the afternoon. Best to squeeze in as many interviews as she could.

* * *

Gabriel A'lle lived in one of a series of tiny houses clustered around the footings of the Victoria Jubilee Bridge, in the heart of the Alley. There was no one home.

The house was well kept, with curtains hanging in the windows and a recent coat of paint on the door. Its neighbors all had smoke coming out of their chimneys, but Gabriel A'lle's house did not. Constance and Murphy peered into the dark windows but couldn't tell if the house was abandoned or if the owner had simply not returned from work. The front walk was shovelled.

"You there!" called a man and they both turned to see an older man—a human—standing on the stoop of the house next door. He held a squared off shovel before him.

The man caught sight of Constance's eyes and the shovel lowered as he relaxed. He was broad-shouldered but his back was beginning to round in the way humans did in their decline. Still, the arms that emerged from the rolled up sleeves of his red plaid wool shirt were muscled and hard, as were the hands holding the shovel.

"What do you want?" he called across the yard. His eyes were brown, Constance noted, and they squinted a little.

"I am with the St-Vincent constabulary," said Constance. "I want to speak with Gabriel A'lle."

The shovel lowered until it rested on the stoop next to the old man's boot. "He's still at the stables," he said. "He usually comes home after dark. What do you want with him?"

Constance made her way back up the walk to the sidewalk and then down the other man's walk. Murphy followed in silence, although she was aware that he kept glancing around watchfully. Her stomach growled so loudly she wondered if the old man could hear it. She hadn't eaten since Madame Maillet's glorious breakfast.

"I am Investigator Constance A'lle," she said, then turned slightly to nod at Murphy. "And this is Constable..." she couldn't remember his first name "...Murphy from the Montreal constabulary. We are investigating the disappearance of Albert A'lle."

The old man's eyebrows raised in incredulity. The door behind him was closed but Constance could smell boiled cabbage and potatoes. Someone was preparing lunch.

"After all this time?" said the old man. "Took you long enough. Al was killed three months ago!"

Al. Constance realized suddenly that this man was a friend of the A'lle brothers. Perhaps he knew something that could help. She wished suddenly that Murphy couldn't overhear the conversation.

"What's your name?" she asked.

"Horace Johnson," said the man promptly. A long-sleeved undershirt poked out from his sleeve and he pushed it up impatiently. He must have been cold standing outside but he didn't shiver.

"Mr. Johnson," said Murphy suddenly, almost startling Constance. "I take it you are friends with the A'lle brothers?"

"For over thirty years," said Johnson matter-of-factly. "From the day I moved in with my bride."

Murphy had stepped up to stand next to Constance. She could see his breath. It was getting colder.

"Were you here the day Albert went missing?" asked Murphy.

Johnson shook his head. "It was a workday," he said. "I was at the brickyard. I come home for lunch."

"So Albert was at work, too?" she asked.

A sharp nod. "He and Gabe own—owned—a stable down by the river," he said. The shovel scraped as he shifted from foot to foot. For the first time, Constance noticed that he was wearing a pair of workboots with the tongues hanging out. He had donned them so quickly he hadn't had time to lace them.

The smells of lunch cooking from neighboring houses were distracting. She could feel the weight of gazes on her. Clearly, they were the focus of attention from the neighbours. She wondered if Johnson's wife was in there, waiting for her husband to return and report.

The brickyard must be close by, to allow him to come home to eat at midday.

"Go on," said Murphy encouragingly. "Gabe and Al were at work at the stables. Then what?"

Johnson sighed sadly. "The vet came to deal with a sick horse, and Gabe went with him to the stall. When he came back to the office, Al was gone. Three weeks later they fished him out of the St-Lawrence." His voice was laced with horror and Constance looked away, suddenly remembering the report.

Albert A'lle's vital organs had all been removed, as had his eyes. Then his body was dumped in the river, where a fisherman found it, three weeks after his disappearance.

Something already tight in her chest wound a little bit tighter. Albert A'lle had been autopsied. Someone had wanted to see what was inside him.

To see how he differed from humans?

The three remained silent for a moment before Murphy cleared his throat. "Nobody saw where he went when he left the stables?"

Johnson shrugged. He looked older, somehow, as if the stirred-up memories had aged him. "He hadn't been feeling well. Gabe thought he'd gone home. It's only when he got there himself that he realized that Al hadn't made it back. He asked around—we all searched for days. Nobody saw Al leaving the stables."

It was gloomy in the shadow of the bridge. This part of the Alley didn't seem to have any electric street lights. At night, pedestrians and drivers would have to rely on headlights and the incidental light from the houses themselves. The smell of woodsmoke now vied with the cooking smells, and Constance was suddenly aware that she did not belong here, that she was intruding on this man, on this community. How had the brothers managed to fit in so well?

"Do you know of any reason why anyone would have wanted to harm him?" she asked softly.

Johnson shook his head sadly. "He was a good man, for all that he was A'lle, if you catch my drift. He and his brother were always ready to lend a hand or a dollar. They stood shoulder to shoulder with us when Paxton's house caught on fire. He didn't deserve to die the way he did."

He straightened suddenly. "I don't think Gabe would appreciate me natterin' on about him and his brother like this. You got more questions, you should come back when he's home or go down to the Wellington Street Stables."

Murphy took a breath as if he wanted to ask another question but Constance beat him to it.

"Thank you, Mr. Johnson. We may do just that. In the meantime, if you remember anything else, I'm staying at the Auberge Maillet, on Ste-Famille." She put her hand out for him to shake.

After a moment's hesitation, he took her hand and shook it, jumping a little at the shock. She held his hand a moment longer, reading, then released it. He was telling the truth. There was a deep anger in his heart but also loss and sadness. The man still grieved for Albert A'lle.

With a sharp nod, Johnson lifted his shovel and went back inside, leaving them to make their way back to the Parker.

"Are you going to keep doing that?" asked Murphy disapprovingly.

"Do what?" asked Constance, startled. Did he know about the reading? It was bad enough she was breaking her people's taboo, but to have a human learn of it...

"Telling people where you're staying." Murphy opened the car door. "I don't like it."

Constance sat down and closed the door. "We need information," she pointed out. "The witnesses may not want to be seen talking to us in their own neighborhoods. They may want to come to us. Somone knows something about the people responsible for the disappearances."

"Who the hell are these people?" Murphy's voice rose in sudden anger. "They kidnap, murder... What are they after?"

Constance had no answer for him. She was thinking of her family in St. Vincent and of her isolated home on the side of the hill.

❧ TWENTY-THREE ❦

DESAUTEL read over his notes once more, to be certain he had missed nothing. Part of him chafed at having stayed behind at the inn—comfortable as it was—while the young constable and the A'lle girl chased down interviews, but the tedious details had to be tended to, as well. He had learned to ignore the less exciting parts of an investigation at his peril.

Armande stepped into the parlor, wiping her hands on her apron.

"Du thé?" she asked.

Desautel shook his head. "Non, merci," he said. He had a slight headache and would rather have had a glass of water, but he was impatient to get on with his phone calls.

With a nod, Armande withdrew back to her kitchen, closing the door between kitchen and parlor firmly behind her. They had the entire inn to themselves. The man who had been here yesterday—sitting in this very chair, reading a newspaper—had left early this morning, while the woman who had checked in late last night had only just left to take the train to Quebec City. To visit her mother, if he recalled correctly.

Which meant he was now free to use Armande's telephone to make his calls.

His first call was already crossed off the list. He had contacted Louis in St-Vincent and asked him to arrange for someone to interview the conductor, porter—anyone who had worked the train on the day Frederick A'lle had arrived in St. Vincent.

Next, he asked the operator to connect him to the head office of the Montreal Constabulary. When the connection was made, he identified himself and asked the constable at the other end if Chief Investigator McReady was available.

"No, sir," said the constable. "He is not in his office."

Desautel leaned back in the comfortable wing chair and stretched out his legs. Armande had started a small fire in the fireplace and the room was quite cosy. No doubt Constance A'lle would have been too hot.

"Did you want to leave a message?" asked the voice at the other end.

No, he didn't. In fact, this might be a fortunate twist.

"May I speak with the duty officer?" he said in response to the constable's question.

"Just a moment, sir."

The handset was set down on a hard surface and Desautel heard footsteps receding. A moment later, two sets of footsteps could be heard approaching. The handset was picked up and an older, deeper voice came through.

"This is Sergeant Alphonse Tessier. How can I help you, Chief Investigator?"

"Sergeant, I need a favor," said Desautel. "You may know that I am here investigating the death of a young man in Backli's Ford."

"The A'lle boy who was beaten to death." The sergeant's voice was flat and unemotional, and Desautel wished he could have done this in person. It was almost always better to ask a favor in person, especially when you didn't know the person of whom you were asking the favor. But Constance needed the car for the interviews.

"Yes," Desautel confirmed finally. He had gotten to his feet without realizing it and now he stared out the window onto

Ste-Famille Street. Above the rooftops across the street, the sky was blue and cloudless. A coal man was loading coal into a barrow from his horse-drawn cart. His breath puffed out in steam as he worked.

"What about him?" continued the sergeant, his voice still carefully neutral.

Desautel's headache was growing more pronounced and he rubbed the deep groove between his eyes. There was no help for it, he finally decided. He would have to presume the sergeant was not of McReady's ilk.

"He traveled from Montreal to St-Vincent on the train," said Desautel. "Last Wednesday. I would appreciate it if you could assign two constables to speak to anyone at Bonaventure Station who might have worked that day."

There was a silence at the other end and Desautel held his breath.

Finally Sergeant Tessier spoke. "What do you want them to ask?"

Desautel relaxed a little. Tessier could have objected immediately that he didn't have the manpower to spare.

"I need to know if the boy spoke to anyone on the train," he said. "Or if anyone paid particular attention to him on the trip."

Again the sergeant remained silent as he considered Desautel's request. Desautel could hear him breathing at the other end of the line and could imagine what was going through the man's mind. He would be wondering what Chief Investigator McReady would have to say when he returned to find that his duty officer had despatched constables to do Desautel's bidding.

"I see no problem," said Tessier suddenly, almost startling Desautel. "I'll send two men to Bonaventure Station immediately. They can speak to the staff there. You realize the train won't be pulling in for a few hours?"

Desautel grinned at the man's cheerful tone. It would seem he had hit upon a true police officer, unlike that excuse for a chief investigator, McReady.

"My men in St-Vincent are already speaking to the workers on the train," he assured the sergeant. "Between the two ends, we will surely find something useful."

"Here's hoping, sir," said Tessier. "That was a terrible thing, what was done to that boy."

"Yes, sergeant, it was," agreed Desautel gravely. He wanted to say that what was being done to many, many of the A'lle in Montreal might be even worse, but he kept that to himself. This man might not know of the attacks, though that wasn't likely. And if he did know of them, he might not be in a position to defy the direction Chief Investigator McReady had taken.

Perhaps that was why he had agreed so readily to Desautel's request.

"How can I reach you to report?" asked Tessier.

Desautel gave him the name of the inn and they rang off. He stood staring down at the receiver in its cradle, reluctant to make his next call. But he had no choice. Something big was happening to the A'lle population of Montreal. He needed to know if the same was happening elsewhere in Lower Canada. Only the magistrate could provide answers.

A knock at the door startled him and he turned to see Armande at the hallway door. She had removed her apron.

"There is a young woman here to see Mademoiselle A'lle," she said. Her green eyes sparkled with curiosity. "Shall I invite her in?"

"Yes, of course," said Desautel. He shared Armande's curiosity. Who could the A'lle girl possibly know in Montreal? "Please," he remembered to add.

A moment later, Armande ushered into the parlor a tall young woman with thin features that emphasized her enormous A'lle eyes. Her black hair was swept into a loose braid behind her head. She wore a smart gray coat and carried her gloves in one hand. She had removed her boots at the door and her stockinged feet made her look absurdly vulnerable.

"Mademoiselle Odile A'lle, this is Chief Investigator Médéric Desautel," said Armande formally.

Desautel would judge the young woman to be perhaps fourteen, which meant she was likely closer to twenty.

"Mademoiselle," said Desautel as she entered. "How may I help you?"

She glanced around the parlor, then settled her gaze on him. "I would like to speak with Constance A'lle."

Armande stirred herself. "I'll bring tea," she said to no one in particular and left the parlor by the hall door, closing it behind her.

Desautel smiled but the young woman didn't reciprocate.

"Mademoiselle A'lle is away for now," he said. "Perhaps I can be of assistance?"

He could not read the expression that flitted across her features but her words left him with no doubts as to her desires.

"Non, merci," she said politely, and turned to leave.

"Mademoiselle, wait!" Desautel reached out a hand and took a step toward her but stopped when she recoiled. His hand dropped to his side. He had never elicited that response from anyone, man or woman, A'lle or human, and to see it now in this girl placed him off balance, so that his next words were more direct than he would normally have chosen to be.

"Is it to do with the disappearances?"

She grew very still, her huge eyes watching him carefully, her hand poised over the doorknob.

"If so," he continued gently, ignoring the headache that was beginning to throb behind his eyes, "please stay. If you know anything at all that could help us with our investigation, please tell me."

She remained caught between standing still and fleeing for so long that he almost spoke again, but some instinct kept him quiet, patient, while she worked it out for herself.

At last, her hand withdrew from the doorknob.

"The constabulary is not investigating," she said at last.

"I am not with the Montreal constabulary," he said gently. "I am chief investigator for the Baudry region." He indicated the settee in front of the window. "Please, Mademoiselle, sit."

Again Odile A'lle hesitated, but then she moved toward the settee, as far from the fireplace as possible, and perched on the edge of the seat, ready to leap up and flee. She wore a dark woolen skirt that came down below her calves, with button detailing down the front and heavy black embroidery at the hem. A white, fitted blouse with pearl buttons and a lace collar and heavy black stockings completed the outfit. It seemed more like a uniform to him and he wondered if she were a store clerk.

"I was told that you are not investigating the disappearances," she said stiffly.

Desautel prided himself on being a good judge of character. It was only with Constance A'lle's arrival at the St-Vincent constabulary that he realized how much of that skill came from his ability to read nuances on people's faces. Human faces.

Staring at this young A'lle woman, he suddenly felt adrift, a sailor with no stars to guide him.

"We did not start out investigating the disappearances," he said slowly. Then he added, "The murders."

The girl's chin rose and he kept going, afraid he had already said the wrong thing, but not knowing what else to do.

"An A'lle boy was murdered in my jurisdiction," he said carefully. Like her, he perched on the edge of the horsehair chair, resting his elbows on his knees and allowing his linked hands to dangle between them. "In the course of our investigation, we learned about the disappearances, and the murders, taking place here. The boy's murder, these disappearances... they are linked, somehow."

He stopped then, surprised. When had he decided that? Why had he decided that? Hadn't he argued against this assumption with Constance A'lle? Hadn't he insisted that there was no evidence connecting the boy's murder to the Montreal disappearances, no matter what he'd told McReady?

And yet, he had come to believe that there was a connection, that if he could learn who was kidnapping and murdering

Montreal's A'lle, he would learn who had murdered Frederick A'lle in Backli's Ford. And why.

"My sister is missing," said Odile A'lle and the pain in her eyes transcended all barriers.

Desautel controlled a sudden urge to reach for the young woman's hand to comfort her. He saw now that what he had taken for composure was barely controlled panic.

"Tell me," he said.

At that moment, Armande entered with a tray. Desautel almost sighed but stood up to take it from her. He set the tray on the table in front of Odile A'lle and Armande proceeded to pour tea for the young woman and Desautel. The A'lle girl thanked Armande and picked up the cup, but did not sip from it.

"Lunch will be ready shortly," Armande told Odile A'lle with a smile. "Would you care to join us?"

"Non merci, madame," said the young woman. "I must return to work."

"Ah." Armande smiled and, apparently oblivious to Desautel's impatience, asked, "And where do you work, mademoiselle?"

"At Brabant and Sons."

That piqued Desautel's interest. Brabant and Sons were the biggest publishers in Lower Canada, rivaling Upper Canada's Stuart Brothers for the size of their inventory and the fame of their authors. If he remembered correctly, Brabant and Sons were located on Ste-Catherine, near Aylmer—quite the walk for the young woman. Which meant she would be expected back soon.

Armande opened her mouth to ask another question but just then she caught sight of Desautel's expression and smiled instead.

"Well, perhaps another time," she murmured and left them alone.

Odile placed the tea cup back on the tray without drinking from it, prompting Desautel to wonder if tea had the same effect as coffee on A'lle physiognomy.

"When did your sister go missing?" he asked.

"Almost a week ago," she replied. Her hands found each other in her lap and clasped together tightly. "On Wednesday. We left for work at the same time as usual, but she never arrived at the bank where she works."

Odile and her sister Lucie lived on Lexington Street, again in the Alley. Both took the tram to work every day, parting at St-Denis where Odile walked down to Ste-Catherine and Lucie to Ogilvy Street, on the corner of which stood the Bank of Montreal.

But Lucie never arrived at work, and it was only when Odile returned home at dinner time that she realized something was wrong. So while Frederick A'lle was losing the battle for his life in Backli's Ford, Odile A'lle was frantically and unsuccessfully searching for her sister.

"Did you report...?" asked Desautel. The look she gave him answered his question and he moved on to the next one.

"Had anyone seen her that day?"

"Yes, of course," said Odile A'lle. "The same people who saw me walking to the tram stop, the regulars on the tram... It is only a ten-minute walk to the bank from the tram stop. I've asked at every shop along the way, but no one can recall seeing her. It was still early and many of them weren't open yet."

Desautel sat back and stared out the window onto the street. Most shops in downtown Montreal opened at nine o'clock, as did most businesses.

"What time did you part ways?" he asked abruptly.

"The tram drops us off at five minutes past eight thirty," she replied. He noted absently that she had picked up the cup and wrapped her hands around it, as though to warm them. She had also kept her overcoat on, as if chilled. It was so unusual that he wondered if fear and pain kept her cold.

So. Eight-thirty-five. Odile had said it was a ten-minute walk to Ogilvy Street. A young woman could be forgiven for lingering in front of a display window. Still, even if she had been accosted while she lingered in front of a window, there would have been dozens of people all around her. Hundreds, perhaps. All walking to work.

No. Not everyone walked to work. There were more and more cars in Montreal now. Could Lucie have gotten into a car with someone?

He glanced at Odile A'lle, who sat patiently on the settee, watching him out of those unnaturally large eyes. She was the portrait of a correct, modern young woman. He could not imagine her getting into a car or a carriage with someone she did not know.

Would her sister?

Perhaps Lucie A'lle had a secret life, one her sister knew nothing of? It wouldn't be the first time a young woman turned to prostitution out of desperation.

But no. Odile's clothing were not expensive but they were of good quality. She had a position with one of the most prestigious publishers in Lower Canada. If her sister had fallen on hard times, Odile A'lle would have helped. Any of the A'lle would have helped.

He had never heard of an A'lle prostitute. Which left only one reason she would have gotten into a car or a carriage. She knew the person driving it.

"Had anything unusual happened in the days preceding her disappearance?" he asked slowly, still formulating the thought. "Any strange event or encounters that she reported to you?"

Odile dropped her gaze to the floral carpet, frowning. After a moment, she looked up.

"I can't think of anything untoward, Monsieur," she said.

"No break in her routine? No new people in her life?"

Odile shook her head. "Non. There was nothing..." She stopped and frowned again.

"Have you thought of something, mademoiselle?" Desautel prompted when she didn't speak.

The A'lle girl shook her head. "Not really," she said. Disappointment tinged her voice and she returned the cup to the saucer with a clatter that spilled tea over the edge. "She did visit Monsieur Harper the night before. He is our neighbor and has been ill. She brought him soup."

"Are they in a relationship?" he asked.

Odile A'lle smiled, making Desautel think of Prudence, Constance A'lle's sister. But Odile did not have the same warmth behind her smile as did Prudence.

"Monsieur Harper, while a charming man, is seventy-eight."

Desautel sighed. From the kitchen came the smell of ham, alerting his stomach to the possibility of getting fed.

"He has been very ill," continued Odile. "And besides the priest and the doctor, we are the only ones to visit him."

He stood up and began to pace. How were all these people disappearing without a trace? How could they possibly be taken without anyone being aware of it?

The only thing that made sense was if they went with someone they knew and trusted, without making a fuss. He could not be certain, of course, but he doubted any of the A'lle trusted easily.

"Let's take down the information," he said finally, reaching for the loose papers Armande kept by the telephone. "I will also want to know where you live, should I need to contact you."

He saw the droop of her shoulders and the pain in her eyes before she dropped her gaze.

"Of course," she said.

He had disappointed her. Try as he might to reason with himself that he was not likely to find Lucie simply by questioning Odile, he couldn't help feeling he had disappointed himself, too.

* * *

After she had seen Odile A'lle to the door, Armande returned to the parlor and stood in the doorway, hands clasped at her waist.

"Bad news?" she asked softly.

Desautel sighed and replaced the papers on the table. He began gathering up the tea cups and placing them on the tray. Armande let him.

"It's certainly not good news," he said finally. He straightened, holding the laden tray. "Everything about this case is hearsay. The only evidence we have is three bodies and the constabulary never examined them, so there is no coroner's report."

Armande's pink cheeks drained of color, but her voice remained even. "Is there anything you can do to help them?" she asked.

Desautel shook his head in frustration and headed into the kitchen. A pot of soup simmered on the stove, filling the kitchen with the wonderful aroma of pea soup. He set the tray down on the counter and stood looking down at the dishes.

Armande's firm hand on his shoulder drew him back.

"Médéric, if anyone can find out who is doing these horrible things, you can."

He smiled and turned to give her a quick hug. As he stepped back, his gaze caught on the small gold crucifix around her neck.

"Armande, do you still attend mass?"

Her eyebrows rose is surprise, reminding him of the young woman she had been.

"Yes, of course. I go to the Church of the Assumption during the week and the basilica on Sundays."

The Church of the Assumption was on Ste-Catherine, within easy walking distance. The basilica would be Notre Dame Basilica on Notre-Dame. Farther away, but easily walkable on a nice day.

"What is the feeling within the Church about the A'lle?"

Armande looked away and some of the color returned to her cheeks. After a moment, she sighed and looked at him.

"The priest at the Church of the Assumption never mentions them. I have even seen a few A'lle attend mass. They always sit at the back, however, and never take communion."

"And at the basilica?" he prompted.

She turned away from him to empty the almost full teapot and clean the cups. "It depends on which priest is officiating," she said finally. "Father Brennan never speaks of them, but I've heard Father Vézinas and Father O'Doule mention them in their sermons." She glanced over her shoulder at him. "Never incitingly, of course. But they speak of the A'lle as not being part of the shepherd's flock and therefore having no soul. They are always careful to say that this doesn't mean the A'lle are evil, but..." she shrugged and turned back to her cleaning up.

A passing car honked out on the street. Armande glanced at the watch pinned to her bodice.

"Oh! I'll be late!" She reached for a cloth threaded through the handle of the nearest drawer to wipe her hands.

"Where are you off to?" he asked, wondering if she was inventing an appointment to avoid discussing the issue any longer.

"My solicitor's," she said. "I'm selling the house on St. Antoine."

It was his turn to raise his eyebrows in surprise. "Do you need the money? I can—"

She smiled and patted him on the arm. "My finances are sound, old friend. I want to buy a warehouse on Bord de l'Eau. The port district is growing and I think this is a good time to buy."

Desautel smiled. Armande had turned into a good business-woman, something he would never have suspected in the days she and Françoise would trade recipes and walk to the park with the children.

She left him alone, with hurried instructions about lunch, and he returned to the parlor to complete his notes of the interview with Odile A'lle.

This case was beyond the resources of two investigators and one constable. He needed the full resources of the Montreal constabulary behind this investigation. However, Alastair McReady had already made his position clear.

But eight people were missing—nine now with Lucie A'lle... How many more had not been reported because it was pointless? And with three bodies, there was clearly a murderer at work, if not a gang of them. Something bigger was going on here than McReady's dismissive theory that the A'lle were settling their own accounts. If that were true, the corpses would not have been autopsied.

And now there was a new sense of urgency, muted though it was. Lucie A'lle had disappeard less than a week ago. He hadn't wanted to raise Odile A'lle's hopes but if there was any chance that she might still be alive, he had to do everything in his power to find the young woman.

It was time to pull in the magistrate.

* * *

Constance and Murphy drove back to the Auberge Maillet in silence. She had wanted to go to the next interview, Thibault and Clémence A'lle, but her hunger was almost overwhelming her ability to think. Even Murphy's stomach clamored loudly for attention, much to his embarrassment.

Besides, the interviews were taking on a terrible similarity. She doubted they would learn anything of value, no matter how many A'lle they spoke to.

The murderer—or murderers—was too clever. Too careful.

Too organized. She had trouble imagining the Ferret behind that level of organization. His actions to date had seemed impulsive to her, as though he were reacting to events.

They trudged up the steps and opened the door to the inn, leaving behind the sunshine and mild breeze. Water ran in the roof gutters as the sun melted the snow on the roofs.

The delicious smells that greeted them almost pushed all other thoughts out of her mind, but before she closed the door behind her, Constance took a long look at the street. Children were walking back to school after lunch. An old man across the street took advantage of the warmth to chop away at accumulated ice on his sidewalk. A postman ran up the steps of a business two doors down. A lorry drove by.

There was no sign of the Ferret.

She hadn't seen him since last night. Was he still here? Or had he headed back to St-Vincent to help his partner kidnap her sister?

No. He must still be in Montreal. There was only one train to St. Vincent and it was at dinner time. He could have taken a horse or a carriage, of course, but that would take much longer than by train, and some parts of the road would be starting to be impassable with the spring melt.

He was here, somewhere.

Her gaze drifted up to the roofline of the brownstone across the street. It stood out in stark contrast to the blue sky. It was hard to believe that bad things could happen on a day this beautiful. But she knew better.

Renaud and Dallaire had been murdered on a day this beautiful.

She needed to find out if Roland A'lle had made it to St-Vincent last night and managed to transmit her message to her family. If she knew for certain that they had been warned, she could focus more closely on the investigation.

Perhaps she could convince the chief investigator to let her go home on the evening train. But even as she thought it, she knew it was hopeless. They were only three to investigate what was turning into a crime of massive proportions. He needed her here.

Even if she could be alone in the parlor to place a call to the St-Vincent constabulary, she couldn't be certain that the Ferret didn't have a contact there. She didn't want her call to trigger the Ferret's companion.

Her only choice was to drive back to Roland A'lle's home to see if he had returned with his son's body.

"Are you going to stand there all day?" asked Murphy.

She turned to find him staring at her quizzically. Instead of replying, she closed the door and took off her boots.

* * *

She and Murphy filled in the chief investigator on the interviews they had done over excellent pea soup, fresh bread, and apple pie. Constance had three bowls of pea soup.

When she got to the part where Amanda A'lle told her that there were many more disappearances than had been reported, Desautel simply nodded.

"Did you know about this?" she asked him, almost accusingly.

"Yes." He finished slathering molasses on his bread. "Continue. I will catch you up afterward."

They finished their report and by then, they were at the pie. It was good, but not as good as Prudence's pie.

"I had a visit not long before you returned." Desautel pushed away his half-finished pie. "An Odile A'lle. She wanted to speak to you," he continued, nodding at Constance. "Instead, she spoke to me."

He proceeded to relate her story and neither Constance nor Murphy interrupted. It was by now an all too familiar story, after all. When he was done, Murphy spoke up.

"Sir, the abduction was less than a week ago. People's memories will still be fresh. We could go talk to—"

Desautel waved a hand to stop him. "I agree, constable. But the case is now in the magistrate's hands. He and his investigators are arriving after dinner on the Quebec City train. They will be staying here and taking over the investigation from this end. No doubt they will be wanting your services, Constable Murphy, as you are so familiar with the case. Investigator A'lle and I will return to St-Vincent tomorrow evening and try to trace Frederick A'lle's path from there to Backli's Ford."

Constance's breath caught in her throat. Home? They were going home?

"I could return on today's train," she said. "Help with the investigation at that end..." She trailed off when he again waved a dismissing hand.

"Non. I will need you here to report to the magistrate when he arrives. He may even ask that you remain on to help."

"No!" The word shot out of her mouth, startling all of them.

Desautel frowned and waited for her to explain herself, while Murphy just sat there, his mouth open.

Constance swallowed hard. She had to control her emotions. Make him understand.

"Sir, I need to go home," she said calmly, trying keep her breaths shallow. He couldn't make her stay here. She had to be in St-Vincent before the magistrate arrived. The moment the magistrate descended on the auberge with his team of investigators, the Ferret would realize the investigation had escalated. He would call his partner in St-Vincent, who would do his best to hurt one of her sisters.

She stood up, unable to remain sitting, and returned her dishes to the counter. She kept her back to the two men at the table. "I respectfully request to return to duty in St-Vincent."

For an old man, he moved quickly and silently. When he next spoke, he was standing less than two feet behind her, and she had not heard him move.

"Constance, what is it?"

It was the concern in his voice that undid her determination. She turned to look at him and saw a strong human man who had shown her respect, if not always fairness. She knew him to be an able investigator and a man of honor.

But was she willing to risk her family's safety on his sense of honor?

"I have an... ability. A talent," she began, looking him in the eye. She could smell molasses on his breath, and see the gray stubble breaking through his chin and cheeks. "I can tell whether or not a person is honest. I can read the truth of their hearts."

Chief Investigator Desautel blinked. "I beg your pardon?"

Out of the corner of her eye, she saw that Murphy's mouth was still open. He hadn't budged from his chair. She was growing uncomfortably warm next to the electric range, which was on low heat to keep the soup warm. But she knew instinctively that this was her one chance to convince the chief investigator, and that if she moved away, she would lose him.

She raised her right hand and rubbed her fingertips with her thumb.

"It's something to do with my body chemistry," she continued. "If I touch someone's skin, I can tell. Different emotions release different chemicals in the body. And something about this planet's soil, different amino acids, I suspect, combines with my chemistry to make this ability very strong, and very accurate."

Murphy made a slight choking sound and she turned to look at him. His face was scarlet.

"Do you mean...?"

She shook her head. "I have not touched you, Constable Murphy. Even if I had, I can only sense these things if I concentrate. It must be wilful touching."

She turned back to the chief investigator and almost recoiled at the look on his face. It was cold and controlled, but there was no hiding his anger.

"Why have you kept this hidden from me?"

Unlike Murphy, the chief investigator's face was white. Even his lips, pressed together so tightly, were rimmed with white. Constance swallowed and wished she could move away, but she had trapped herself against the counter.

"Sir," she said softly, "it is no different than my parents' ability to find lost children, or Prudence's ability to know where each of us is."

"Does every bloody A'lle have this 'talent'?" Desautel's words came out clipped but there was no disguising the accusation in his tone.

A matching anger reared within her. How dare he be angry with her? Was it his people who were being hunted and killed? Had his people been hanged as witches?

"In my family the talent is strong. It manifests as an ability to find. We find lost children, family, or in my case, the truth. In other families, the talent is weaker and manifests differently. Just as it does among humans." She stared him in the eye, daring him to contradict her.

Which he did.

"No human I know can tell the truth of a person just by touching them!"

"Perhaps not," she said coldly. "But no A'lle can look out the window and paint what she sees. Or hear music in her head and transcribe it for others to play. Talent is talent. We are no more responsible for the talents we are born with than you are."

He took a deep breath, visibly trying to control himself. His reaction unnerved Constance. She had not expected his reaction to be so... visceral. Had she made a mistake in trusting him? Was he akin to Père Noiron in his mistrust of the A'lle?

"Why are you telling us now?" asked Murphy suddenly. He leaned back unconsciously, as though afraid she might try to touch him.

Constance closed her eyes. She did not want to do this, but it was the only way. She needed to know if she could trust him. Them.

"Because she wants to do it to us," said Desautel slowly. She looked at him and winced at the hard look in his eyes. "Isn't that right?" he asked.

She nodded, not trusting words.

Desautel looked grim. "You do *not* want to know what I am thinking now."

She smiled tightly. "You misunderstand my talent, sir. I cannot read your thoughts. I can only read your emotions."

They remained silent for long moments, studying each other. Suddenly, Murphy stood up, startling her.

"Why now?" he asked, his arms spreading out to express his bafflement. "Why today?"

Almost she gave in to his distress, but the thought of the Ferret's partner kept her strong. She turned back to Desautel. "You asked what was the matter, sir, and I want to tell you, but first I must do this."

"Why not just do it and not tell us about it?" asked Desautel. "You could have done it at any time." His anger was still present but now it seemed tempered with puzzlement, as if he truly wanted to understand her.

Her chin rose. "Among my people, it is forbidden to use this particular talent without the person's permission, unless sanctioned by a council of seniors, and then it is only in rare cases, as when a crime is suspected."

From the day Constance's talent first manifested, when she was five, Grandmother Esther had emphasized the ethical use of it until Constance would no more have invaded someone's privacy by reading their emotions than she would have spied on a couple being intimate.

She was A'lle. She did not abuse her talent.

And yet, she had, she suddenly remembered. The day Thomas, the Backli's Ford innkeeper had found her. She had wilfully touched him before allowing him to help her. And she had touched that old man, this morning.

It would seem that her ethics were contingent on her sense of safety.

"All right, then," said Murphy. He came to stand before her and stuck his hand out, palm open. "Go ahead."

She couldn't read his expression, where before it had been open for all to see. As much as he was willing to allow her access to his innermost feelings, he was clearly not willing to allow her access to his thoughts.

She sighed softly and nodded. "Thank you."

Without hesitating, she took his hand in both of hers, closed her eyes and opened herself up. She felt the strength in his hands, the solid bones, the length of his fingers, the rough texture of his skin. Then the familiar shock ran through her as his skin's amino acids mingled with hers, sending messages like a lightning storm to her brain.

Anger, resentment, attraction. Hurt, but no hatred. No attempt to hide.

She opened her eyes and found Murphy looking steadfastly at her, his brown eyes serious and questioning. She squeezed his hand and he squeezed hers back. Then she released him and turned to the chief investigator.

He was looking at Murphy.

"A tingle, sir," said Murphy. "Like you sat on your hand and now it's pins and needles." He hesitated, then glanced at Constance. "Only stronger."

Desautel turned back to Constance. Without a word, he held out his hand.

It took all her courage to clasp his hand in both of hers, but she did. The chief investigator's hand was bigger than Murphy's, and callused, and Constance wondered what work the man did when all she ever saw him do with his hands was write.

Then she closed her eyes and concentrated.

Anger, yes. An even greater curiosity. Frustration. Fear. Disappointment.

Constance broke the connection abruptly, shaken by the knowledge that the chief investigator was disappointed in her. And perhaps fearful of her, though that emotion was faint and truly, she couldn't be certain that it was aimed at her.

The disappointment, though—that was most definitely aimed at her.

"Thank you," she said stiffly.

"Now," said Desautel, at last stepping away from her, "what was so important that it was necessary to impose in this outrageous way?"

Constance began to tremble in reaction to doing two intense readings in a row. She walked toward her chair, but her knees buckled before she could reach it. Only Murphy's quick hand on her elbow kept her upright. She nodded her thanks and sank into the chair.

Desautel sat down across from her, studying her face and her trembling hands.

"Your sister," he said abruptly. "Prudence. She reacted similarly when she searched for you."

Constance remembered to breathe deeply to replenish the oxygen in her blood. Finally she nodded. "Yes. Hers is an unkind gift. She is weak for hours after using it."

"And you?" asked Murphy, handing her a glass of water.

She drank deeply then set the glass down. "Normally, for me, the weakness passes quickly, but when I do more than one, or the emotions are... strong..." She smiled briefly at Murphy. "I will recover momentarily."

"Investigator A'lle," said Desautel, "I want to know now."

She did not need to touch him to see that he was still angry. She took one more deep breath, and began.

"On the way to Montreal, on the train." She waited for Desautel's nod. "While you slept, I returned the dirty cups to the dining car."

She continued, telling them both about the Ferret and his threats to harm her family should she not do as he ordered and impede the investigation.

"And did you?" asked Desautel. "Did you impede the investigation?"

Constance studied his expression but could glean nothing from it.

"No sir," she said.

"Did you not fear for your family?" he asked softly. Even Murphy glanced at him questioningly at that.

Constance sensed danger around her but could not tell which direction it was coming from.

"Yes, of course I feared for their safety," she answered. "That is why I asked Roland A'lle to warn them."

At that, Desautel sat back, but it was Murphy who exclaimed, "So that's why he changed his mind and decided to go to St. Vincent!"

She nodded but kept her gaze on the chief investigator. She could not guess what he was feeling. It was as if he had erected a barrier between them. She was surprised at how much the thought hurt.

"And you did not confide is us," said Desautel softly, "in me, because you did not trust us. Not until you did your little parlor trick."

Constance looked away. He was deliberately belittling her talent. Why?

Perhaps it was the bewilderment, or the weakness, or if she were to be completely honest, the hurt that she felt at his words that prompted her next statement.

"You will forgive my saying so, Chief Investigator, but you have given me no reason to trust you."

The chief investigator's face paled and Murphy's hand rose as if to snatch the words back from the air, but it was too late.

She had gone too far, but in the past few days she had fallen off a cliff, survived an attack in a cemetery, had her family's safety threatened, and now, had the talent that defined who she was as an A'lle belittled.

She no longer cared how far she had to go.

"Now you understand why I need to go back today. The moment the magistrate arrives here, my family will be in even greater danger."

The color had returned to the chief investigator's face and his eyes had narrowed. Now he stood up. "There's no need to worry, Investigator A'lle," he said coldly. "I will ensure that your family is well guarded. We will proceed as planned."

Then he left the kitchen for the parlor, where the telephone sat.

"Was it necessary to insult the man?" asked Murphy. The look he gave her was full of reproach. Then he got up, too, and left the kitchen.

❧ TWENTY-FOUR ❧

WHEN they arrived at Thibault's home, the sound of an axe thumping against wood drew Desautel and Constance A'lle down the neatly shoveled path to the side of the house and to the back. They found Thibault A'lle splitting wood while his wife stacked it in a neat pile on the porch next to the back door.

Like most of the Montreal A'lle, they lived in the Alley in a two-story house that could use a coat of paint but otherwise was in good repair. Desautel had ordered Murphy to stay with the car, not wanting to alarm the old couple needlessly. Besides, he was tired of the reproachful glances the young man kept giving him.

According to the A'lle girl, Thibault and Clémence were ninety and eighty-six, respectively, but Desautel didn't believe it. They looked thirty years younger, closer to his age.

The woman was the first to notice them. She was dressed like a man, in sturdy canvas pants and workbooks, but with only a light woolen shirt with the sleeves rolled up, and a pair of work gloves. Incongruously, she wore a short apron around her waist. She had just emptied the canvas carrier and was rearranging the split logs so that they stacked better. She stopped when she became aware of their presence and said something to her husband, who turned around, gripping the axe and frowning.

His stance relaxed somewhat when he caught sight of Constance A'lle. He spoke to her in their language and she responded. The yard was large and although there were houses on either side, it felt private. The tall fence contributed to the effect.

"In that case," said Clémence A'lle in English, "you may as well come in." There was no welcome in her voice.

As they turned to follow the woman inside, Constance leaned over.

"They are the grandparents of Edith," she whispered. "Their son-in-law is at work and their daughter is gone to Quebec City with her three remaining children to visit her sister."

He nodded stiffly. He did not know how to behave around her now. Part of him was ready to admit that he was a hypocrite for being insulted that she hadn't come to him when she was threatened. After all, he hadn't trusted her from the moment she arrived at his constabulary. Wasn't that why he had wanted her close by? So he could keep an eye on her?

He had failed to treat her as he would have treated any other investigator. It had to do with having her thrust upon him with no warning, but he was honest enough with himself to know that she made him uncomfortable. Her whole family made him uncomfortable.

Except perhaps for Prudence. For some reason, her presence eased him.

He followed the older woman into the kitchen and they all removed their boots. His stockinged toes immediately curled up in protest against the icy kitchen floor. A wood cookstove stood against the far wall, not presently in use although the ghosts of woodsmoke and meat pie filled the air. A small electric range sat at the end of the counter. It was a big kitchen, with black and white tiles and a big table taking pride of place.

He seemed to be spending all his time in kitchens lately.

Clémence A'lle offered them a seat at the table while her husband closed the door behind him. He set the axe down next to the door—a gesture not lost on Desautel.

"Would you like some tea?" offered the woman.

Constance A'lle glanced at Desautel, who wondered how genuine the offer was. Still, he would need something to help him keep warm.

"Merci, Madame," he said formally.

Clémence A'lle turned the burner on beneath the kettle and pulled a teapot toward her. It clanked loudly in the silent kitchen.

Desautel almost sighed. The hostility was almost palpable and he could understand it. They knew why he was here. His very presence was stirring up raw pain. He knew enough about the A'lle to know they grieved as keenly as humans did.

And, as Constance A'lle had made plain, they had no reason to trust him.

She looked at him questioningly, her own expression cool, and he nodded imperceptibly. They would get better results if she spoke to them, he thought.

She began to speak in her tongue. Clémence A'lle listened for a moment, her face growing tighter and tighter. Finally she waved a hand and said, "Stop, stop!"

Constance faltered to a stop. Clémence A'lle frowned. "Your A'lle is terrible," she said.

Desautel slid a glance over to the girl. She had grown very still.

"Then we shall speak English," she said finally, and nodded to Desautel.

Thibault A'lle said something sharp to his wife and she responded in kind and turned her back to him, busying herself with the teapot. Thibault sat down across from Constance and shook his head.

"You will have to forgive my wife's blunt manners," he said gruffly. "We were taught the mother tongue by our grandparents, who were born on the home world. Every generation since has lost a little bit more of the language."

Constance nodded once, accepting the apology, and the implied rebuke. Over by the range, cups clattered dangerously on saucers.

"If you will permit?" said Desautel, and it was in that moment that he accepted the fact that the man sitting across from him was much older. He only felt this level of deference for men and women old enough to be his parents.

Thibault nodded at him to continue.

Desautel had given some thought to how to approach these two, but it was only then that his method crystallized. Not for these two the tiptoeing around the sore subject. He would aim directly at the heart of the matter.

"In the course of investigating the death of Frederick A'lle," he said, "I learned that there have been a number of disappearances and murders of A'lle in this region."

His words were met by silence. Clémence A'lle turned to glance at her husband.

"Fifteen are missing," said Thibault finally, grimly. "And three have been returned to us, dead."

Fifteen! Desautel felt the weight of Constance A'lle's surprise but was too shocked to look at her. Fifteen gone. After speaking with Odile A'lle, he had suspected there would be more than the ones that had been reported. It would seem that John A'lle's information was out of date. For a moment, he wondered if the fifteen included the missing Lucie A'lle but did not ask.

"Including the little one," whispered Clémence A'lle, turning her back. Her words were uncomfortably close to his thoughts. Her hands had stilled and she stood with her head down.

Thibault nodded. "Including our little Edith," he said quietly.

Gone was his anger against Constance A'lle, overwhelmed by the pity he felt for these two. If he allowed it, their grief would undo him, make him unable to ask the questions that needed answering. He steeled himself against their pain, shifting in his chair.

"If you please," he said firmly. "Tell us what happened." He kept his gaze on Thibault A'lle but noticed out of the corner of his eye that the A'lle girl had taken her notebook out and was ready to take notes.

The water in the kettle began to boil and with the sounds of Madame A'lle preparing the tea as accompaniment, Thibault began to speak. His voice grew rough, and low, as if he had to push the words out past an obstruction.

"Matthieu, our oldest grandchild, was watching the younger children that day," he said. His gaze was on something in the distance above Desautel's shoulder. "He is eleven. Normally Clémence looked after the two youngest ones, Edith and Jeanne, but that day she had gone to the doctor's because she wasn't feeling well and I was helping my son-in-law on a construction site. He is an electrician," he added.

"And your daughter?" asked Desautel.

"Aline was working, too," said Thibault. "She was the book-keeper at the Cecil Hotel on Notre Dame." He shook his head. "She lost the position when she stayed away, looking for her baby."

"So there was only your eldest grandchild in the house, with his two young siblings?" asked Desautel resolutely. He could not allow his sympathy for this man to prevent him from doing his job. He wanted to rub his hands together to work some warmth back into them but felt that would be disrespectful.

A bone china cup appeared before him as Madame A'lle set out the tea cups and tea pot. She poured the tea and pushed a jar of honey toward him. Finally she sat down next to her husband, her face carefully neutral.

Thibault clasped his hands together on the table. "It was June," he said softly. "And hot."

The older brother had taken his two young sisters, Jeanne and Edith, down to the public pool. School was out and there were many children playing there. Jeanne, the three-year-old, was able to walk with him, but he pushed Edith in the stroller. When they got to the pool, he set the stroller beneath the tree while he helped

Jeanne out of her dress and into the wading pool. The baby was sound asleep and there was no one nearby. When Jeanne was sitting down in the water, he returned to the tree but Edith was gone. She was six months old.

Her body was discovered two weeks later. As with Albert A'lle, her organs had been removed. Unlike Albert, her eyes had not been touched and her body cavity had been sewn up. She was dressed in the clothes she had worn when she was taken and her body was wrapped in a clean white sheet. It was left at the door of the local church, where the A'lle-friendly priest found it.

That was eight months ago.

Desautel's best intentions deserted him as the story unfolded. He found himself swallowing down cries of disbelief, of denial. Who would do such a thing to a baby?

That damned McReady was an accomplice to these murders, as surely as if he had helped kidnap the victims himself. He not only disgraced himself, but the magistrate's uniform, as well.

"Did anyone see anything strange around the swimming pool?" Constance A'lle's words dropped into the silence. "Anyone who did not belong?"

Thibault's hands clenched into fists. His wife leaned toward him slightly, her shoulder barely touching his. The touch seemed to brace him.

"A child noticed a man near the tree, though she didn't see him take Edith," he said calmly. "She noticed him because he was not there with a child of his own and was fully dressed."

"Did you obtain a description?" asked the girl.

Thibault's hands opened and he rubbed his face wearily. "A child's description," he said flatly. "He was small and mean looking."

Desautel glanced at Constance A'lle, but she was looking down at the table. She had described the man who had accosted her on the train as small and ferret-like. That would qualify as mean looking.

"Has anyone else asked about your granddaughter's death?" he asked on impulse.

Clémence A'lle slapped the tabletop, startling everyone.

"What does it matter?" she said in a low, fierce voice. "Will all your questions bring the child back? Will they heal my daughter's anguish?" She took a quick breath. "Where were you eight months ago, when your constables could have made a difference in finding her while she yet lived?"

Desautel fought against the urge to drop his gaze under the onslaught of her accusations. As with Roland, a part of him pitied these people for their inability to weep. Surely, they deserved the release.

"Eight reported taken," said Constance calmly. "Many more not reported. Three dead, that we know of. And now Frederick. Someone is after the A'lle. We can do nothing to change the past. But the help you give us now may help prevent further disappearances."

Desautel glanced at her sideways. She had put into words what he had been feeling since yesterday. The scope of their investigation had expanded from the beating death of one boy to finding a multiple killer.

They had to find out what was happening before more A'lle were lost.

* * *

Bertrand A'lle was seventy and lived alone above the small tobacco shop he owned. It was a prime location, on the corner of St. Antoine and McGill. A tram ran by it and Desautel noticed a steady sound of traffic throughout the interview. It was close to dinnertime and people were hurrying home.

The shop could not be more than ten feet by twenty. It consisted of a counter—a weathered, dark wood, probably mahogany—and tall shelves along both walls, stacked high with tins and pouches and pipes and cigarette holders and humidors. At the far end was a closed door, presumably leading to the living quarters upstairs.

Desautel was glad they had left Murphy with the car, again.

Really, there was barely enough room for two people on the other side of Bertrand A'lle's counter.

The man refused to leave his spot behind the counter to go somewhere more private. Desautel and the girl had to conduct the interview in between customers and amid the intoxicating smell of exotic tobacco. The whole time Desautel stood there, he had to fight back the demons of his youth, who demanded he buy pipe tobacco—right now—even though he had gotten rid of his pipes ten years ago.

Bertrand A'lle's wife, Mathilde, had disappeared before Christmas, on her way downtown to do some shopping at Eaton's. When she wasn't home by evening, Bertrand had searched for her, then called on friends and family. No one ever saw her again.

He never informed the Montreal constabulary.

The bitterness was so strong in this one that he refused to speak to Desautel, and would not speak English, though he understood it perfectly.

"Sir," said Desautel, "did you notice any strangers about on that day?"

The man gave Desautel a look of contempt, then turned his attention to Constance A'lle. She translated, and he replied in their tongue, then she turned back to Desautel. She had given up apologizing with her eyes and now concentrated on keeping him abreast of the information.

"He says this is a tobacco shop and he sees strangers every day."

Desautel could imagine that the man hadn't used quite those words but let it pass. "Did anyone stand out?"

Constance glanced at Bertrand A'lle who remained stubbornly mute until she translated the question. It was becoming irritating.

Bertrand started to shake his head, then hesitated. At that moment, a customer came in and Desautel and the girl moved away from the counter to allow the shop owner to conduct his business. When the customer left with his purchases, Bertrand looked at Constance.

She listened while he spoke and when he fell silent, she turned to Desautel. "He says he didn't notice anyone special that day but on the previous day he did see a man standing across the street, watching. He'd never seen him before and hasn't seen him since."

"Can he describe him?" asked Desautel. He had been growing discouraged—and almost ready to give in to the temptation of the tobacco—but now he leaned forward, his attention fully engaged.

The man listened to Constance A'lle, then replied.

"He says he couldn't tell much from across the road, but he had dark hair and was tall for a human. Slender. It was too far to make out eye color." She listened again and he could tell at once that she had something. "He says he thought the man wore a clerical collar, even though he did not wear a cassock."

A priest? Desautel frowned, listening absently as Constance tried to elicit further details. But Bertrand A'lle was done.

"He didn't think anything of it," said Constance finally. "It seemed to him that the priest was waiting for a ride. He hadn't even remembered until our questions jarred the memory free."

Finally, Desautel thanked the man for his time and turned away.

And then Bertrand said softly, in English, "They took my Mathilde. We will find her one day, as we will find the others. She will have been cut open, her organs removed, perhaps her brain. What kind of person does that?"

A scientist. The answer popped into Desautel's mind with the weight of truth.

"Someone who wants to learn about the A'lle," he replied just as softly, looking Bertrand A'lle in the eye.

"Someone who sees us as nothing more than mice to be experimented on," said Bertrand bitterly. "Perhaps it's time the mice fought back."

It sounded threatening to Desautel and he did not know what to say. The man came from a race of people who had built great vessels and traveled vast distances. Surely such people had defences. Perhaps even weapons, although it was well known that the A'lle were peaceful.

But in the A'lle he had spoken to here, he had seen great rage.

He moved closer to Bertrand A'lle until all that separated them was the counter. They stared at each other.

"Sir, I promise you that I will find out what is happening to the A'lle. And I will bring the culprit to justice."

All the fight seemed to drain out of the man. His eyes filled with a dull despair. "Chief Investigator," he said, "what justice can we have when even men of God see us as less than human?"

Desautel had no answer.

* * *

The mention of the priest rattled Constance. Bertrand A'lle had mentioned his presence as if it were commonplace, and perhaps it was, here. But this was the second or third time priests or bishops or the Church itself had been mentioned in the course of their investigation and it was important. She could sense it.

They made their way back to the car. Desautel was apparently content to sit and think while she filled Murphy in on what they had learned.

"A priest?" said Murphy doubtfully. "The tram stops across the street from the tobacco shop," he pointed out.

Constance pulled out her notebook. "I'm sure some other witnesses mentioned priests," she muttered, flipping through the pages.

"Today," said Desautel, startling her. He looked at her, then at Murphy. "Odile A'lle mentioned that her neighbor was ailing, and that a priest had attended him."

Constance nodded. "And the old woman. The first interview we did on Jubal Street." She kept flipping, trying to find the exact page. "Here it is," she said finally. "She described a man who asked the same questions we did. She said he was taller than the chief investigator, with shaggy hair and shabby clothes." She looked up from her notes. "That could easily describe Père Noiron."

"Now, wait," said Murphy. He had twisted in his seat to look at both of them, and now his eyes looked troubled in the failing light. "It's a long way from shabby clothes and long hair to a priest! And why would you even *think* that?"

Constance smiled. "The Church is no friend to the A'lle." The car was uncomfortably warm and she pushed her coat open.

"But to suggest that they would be involved in something this terrible..."

He sounded genuinely shocked. Offended, perhaps.

She would never understand the human need for religion, or their invention of God. Father and Mother had trained them never to offend human sensibilities around religion, but part of her always wanted to try and talk sense to them. But as Father said, religion had nothing to do with logic, or scientific proof. It had to do with faith.

No wonder she didn't understand.

She glanced at the chief investigator but he was looking out at the busy street. The streetlights had come on and there were fewer cars on the street. An occasional beam of light would catch his profile and limn his craggy nose and prominent chin.

"And who is Père Noiron?" continued Murphy plaintively.

"He is the priest in Backli's Ford," said Constance. "He tried to make Monsieur and Madame Pelletier throw me out of their inn when I was injured. He worried that I would endanger their souls."

The words left behind a deep silence. How could they have lived with the A'lle in their communities for so long and not realize how the Church hated the A'lle?

Murphy cleared his throat. His face was now in shadow, only lit up when an occasional car passed by. The tobacco shop was now closed, its lights off, while the upstairs apartment had lights on.

"Not all priests think that," said Murphy finally. "Do you really believe priests kidnapped and cut open all those people? To what end?"

Constance wished she could shrug. The human shrug was so expressive, of so many things. But she had seen too many A'lle attempt the shrug and succeed only in looking awkward. The A'lle shoulder simply wasn't hinged to allow a proper shrug.

"Your Jesuits are scientists," she said. "Bertrand A'lle is right. Whoever is doing this thinks of us as nothing but mice to be experimented on."

She sensed the chief investigator's gaze on her and turned to look at him.

"Are they right, sir?"

* * *

The offices of the archdiocese—and the home of the Archbishop of Montreal—were in a grand building behind Notre Dame Basilica, the smaller cousin to the basilica in Paris, in front of Place d'Armes. A narrow pathway connected the buildings.

A tall, thin cleric opened the door to them and stood looking down at them in a way that reminded Constance of Louis, Desautel's assistant.

"Chief Investigator Médéric Desautel," said the chief investigator. "I would like to see the bishop, please."

"You mean the archbishop, of course," said the man stiffly. "Do you have an appointment?"

From inside came the smells of meat roasting, and Constance's stomach stirred with interest. The outside light was right above the cleric's head, casting deep shadows beneath his eyes and cheekbones. He seemed young to Constance, but it was not always easy to tell.

Constance didn't know enough about their uniform to identify what rank he held within the Church. He had one of those thin, round black flapjacks covering the crown of his head and a long, black cassock, the kind Père Noiron wore.

She glanced at Desautel.

"Non," he said, and nothing more.

The cleric seemed confused for a moment, as though he had

expected Desautel to plead to be admitted. But he quickly regained his composure.

"The Monseigneur is about to sit down to dinner," he said stiffly. "If you would like, I can set up an appointment for tomorrow."

Desautel shook his head. "This can't wait. I am investigating a series of murders."

"And what does this have to do with the archbishop?" asked the cleric. If anything, he seemed even less inclined to allow them in.

Murphy bristled next to her, but Constance waited. She had learned that the chief investigator was rarely thwarted, and certainly not by a minor official, from the Church or not.

"That is what we are here to find out," he said.

"What do you mean?" asked the cleric sharply. He was younger than Constance had first thought, with curly brown hair peeking around the rim of his little hat and blue eyes suddenly wide with alarm.

Desautel leaned forward slightly, giving the man the full benefit of his attention.

"Do you really think the archbishop would appreciate us discussing this on the stoop?"

The cleric hesitated for a long moment then stepped back. "Come in," he said stiffly. They trooped inside and he closed the door. "I will see if Monseigneur Pinard can see you. Wait here."

He turned with a swish of his robe and walked to a door at the far end. He knocked twice and then entered. Constance had a glimpse of a white wall before the heavy wooden door closed behind the cleric and they were alone in the hall.

Murphy glanced at her and waggled his eyebrows but they all remained silent. Murphy had offered to wait in the car, but even Constance could see he wanted to hear what the archbishop had to say.

They were in a dark, wood-paneled hall with the closed door at the far end and two open doors off to the right. Through the nearest one, they could see a small desk and chair, and a lamp with a green glass shade. It was warm in the hall, though there was no evident source of heat.

Five minutes later, the cleric returned.

"Please remove your footwear," he said primly, indicating a mat next to a coat tree by the side of the door. "Monseigneur Pinard can only spare a few moments."

"That is all we will need," murmured Desautel.

The cleric waited while they removed their boots and set them on the mat.

Desautel removed his coat and hung it up on the coat tree. Then he glanced at the two of them. Constance smothered a grin and she and Murphy removed their coats, too. Murphy stuffed his cap and gloves in the sleeves, taking his time.

The cleric examined her bloodstained coat disfavorably. Perhaps that was why he didn't object to their presumption. After all, he wouldn't want to expose the bishop to the evidence of her profession.

Without a word, he led them past the first door and through the second. This, too, was an office, but the desk was enormous, a lovely expanse of polished dark wood, with a brass lamp on one side and a pile of papers on the other. A hardwood chair with a high, carved back waited behind it while two comfortable wing chairs unpholstered in a red velvet sat before it. The archbishop either thought more highly of his guest's comfort than his own or wanted it to appear that way.

Bookshelves covered every square inch of wall but for two windows, one behind the desk and the other opposite the hallway door, and a door that connected to the other office, presumably the cleric's. There was a tall grandfather clock ticking in the corner.

"Please be seated," said the cleric stiffly. "The archbishop will be here as soon as he can free himself."

He left them alone, closing the door firmly behind himself.

Constance felt tension tighten her shoulders with the clicking of the door latch. Desautel stood in the middle of the room with his hands clasped behind his back, but Murphy prowled around the archbishop's office, examining the titles in the bookshelves, peering out the windows. The chief investigator cleared his throat and Murphy finally came to stand next to Constance. She kept her hands clasped behind her back, too. She would never take the kind of liberties Murphy had just taken.

Grandmother Esther had drilled it into each one of her grand-children. "Treat the Church with respect. They could wipe us out with one edict."

Like the Separatist Church had done to the A'lle who had settled in the United American States. Grandmother Esther had been a child during the last Purge. She had seen what the Church could do.

The room filled with the sound of the grandfather clock.

At last the door opened behind them and they all turned to face Monseigneur Pinard, the Archbishop of Montreal.

The archbishop was a head shorter than she was, with iron-gray hair cut so short it was a wonder his little cap stayed on. Unlike the cleric's, this cap was wine red. Constance knew there was a significance to the color, but aside from indicating he was of higher rank than the cleric, she did not know what the significance was. He wore a robe that was no different from the cleric's, as far as Constance could tell.

His pale blue gaze took in Murphy and Desautel at a glance, then moved on to her where it lingered on her eyes. She couldn't tell what he was thinking.

He closed the door and advanced upon them, stopping a few feet shy.

"Monseigneur," said Desautel. "I am Chief Investigator Médéric Desautel, from St-Vincent. This is Constable Murphy, from the Montreal Constabulary, and Investigator Constance A'lle, also from St-Vincent."

"Chief Investigator," said the archbishop. Then he put his hand out toward Desautel. He wore an enormous ring on his finger. It was made of gold and some pearl-like stone. To her surpise, the chief investigator took the archbishop's hand, stooped over it, and kissed the ring.

"Monseigneur," he murmured as he straightened.

Then Murphy followed suit and stepped back.

She had never met a church official of this man's rank before. Once, a visiting bishop had come to St. Vincent when she had been a little girl, but no one had been required to kiss him. The thought repulsed her and she almost took a step back when he turned that pale gaze on her and held his hand out.

As she hesitated, Murphy shifted from foot to foot, his growing anxiety evident.

What protocol would she breach if she refused to follow this ridiculous custom? Did the Church expect everyone to bow to their customs, even those of other faiths? She glanced at Desautel for a clue and saw him nod imperceptibly.

And then the thought struck her. To kiss the archbishop's ring, she would have to take his hand.

She took a shallow, silent breath and took the man's hand. It was warm and dry, like a wasp's nest in the sun. As she bent to kiss the ring, she focused her attention on the texture of his skin, allowing her skin to absorb the oil, sweat, and impurities exuded by his skin. She closed her eyes just as her lips touched the ring. He smelled of talcum powder.

The archbishop gasped and jerked his hand away, forcing her to straighten up. She tried to look surprised at his reaction.

"Is everything all right, Monseigneur?" asked Murphy. He gave her a look that could have curdled milk but there was no expression on Desautel's face. She had taken his nod for tacit permission. Had she misread it?

The archbishop's face had paled but the color now seemed to be returning. He shook his head.

"Merely a shock," he said dismissively. "Static electricity, no doubt." His voice carried the accent of eastern Lower Canada, or perhaps even that of the Maritime colonies. He was far from home.

"Thank you for taking the time to see us, Monseigneur," said Desautel.

"Please, sit," said the archbishop as he strode around the desk. He waited for Desautel to sit down in the wing chair before taking his own seat. When he did, the high back of the chair extended past his head.

Murphy nodded at her to take the other chair and rather than argue the point, she did.

Constance found herself relaxing for the first time. Despite her distrust of the archbishop and all he represented, she had sensed none of the toxins in his skin that would indicate ill will.

They might as well leave now. She had learned everything she would from the man with just one touch. He knew nothing.

"You will forgive me," said the archbishop, "but I truly only have a few moments to spare. Michael tells me you want to ask me about a murder?" There was curiosity and sadness in his eyes. But no surprise.

Desautel nodded. "We are investigating a series of kidnappings and deaths within the A'lle community," he said. "Do you know of this?"

The archbishop looked down at his hands clasped on top of the desk. He remained silent for a few moments. Then he looked up.

"I have recently been made aware of this," he said in a low voice. He shook his head and his voice grew low. "A terrible thing."

"Yes," agreed Desautel. He hesitated. "We have learned that a priest may have been asking questions about the murders. Would you know who this is?"

The archbishop glanced at Constance, as if to gauge her reaction. "When I learned of these crimes, I charged all my priests with reaching out to the A'lle among their flock."

A very careful answer. One designed to state the truth but not the whole truth. What was he hiding, and why? She had not sensed in him the same near-fanatic distrust evident in Père Noiron, but he had not reached the status of archbishop without learning a trick or two from politicians.

"To what end?" asked Constance, earning a hard look from the chief investigator.

The archbishop's eyebrows rose in surprise. "My daughter, we are all God's children. Of course we would reach out to you in this trying time. Would you rather be alone?"

His answer caught her by surprise—as did his question. He was not cut of the same cloth as the Backli's Ford priest. And yet, he hid something. What was it?

It seemed logical enough that he would have sent his priests to visit the families of the missing and murdered ones. Still, the description the tobacco shopkeeper had given of the priest was too similar to Père Noiron to be a coincidence. And the description from the old woman on Jubal Street...

"Monseigneur Pinard," said Desautel, turning back to the archbishop. "Do you know a priest named Noiron?"

Constance swallowed a groan of dismay. That was too direct, even for her. She did not want the priest aware that they knew of him. But the archbishop thought for a moment, then answered.

"From Backli's Ford, yes? Of course I know him. Why?"

Desautel leaned forward.

"His views on the A'lle do not seem to match yours."

The archbishop looked down at his linked hands on the desk. Finally he sighed. When he looked up again, his gaze found Constance. "You must know that the Church is divided on this... issue," he said softly. "The Holy Father has yet to pronounce himself and neither faction wishes to push, for fear he will decide in favor of the other side."

Constance's breath grew shallow and quick. He spoke of things she knew—had known for a long time—but she had never heard any Church official be so honest about Church politics. She could not tear her gaze away from his.

"While I cannot govern what a priest's heart tells him, I can govern his behavior. If Père Noiron has been disrespectful, I can recall him. Perhaps assign him a different parish."

And thus transfer the problem to a different village. Such a political solution. She opened her mouth to tell him so, but to her surprise, instead she said, "He saved my life."

All three men stared at her. Desautel and Murphy in surprise, and the archbishop with understanding.

❧ TWENTY-FIVE ❦

THE drive back to the inn was short. Darkness had fallen and they drove in silence, each lost in thought. Desautel ran through the few facts they had, trying to put order, or some kind of logic in them, but he kept coming back to the archbishop and Constance A'lle.

The A'lle girl seemed convinced that the Church was somehow involved, but he wasn't. Certainly, priests were men, too, and subject to the same likes and dislikes as other men. But priests were men of God first. He could not imagine a man of God—no matter his scientific bent—dissecting a child simply to see how her organs worked.

If the Church were involved in something so heinous, surely a senior officer of the Church in the archdiocese of Montreal—in the heart of the disappearances—would know. Yet Constance had grudgingly admitted that she had sensed nothing wicked in the prelate.

Part of him had the grace to be embarrassed at how willingly he had allowed her—*encouraged* her—to practice her arts on the man of God. He had been so offended that she had wanted to... to what?... *read* him? And yet he had tacitly allowed her to do the same to the archbishop.

At least she had asked him and Murphy for permission before reading them.

He was a hypocrite. He almost shook his head in impatience. Now was not the time to worry about his sins. A'lle were being taken, tortured, and killed. The priority here was to find out who was doing it and end it.

They were on the wrong path. He knew it, but could not see where the right one was.

If they could find this "ferret," they might stand a chance. Otherwise, the killer—or killers—were ghosts.

For the first time in his professional life, first as a lawyer and then as an investigator, Desautel feared that he might not find the answer he sought.

He looked up when Constable Murphy stopped in front of the Auberge Maillet. The evening had turned cold and their mingled breath now condensed on the windows of the car, with the result that the street lights seemed diffused and watery.

He sighed. "Come inside and eat, Constable," he said. "We'll plan our next steps."

"Yes, sir," said Murphy. He sounded as dejected as Desautel felt.

They emerged from the Parker and headed up the stairs, with Constance A'lle trailing behind. Ste-Famille Street was quiet. Businesses were closed for the day and most people were inside, having dinner. He wondered what Odile A'lle was doing.

She would probably be dispirited if she saw him heading inside a cozy inn for a hot meal while her sister remained missing.

Behind him, the girl's steps paused and he turned to find her watching the street carefully. The wind had picked up and now sent small pellets of snow to sting his cheeks. He raised his collar but stayed on the stair, carefully examining each home and building within sight.

Nothing. Her ferret had left, it would seem.

Constance A'lle turned back and seemed startled to find him

looking at her. Without a word, he joined Constable Murphy on the stoop and pushed open the door.

The murmur of male voices that greeted him told him that the magistrate had arrived. He quickly removed his boots and set them on the rubber mat by the door while Constance A'lle came in after Murphy and shut the door. By the time he had removed his great coat and muffler and hung them up on the coat rack to join the four others already there, the voices had dropped to a murmur.

"Sir," said Murphy, and Desautel turned around to find Felix Latendresse, Magistrate of the Baudry Region, standing in the doorway to the parlor.

"Hello, Médéric," said the magistrate.

Desautel's welcoming smile faded at the man's expression. He had seen that expression too often on the constables who informed families that their loved ones had died. He steeled himself. "Sir?"

Behind Latendresse, three men held back, their own expressions somber. When he realized that they weren't looking at him, Desautel followed the magistrate's gaze. The man was looking at Constance A'lle. Desautel's heartbeat slowed in dread as if to delay the inevitable. He saw Murphy glance at him, then at the magistrate, but Constance A'lle had eyes only for the magistrate.

"Sir," she said, and only then did Desautel remember that she knew him. Of course she knew him. He had hand-picked her to come to St. Vincent.

"Investigator A'lle," said the magistrate evenly. "We have just received word from the St-Vincent constabulary. One of your sisters is missing."

* * *

Constance took deep breaths to control her fear and anger. The chief investigator had taken her by the elbow and led her to the settee in the parlor and now five men hovered over her as if waiting for her to faint. Only Murphy stood in the parlor's doorway, watching her gravely, an island of calm in the sea of solicitude.

Something clanged in the kitchen as Madame Maillet prepared

a late dinner. She would probably set dinner in the dining room to-night, since there would be so many guests. Did she have enough rooms for everyone?

Why had the magistrate only brought three investigators with him? Did he not know how vast a crime they were dealing with?

At last she recognised that she was in shock. She accepted the cup of tea that was placed in her hands and almost drank from it before she regained her senses and placed the cup and saucer on the side table.

Somehow, the magistrate had managed to sit beside her on the settee without her noticing. Now she turned to him and said, as calmly as she could, "Tell me."

The soft light from the torchiere gleamed on his bald head. Like Desautel, he only ever wore the magistrate's uniform on for-mal occasion. Tonight he wore a sturdy brown wool suit and a brocade vest in dark greens, browns, and blues. It made his brown eyes look even darker and more penetrating. He was the only hu-man whose intentions she could always read on his face and now she sensed that he wanted to take her hands in his. She reached over and picked up the cup again before looking at him enquir-ingly. It took all her concentration to keep her hands from shaking.

"An hour ago," began the magistrate, "the St-Vincent con-stabulary called." He took a deep breath. "Someone came to your home and took one of your sisters while she was alone."

"Which sister?" she asked at once. "Were there signs of a struggle? Why were no constables assigned to protect my family?"

The last was asked in a fierce whisper that barely contained her growing rage. She looked up but Desautel was gone. As was Murphy.

"I am sorry, Investigator A'lle," said Latendresse calmly, "I do not have the details. They had just learned of the abduction and were investigating. We will know more as soon as they do."

Nonsense. It would be hours. For whatever reason, and de-spite Desautel's promises, no one had been guarding the house.

Therefore constables would have to make their way to the house, question her family, examine the scene, organize a search party... it would be hours before anyone reported back to the constabulary with news.

Hours.

Which one of her sisters had been taken? It didn't matter. She had to find a way to get back home, help with the search before...

Her eyes closed tightly, but that only made the images in her mind more vivid as she remembered the three A'lle who had been found.

Her hands began to shake and she quickly returned the cup to the table. A horse. Or a small sled. If she drove all night, she could be home by morning.

She could have been home now, if Desautel had let her go.

The thought formed and was released as useless.

Which sister?

Her family...

And only then did the thought finally occur to her. She looked around again for Desautel, but the chief investigator was still conspicuous by his absence. All she had was the magistrate, who had taken a personal interest in her during her training—though she had no doubt that it was for his own political reasons—and the three strangers he had brought with him, men who, despite their disparity in age and looks, reminded her chillingly of Renaud and Dallaire.

She stood up abruptly, startling the magistrate.

"Investigator A'lle...?"

Ignoring him, she walked out of the parlor and into the hallway, heading for the kitchen, certain that was where she would find Desautel and Murphy. But before she reached the kitchen door, she passed the door to Madame Maillet's private quarters. It was slightly ajar and light spilled from it.

She paused when she came abreast of the door, aware that the magistrate had followed her into the hallway. Then she heard the deep tones of Desautel's voice, and she pushed open the door and found herself in a small sitting room.

It was furnished with two overstuffed wing chairs upholstered in a tapestry-like fabric. Each one had a matching footstool. A small table stood between the chairs, upon which was a reading lamp and a small stack of books. Constance spied a bookmark peering out of the top one. Behind the chairs was the only window in the room, now obscured with drapes patterned in a rich blue and yellow, to match the colors of the chairs. Another door, presumably leading to Madame Maillet's bed chamber, stood closed to her right. Aside from a few photographs on the wall and a bookshelf against the wall on either side of the doorway in which she stood, the only other piece of furniture in the tiny room was a long, narrow table and a dainty white wooden chair at the far end of the room, opposite to the bed chamber door. On the table stood a pile of writing paper and envelopes, a nib pen and an inkwell, and another telephone.

Desautel sat at the table, his back to the door, talking on the telephone. Murphy stood next to him, jotting down notes with a pencil in his notebook as Desautel spoke.

Murphy looked up as she entered. Glancing over his shoulder to see if Desautel had noticed, he walked over to Constance.

"Who is he speaking to?" she asked.

"Someone named Louis," whispered Murphy. "I take it he works for the chief investigator."

Constance nodded and edged past the constable so that she stood next to Desautel. He sat with the heavy black telephone receiver tucked between his ear and his shoulder and was busy writing something down on Madame Maillet's rose-edged writing paper. The nib of the pen scratched as he quickly jotted down notes.

He glanced up awkwardly at her. Finally he blinked. "One moment, Louis," he said. He set the pen down, then placed his hand over the mouthpiece and pulled the telephone away from his ear.

She could not read the expression on his face.

"Where are my parents?" she asked.

Desautel stared up at her. "Your parents?"

"Are they at the house?" she asked. "Or have they gone after my sister?"

The chief investigator blinked up at her, clearly puzzling out her words. At last his expression cleared. "Oh."

At once, he turned back to the telephone.

"Louis, where are Monsieur and Madame A'lle?"

He listened in silence for long minutes. When next he spoke, his voice was cold and hard. "Listen very carefully, Louis. I want a permanent detail assigned to the remaining A'lle siblings. I want the elder A'lle found and brought back. While they can find their daughter more quickly than we can, they are in as much danger as she is. Be quiet," he said firmly, clearly interrupting the other man. "Their skill is not in question."

He looked up at Constance before adding, "We will be returning tonight." Then he hung up.

He stood up and the little room felt suddenly much smaller.

"The Monteal constabulary will lend us their sled," he said. "We can leave as soon as it arrives."

A great weight lifted from Constance's chest and she nodded. She would be home tonight.

"Sir, which sister...?"

Desautel looked her in the eye and this time, she recognized the expression in them. It was horror.

"Prudence," he said. "They took Prudence."

* * *

"I'm sorry, Médéric, but I need her here."

Desautel straightened from the leather overnight case on the bed. He had very little to pack, really. His shaving kit, his toiletries, the extra shirt, and the long johns. Unfortunately, he had not brought a sheepskin coat or the right boots for an all-night ride in a sled.

The magistrate sat on the straight chair by the window, watching him pack. They had been arguing for five minutes, each one trying to outdo the other's reasons for wanting Constance A'lle with him. Desautel wondered how she would feel knowing that she was being fought over like a prize at a penny arcade.

He had known Felix Latendresse for over forty years. They had been at grade school together and had studied law together at McGill. After two years, however, Felix had decided he would rather enforce the law than argue it and began his career in law enforcement as a constable in Lachine. As Desautel climbed the rungs until he owned his own law practice, so did Felix climb the rungs of his own profession until he became the magistrate, almost coming full circle to the study of law.

It had been Felix's idea for Desautel to join the constabulary as an investigator when Françoise died.

They had been friends for four decades, and for four decades they had argued over the proper course to take. But in this matter, Desautel was in deadly earnest. He turned to face his old friend.

"You have a copy of my notes. You have Constable Murphy, who has proven himself an able assistant in this matter. You may draw from the entire contingent of the the Montreal constabulary. Surely you won't begrudge me one investigator."

"She is an A'lle investigator," Felix pointed out calmly. His reflection in the window waved a hand, matching his movement. "I want her with me for the same reason you brought her with you. She can speak to her own people in their own language."

Yes. Well apparently not as well as one would have hoped, judging by the reaction of Clémence A'lle.

Felix's idea of incorporating A'lle into the Baudry region constabulary was revolutionary. Dangerous, almost. Yet, if it worked, it would ease the tensions between the A'lle and constabularies throughout Lower Canada. Just knowing that an A'lle could become a constable, or an investigator... It was a good idea. A difficult one to implement, but a good idea.

"If it were you, Felix, would you allow anyone to keep you away from your family?" Too late, he realized what he had said. Felix, too, had lost his wife. They'd never had any children, so that he had thrown himself even more fully into his work. He had no family to speak of.

"She is an investigator," said Felix coolly. "Her duty is to assist me in this investigation. The St. Vincent constabulary will find her sister."

And there it was, the crux of the problem. Felix, as wise an old politician as he was, did not understand just how alone A'lle were here. They could only really count on each other. Humans had betrayed them too often.

Constance could no more believe that her fellow constables would rush to her family's rescue than she could fully trust Desautel before she 'read' him. She was right. He had given her no reason to trust him. None of them had.

"Felix," he said slowly, "don't do this. If you try to keep her away, she will resign and you will have lost your only A'lle investigator." He could have tried to explain the insight he had just gained but there was no time. His friend would have to trust his judgment on this matter.

Felix closed his mouth and Desautel thought he heard his teeth clack. The magistrate watched him out of narrowed, suspicious eyes. Finally he sighed.

"Very well. I should know better than to argue with a lawyer."

Desautel grinned and finished putting his dirty socks in the bag. Then he closed it with a snap and set the bag down on the floor by the foot of the bed. He sat down on the side of the bed, as Felix had the only chair. The two eyed each other in silence. Finally Felix spoke.

"Do you really believe that McReady is involved in the A'lle disappearances?"

Desautel glanced at the door, even though he had closed it himself. These were not allegations to be made lightly, or in the presence of any but the most trusted person.

"I don't know." He shrugged. "At the very least, the man displayed a criminal dereliction of duty, which may have led to more deaths." He shook his head and thought again about the names on the scribbled list John A'lle had given him. Only now, they knew there were many more than the eight recorded on the list.

"Use Constable Murphy," he said in a low voice. "He's a good man. I am convinced he knew nothing of the disappearances and murders. He can recommend others in the constabulary who are trustworthy. I wouldn't share information with McReady, just in case."

Felix shook his head and looked down at the floor. His bald head gleamed dully in the overhead light. "It's an ugly business, Médéric. I don't like thinking that one of us could..."

Desautel nodded, even though Felix still had his gaze fixed on his feet.

"Go back to..." Desautel pulled his notebook from his bag and riffled through the pages until he found the right one. "...Amanda A'lle. She seemed to know about a number of other A'lle who had gone missing. There's a common thread here somewhere, Felix, but I just can't find it."

His frustration must have been evident because Felix looked up at last with sympathy in his eyes. "We'll find the bastards, Médéric. I brought my three best investigators. Between them and your constable Murphy, we'll find out what's going on. And I'll personally see to Chief Investigator Alastair McReady."

☙ TWENTY-SIX ❧

THE temperature dropped with every mile they drove. Constance eventually donned her gloves and closed her sheepskin coat, but she refused to put her hat on. The chief investigator, on the other hand, was buried under a heavy wolf pelt, with only his eyes peering above it. Of necessity, he spoke very little, which suited her.

With every mile closer to St-Vincent, she grew angrier.

They had taken Prudence.

Every hour they had her increased the chances that she would end up dead. Prudence's only hope was that Mother and Father could find her. Perhaps they already had.

She didn't know if that thought was any better. Her parents did not know how to fight. No A'lle did. It was against their nature. How could her parents rescue Prudence? It was more likely that they, too, were now prisoners of those two murderers.

Or dead.

The moon shone out of a clear sky, reflecting off the snow and lighting their way. It took nearly an hour to reach the outskirts of Montreal, and then another half-hour to leave behind the last of the straggling businesses and liveries. After a while, all they saw was the occasional lighted window in a farmhouse far down a long

road. Then they left the farms behind or it grew so late that everyone was in bed.

They stopped occasionally to let the horses rest and feed them
a little. Normally the trip would take only four hours, but it was
night and it was cold. Thankfully, the road was hard-packed and
mostly smooth.

Prudence might be dead by the time they reached St-Vincent.

"They will not kill her," came Desautel's muffled voice, startling her. She looked at him.

"They have killed every A'lle they have taken." Although they
had found only three bodies to date, it was logical to assume all the
missing ones were dead, too.

Desautel pulled the heavy pelt away from his mouth and chin.
His breath plumed out. "They need her alive."

Constance frowned at him. "I failed to do as the Ferret said,"
she explained, wondering if the cold had addled his brains. "He
told me they would take one of my sisters if I failed. And he did."

Desautel watched her out of those blue eyes that missed so
very little.

"It is not in their interest to kill her," he said. "They need a hostage while we chase them. They will only kill her if they get away."

Constance blinked at him, considering his words. At last she
decided that his logic was sound. Prudence was of more value to
them alive than dead. The knowledge gave her comfort, as did the
realization that Desautel had not sought to give her false hope.

Of course, if the Ferret had her parents, as well, he might
choose to kill one or two of his hostages in the interests of expedi-
ency. If she were in his place, she would kill Father, so that he
could not attack them. The Ferret did not know that the A'lle did
not fight.

Except for her.

She turned back to the road, willing the horses to go faster.

* * *

It was still four hours til dawn by the time Desautel pulled on the leads and the horses slowed to a stop, then stood quietly with their heads drooping. The A'lle girl jumped off the sled and walked around to the stable door. Before she could touch it, however, the wide door opened, spilling light on the trampled snow in the court-yard behind the St-Vincent constabulary.

A boy stood in the doorway, blond hair rumpled with sleep and with straw sticking to his clothes.

"I've been waiting for you," said John Lambert.

Desautel smiled and slowly climbed down the sled. His hips were stiff from sitting so long. And from the cold. "I expected no less of you, Mr. Lambert," he replied.

But the stable boy had already handed the lantern to Constance A'lle and was examining the horses with a critical eye. Finally he looked up at Desautel.

"That was a long ride." There was a note close to censure in his voice. In the uncertain light of the alley, his grey eyes looked almost white.

"It was necessary," said Desautel. "Let's get them inside. They deserve a good feed and a rest."

John Lambert glanced over his shoulder at Constance A'lle, then back at Desautel.

"You go on in, sir. I've got this."

Without a word, Constance A'lle handed him the lantern and headed for the back door to the constabulary. It was normally locked from the outside at night, but this night was different and it opened under her touch. Desautel nodded his thanks at the boy and followed her inside.

The door opened onto a dimly-lit landing, with a staircase to the left leading down into a storage area for items not in use by the constabulary, such as bicycles, and the file morgue. The staircase on the right led to a closed door that opened onto the duty room. Constance opened the door and stood blinking in the light. Desautel gave her a gentle nudge to get her moving again and she took an uncertain step in.

He glanced at her as he eased past and was startled to see tears in her eyes. The he noticed the furious blinking and realized that the light had blinded her. It seemed a serious disadvantage to him that she could so easily be blinded, simply by entering a lit room.

But then again, she could see extremely well in the dark, where he stumbled along like a blind man.

"Maître!"

He turned to see Louis bearing down on him. His assistant's light brown curls were dishevelled, revealing the thinning at the top of his head, and his eyes were bloodshot.

There were only two other people in the duty room: a young constable recently graduated from the academy and a sergeant from day shift who had to be at least sixty-five. Morgan, Desautel remembered. Both men turned in their direction and Morgan nodded respectfully. Desautel nodded in return and turned back to his assistant.

"Hello, Louis." He knew his voice retained some of the coldness he had felt for the man during their last conversation. Louis had actually tried to talk him out of assigning constables to protecting the A'lle. For a moment during that conversation, Louis had reminded Desautel of McReady, not an association he wanted with anyone who worked for him.

Whatever Louis had been about to say, he clearly thought the better of it. He came to a stop a few feet from Desautel, his mouth pressed down, keeping the words in.

Desautel wondered what he must look like, to stop his assistant in his tracks like that. But then he realized Louis was looking at Constance A'lle. He glanced over his shoulder at her.

He had never seen an expression like that on anyone. It stopped the breath in his throat, stealing his own words.

"Tell me," she said, staring at Louis. Her face looked carved in marble.

Desautel prepared to intervene as soon as his assistant opened his mouth but to his surprise, Louis took a deep breath and forged ahead.

"No sign of your sister," he said bluntly. "But we caught up with your parents a mile out of town. We have them and the rest of your family here at the constabulary. They are in the kitchen." He glanced at Desautel. "Sergeant Morgan felt it would be safer for them."

Without a word, Constance turned and headed toward the back of the duty room and the door that lead to the kitchen.

Desautel watched her thread her way past the desks for a moment then turned to his assistant.

"Report."

"Sergeant Morgan called in all the shifts, sir. It took a little while to organize," he added apologetically. "He placed men on all the roads out of St-Vincent. We've had men knocking at doors all night long, checking with the livery stables, getting citizens out of bed to check their private stables. He widened the pattern out to the nearest farms." Louis shook his head. "Nothing, sir."

"Nothing yet, Louis," said Desautel firmly. "These men are not ghosts. We will find them. What of Mr. and Mrs. A'lle? Where they able to say where their daughter is?"

Louis' gaze dropped. "They won't speak to us, sir."

A great ball of despair settled in Desautel's chest. Was it possible that they would not find Prudence in time? He shook off the feeling, recognizing the danger. There would be time for grief later, after he had done everything in his power to rescue the young woman.

* * *

Constance pushed open the door to the kitchen and to her intense relief, her family turned to look at her.

Her siblings sat at the long refectory table, on benches. Mother sat in a hard wooden chair at one end of the table. She looked up at Constance, her gaze filled with misery and anger.

A movement at the window caught Constance's eye and she glanced over to see Father standing there. Confused, she looked back at the table and realized that the man she had seen sitting there was Roland A'lle. Of course. In her anxiety to get home, she had completely forgotten that he had come to St. Vincent. She nodded at him and he nodded back gravely. There was a vast pain in his eyes and she turned away, unable to deal with it now. She looked around at Father.

The expression on his face stole her breath away. His eyes were narrowed and his lips pressed tightly together. There were lines bracketing his mouth that she had never seen before.

She was no longer certain that he was incapable of violence.

"When was she taken?" asked Constance to the room in general.

Eloise rose from the bench and stepped over it to come stand in front of her.

"About seven hours ago," she said grimly. Her hair was pulled back in an untidy braid and her normally thin face looked drawn under the electric lights. She wore her heavy canvas pants and work boots with her favorite shirt, a fine cotton, long-sleeved one with a cornflower pattern that mother had made for her last birthday.

"We were all in the sitting room," said Mother. "With Roland. She had gone to the kitchen to check on the chicken."

Eloise nodded. "We found the door to the back open. Her boots were gone. We think she went to get wood for the cookstove, and that's when she was taken."

"We went after her," said Mother. "As soon as we realized." There was a brittleness in her voice that frightened Constance. Gemma's hand stole out to cover Mother's.

"They brought us back," said Father, a deep rage in his voice. "As if we were children running away from home. My daughter is gone and they treat us like prisoners!"

Constance swallowed. She did not want to tell them that she was glad the constables had caught up to them and brought them back. "Where is she?"

The muscles along Father's jaw stood out as he grit his teeth.

It was Eloise who answered.

"She's in Backli's Ford."

Backli's Ford. Again, Backli's Ford.

"Did you tell them?" Constance nodded at the door, beyond which was the common room.

The silence stretched on for a few seconds before Roland A'lle spoke. "No. We did not know whom to trust."

* * *

Prudence awoke to a darkness so profound even her A'lle eyes could not penetrate it. Her head throbbed to the beat of her heart. A smell of dampness pervaded the air, along with mustiness and the faint, unmistakeable stink of death, but there was also a breath of fresh air, as if through a badly sealed crack. There were no sounds that she could hear.

She was lying on her side on something cold and she tried to push herself up to a more comfortable postion. It was only then that she realized her hands and feet were bound. A cloth covered her mouth and was tied tightly behind her head. It tasted of old sweat and she gagged, barely controlling the urge to throw up.

❧ TWENTY-SEVEN ❦

THE last few miles into Backli's Ford were traveled without the benefit of moonlight, but the lightening of the sky in the east promised more light soon.

It didn't matter to Constance. She was able to see well enough to tell that there was no way of discerning who had been on the road before the twelve constables, Bérubé, the chief investigator, and herself. There were hoof marks and sled tracks, but it was impossible to tell how old they were.

The chief's right hand man, Bérubé, and his men had returned to St. Vincent yesterday morning, having found no traces of the Ferret and his partner. Constance avoided looking at him, afraid that her thoughts would be plain on her face.

They rode in silence, with only the thudding of the horses' hooves and the swooshing of the sled's skis filling the night air. Bérubé and Constance rode on either side of the sled while the rest of the constables followed. The chief investigator drove the sled they had borrowed from Montreal, but with fresh horses.

The stable boy had had to send to a nearby livery stable to borrow another three horses, as the constabulary did not have enough to fill the need.

Constance glanced at the sled, and its silent driver. She hadn't asked Desautel why he had taken the Montreal sled. It was bigger than the one at the St-Vincent constabulary. The last time that one had been used, it had taken home the bodies of Renaud and Dallaire, while Frederick's body had traveled on the innkeeper's sled. Had someone returned it to Thomas and Marie Pelletier? She couldn't remember seeing it in the stables.

When they reached the spot where Renaud and Dallaire had been killed and she went over the cliff, Bérubé crossed himself.

Half an hour later, they rode into Backli's Ford with the sky rosy with impending sunrise. The village stirred with signs of life: an occasional lit window, a young boy fetching wood, a dog trotting down the center of the main street.

Desautel pulled the sled to a stop in front of the Bartolomée Inn and draped the leads loosely around the brake. He clambered down stiffly, and Constance dismounted as well to tie her mare's reins to the seat of the sled. The horse snorted and Constance fished through her pockets for the last of the dried apples the stable boy had given her. The mare plucked it daintily from her palm and crunched down on the treat.

"You men stay here," Bérubé ordered as he dismounted and tied off his own roan to the sled.

Then she, Desautel and Bérubé walked up the snow-packed walk and climbed the steps to the porch. Before Desautel could knock on the front door, it opened to reveal Thomas Pelletier in a pair of gray wool pants held up by suspenders and a wrinkled nightshirt stuffed into them.

His hair stood out on either side of his head, but he smiled in welcome until he saw the men on horseback on the street.

"Chief Investigator," he said, stepping back. "Come in out of the cold. Will your men be coming in, too?"

Desautel stepped inside and moved aside to allow Constance and Bérubé to enter behind him.

"Non," said Desautel. "Nor are we staying," he added as the innkeeper closed the door behind them.

A noise caused them all to look up. Madame Pelletier stood at the top of the stairs, a dressing gown wrapped tightly around her round body. Her hair hung over her shoulder in a loose braid. She looked down at them, clearly aware that something was wrong.

"Shall I put the kettle on?" she asked.

Desautel spoke for all of them. "Thank you, madame, but we are not staying. I apologize for dragging you out of your beds but we have ridden all night in pursuit of two men who have kidnapped a young woman. Have you seen any strangers in town?" he asked.

Madame Pelletier blinked in confusion and glanced at her husband. Thomas Pelletier's mouth was set in a grim line and he was looking at Constance.

"The same two...?" he asked her. She nodded and he visibly braced himself. "And the girl...?"

"My sister. Prudence." Her voice came out low and tight.

"Oh, my dear!" said Marie Pelletier. She came down the stairs, her slippers making soft slapping sounds on the carpeted treads. "When? How?"

"Madame." The chief investigator reclaimed their attention. "Have there been strangers about in the last few days? Monsieur Pelletier, have you seen either of the two men who accosted you on the road last week?"

But both of them shook their heads. "Nothing since your people left yesterday." He nodded at Bérubé, whose face reddened.

Constance looked away. She knew him for a capable investigator and an honorable man. She believed he had searched as well as he could for the two men, but the Ferret had made his way to Montreal on the train with her and Desautel, leaving behind the big man. How difficult could it be to find a stranger in a small village like Backli's Ford?

"Very well," said Desautel. "My men will search every house in this village. Starting with this inn, if you will permit, Monsieur Pelletier."

The request was polite but his blue eyes looked unapologetically at the innkeeper and his wife. Madame Pelletier's mouth grew stern and she and her husband exchanged a glance before turning to look at the chief investigator.

"We have nothing to hide," he said stiffly. "Search all you want."

Constance almost felt bad for these two kind souls, but then she remembered that Prudence was somewhere in Backli's Ford.

Which meant that someone in Backli's Ford harbored murderers and fugitives.

She would search every attic and cellar in this village if she had to.

* * *

When they returned outside, Constance was momentarily blinded by the sunlight so that she missed the arrival of the old man who ran the general store. She couldn't remember his name. One of the men still on horseback directed him to the chief investigator and they met where the front walk met the street.

"Monsieur Patenaude," said Desautel in greeting. "How can I help you?"

The merchant had slipped his boots on but hadn't taken the time to fasten them. His wispy gray hair stuck out at odd angles from under his cap and he had rushed out of his store with only a sweater covering his cotton shirt. Still, he seemed unaware of the cold as he shuffled toward the chief investigator.

"Monsieur Desautel," said the old man. "There is an urgent phone call for you."

Desautel nodded, his face calm.

"Jean," he said, turning to Bérubé, "start the search at the inn. Spread out from here. Never fewer than two to a house."

"Oui, Maître," said Bérubé, immediately taking charge. As he walked over to the men waiting on horseback, Constance watched in dismay as Desautel crossed the street with the old merchant. Bérubé had already tried and failed in Backli's Ford. Why was the chief investigator giving him another chance?

"Constance."

She turned to find Bérubé looking at her and the rest of the constables spreading out to the houses across the street. He had never before called her by her given name. "Yes?"

"You and I are starting with the inn."

She nodded. "Yes."

*　*　*

Prudence could not rest on her back, nor could she sit up. Every time she tried, the world spun around her and she wanted to throw up. It became harder and harder to breathe as she struggled to keep from gagging on the cloth.

The darkness seemed to be easing and by that, she suspected that she had first awakened at night but now night was passing.

Where was she?

Father had told them about the abductions in Montreal. And the bodies. Was this how it happened? Did it start with waking up in a dank cellar? If that was where she was?

The details of the deaths floated through her mind and she shuddered at the thought of having her eyes removed, or her heart.

The trembling started in the pit of her stomach and spread to her limbs as fear took hold of her but before she could give way to panic, she had a sudden memory of Médéric Desautel sitting at her table, eating her pie, his eyes tired but his smile warm as his gaze lingered on her. The thought of the chief investigator braced her and pushed the panic away.

He could have sent someone else to the house that night to tell them Constance was safe, but he had come himself.

He would come for her.

Comforted, she tried to relax by taking deep breaths. Her heart still beat too fast and she was losing feeling in her hands, but if she focused deeply, she could turn her attention to St. Vincent.

There.

Gemma's steady blue flame appeared in the vast darkness, followed by Patience's fiery orange and Felicity's green flame. And there—there was Eloise's deep red, and the bonfire that was Mother and Father.

A trickle of unease crept through her. Where was Constance? She expanded her search and to her surprise, found Constance's bright white flame in Backli's Ford. Only then did Prudence realize where she was. She was in Backli's Ford, too. How long had she been unconscious? She remembered going out to the woodpile to fetch a load for the cookstove, then a sharp, bright pain at the back of her head.

Someone had hit her, clearly, but why bring her to Backli's Ford?

❧ TWENTY-EIGHT ❧

CONSTANCE and Bérubé were still searching the top floor of the inn when Madame Pelletier called them to the stairs.

"Monsieur Desautel wants you," she said and stepped aside to let them run down the stairs. They hurriedly donned their boots and walked out onto the porch in time to see the chief investigator crossing the street.

"He has something," said Bérubé, almost to himself.

Constance's heart leapt in hope but then she caught sight of the chief investigator's grim expression.

She was down the porch stairs before she even knew she was moving.

"What is it?" she demanded.

He didn't even pause as he reached the walk. "Bérubé, carry on the searches," he ordered. He looked at Constance. "You're with me."

She fell into step behind him, alarmed. "Where are we going?"

"To speak to Père Noiron."

The priest. Constance stretched out her legs to match the chief investigator's pace. What had Desautel learned about the priest?

By then they were turning into the church's front walk and

from there down the sidewalk to the rectory. Desautel climbed the three steps to the rectory door and knocked firmly. Constance stood on the bottom step, waiting. She could not have said a word if she had wanted to.

A woman with an imperious nose and jet-black hair in a severe bun answered the chief investigator's knock. Desautel, standing on the stoop, removed his cap.

"Bonjour, Madame," he began politely.

The woman frowned, her glance jumping immediately to Constance.

"Do you know what time it is?" asked the woman sharply. "It is barely seven o'clock."

And yet she was fully dressed, in a black dress and a white apron. This then would be the priest's housekeeper. Constance could not recall the woman's name, if she ever knew it.

"Oui, Madame." Desautel smiled, which only elicited another frown. "However, we need to see Père Noiron right away."

"Come back in an hour," she said and would have closed the door on them if not for Desautel's arm shooting out to bar the door from closing.

The housekeeper took a step back, startled and no doubt alarmed. Constance schooled her features to reveal none of her surprise. She had not known the older man had such quick reflexes.

"Madame," he said, without a smile this time. "I must insist."

"What is it, Madame Demers?" came the priest's voice from the back of the house.

Before the woman could speak, Desautel raised his voice.

"Chief Investigator Médéric Desautel, of the Baudry Region," he said loudly. "I have a few questions for you, mon père."

Constance braced herself for what was to come.

The sound of footsteps approaching heralded the priest's arrival and Père Noiron nodded to his housekeeper to step back. When she did, after giving Desautel a reproving look, the priest opened the door wider. Only then did he see Constance. His face grew stony.

"Would you like to come in, Chief Investigator?"

"Thank you," said Desautel, stepping over the lintel.

Constance made a move to follow the chief investigator, but the priest moved quickly to bar her way.

"You must wait outside."

His bare hand was braced on the door frame. All she would have to do was reach out and touch him. Then the door opened wider and Desautel stepped close to the priest. His face was red beneath the stubble and there were lined circles beneath his eyes. With his hair dishevelled from removing the cap, he looked old.

And yet the look he gave the priest shook her in a way she did not understand. She almost stepped back from the fury in his gaze.

"I believe you have met Investigator Constance A'lle," he said, his voice cold. "She also represents the Magistrate of the Baudry Region. Are you attempting to bar her from her duty?"

Constance was not sure she could have stood up under the onslaught of the chief investigator's rage. Yet the priest did not flinch. From her position on the lower step, he seemed impossibly tall. Despite the shaggy mane of gray hair and his black robe, he seemed warrior-like. His pale eyes could have struck a spark on flint.

"This is a house of God." He faced Desautel. "I will not allow the godless within its walls to defile it."

The priest had to be cold, standing in the open doorway. Yet he did not shiver, did not shrink. He filled the doorway with his forbidding presence, daring the devil to breach his defences.

He believed her godless, and he would fight to keep her out of the house of his God.

And yet he had saved her life.

"Then we shall speak outside, Père Noiron, if you would care to fetch your coat."

Outside? Were they not going to search the church and rectory?

The priest stared at Desautel for a moment, then at Constance. He nodded, agreeing to the compromise. A moment later, they stood on the narrow walk.

Desautel was not a short man, yet the priest towered over him by half a head.

"Have you heard of the A'lle disappearances in Montreal?" asked Desautel. Constance glanced at him, but the chief investigator was staring at the priest.

"Yes," nodded Père Noiron. "The archbishop has informed us and asked us to reach out to the A'lle in our congregation."

Constance's lips tightened against a sigh. The thought of Père Noiron ministering to the A'lle beggared the imagination.

"Père Noiron," said Desautel, "when was the last time you were in Montreal?"

The priest looked as surprised as Constance felt. Why was the chief investigator asking about this? What did it matter?

"Last week," replied the priest. "Why?" His eyes had taken on a hooded look, as if he wished to hide what he was thinking. Constance found herself leaning forward slightly.

"When last week?"

Père Noiron shifted from foot to foot, as if his feet were getting cold, but Desautel waited patiently, unmoving. Unlike the priest in his long woollen overcoat, the chief investigator wore a thick sheepskin coat, with his fur-lined cap and warm mittens. He could outwait the priest.

Finally Père Noiron crossed his arms over his broad chest. "Last Tuesday. I have a monthly meeting with the archbishop of Montreal."

"And when did you return?"

The priest blinked slowly, then looked at the door to the rectory. "I returned the following day, on Wednesday," he said calmly. He looked back at Desautel, expectantly.

Constance took a deep breath. Wednesday. The priest had returned on Wednesday.

"And how did you travel, mon père?" asked Desautel softly.

Père Noiron smiled slightly. "By train, of course."

"From St-Vincent to Montreal, no doubt," agreed Desautel. "And from Backli's Ford to St-Vincent and back?"

"Monsieur Henderson kindly allows me to use his horse for these monthly trips," replied the priest. "And the archdiocese pays for the mare's stabling in St-Vincent."

Desautel nodded. "And on your trip back from Montreal," he asked gently, "did you see Frederick A'lle on the train?"

And there it was.

The priest was silent for a long moment. Finally he nodded.

"And did you see him get off in St-Vincent?"

This time, the nod was very slight. Constance's breath grew quick with anticipation. He had seen Frederick.

"And what did he do when once he arrived in St-Vincent?" The chief investigator asked the question as if it were part of an idle discussion about the weather.

The expression on Père Noiron's face changed subtly and he sighed, for all the world as if a great weight had been lifted from him.

"I saw him at the stables, where I had left Mr. Henderson's mare. He was renting a horse."

"And then?"

"And then he left," said the priest. He glanced toward the cemetery with its snow-shrouded headstones.

Constance itched to clamp a hand on his cheek and read him. Frustration flooded through her at the thought. All that would tell her was how he felt, not what he knew.

Desautel stared at the priest as though looking alone would draw the words out of him.

"What about on the train?" he asked softly.

The priest remained silent. Constance had to fight down an overwhelming urge to shake the man. He knew something, something that might help her find Prudence. She glanced at the chief investigator but his gaze was focused on the priest and for a moment, she saw the lawyer he had once been superimposed on the lawman. Both professions were but facets of the same coin.

And then the words tumbled out her, without her volition, startling the priest and the chief investigator no less than herself, but once started, she could not stop.

"I believe you are a good man," she said, looking up at the priest. "Despite the fact that you believe me evil, you saved my life." She took a deep breath. "My sister is missing." He frowned, clearly surprised, but she continued without giving him a chance to speak. "She was taken from our home in St-Vincent and we believe she is here in Backli's Ford. Please, Père Noiron. If you know something about these disappearances, even a little thing, please tell us."

She looked at him steadily, hoping he would hear the plea of her heart, hoping he would rise above his prejudice. She grew aware of Desautel's gaze on her but kept staring at the priest.

"Mon père?" prompted Desautel finally.

A light wind had picked up with the rising of the sun, fresh to Constance but raising blooms in the men's cheeks. The priest began to shiver in his inadequate great coat and he shoved those big hands of his in the pockets. The tips of his ears were beginning to turn white. Out of the corner of her eye, Constance caught the housekeeper peering out of the rectory window.

"I saw him on the train," he finally said. "He seemed to be watching a man."

Constance glanced at Desautel.

"And?"

"Once we arrived in St. Vincent, the boy asked directions to the nearest stable, which was of course where I stabled Monsieur Henderson's mare. He paid and saddled the horse quickly and left before I did." He glanced from Constance to Desautel. "I believe he meant to follow the man."

"Did you see where the man went?" asked Constance before the chief investigator could.

The priest nodded. He hesitated barely a moment, then looked down at the ground. "Yes," he said, his voice low. "He got into a sled. There he was joined by two men, rough-looking sorts. A very tall one who laughed too much and a shorter one who looked sour. I had seen them on the train earlier. They clearly knew each other but acted as if they did not know the man. Yet once they were in St-Vincent, they all drove away together."

The pause that followed was filled with too many emotions for Constance to identify. Thankfully, Desautel broke it by asking, "Who was the man, mon père?"

The priest sighed a great sigh, one filled with regret and pain and sorrow. "Docteur Saunders."

❧ TWENTY-NINE ❧

CONSTANCE turned and ran, not waiting for the chief investigator. She turned left at the church gates and almost tripped on the dog. He jumped out of the way in time and woofed in greeting.

"Hello, boy," she greeted then turned toward the doctor's house. Behind her sounded three sharp whistles and she glanced over her shoulder to see Desautel standing in front of the church gates. He was looking away from her, toward the homes across the street. Within seconds, heads popped out of doors as the St-Vincent constables recognized Desautel's call for attention.

"To me!" yelled Desautel, and a moment later, Bérubé came running up to the chief investigator.

Constance didn't wait. She ran toward the doctor's house, the mutt by her side, and up to his porch two steps at a time. She banged on the door and tried the handle. Locked.

"Docteur!" she yelled. Then she turned and ran around the porch to the back of the house and banged on the back door.

She didn't know what to believe. Père Noiron seemed to imply that the doctor knew the two ruffians, whose description exactly matched that given by Thomas Pelletier. It also matched what she knew of the two men who had tried to kill her in the cemetery. But if they were the same men, what was the doctor doing with them? The priest had said that Frederick was following the doctor, not the two men. As if he had recognized him.

The priest had to be wrong.

The house remained resolutely silent and dark and Constance wanted to scream her frustration. She was about to kick at the handle when Desautel and Bérubé came running around the corner.

"Move aside," ordered Bérubé and without waiting for her to obey, he pushed her aside. The dog skittered out of the way of his big boots. Before she could get angry, the sergeant raised his foot and kicked the door in. Pulling a baton out of his coat, he led the way inside, followed by Constance and Desautel.

From inside the house came the sound of the front door splintering open as more constables battered it down.

The mutt had stayed outside, on the porch. She looked back at him, aware that he was whining in distress.

The sounds of half a dozen men in boots filled the doctor's little house and Constance knew they would not find the doctor. He was gone. She glanced out the back door again, past the mutt to the trampled snow in the back yard.

There were fresh tracks in the snow, leading to the fence beyond the stone shed. She took in the whole scene—the path to the shed, the large back yard that shared a forged iron fence with the church on one side and a tall picket fence at the back and on the other side, and the snowshoe tracks from the hunt for the two men who had attacked her.

And in her mind's eye, she saw the two men emerge from the doctor's back door, look around furtively and quickly fasten their snowshoes only to clamber over the fence and disappear into the night.

Her heart sank.

What she had taken for Docteur Saunders' clumsy attempts at showshoeing had been the tracks of the two men confusing their trail before going over the fence and into the woods.

The doctor. He had hidden the men after they had killed Renaud and Dallaire, and after they had attacked her in the church yard. But why?

Was he being coerced?

"What is it?" said Desautel next to her and she jumped in alarm. The mutt barked a warning at the chief investigator and she put out a hand to let him know it was all right.

"He's gone, isn't he?" she said.

Desautel nodded grimly.

"They must have forced him to go with them," she said. Desautel gave her a look under lowered brows.

The mutt whined again and trotted a few feet toward the shed. Desautel turned to look at him for a moment, then climbed down the porch. From inside the house came Bérubé's voice calling for the chief investigator. Constance ignored him and followed Desautel toward the shed.

A few feet from the small stone building, he turned to look at her and placed a finger against his lips to indicate silence. Constance looked beyond him and only then did she see what he had noticed.

The lock was gone from the door.

Her heart rate sped up and her mouth parted. She looked around for a weapon but she didn't even have a baton like Bérubé's.

It didn't matter. Clearly reaching the same conclusion, Desautel stepped up to the door, and rearing back, kicked it open.

An empty can clattered to the floor of the shed, knocked off by the force of the door slamming against the shelves.

As Bérubé came running down the porch steps toward them, Constance and Desautel crowded the doorway to take in the sight of Prudence, gagged and bound on the same table where Frederick A'lle had lain dead only a few days ago. A pool of blood slowly spread around her from the knife sticking out of her chest.

* * *

The weight of her in his arms... Desautel tried not to think that she was a dead weight, but Prudence A'lle's head lolled back, exposing her blood-spattered neck, as if she were dead. Only the fact that blood still seeped from around the knife blade where it plunged into her chest allowed him to hope that she lived.

The world narrowed to a dark tunnel through which he carried the girl, seeking desperately for help.

She would die, if she wasn't already dead. She was A'lle, yes, but she was not indestructible. Frederick A'lle had died of his injuries...

The smell of blood filled his nose and all he heard was the sound of his heart laboring in his chest.

She would die.

A hand suddenly grasped his elbow and forced him to turn and only then did he realize he had reached the Bartolomée Inn. He obediently carried Prudence down the walk and up the stairs to the porch. Someone held the door open and he stumbled across the stoop, righting himself before he could drop his precious charge. A hand on his arm directed him toward the sitting room. He stopped when he reached the settee and automatically lowered her down until she rested on the padded surface.

As if releasing her were a signal of sorts, he suddenly became aware of voices all around him. He blinked and looked around. The Pelletiers, Constance, Bérubé, the old man from the general store, a few others he vaguely recognized from the last time he was in Backli's Ford.

Too many people. They were crowding the girl.

"All right," said Marie Pelletier firmly. "Thomas, set water to boiling and bring me my kit." She looked around and fixed her gaze on a short man with a shock of black hair. "Zacharie, go fetch the doctor. Monsieur Patenaude, upstairs in the hall closet, bring me blankets. Everyone else, out."

Thomas and Monsieur Patenaude hurried out the room to do her bidding, the third man, Zacharie, behind them. Constance caught his arm to stop him before he could leave.

"The doctor is not there," said Constance grimly. She moved close to the settee and looked down at her sister. "We must care for her ourselves." She looked around at the room. Her gaze landed on Desautel. "We must remove the knife."

Desautel swallowed and forced himself to look down at Prudence. Her long hair had come undone from its braid and now surrounded her too-white face like a dark halo. Her arms lay by her sides, hands curled slightly, like a child's hands in sleep. Someone had wrapped a towel around the knife hilt in her chest and it had turned red. Funny that, that her blood should be red like his.

Only the slight rise and fall of the knife hilt reassured him that she still lived.

"It will kill her," objected Bérubé. And Desautel knew this for the truth. He had seen other wounds like this, where the blade acted to stop the worst of the bleeding. Once removed, it allowed the blood to flow freely and abundantly until the wounded one died.

"He is right," said Desautel. He cleared his throat, which seemed constricted. "Her only hope is to bring her to St-Vincent."

Constance looked over her shoulder at him and he saw the same dark knowledge in her eyes as in his heart. Prudence A'lle would not survive a sled trip into St-Vincent.

"She is A'lle," said Constance. "She may yet live, but we must remove the knife so her body can heal itself."

Monsieur Patenaude returned bearing half a dozen woolen blankets and set them down on the horsehair chair.

"Maître!"

Constance A'lle's sharp voice started him out of his spiraling thoughts and he straightened his back.

"Very well," he said. "We will need to hold her down. Bérubé, pin her shoulders and arms down. Zacharie, please take her legs. Constance, help him. Pin her hips down. I will remove the knife." He turned to Marie Pelletier. "Madame, do you have a disinfectant? Strong liquor will do."

The woman nodded and bustled off to the kitchen, passing her husband in the doorway, who entered with a huge metal bowl full of steaming water and a pile of clean dishcloths hanging over his forearm. Pinned under one arm was a small case which presumably contained supplies for treating wounds.

Soon everyone was in place, except for Constance. She had found a pair of scissors somewhere and, working around Bérubé, cut open Prudence's blouse. Then, without hesitation, she cut open the bodice of the undershirt and spread it open, revealing Prudence A'lle's blood-soaked chest and the knife sticking out to the right of the breast bone.

The men blinked in silent discomfort, but Marie Pelletier immediately pushed Constance out of the way and began to clean the flesh around the injury. She poured liberally from a bottle of whiskey and wiped it clean. Fresh blood seeped around the wound and suddenly, Desautel was struck almost physically by the obscenity of it. He swallowed hard.

"Are we ready?" he asked gruffly.

Madame Pelletier stepped back and handed the bloody cloth to her husband, who immediately handed her a fresh dry one. She nodded at Desautel.

Without giving himself a chance to doubt, he grasped the hilt of the knife and pulled with one smooth, upward motion.

The knife came out with a sickening, sucking sound that would stay with him until the day he died. Prudence gasped and screamed, and would have bucked but for the three people holding her down. Then she stopped moving. At once blood welled out of the wound, rich and dark, carrying with it Prudence's life. Desautel glanced at her still, still face and swallowed hard. He could see no movement of air.

"Is she dead?" he asked.

"No." Constance pushed him out of the way and someone gently took the knife from his hands.

"Maître," said Bérubé at his elbow. Then, louder, "Maître."

Desautel could not seem to tear his gaze away from the work

Constance and Marie Pelletier were doing on Prudence's chest. The rich, copper smell of blood filled his nose.

"What?"

Bérubé took his elbow and gently turned him away from the bloody scene. Only then did he note that the old shopkeeper, Patenaude, and the other man, Zacharie, were still present, hovering by the door, watching the ministrations with grim faces. Desautel wanted them to leave, to not see the girl this way. He focused his gaze on his lieutenant. "What is it, Jean?"

"The doctor's house," said Bérubé. "There was a trap door in the bedroom. It led to a cellar. There were cots and dirty dishes. Someone was hiding there."

Desautel stared at Bérubé a moment longer and then the words penetrated. "Does the doctor own a horse?"

"Non," said Zacharie, shamelessly eavesdropping. He stepped up to them, turning his back on Prudence. "He rents a horse from the ferry master when he needs one."

Desautel considered his words. The ferry master, from whom the priest also rented a horse. "And does the ferry master rent a sled, as well?"

The other man nodded. "Yes. Sam Henderson keeps a small stable. He owns a cart, two sleds and a buggy that he rents out. He also keeps three horses. Most of his business is in the summer, when the ferry operates."

Desautel blinked at the man. The ferry. He had forgotten that Backli's Ford was located at the only safe ford for miles. The Bartolomée River was too fast for most of its course. From here, it was only a few short miles to the border of the United American States.

Had those men chosen Backli's Ford because it was close to the border? There was one road surrounded by brush and forest between the Bartolomée River and the nearest American town, Gideon's Reach, twenty miles away. Were these men based out of the American States? What of the doctor?

"I need to make a call," he said slowly. He turned to Bérubé. "Get the men together. We need to organize a search party. The starting point will be the doctor's back yard."

* * *

The bleeding finally slowed to a trickle. Constance and Madame Pelletier worked together to secure a thick pad over the wound, running a bandage around Prudence's shoulder and under the opposite arm, to knot over the pad.

Madame Pelletier took a corner of the last clean cloth and began to wash Prudence's face and neck, still splattered with blood. Beneath the blood, Prudence's flesh was ashen and cold to the touch. Constance went to the horsehair chair and grabbed the pile of blankets. She tucked all three over her sister and then went over to the fireplace and added another log. She was sweating from spending too much time by the fire, but Prudence would need heat if her body was not to spend precious resources trying to stay warm against the encroaching shock.

She would need every ounce of strength, every A'lle resource her body possessed to survive.

Finally Madame Pelletier straightened and looked around. The floor was covered in bloody cloths and bandages, not to mention the remains of Prudence's clothes.

"If she wakes," said Constance, "you must feed her."

Madame Pelletier allowed herself a small, humorless smile. "Yes. I recall." Her gray hair was dishevelled and there was a streak of blood on her cheek. Her hands were tinged pink up to her wrists and Constance had to look away.

"She must be kept warm," she continued. "For the moment, that is all you can do for her. That and food. She must do the rest."

"I will get Camille to help me," she said. "You stay with your sister."

But Constance shook her head. "Non, madame. I have done all I can for her." She took a deep, steadying breath and reached for her sheepskin coat, abandoned on the floor at the foot of the settee. "It's time to find whoever did this to her and the others."

❧ THIRTY ❧

"THEY crossed the river," said Bérubé when Constance and the chief investigator emerged from the trees.

Desautel had ordered part of his constables to stay behind in Backli's Ford and continue the search, just in case. He had called Montreal and finally located the magistrate, who promised to call his counterpart in New Amsterdam and have them send reinforcements from Gideon's Reach. Then he, Constance, Bérubé, and half a dozen of his constables had fanned out from the doctor's house to find a trail.

It was Saint-Amand, the tracker, who found the trail amid the myriad tracks left over from the earlier search. He spent a few minutes studying the snow beyond the doctor's fence before pointing to a stray snowshoe print. From there, it was a question of following where the trail led—not easy, since none of them wore showshoes and the trees were too close for horses.

Now they stood on the frozen river bank, their boots having broken through the crusted top layer to sink a few inches. Across the river, the sun played on swaying tree branches, casting blue shadows deeper into the trees.

The river here had frozen in great slabs that had then shoved up against each other, creating a maze of ice and deep snow. The tracks disappeared into that mess.

Saint-Amand shaded his eyes and peered across the river. "There." He pointed, and squinting against the glare, Constance managed to make out a disturbance in the snowy bank on the other side.

"The river should be safe enough," said Desautel, "but I want fifty feet between each man. Then we wait for each other on the other side."

They moved swiftly but carefully. Desautel was right; the ice was solid but it wouldn't be long before sun and heat did its work. Another month of this weather and the river would be clear.

As she clambered over and around the ice pack, Constance's eyes roved the surface of the river, looking for clues as to what had transpired, but the surface was too windblown and frozen. They may as well have been trailing ghosts.

She felt as if the knife that might yet kill Prudence had been plunged into her own chest. She thought of the tobacco shop owner and his bitter assertion that it was time the mice fought back. Perhaps, but unlike humans, the A'lle did not have the right instincts to meet violence with violence. Violence in A'lle culture was abhorent and aberrant. They were ill equipped for it.

But they would have to learn, if they were to survive this latest attack.

She stumbled and righted herself, aware that Desautel was watching her from the far bank.

She was equipped to meet violence with violence. She had been trained to do so at the academy. It had been difficult but she had learned to notice the signs that someone intended her harm and had learned to defend herself, even it it meant harming another.

She knew of no other A'lle who could do so.

* * *

"They split up." Saint-Amand straightened from his crouch and pointed to his right, toward the east. "Two went that way."

Then he turned to point south, toward Gideon's Reach. "And one went this way."

Three, thought Constance. The doctor, the Ferret, and his big companion.

Desautel glanced at her, then looked at Saint-Amand. "They split up, to split us up," he said flatly.

Yes, of course they had. They knew they were being pursued. That was why they had stabbed Constance, to delay pursuit. Now they hoped to increase their chances by dividing their group. But it was risky. With only one of them with the doctor, he might overpower his captor.

Saint-Amand stood with hands on hips, looking first one way then the other. Inside the forest, the shadows were thicker and the air was cooler. Constance could smell woodsmoke from the village. There was no discernible trail that she could see. It seemed to her the fugitives had struck through the forest with no plan at all.

Bérubé came closer. He pointed to the left, where the tracks disappeared into the shadows. "The old rum runner's trail is less than a quarter mile that way. It meets up with the road to Gideon's Reach. It's not kept up in winter, but it's an easy go of it for a man on snowshoes. He could be making for it."

That would be the Ferret. It could be the other one, she supposed, but Constance had no doubt that the lone track belonged to the Ferret. She could easily imagine him leaving his big friend to deal with the doctor.

And if the doctor became troublesome? It would be easy enough to despatch him and rendezvous with the Ferret later.

Constance suddenly wished they had accepted the village men's offer to help search. She understood why Desautel had turned them down, however. He didn't know who, if anyone, from the village had helped the fugitives. He could not trust any one of them.

He believed the doctor had gone with the Ferret and his companion willingly.

Constance, on the other hand, felt that Desautel was too quick to assume the worst. Docteur Saunders had taken good care of her, had seemed genuinely disturbed by Frederick's death. The Ferret must have forced the doctor's cooperation.

"Very well," said the chief investigator finally. He looked around at the small group. "Mackenzie, Johnson, and Saint-Amand, go with Bérubé. Follow the east trail. Fire a shot if you find anything, and remember that these people are killers."

"Sir," said Bérubé, acknowledging the order. He nodded Saint-Amand ahead of him and without another word, the four set off to follow the trail.

Desautel took a deep breath and turned to his group. "Let's go."

* * *

Constance ran ahead of the chief investigator and the others, aware that they were lagging farther and farther behind, but unwilling to wait for them. The path was well packed by now, but she had to pay attention to avoid low branches and hidden roots.

Her breath felt too thick for her lungs, as if she were drowning in it. The horror of Prudence's wound and Frederick's death, and all the other attacks on A'lle merged into a great ball of fear and rage that settled in her chest, preventing her from breathing properly.

She hoped Bérubé would find the doctor quickly, and bring him back to Backli's Ford. He would be able to help Prudence.

But the Ferret was hers. She had no doubt he was the one who had tried to kill Prudence, just as he had tried to kill her in the cemetery.

She heard the chief investigator call her name, but the anger propelled her faster and faster until she was taking reckless chances. At last the inevitable happened: her heel landed on a barely covered root and slipped off, throwing her off balance so that she sprawled face first in the snow.

She sat up, gasping for breath, her face wet with melting snow.

The chief investigator caught up and stopped next to her, hands on his knees, trying to catch his breath. His face was ruddy with exertion but he stuck his hand out and wordlessly hauled her up.

Charlevoix, Joliette, and Rupert caught up and stood catching their breath, too.

Then a shot rang out and they all ducked. As one, their heads turned toward the east, the direction from which they had come.

"Bérubé's group," gasped Desautel. He looked at Joliette. "Take Charlevoix. Go help. We'll continue. If they are secure, come back."

Joliette hesitated a moment, clearly unhappy about the order, but finally he nodded. He and Charlevoix turned and headed back the way they had come. After a moment, she could not even hear the thudding of their feet.

She began running again, the chief investigator and Rupert behind her. Miles Rupert was a big man, easily six inches taller than she was, with fine brown hair that he kept short and brown eyes that missed nothing. He was also an excellent shot. She had never seen him smile.

Before she could get up to full speed, Desautel caught her sleeve. She glanced back and saw him motion her behind him. She was about to protest when Rupert reached for the rifle slung across his back.

She stepped off the trail and allowered Rupert to precede her. He kept to a fast walk and she and Desautel followed close behind, peering into the trees, listening. The chief investigator had unslung his own rifle and carried it across his chest, barrel up.

Then she heard the moaning. Rupert stopped and held up his free hand. He glanced over his shoulder at Desautel, who nodded. The chief investigator looked at Constance and pointed to one side of the trail. She obediently stepped off the hard-packed trail again and angled to the right, while he did the same to the left. Rupert continued on the trail, rifle at the ready.

They approached cautiously until they reached a small clearing and found a crumpled figure in the snow.

Constance glanced around the small clearing but saw no one else. Rupert emerged from the trail and held his rifle at the ready.

Still scanning the clearing, Constance approached the figure just as the chief investigator emerged from the trees on the other side of the trail.

She noticed the showshoes first—one had fallen off but the other was still strapped to the man's foot, twisting it uncomfortably. Then she noticed the calf-high moccasins and the tweed pants tucked into them, but it was when she noticed the long black great coat that she finally realized who it was.

She turned to look at Rupert and the chief investigator. "It's the doctor."

* * *

Constance, Rupert, and the chief investigator took turns carrying the doctor two at a time. As near as she could tell, he'd only been shot in the arm but he remained unconscious for the first fifteen minutes. Then Joliette and Charlevoix returned and the doctor finally regained consciousness.

Bérubé's group had found one of the men. He had shot at them but gave up quickly when he saw he was outnumbered.

To Constance's chagrin, the one they had captured was the big one.

The Ferret had escaped.

Desautel glanced at Constance when they heard, but she refused to look at him, afraid he would see the anger in her.

The Ferret had killed Renaud and Dallaire. He had tried to kill her. Twice. And now he had tried to kill Prudence.

She remembered his cruelty as he pressed her face against the hard edge of the railcar door, and described what his partner would do to her sister if she did not cooperate.

She wished him dead. Bérubé had sent three men after him and it was only a question of time before they found the Ferret, or one of the chief magistrate's patrols found him. Even if he managed to double back and head for New Amsterdam, the New American officers out of Gideon's Reach would get him. And he would be a fool to return to Backli's Ford.

It was only a question of time.

But the knowledge failed to satisfy her. As long as he was free, she would fear for her family.

It was a grueling trudge back. The doctor clutched his arm and shivered the whole way, stumbling often, despite his snowshoes. Desautel placed him in the middle of the group. No one spoke to him.

Constance trailed the group. Despite her exhaustion, she wanted to talk to the doctor and find out what had happened. They had found no rifle next to him. Clearly someone had shot him, but who? Certainly not the Ferret and his friend, since they had been half a mile away when the shot rang out. A shot that clearly came from the east.

They had heard only one shot. Had the doctor been shot before they even set out in pursuit?

One touch, and she would know if the doctor was innocent or not, but one look at Desautel's grim face warned her not to even try.

When they arrived in Backli's Ford, the men of the village took over silently, tying the big man up behind the inn to await questioning.

While Bérubé supervised the guard detail, Constance and the chief investigator met Thomas Pelletier on the front porch of the inn.

"If I may impose one more time," said Desautel. "I would need the use of your kitchen for a time. The doctor is wounded."

Thomas nodded silently and moved aside to let them in.

The doctor smiled reassuringly at Thomas but the innkeeper looked away. As they passed the doorway to the parlour, the doctor glanced inside and stopped in his tracks.

"Who is that?" he gestured at Prudence. "Is she hurt?"

Constance studied his face in silence. Could anyone play the role so well if he were guilty? Her hand twitched but she she bided her time.

"There is nothing for you to do," said Desautel gruffly and he pushed the doctor toward the kitchen.

Constance slipped to Prudence's side for a few seconds, but her sister was still unconscious. Her face was pale and very thin, and when Constance reached under the blankets, she found the flesh of her arm clammy and cold. She added another log to the fire and tucked the blankets more securely around her sister. Then she stroked Prudence's cheek.

"Fight, sister," she whispered. "Please fight."

She joined the chief investigator in the kitchen. Madame Pelletier was just turning away from the back door, where she had been watching the big man being tied up. She blinked in surprise at the doctor, then frowned when she saw the hole in his sleeve and the dark stains.

"Madame," said the doctor with a pained smile. "It would seem I now need your ministrations."

Madame Pelletier glanced at the chief investigator.

"He has been shot," explained Desautel. "A graze, really."

Madame Pelletetier studied the chief investigator's face uncertainly, then glanced at the doctor. Finally she turned the burner on beneath the kettle.

Half an hour later, the wound had been cleaned and dressed and the doctor smiled at Madame Pelletier.

"Merci, Madame," he said as she helped him back into his bloody shirt.

Madame Pelletier nodded stiffly and left. Constance had watched as the innkeeper cleaned the doctor's wound in the uncomfortable silence. The chief investigator was right. The wound was just a graze.

At that moment, Bérubé entered the kitchen carrying a length of rope. At Desautel's nod, he headed for the doctor.

"Is that really necessary?" objected the doctor, with the look of a man who was starting to lose patience with the foolishness of others.

"I'm afraid it is," said Desautel.

Moments later, the doctor's hands were tied behind his back and his legs tied solidly to a straight chair. He looked angry and uncomfortable and in pain.

"Sir, this is unacceptable," he said. "I am an injured man!" He only managed to control himself with an effort. "There is no cause to truss me up like a pig."

"I will be back for you shortly," said Desautel with no inflection in his voice. He nodded to Bérubé, who nodded back. Then Desautel ushered Constance out the back door, to where the big man awaited.

Before the chief investigator closed the door, she glanced back at the doctor. Surely only an innocent man would be so offended.

* * *

The big man's name was Theophilus Blaine.

If Desautel had worried about obtaining a confession, he needn't have. Blaine was quite willing to speak his piece.

"Where is your friend?" asked Desautel. It was barely noon. They still had time to find Constance's so-called Ferret, but only if they knew where to look.

Blaine shrugged. "Halfway back to Montreal by now, is my guess," he said. There was a trace of bitterness in his voice.

"Did he abandon you?" asked Constance. Desautel controlled an urge to frown at her. She would not even have noticed. Her attention was fixed on the prisoner.

"Little bastard," muttered Blaine, looking down at his feet. "Said we should make our stand. Said he'd circle around through the woods to catch the constables by surprise."

"Instead," said Desautel sympathetically, "he left you there to deal with the law on your own."

Blaine shrugged again. "Never did like that little pissant."

Desautel tried another tack. "Why did you take the doctor prisoner only to shoot him?"

"Prisoner?" Blained looked up in surprise. "You got it all wrong," he insisted. "Stoker an' me, we worked for the doc. He's the one who split us up. And he weren't shot when I saw him last. Maybe Stoker did it."

Desautel saw Constance A'lle's start of surprise out of the corner of his eye, and almost felt sorry for the girl. He knew she had harbored a hope that the doctor was innocent.

"How did the doctor hire you?" he asked. "He lives here in Backli's Ford, but you don't. And what did he hire you for?"

"The doc used to live in Montreal," Blaine pointed out. "He hired us to follow him whenever he went on a house call to an A'lle house. Sometimes, nothing would happen, but other times an A'lle would leave with him. We would follow with the car and nab the poor sap. Hell, the doc even helped us sometimes!"

The sun beat warm on Desautel's bare head but he felt chilled nonetheless. He had been standing in front of Blaine, forcing the big man to look up. Half a dozen of his constables were arrayed around the yard, watching Blaine for any sudden movements. The dog that seemed to have adopted Constance sat in a sunny patch, watching everything with those intelligent eyes of his.

Desautel took a deep breath and sat on the stump that Rupert had provided. It was five feet from Blaine, close enough to see the man's bloodshot eyes.

"Why?" he asked finally. "Why did he hire you to kidnap A'lle?"

At that, Blaine glanced uncomfortably at Constance. "He said he wanted to study them."

"But the doctor has been here six months," said Constance, and Desautel gritted his teeth. "And A'lle are still disappearing from Montreal."

Blaine nodded. "Oh, we didn't just work for him. And we weren't the only ones doin' it, neither. The doc was part of a group of mucky-mucks. They all wanted to find out more about your kind."

Constance slowly turned to look at Desautel, her mouth open in shock. He knew his face mirrored hers. A *group*?

Dear God in heaven. What had they stumbled onto?

His hands were trembling, he noticed. He placed them deliberately on his knees.

"Why kill my two constables?" he asked. "Why try to kill Investigator A'lle?"

Blaine sighed. "That was just bad luck," he said. "Things were starting to get a little hot in Montreal, with all them priests sniffin' around. So we got sent here to lay low. The A'lle kid followed us from the train station. Stoker 'an me, we didn't tell the doc, on account he gets a little funny about our work. So we caught the kid and tried to find out if he told anybody that he seen us." He shrugged a little. "I guess we got carried away, but they're supposed to heal and all." He shrugged again. "The doc was real upset when he found out."

"Especially when we were called in," murmured Desautel.

Blaine nodded. "Yep."

"But why kill the constables?" demanded Constance. "You must have known it would only result in more of us coming."

"We was supposed to be long gone by then," said Blaine glumly. "But we couldn't leave without the doc's help and the doc had patients and was never alone long enough for us to tell him. And then you got here." He gave Constance a sour look.

Yes, indeed. Constance had arrived and insisted on beginning her investigation right away, despite her injuries.

Good girl, he thought. Good girl.

ᕔ THIRTY-ONE ᕖ

CONSTANCE glanced at the chief investigator. He had ordered the guards out of the kitchen and they were alone with the doctor. It was now or never.

Desautel nodded at her.

With a deep breath, she took a chair from the table and placed it so that she could sit facing the doctor. He frowned at her and glanced from her face to Desautel's.

"I have a few questions, Docteur," she said softly. "Let's start with my sister."

"Your sister?" He blinked in bewilderment. "I'm afraid I don't know your sister."

"According to Monsieur Blaine," said Desautel coldly, "you ordered Stoker to stab her."

"Me?" cried the doctor in outrage. "What nons—"

Constance abruptly placed a hand on his stubbled cheek and he jerked back, but there was nowhere for him to go and her hand followed his movement. She focused, giving herself over to the awareness of her flesh on his, her oils mingling with his, her essence interacting with his.

The smell of breakfast lingered in the kitchen, as did the smell of the scrap bowl Madame Pelletier kept on the counter. Constance eliminated the distraction from her mind, eliminated the sound of the chief investigator shifting from foot to foot, and concentrated on the doctor's shallow breathing.

Then it came, the sudden tingling that told her she had connected. The doctor jumped in surprise and suddenly she was swamped with a myriad of feelings: anger, disgust, guilt, arrogance and a vast sense of grief.

Constance opened her eyes and stared at the doctor. He was so close she could see the pores in his skin.

"Tell me, Docteur, how long have you been torturing A'lle?" asked Desautel. He stood to one side of Constance, his hands clasped behind his back, examining the man with curiosity.

To her surprise, the doctor's emotions immediately stilled, as if he were holding his breath even though she could hear his steady breathing. She had never encountered this in anyone before.

"What are you talking about?" he asked softly. "Who has been tortured?"

And it was at that moment that Constance knew that he was responsible, or at least involved in it all. There was no surprise in the man at all. Only watchfulness.

And grief.

Bile rose and she released him to go stand by the counter. When Desautel came to stand beside her, watching her with concern, she looked at him and nodded.

"Yes," she said. "He's in this up to his neck."

Just then, a knock sounded at the door between kitchen and parlor, and Bérubé came in. He gave the doctor a cold look, then turned to chief investigator. Only then did Constance realize he was carrying a rifle.

"Saint-Amand found it," he reported. "The doc had tossed it in the woods a ways from where you found him. There were rags wrapped around the mouth of the barrel, to muffle the sound of the shot."

They all turned to look at Docteur Saunders. He had shot himself, to make it seem as if he had escaped Blaine and Stoker. There was no disguising the regret on his face as he looked at her.

"Why?" she asked. Her hands went out in the universal gesture of beseeching. At the moment, it felt as though they were the only two in the room. "Why did you hurt my sister? Why kill all those A'lle?"

His eyes closed as if he could no longer bear to look at her. "Because of Alice," he finally murmured.

"Who is Alice?" said Desautel, startling her.

Saunders' eyes opened and a tear escaped. "My sister," he said, apparently unaware of the tear coursing down his cheek.

Constance frowned. "What of her?" she asked. What did his sister have to do with the kidnapping and murder of A'lle?

Deep lines appeared between the doctor's eyebrows and his cheeks suddenly seemed gaunt, as if grief hollowed them. His blue eyes were bloodshot.

"She was injured in a fall from a horse," he began. "Two years ago. The fall broke her back and left her an invalid."

Constance drew in a sharp breath but he continued, oblivious to her dawning realization.

"I knew of the A'lle ability to heal." He looked up at her. "To regenerate." The smile he gave her twisted something inside her. "I know of only one creature on earth that can regenerate itself. The lowly earthworm. Is that not ironic?" he said with a harsh laugh. "The basest creature can heal itself but we cannot."

The room filled with silence, broken only by the sounds of breathing.

Bérubé shifted by the door, breaking the spell and Desautel cleared his throat.

"That tragedy does not excuse you, Docteur," he said firmly. "Torture is never accep—"

"I am not a torturer!" said the doctor. His cheeks flushed and he sat up straighter, only to slump again when the movement placed a strain on his injured arm. "I only ever needed A'lle blood."

"From unwilling subjects," said Desautel crisply. "And the organs? Why take those if you only needed blood?"

Constance found herself taking shallow breaths. They were discussing her people as if they were nothing but cattle.

Or mice.

Suddenly Bérubé was by her side, and while he did not look at her, he stood so close his coat sleeve brushed against hers, lending her his silent support.

Saunders looked at her. "I needed to analyze the blood, you see. I know—know—the key is the blood. But I needed a laboratory, and money. There were others who were also interested, who promised to help. They had a great deal of money, and they wanted to know how A'lle manage to live so much longer than we do."

Constance swallowed hard. The humans had gone from lynching and burning the A'lle to subjecting them to experiments.

"Who are these others?" demanded Desautel. "These people who helped you—tell me their names."

The doctor shook his head sadly but firmly. "I am very sorry, Chief Investigator," he said softly. "This promise I cannot breach. If I do, they will kill Alice."

ॐ THIRTY-TWO ॐ

CONSTANCE twisted slightly in the saddle, scanning both sides of the road, looking for disturbances in the snow.

Next to her, the chief investigator did the same, as did Bérubé and Johnson, riding behind them. The chief investigator had decided they had time enough to help search for Stoker. Constance suspected that he, like her, would feel much better once Stoker was in custody.

The early afternoon sunlight streamed down, so warm that she rode with her coat folded in front of her while the others unbuttonned theirs. Hoofprints and sled imprints scarred the snowy surface of the road. Already the snow had grown granular. Soon it would begin to melt and soon after that, the road would become impassable for a few weeks.

They were a few miles outside Backli's Ford. Constance tried to estimate how quickly Stoker could travel, but it was difficult. According to Blaine, Stoker would head for Montreal. Unless he planned to stay in the woods the entire journey, he would eventually have to emerge from tree cover to use the road. Perhaps he had found a place to hide and wait. As far as they knew, he had no horse, not even snowshoes—he couldn't have gotten very far.

They would have to turn around soon and go back to Backli's Ford for the prisoners. It would be foolish to travel in darkness, especially with Stoker still free.

Her shoulders ached and she realized that she was tense. Her gaze kept returning to the trees bordering the road. He could be anywhere.

"This is where it happened," said Desautel, his voice pitched to carry over the sighing of the wind through the pines.

She looked at him and he nodded at a wide opening in the trees to their right. "There. You were ambushed." He pointed to the far end of the open space. "You can't tell from here, but there's a cliff on the other side of those bushes."

Constance swallowed hard and stared. That was where she had fallen, after Renaud and Dallaire had been shot. A memory flitted by and she clasped it to her.

"After Dallaire fell, Renaud slapped my horse," she murmured. "To get it going. If he hadn't, I would have been killed, too." She took a deep breath of pine-scented air. One memory reclaimed. Perhaps more would come.

Desautel smiled wryly. "The horse threw you," he pointed out, just as Constance caught a glint of sunlight on metal in the trees to her left.

Bérubé called out, "Down!" just as a shot rang out.

"Left!" shouted Bérubé. "In the woods!"

Another shot rang out and the coat flew off her lap. Then Desautel shoved her off her horse and jumped down from his.

"Take cover!" he ordered. Constance did not wait for him to repeat himself, but scrambled as fast as she could into the nearby ditch.

A third time the rifle fired and Constance realized with horror that her rifle was still in its scabbard on the horse... which was now galloping down the road toward Montreal with the other three.

She risked raising her head only to see three other heads rising above the ditch across the road. Another shot rang out and they all ducked. She was alone and weaponless on the same side of the road as the shooter. However, the land rose on her side, keeping her out of sight of the shooter, while the chief investigator and the other two were pinned down.

This was how Blaine and Stoker had done it before, she suddenly realized. One of them would have waited where Stoker waited now, while the other waited in the trees across the road. A perfect ambush.

She ducked down to consider her options. With any luck, at least one of the others had had the presence of mind to grab a rifle. If so, and if they could distract the shooter—she had no doubt it was Stoker—then perhaps she could work her way around him and catch him by surprise.

As if in response to her thought, a sharp report tore through the clear air, so close that she jumped. That had come from the other side of the road. Without giving herself the chance to change her mind, she began to crawl through the snow at the bottom of the ditch. Within seconds, her pants were soaked. When she judged she was far enough, she risked looking over the top. She had crawled perhaps a hundred yards from her original position. As she watched, Bérubé lifted his head and shoulders above the ditch and fired a shot at the woods across the road. As soon as he ducked down, Desautel emerged, rifle in hand and shot at the trees.

Constance swallowed her trepidation. It appeared they had two rifles among them but Desautel, Bérubé, and Saint-Amand were pinned down. If Stoker had enough ammunition, he could pick them off if they tried to rush him.

Why had Stoker attacked them? He could easity have let them pass by. They wouldn't have known he was there.

And then she realized she knew why. The horses. He had to get a horse or be trapped in the woods.

He had the perfect spot. All he had to do was wait for passersby and kill them. And if no unsuspecting traveler came by? Then he would have to settle for four constables.

Poor planning. Poor execution. Without the doctor to give him direction, he made poor decisions.

With a deep breath, she crept out of the ditch and rose to her feet just as another shot rang out, but it was Bérubé again, and Constance ran to the trees a few yards away, praying that Stoker hadn't seen her.

She entered the cover of the trees as more shots were exchanged and hurried toward Stoker's position. She hoped Bérubé and Desautel had seen what she was doing and would stop shooting, else they might hit her.

She crept through the forest as silently as she could, her boots filling with snow. Gradually, she became aware that the shooting had stopped and looked around. There were no sounds except for the sighing of the wind. Then she caught a movement out of the corner of her eye and twisted.

The movement was just enough to keep the rifle butt from striking her head. Instead, it cracked her on the tip of the shoulder, shooting excruciating pain down her arm. She cried out and turned in time to see the Ferret raise the rifle to strike her again. There was no mistaking the gloating in his eyes.

"To me!" she cried. "To me!" Then she launched herself at him.

He struck at her again but she was too close to him and the blow glanced off her back. Her momentum carried them both down into the deep snow and Constance heard the breath whoosh out of him as she landed with a knee on his stomach. The rifle flew out of his hand.

Her shoulder screamed a protest but she gathered herself into a sitting position on his abdomen, preventing him from taking a deep breath. She had his right arm pinned beneath her knee but could do nothing about his left arm, as her arm was useless. He struggled to reach his fallen rifle but it was too far.

"Get off me!" he grunted, shoving at her, but Constance had had enough. This man had taken part in a great crime against her people, had murdered an innocent young man and two fine constables, tried to kill her twice, and stabbed Prudence.

She could not allow him to go free, even if she had to harm him to keep him prisoner.

Then he punched her in her injured shoulder and she screamed in pain. He scrambled out from under her and she clutched at his leg, tripping him. He fell with a curse but leapt up almost immediately, rifle in hand.

"You A'lle bitch!" he yelled. "I've had enough of you!"

He raised the rifle to take aim at her and Constance frantically scrambled to her feet.

Then he jerked forward as if pushed from behind, just as a shot rang out, making her ears ring.

He crumpled to the snow-covered ground, a look of immense surprise on his face, and lay staring up at the trees. The snow around him immediately turned pink.

Constance looked up to find find Chief Investigator Desautel slowly lowering his rifle.

≈ THIRTY-THREE ≪

DESAUTEL rented the ferry master's cart and the innkeeper's sled, promising they would be returned the next day. He forced Blaine to travel in the back of the cart with his dead partner, and kept the doctor trussed up in the sled. He did not want them concocting stories together.

He sent the rest of the men back to St-Vincent, having decided he would spend the night in Backli's Ford. He told Bérubé to keep the doctor in isolation and not allow him to speak to anybody until he arrived in the morning.

Desautel planned to call the magistrate and fill him in, but first he wanted to check on Prudence. She was in no condition to travel, might not even survive the day, although when he last checked on her, her breathing was strong and steady.

As for Constance, she was already recovering from the injury to her shoulder. At least it was not the shoulder so recently dislocated.

He stood up from the kitchen table where he had been taking notes, trying to record everything while it was fresh in his mind.

The door to the parlor swung open and Madame Pelletier backed in, carrying a tray. She jumped a little when she saw Desautel standing there.

"She is still with us," said the woman, nodding decisively. The tray supported a heavy bowl filled with bloody water and rags in various stages of discoloration. He took the tray from her and set it on the counter, trying not to see. Or smell.

Desautel swallowed. "Does she still bleed?" How much blood could she lose and still live?

"It has almost stopped," said Madame Pelletier. She sat down on the chair the doctor had occupied and her shoulders slumped.

"Do you think she will be able to travel tomorrow?" he asked.

She frowned, then shrugged. "Anyone else, I would say definitely not. Them?" She shrugged again and he realized she was referring to the A'lle in general. "You had best ask Constance, but I don't think that girl should travel anywhere for a while."

He nodded and walked to the door through which Madame Pelletier had just entered, then paused. "Madame, you are very good to take these strangers in and care for them."

Madame Pelletier gave him a half-smile. She had lovely green eyes and Desautel could see the young woman peering out at him from them. "What should I have done?" she asked philosophically. "Turn her out, as Père Noiron would have had me do? Let her find her way back home injured and helpless?" They were no longer talking about Prudence, but Constance.

Madame Pelletier shook her head. "Besides, I am growing accustomed to these strange ones. When you consider it, they are not so different. They bleed just like we do. And they die."

Her smile disappeared in sadness and they looked at each other for a long silent moment. Finally she stood up. "Well, I'd best prepare something to eat. With two A'lle in the house, I will be cooking for the rest of the day."

Desautel smiled but before he could push the door open into the parlor, she spoke again.

"Are you certain about the doctor?" she asked softly. "He was shot, after all..."

"Yes, Madame, I am certain," he said decisively. "He knew it was only a matter of time before we caught up to him. So he shot himself in the arm, muffling the sound. It's no easy feat, and you have to be careful, but it is possible. Besides, there were powder burns on his coat. He was shot from a very close distance. Then all he had to do was toss the rifle into the trees and keep moving, only to pretend to be unconscious before we found him."

Clever man. Clever enough to know that stabbing Prudence in the chest would not kill her right away. According to Constance, the A'lle heart was lower than the human one. No, the wound might not kill her, but it had provided an excellent distraction, delaying the pursuit.

The sheer cold-bloodedness of it made him shiver.

* * *

The fire in the parlor kept the room overly warm but Constance had said it was necessary. Prudence lay so very still under a pile of blankets. Her face was pale and she seemed to be almost frowning, as though she were concentrating.

Someone had moved a hard-backed chair by the settee and he sat down in it. He wanted to brush the hair away from her forehead but did not want to disturb her.

The windows above the window seat brought in the bright sunshine of late afternoon. Dust motes danced in the air currents. From the kitchen came the sounds of pots being set on the range. He had no idea where Constance was. He felt, for the moment, as if he were all alone with Prudence. He suddenly felt alone, and lonely.

"I knew you would come."

The voice was so faint that at first he thought he had imagined it. He looked down to find Prudence watching him. She was very pale still, but there was faint color in her cheeks. The sight cheered him.

"How are you feeling?" he asked gently. He leaned forward, elbows on his knees, hands clasped, so that he could examine her more closely. That bloom of color didn't mean fever, did it? He risked a hand to her forehead but found it cool to his touch.

"Like I was hit by a train," she said, and smiled.

Desautel found himself smiling back. "I am told you will recover," he lied.

"More than likely," she agreed. "Although I am very hungry." She looked at him beseechingly.

He laughed. "Madame Pelletier is already preparing for the onslaught of your appetite," he said. "But I will tell her you are awake." He made as if to get up but her hand slipped out from under the blankets and caught his. Her fingers were icy cold and he automatically wrapped both of his warm hands around hers. He settled back down.

"What day is this?"

He had to think about it. "Tuesday," he said finally.

She frowned. "Truly? I thought it was much longer." She sighed. "Even throughout the night, I always knew you would come."

Desautel's hands tighted on hers and he felt his cheeks flush. Finally he cleared his throat. "Can you tell me what happened?"

The smell of frying ham reached under the kitchen door and Prudence's head turned toward the kitchen. Her cheeks seemed suddenly thinner, as if hunger hollowed them as he watched. But she turned back to him and answered readily enough.

"I went out to the woodpile," she said. "To fetch wood. Dinnertime was delayed by Roland's arrival and I was alone in the yard. Someone placed a bag over my head and then something hard hit me in the back of the head." Her hand had begun to tremble and Desautel patted it soothingly.

"And then?" he prompted.

She took another deep breath and glanced at the kitchen door again. Desautel wasn't certain but he thought he could smell baked beans.

"I woke up in darkness. There was a window above me. I could see that it was night time. I was tied up and gagged, on some kind of table."

Desautel looked away, unable to bear the memory of how they

had found her, gagged, bound, and bleeding from a stab wound to the chest, in the doctor's makeshift mortuary.

"And your injury?" he asked softly.

She remained silent for long minutes and he finally stole a glance at her. She was staring out the window. At last she looked back at him.

"I must have fallen asleep at some point," she said. "I woke up when someone opened the door. It was a man. I had never seen him before. He came to stand over me. I remember thinking that I had never seen such a strange look on a person's face before. Then another man came in, smaller. The first man pointed at my chest, and then the second one stabbed me." Her voice hitched on the last part.

Desautel jerked in horror and then cursed himself when his sudden movement caused her to hiss in pain. He tried to release her hand but she clung to him. Her forearm was slender but muscled and he suddenly remembered that they had cut her shirt and petticoat off.

"What did he look like, this first man?" he asked finally.

"Tall, I think. Black hair, blue eyes. The second one had a sharp nose and mean eyes. He was in shirt sleeves and had a canvas apron over his clothes."

So as not to get his clothing bloody, Desautel thought grimly.

"Do you know who they were?" asked Prudence.

He nodded. "The first one is—was—the doctor in Backli's Ford. He and his two partners are involved in the A'lle disappearances in Montreal. The one who stabbed you is dead."

Prudence took a long, tremulous breath. "What did they want with me?"

Desautel shook his head. "I believe they wanted you as a hostage, to force your sister to do what they wanted." He gave her a brief overview of their investigation in Montreal, and Constance's encounter with the late Ferret.

"And so, they decided I would be more useful as a half-dead

patient than a live hostage." Her voice was growing more tired but she seemed reluctant to stop talking.

"I expect you are hungry," said Constance from behind him. He jumped and jerked his hand away from Prudence's, for all the world like a schoolboy caught stealing cookies. Constance had been leaning against the doorway that led to the hall. Now she straightened wearily and walked over to them. He stood up to give her the chair, which she accepted with a grateful smile.

"What of the others?" asked Prudence. "Mother...?"

"All safe," said Constance. "All waiting for us at home."

The sisters stared at each other for a long time.

Finally, Desautel left them alone and went to find Madame Pelletier.

* * *

"What I fail to understand," said Marie Pelletier, "is why the doctor moved here."

They were sitting at the kitchen table, having devoured a dinner of mashed potatoes, baked beans, fried ham and fresh bread. Prudence had been fed and was resting. Constance doubted that her sister would be able to travel in the morning but Gemma had promised to return with the sled in the morning, to help care for her.

Desautel had spent at least an hour on the telephone, speaking to the magistrate. Now he shrugged, drawing her back to the here and now. "I will know more when I interrogate him tomorrow," he said. "But I suspect he left because of growing suspicions in Montreal. Many of the people we spoke to mentioned a doctor. When we show them a photograph of Saunders, they will surely name him as the doctor in question. He was the only common factor in most of the disappearances. Always, someone near the person taken had been sick. Sometimes the person who disappeared had been sick."

"There was often a priest, too," Constance pointed out.

"Yes," nodded Desautel, "but we know why."

"Why?" asked Thomas, rising to bring the tea pot to the table.

"The archbishop of Montreal had enjoined the priests to reach out to the A'lle among their flock," said Desautel, as if that explained everything. Thomas and Marie nodded as if they understood, but Constance reserved judgment.

The Church would not be sorry to see the A'lle gone.

"And Theophilus Blaine and John Stoker were sent away for the same reason," continued Desautel. "They were becoming too visible in Montreal. I suspect they were trying to make their way to the United American States."

"But the terrible things they did to the A'lle..." Marie Pelletier shook her head when her husband offered to refill her cup. "For what earthly purpose...?"

Constance wrapped her hands around her cup, for once glad of the added warmth. "The first time I met him," she began, "here, the doctor spoke of his roommate at university. He knew a great deal about A'lle physiology. When his sister was injured, he hoped to find a way to help her by studying our ability to heal quickly. He would not be the first scientific mind to wonder if that ability could be transferred." She stopped talking when she recognized the note of bitterness in her voice.

Desautel sighed. "I'm afraid it's much more than the idle curiosity of a diseased mind," he said quietly. "Blaine, the Ferret's partner, told me that there is an underground organization that pays thugs like him to kidnap A'lle."

Marie Pelletier stared at him in growing horror.

"More?" she exclaimed. "There are more of them out there, kidnapping and... and... cutting people?"

Desautel nodded grimly. "And the doctor was not the only one experimenting. Some are experimenting with breeding."

Constance looked down at her empty plate, trying to make sense of what he had said. Then she ran through the names of the A'lle who had been taken and realized something.

"The ones who went missing..." she began slowly.

Desautel looked at her and nodded. "Yes. Of the young women who went missing, none have been found."

Constance swallowed hard and Thomas Pelletier made a small sound in the back of his throat.

"They are trying to... to *breed* them?"

"But why?" asked Constance at the same time. "If they hate us so much..."

Desautel shook his head. "They don't want the babies. Or at least, they don't want the babies alive. They think they might be able to extract whatever it is that helps you heal so fast from the blood of the half-breeds. Apparently analysing the blood of their captives hasn't helped."

"They can rape us all they want," said Constance bluntly, "there is no interbreeding between our two species. Our differences are slight, but they are enough to prevent it."

A shocked silence followed her words.

Desautel finally sighed. "It would seem we have stumbled upon a ring of people willing to go to great lengths to learn more about the A'lle. I spoke with the magistrate earlier. He is launching an investigation throughout Lower Canada. If the evidence warrants it, he will speak with his Upper Canada colleague. We will eventually find who is at the bottom of these terrible deeds. And they will be brought to justice."

Constance studied his profile for a moment and looked away when he turned toward her.

They would indeed be brought to justice, even if she had to do it herself.

* * *

The morning dawned bright and warm. Constance tucked the food and drink Madame Pelletier had provided in a basket under the seat of the sled they had borrowed from the Montreal constabulary and turned toward the innkeepers.

"My sister Gemma will be here shortly to look after Prudence," she told Madame Pelletier.

The woman smiled reassuringly and patted Constance's hand. "Stop worrying," she said. "Prudence is doing much better than anyone had a right to expect—well, except you, I suppose."

Constance smiled in return. "A'lle don't worry," she said. "It is pointless and wastes energy."

Madame Pelletier glanced at her husband, who smiled at her.

"Take care of yourself, Constance," he said and patted her on the arm.

His wife, less shy, reached up and gave Constance a hug. "Come back and see us when no one is trying to kill you."

A soft woof alerted Constance to the mutt's arrival and she grinned.

"There you are," she said. "Are you ready to go home?" She had worried that she would have to go looking for him. She went to one knee and rubbed his soft ears. He leaned into her hand, clearly pleased with her ministrations.

"He seems to like you," said Madame Pelletier.

"Home?" asked Thomas, clearly curious.

Constance looked up. "I believe this is Frederick's dog. His father told us that Frederick had taken the dog with him."

"Ah," said Madame Pelletier. "We wondered where he had come from."

Constance smiled at the dog. "What do you think, pup?" she asked him. "Shall I take you back?"

As though in answer, the dog licked her hand. She laughed and stood up just as Desautel came out onto the porch. He looked inordinately cheerful.

"Ready, Maître Desautel?" she asked. She wondered if he'd gone up to see Prudence, whom he had carried to one of the bedrooms earlier that morning.

"Ready, Investigator A'lle." He shook hands with the two innkeepers, assured them the constabulary's accountant would be kept apprised of the expenses incurred on their behalf and climbed into the sled to settle himself on the bench.

"Well, Investigator A'lle? Shall we go?"

"Yes, Maître." She picked up the dog and handed him to the surprised chief investigator before climbing in, too.

"Is this our missing dog, then?" he asked.

"Yes, sir," said Constance firmly. She scooted over to make room for the dog and he sat between them, tongue lolling, clearly ready for an adventure.

Roland A'lle might already have returned to Montreal with his son's body. If so, they would need to make arrangements to return the dog to him. Perhaps it would take a long time to make the arrangements.

With her arm around the dog, she looked out at the road ahead. She was heading for an adventure, too, a dark one in which she would seek to discover those who were hurting her people. But for now, her family was safe and she felt as if she and the chief investigator had finally reached an understanding. That would do for now.

With a final wave at the Pelletiers, Desautel clicked the horses into motion and they started back for home.

THE END

ABOUT THE AUTHOR

Marcelle Dubé writes mystery, science fiction, fantasy, contemporary and—occasionally—romance fiction. She grew up near Montreal and after trying out a number of different provinces (not to mention Belgium) she settled in the Yukon, where people outnumber carnivores, but not by much.

Her short stories have appeared in magazines and award-winning anthologies. Her novels include the Mendenhall Mysteries series.

To find out more about her, visit:
www.marcellemdube.com.

BOOKS BY THE AUTHOR

Mendenhall Mysteries series:
The Shoeless Kid
The Tuxedoed Man
The Weeping Woman

Kirwan's Son
Obeah
On Her Trail

Made in the USA
Charleston, SC
21 November 2013